Alone and Making It . . .

"My wheels are turning, Jennifer," Oliver said, looking around the crowded room. "I think a place like this would go over big. What do you think about opening another Tavern?"

"I've never thought about it. I have more than I can handle with this place," she told him.

"I don't mean run another place. Franchise it out. Start a chain of Taverns. You're onto something here, and the timing is right. I've heard a great deal about you, how you took this place from nothing and built it up in record time. It's as if one of my publicity men wrote the copy himself!"

"I know, but I don't think I could do it again. I'm not sure I want to," Jennifer said doubtfully.

"I'll let you think about it. I could make you a household word, merchandise your shirts, start your own recording label, make you the toast of the country. You're a young, pretty woman. Trust me. I've got lots of money behind me, and I'm the best promoter that ever lived," he stated. "Together, we can make a fortune!"

Jennifer was intrigued. She either had to be dreaming this whole thing, or Oliver was the biggest con artist she'd ever met. If she went along with him and the venture was a success, she'd never have to settle for second best again . . .

SHORTER DAYS

It has never been my intention
   to burden you with pain or anger
   neither mine nor your own
Yet to escape, to flee or perhaps
   just to leave was somehow forgotten.
Forgotten, if only for a moment
   until somehow it seemed too late.
Too late because your emotions
   grew too strong
   and my distance too close.
Not able to fee over man made miles
   my journey became the distance
        of time—
   time that is limited like the day
       by work
       my work
     by my sleep
   and my sleep
      by my escape.

Peter Stoutenburgh

NOTHING BUT THE BEST

Diane Masters

LEISURE BOOKS ∞ NEW YORK CITY

To dear friends, Judy, Tom, Jane, and Peter. With their help I was able to make my way as a bartender and gather the material to write this book. Thank you.

A LEISURE BOOK

published by

Dorchester Publishing Co., Inc.
41 E. 60 St.
New York, New York

Printed in the United States of America

ONE

Jennifer smiled to herself as she started her long drive home. She waved goodbye to her father and mother, and watched them disappear in the rear-view mirror. She thought of Cassy and Jonathan, and how much she missed them, then looked at her watch and timed her arrival with theirs. She'd be pulling into the driveway as they got off the school bus. She could feel their presence even now. She wondered what long tale they'd tell, expounding in great detail on the Halloween play the second grade was putting on. And Jonathan, grumpy about why he had to go to school, when playing outside was so much more fun. After all, baseball players didn't have to go to school. He should be spending his time practicing.

Maybe Frank, she prayed, had had a change of luck and made a big score in the market. Her heart danced at the prospect of her homecoming, beating with excitement at all she had to catch up with.

Jennifer stopped at the light. She smiled and gave a friendly wave to police officer Davidson, who was directing traffic. The short, stout man waved back.

"How was your vacation?" he shouted.

"Wonderful, but it's good to be home," Jennifer called back, rolling down the car window and feeling the cool breeze of the October air. The light changed, and he signaled her to proceed. She gave Officer Davidson one last quick smile and drove off. She was glad to be home, though it was nice to get away from the daily routine of the kids, her home and Frank. It was the first time since the children were born that she had left them alone and taken some time for herself. She had missed them all terribly. Jennifer felt anticipation welling up inside her as she approached their street. She could almost hear her children's voices, see them running to her, giving her a big hug, their adorable faces smiling at her. The children alone made life with Frank almost bearable lately.

Jennifer turned the familiar corner of Ackerly Drive and saw the large white house set back behind an abundance of shrubbery. The Wells' home. The old house, handed down from generation to generation, had been built by Frank's great-grandfather. The beauty of it always took her breath away. She pulled into the circular driveway, her eyes fixed on the large bay windows. Something about the house bothered her. It was too still. A cold chill ran up her back. She felt the same sinking feeling she had when she awoke this morning, a feeling she couldn't quite shake during the three-hour drive home. She had hoped she'd feel better when she saw the house, knowing she was home.

Jennifer got out of the car, remembering how many times she'd tried to call the house today, but there had been no answer. She fumbled with the keys, finally unlocking the front door, then walked into the foyer. Looking to the left toward the dining room, and then to the right toward the large living room, her eyes next scanned the large circular stairway. No one seemed to be home.

"Jonathan! Cassy!" she called, and quickened her pace up the stairs. "Mildred!" she screamed. But no one answered. Where could everyone be? she wondered. Why would Frank take the children out on the day she was due home? He knew how much she missed them and how badly she wanted to see them.

She opened the door to Cassy's room. The bed was made, her toys in order on the shelves. She crossed the hall to Jonathan's room and sensed the same empty feeling. She proceeded down the hall to the master bedroom. Everything was in order, everything in its place. It was as if the entire household didn't need her. There was not a dirty dish, not a messy bedroom, nothing to indicate that she had been gone a week. No telltale signs of a missing mother, organizer, housekeeper.

Jennifer looked around the bedroom again. Her blue eyes caught sight of an envelope on the mantel. It had her name on it. She picked it up, half knowing what the envelope contained. The handwriting was Frank's. She read the note three times, not believing its contents. Frank had taken the children and left her. He didn't say where, and he didn't say why. They were gone.

Jennifer didn't know how long she stood there staring at the note. She seemed to lose all track of time. When she entered the bedroom the sun was streaming through the windows, the lace curtains billowing in the cool air. She needed light to read the note again. She had to pull herself together, had to think. Where could he have taken them? He must have confided in someone. His mother, Jennifer thought. She'd have to know. Frank never made a move without consulting her. Jennifer dialed the number. Mrs. Wells picked up on the second ring.

"Mother Wells, Frank's gone and he's taken the children," Jennifer blurted out, trying to keep the hysteria from her voice. "Where have they gone?"

"Dear. What do you mean, they're gone? On a vacation?" his mother asked.

"No. No vacation. He's taken them away from me. He left me a note. He said he's leaving me for good, and he's taken custody of the children. When I arrived here this afternoon, I found the note," Jennifer continued, knowing it was hopeless. If the old lady knew where Frank was, she was playing a good game. She'd never tell.

"I haven't any idea. I'm shocked. I saw Frank and the children yesterday. They were fine. They looked happy, and Frank talked about your homecoming. I'm sure you must be mistaken. He's probably taken them for a ride. They'll most likely be walking through the door at any moment."

"You don't seem to understand, Mother. They're gone. If all they did was go for a ride, why would he write me a note saying he was leaving me? I have to find them! I want my children with me. If he wants to leave, that's fine. But he can't have the children. They belong to me. I've been a good mother," Jennifer screamed into the phone.

"No one said otherwise, dear," Mrs. Wells said with the same calm consistency in her voice, the control Jennifer always hated. "I'm sure there's a simple explanation. Why don't you ask Mildred?"

"I'd love to, but she's not here either. How can he do this? The children are in school. How irresponsible he is!"

"Now stop getting excited. I'll make a few calls and see what I can find out. I'll call you back," Mrs. Wells told her and hung up.

Jennifer sat staring at the phone. She was sure, in her gut, that Mrs. Wells knew everything. She knew where they were and wasn't going to tell her. Jennifer put the phone down, and ran down the hall toward the children's rooms. She opened the closet doors, the drawers to the dressers. Everything was gone—their clothes, their favorite toys, everything. This was a nightmare. He'd gone and taken everything. They weren't coming back. Jennifer heard the telephone ring. She ran into her bedroom to answer it.

"Jennifer, I just got off the telephone with Herb. He told me Frank didn't consult with him before leaving. He hasn't heard from him in several days. But being Frank's attorney, he'd have to call him sooner or later, and when he does, he'll try to talk some sense into him, and have him come home," Mrs. Wells told her.

"Do you think he let anyone in the office know where he was going?" Jennifer asked.

"I have no idea. But I have to assume he told his

secretary. He'd have to. As you well know, Frank heads the family business. He can't run off and leave everything in a state of confusion. All our interests are at stake."

"But, Mother, you know as well as I do, Frank can run the business from any phone in the world. He doesn't need to be in the office. And besides, if he was so desperate to leave before I got home and needed to take the children, I don't think he was thinking about taking care of business. God, I wish I had a clue! A lead! I feel the longer we wait the farther away he'll be. I don't even have any legal grounds in calling the police. He's the children's father. He can take them anywhere he wishes."

"So you've answered your own question. There's nothing you can do tonight, but try and get some rest. They haven't vanished off the face of the earth. Sit tight. I'm sure this entire mess will be cleared up in a few days."

"I simply can't just sit here. I can't!" Jennifer told her mother-in-law.

"You don't have any other choice. Where would you start looking? They could have taken a plane somewhere, a boat, the car. I mean, the possibilities are staggering. We'll have to wait until Frank contacts one of us. Try to get some rest. I'll call you in the morning, or sooner if I hear anything," she told Jennifer.

Jennifer knew she was right. There had to be something she could do, but nothing came to mind. What if they all knew—Herb, Mother Wells? What if they were stalling for time, letting Frank get to his destination? What if Mother Wells was lying about seeing the children yesterday? Jennifer tried to remember when she had called last. Two days ago. The children were fine. Frank was fine. The entire time he was on the phone with her, he was plotting his escape, laughing at her stupidity. Maybe that was why he didn't put up a fuss about her trip to her parents. Ordinarily he would have hated her being away for a week, even for a few days. Frank never liked her to do anything on her own. She wondered how long he had planned this.

She leaned back on the soft pillows on their bed. She was tired. It had been a long drive, a long day. She needed sleep. She needed to think, to try to put the pieces together. Why was he doing this to her? What had she done to make him hate her?

She could no longer keep her eyes open. Sleep overcame her, and she gave in to it.

Jennifer woke with a start. The sound of the telephone seemed so far away. When Jennifer knew where she was, she reached for it.

"Herb Gardner here," he began.

"Yes, Herb, have you heard anything?"

"As a matter of fact, I have. I don't know how to tell you this," he continued.

"Tell me!" Jennifer shouted, now fully awake.

"Frank called. He wouldn't tell me where he was. He advised me that he wanted you out of the house, he's cut off all bank accounts and charge cards. The utilities will be shut off by the end of the week. In short, that's about how long you have to pack your things and leave."

"I don't understand. Can he do that? I'm his wife and have been for ten years. I have to have some rights," Jennifer stammered.

"You do, when this thing comes to court, but at the moment, everything is in Frank's name—the house, the bank accounts, everything. He has the right to shut you out. Well . . . the 'right' is not the right word. He can shut you out."

"What can I do? How are the children? Where are they?" Jennifer shot questions.

"I don't know. I really don't. I can't imagine what's gotten into him," Herb said sadly. "Did you two have an argument?"

"Nothing more than usual," she started. "Herb, did he say anything to you about filing for a divorce?"

"No, just spouted off a number of orders in his usual fashion. I listened, he talked, and when he finished, he hung up. I'm sorry, Jennifer, truly sorry. If you need a loan or anything, don't hesitate to ask. But as of this moment, I'd advise you to get yourself a lawyer. I'm representing Frank, so that's that," Herb told her but Jennifer had stopped listening.

"Thank you, Herb. But, off the record, please, if you hear where he might be, please call me. I only want to know how my children are. This must be devastating for them."

"I'll do what I can. Good luck, Jennifer, and again, I'm truly sorry. I wish I could say more."

"I know," Jennifer told him, hanging up.

She would have to leave, give up all she had known for the past ten years of her life. She didn't have any money of her own. Why should she? Frank had always provided for her and the family.

Where will I go? she thought frantically. What will I do? She tried to remember back to her last conversation with Frank. What had set him off to stoop to this?

To take everything away, especially her children? With them at her side she'd have the strength to endure anything. She could start a new life, but the not knowing, the aching inside her was too much to bear. She'd have to think, to calm down and logically plot her decision. Herb was right. She needed a lawyer. She needed professional advice. No court in the land would give custody to Frank when she was the mother. She was devoted to Cassy and Jonathan, everyone knew that. "Frank . . . Frank, what has gotten into you?" she whispered to herself.

She knew the pressures of the business were getting to him. He was drinking more than usual, he went nights without sleep. His life was like a mine field, ready to explode at any moment. He'd made some costly mistakes in the past year which had cost the company and his clients a great deal of money. He seemed to be losing his Midas touch, as well as his instincts for commodities. The brokerage firm was becoming a chore, not the game he had once liked to play. Jennifer knew her husband was at loose ends. He had spoken often in the past few months about selling the firm and going away with the children. But she was always included in his plans. Had she missed something? Had she picked the wrong time to go away? Think! she told herself. "Think, maybe he left you a clue," she spoke out loud.

Slowly and methodically, she recreated the last day they were together. Last Thursday. Frank came home at his usual time, five-thirty, went into the den and fixed himself a martini. Jennifer remembered thinking it wasn't his first, as she continued cooking dinner in the kitchen. Mildred was upstairs, bathing the children. He came into the kitchen, grabbed her around the waist and kissed the back of her ear. "So you're really going to desert us for a week," he said.

"Frank, we talked it over for weeks. You told me you didn't mind. You know I'd take the children but I don't want to have them miss school. If you'd rather I didn't go. . . ." she said, staring into his tired face. "What is it really? You don't look well. I think you need a vacation more than I do. Why don't you take some time off and we'll go away together?"

"I can't. I wish I could. I'm tired, really tired. And I'm frightened, Jennifer. I don't seem to make the right decisions anymore. I'm afraid I'm losing my touch," he said, holding her tightly.

"Frank, everyone has bad days. You can't be expected to make the right decisions all the time," she began, but he cut her off.

"Don't patronize me?" he said. "I *have* to make the right decisions. I'm supposed to know how to advise my clients to invest their money. They trust me. I'm handling their futures. I have the ability to make them millionaires, or paupers. So far, I've done right by my clients. But in the last six months I've lost more than I've made. This lousy market, this economy is shit!"

"Maybe you're trying too hard. Relax, go with your gut instincts, like you used to. Sometimes when we panic, nothing we do is right. We falter, wait too long, become overly cautious. Your clients know better. They know they're gambling with their money. Sometimes you win and sometimes you lose. People who invest in the stock market realize it. I'm sure they're not blaming you."

"*I'm* blaming me. What the hell do you know? You haven't done a day's work since you married me. You're isolated in this big house, spending the money I make, going to classes, doing your own thing. You don't have a worry in the world. You should try it out there someday. Then you'll know." He stared at her coldly, his brown eyes becoming almost black. She pulled away.

"I never said I wanted to stay in this house all day. That was your idea. You told me over and over no wife of yours was going to work. It isn't a bowl of cherries for me, either. I get bored, roaming this house all day. The children are gone all day to school. I'd love to have some challenges in my life."

"So you're bored," he said, twisting her words, and poured himself another drink. "Any other woman would give her right arm to have the life you do, but you're bored. Is that why you're going away? To get away from this boring household? Or have you taken a lover on the side to keep you company?"

"Don't be absurd! You haven't any idea what I'm talking about. I love my life. I love you and the children, but I'd like a life of my own. I'd like to be able to come home and converse with you on a professional level. I sometimes worry about *your* getting bored with me. That's all," she said, stirring the sauce on the stove.

Fighting back the tears, her eyes scanned the large kitchen, the room she was most proud of. It was the only room in the house Frank had allowed her to renovate. Her stainless steel appliances, double-door refrigerator and stove, a free-standing central butcher-block island, with all her pots hanging from

15

the ceiling, and a built-in breakfast nook in the large bay windows, her plants cascading over the imported Mexican blue and yellow kitchen tiles. She loved to cook, and she applied her personality and personal needs to her kitchen—a place where the children could sit and do their homework while she prepared the meals, watch television, and have their snacks. They almost never used the large formal dining room anymore.

"Please, let's not fight. I know you're under a great deal of pressure, and I shouldn't have started. I believe even more strongly than I did before that you need a vacation. *We* need a vacation, *together*. When I return from my parents, let's plan one," Jennifer said softly, moving toward her husband.

He grabbed her. "I know. I sometimes feel the children don't even like me anymore. I'm always snapping at them. I'm a bundle of nerves. I'm sorry, and I'm a little jealous of your freedom, to be able to pack up and go for a week. I wish I could."

"You can, and we will." Jennifer placed both hands on either side of her husband's face. She kissed him gently on the lips and he responded and pulled her closer.

"I'm going to miss you," he said softly.

"I'll miss you, too. Frank, if you don't want me to go, I won't."

"No. You haven't seen your sister's baby, and he's almost six months old. God knows you spend more time with my family than your own. You deserve to be with them. Maybe around the holidays we'll all go up," he said.

"Oh, Frank, could we? I know my parents would be so happy to see everyone. It's been years since we've spent a Christmas with them. I'm sure the children would love an old-fashioned Christmas, the way my father does it.''

''Sure. You tell your father we'll be there.'' Frank smiled his boyish grin, looking almost like the man she had married. His chestnut hair curled around his ears, in need of a haircut. She pushed it away from his forehead. She loved touching his soft, silky hair. They were total opposites in appearance. Frank was dark, olive-complexioned, and Jennifer had wheat-colored hair, blue eyes, and a porcelain-fair complexion. The children had inherited the best from both of them.

The sound of the children running down the back staircase that led to the kitchen broke the mood. Frank pulled away from her and turned his attention to Jon and Cassy.

He seemed to be overly tolerant of the children at the dinner table, trying to make Jennifer's last night home a pleasant one. She tucked them in after the dishes were done and joined Frank in their bedroom. He was sitting on the bed, a stack of portfolios in a heap next to him. She reached for a book and climbed into bed. Frank seemed lost in his work, but Jennifer hoped she could get close to him again. If only their compassionate talk had taken place later, here in the bedroom instead of the kitchen. If only he'd take her in his arms again, as he used to. Their lovemaking wasn't up to par. It had been weeks since he'd last touched her, and Jennifer was feeling the strain within her own body. She needed him, and yet she knew how he felt about her being the aggressor—he felt it was unfeminine. She had to wait for him to reach out.

"Frank, why don't you get some rest? Put the papers away and snuggle next to me," she said gently, not wanting to push the issue.

"I will in a bit. I want to go over these annual reports. I'm thinking of putting some of my clients into this company. I want to be sure it's right for them."

Jennifer rolled over, and willed herself to go to sleep. Her body ached for him and if she didn't drop off, she'd force the situation and create another scene. She woke a few hours later and looked at the clock—it was after two. Frank was still at it. "Do you know what time it is?" she asked impatiently.

"I know, I'm almost finished. Jennifer, I realize I'm ignoring you. You don't have to be the timekeeper," he said irritably. "I'm just not in the mood. I have too many things on my mind."

"I didn't ask you. I was only concerned about . . . ."

"Don't. I know better than anyone, I've been neglecting you sexually. Don't you think it's eating me alive? You're a beautiful woman, alive, passionate, and for the moment, I'm not interested. I have to get everything squared away at the office. Everyone is watching me. You know, years ago they said I'd never be able to fill Dad's shoes. He was the best broker on the street. People looked up to him, trusted his judgment. He left the business to me. I can't disappoint him."

"Frank, he wanted you to run the company, not run yourself into the ground. Nothing is that important," Jennifer stated.

"*Nothing* is that important!" Frank shouted, leaping off the bed. "Nothing! That isn't any way to talk

18

about a company that was formed by my great-grandfather and carries the Wells name. WELLS, RICHMOND AND FIELDS is the most prestigious brokerage firm in the country. People look up to us for our knowledge, and *you* call that nothing!''

''I didn't mean it that way. I'm sorry I brought it up. I just don't think anything is worth driving yourself into a frenzy. Look at you! Just look at you. You're a bundle of nerves. You're not the only broker in the company. You said yourself you've been making mistakes. All I want you to do is relax a bit, take your mind away from your work for a while. Then have another go at it, when you feel fresh and relaxed. You'll be looking at things with a new perspective. Frank, you're all tied up in knots,'' Jennifer said, and tried to touch him, but he moved away.

''Please, leave me alone! I'm too much on edge to sleep, I have to unwind, get out of here. You make me feel guilty. I'm going downstairs,'' he said, storming out of the bedroom.

Jennifer wanted to follow him, but knew there was nothing she could do when her husband got into one of his moods. She had to let him ride it out alone. Maybe a week away from one another would do them both some good. She hoped she'd find him in a better frame of mind when she returned, but knew in the depths of her soul she probably wouldn't. He'd gotten himself into a rut, and only time and one big win would get his confidence back. She could do nothing.

Frank didn't come back upstairs for the remainder of the night. He was gone when Jennifer got up in the morning.

Now she sat on her bed, and wondered if she should

have changed her plans. Maybe Frank had expected to find her home when he returned that night. Maybe he was mad at her for deserting him, going away and leaving him with his problems. Maybe he was punishing her for being an unfeeling wife. Thoughts kept flooding her mind as she tried to make sense of her husband's actions. He was punishing her no doubt, but for what, she wasn't sure. All she knew was that she needed money—money to live, hire a lawyer and find her children. She went to the wall safe in the bedroom and opened it, but as she had feared, it was empty. She dressed, rushed downstairs to the dining room, and emptied out the china closet. "Two can play this game," she thought. She piled up all the sterling and china, and decided to bring it to one of the antique shops in the next town. She'd sell everything she could get her hands on in that house. She loaded the car, and started off.

As she drove east, she remembered her fur coat. She hadn't taken it out of storage yet, and if she was lucky, Frank had forgotten about it too. She'd sell it back to the furrier. It had to be worth a few thousand dollars. Between that and the silver, she'd have enough to hire the best lawyer and detective in town. She realized it was only the beginning. She'd need more, but she'd worry about it later. For now, she felt her adrenaline rising. She had a goal, and no one was going to stop her.

She'd call her parents later. She remembered their small cottage in Marble Lake. They'd let her stay there while she got her life in order. She'd have to keep her expenses down; everything she made, she'd have to invest in finding her children. They were her first priority.

The little man peered over his spectacles at her as she walked into the small, cluttered antique shop. She smiled at him, cleared her throat and started her speech.

"I have a few family heirlooms to sell and I was hoping you'd be able to help me," she stated nervously.

"That's what I'm here for. Did you bring the things with you, or do you want me to come to your home?" the little man asked.

"I have them in the car. Shall I go and get them? It's dishes and silver," she told him.

"Well, Mrs. . . . ."

"Wells," she said. "And you are . . . ?"

"Mr. Beardsley. We'll see what we can do." He smiled, knowing he had a live one. He sensed her nervousness. The things were either stolen or she was having financial trouble. Upon eyeing her again, he went with the latter.

Jennifer helped Mr. Beardsley take the china and silver out of the car.

"Are you sure you want to sell these things?" he said upon taking another look at the treasures and another look at Jennifer. "Is it a divorce?" he smiled knowingly.

Jennifer looked away and said nothing at first, then, "I'm only interested in how much you're willing to give me."

"Well, my dear, the silver is of the best quality, heavy." He started picking up the silver tea set and looking at it again. "But, as you can see, all the pieces are initialed. Same with the silver flatware. It makes it a bit more difficult to sell." Mr. Beardsley was

21

adding up the prices in his head. Mrs. Wells had brought in at least eight thousand dollars' worth of silver. In today's market, he could make a pretty penny on it. "I don't know. The most I'm willing to offer is about fifteen-hundred dollars for everything," he said, waiting for her to make the next move. If she protested, he was willing to go another thousand.

"Mr. Beardsley, these pieces have been in my husband's family for three generations. I'm sure you can do better than that. The silver tea service alone is worth over fifteen-hundred dollars, and there are many other pieces—the bowls, the flatware," Jennifer snapped.

"Twenty-two fifty is my final offer, and I'm being generous. I think you need the money. My soft heart keeps me a poor man," Mr. Beardsley sighed. "There isn't an antique dealer in the area that will do better than that," he told her, and she feared he was right.

"What about the china?" she asked, disheartened.

"I'll give you an extra three hundred."

"All right. I was hoping to get more, but it will have to do," she told him. It's a start, she thought. She didn't have any more time to waste. Mr. Beardsley went into the back of the store to his safe. He came back, counting out twenty-five hundred and fifty-dollars.

"Be careful with all that cash," he told her. "I wouldn't want anything to happen to you. You know how people are these days. I don't usually keep that much cash in the store myself, but I had a few people's homes to go to this morning, and most everyone wants cash these days." He shook his head.

"Thank you," Jennifer said, not knowing why. She

22

guessed that Mr. Beardsley had made a good deal.

"Good luck, my dear, and if you have anything else to sell, please give me a call," he told her. "Paintings, furnishings . . . I buy it all."

"I'm sure you do," she said grimly. "But I think that's about it for me," she told him, leaving the store. She got back into her car and headed toward the furrier. With a little luck, she'd be able to catch Vito before he left for lunch.

"Ah, Mrs. Wells," Vito greeted her as she came in the store. "I wasn't expecting to see you. Have you come for your coat?"

"Not exactly, Vito. Can we go somewhere and talk?" she asked.

"Sure, we'll go into my office." He led the way down the small, narrow corridor, passed the workshop where several men were cutting fur. Vito prided himself on buying and making the finest fur coats in the area.

"Sit. What can I do for you?" he asked.

"Vito, I would like to sell my coat. I mean, I don't want to trade it for another. An out-and-out sale," she told him.

"Mrs. Wells, don't you like the coat? It looks magnificent on you. The dark natural ranch mink looks so rich against your blonde hair," he told her, almost in ecstasy.

"Yes, the coat is beautiful, but frankly, I need the money. Something has come up. I'm being as honest as I know how. Vito, the coat isn't even a year old. It's hardly been worn. You could change the lining and resell it," she stated.

"But Mrs. Wells, I don't buy and resell coats. It was

custom-made for you. It wouldn't fit anyone else."

"Vito, you could remake the coat for someone else. It's what you do best. I mean, the fur has got to be worth something."

"Yes, but not nearly what you paid for it. I'd like to help you out, but I don't know what I can do. What I'd offer you is a crime. You could never replace it for that."

"I'm not looking to replace it. I'm looking to get rid of it. Vito, I'm a perfect size ten. There have to be hundreds of women who'd fit into that coat," Jennifer urged.

"Yes, but the arms, the length, the waist—it was hand-tailored for *you*."

"Vito, give me a price. How much will you give me for the coat?"

She watched while he paced up and down his small office for a moment.

"Mrs. Wells, I'd only consider this because you and your husband have been very good clients, and I know someday you'll be back. Eighteen-hundred dollars," he said.

"What? We paid more than triple that last year, and the price of fur has gone up," she shouted.

"Yes, but it's a used coat. I couldn't sell it the way it is. I'm being perfectly honest with you," he said, and Jennifer knew that it was his final offer.

"All right. I'll take it," she told him.

"I'll tell you what. I'll give you a check for the eighteen-hundred dollars, but if anything changes in the next few months, you come back here, give me the money and I'll give you your coat. I won't touch it for . . ." he thought a moment. "Three months. Is it a deal?" he held out his hands.

"It's a deal," she said. "But I'm not promising anything."

"I have faith you'll be back. You know, this market is awful. I'm sure whatever you and your husband are experiencing is a temporary condition. I'd hate to see you lose the coat."

"I appreciate it, Vito, I really do, but it's more than that," was all she said. She took the check and left. She felt degraded and humiliated, having to sell her own things.

If she saw Frank this very moment, she'd strangle him. How could he humiliate her this way? Men! she thought. If Jennifer had her way, she'd never look at another man again. But in her heart, she knew she really couldn't live alone. The whole system was screwy. You spent a fortune on possessions, especially those for investment, and when the time came that you wanted to cash in on those investments, you got one-third of their worth. Well, she had more money than she had this morning, that was the main thing.

Now she was ready to put the second stage of her plan into action—to get herself a lawyer and a private detective. She couldn't afford to waste any more time. Frank had at least a two-day lead. He could be anywhere in the world. She made a mental note to call Monica, Frank's secretary. He must have called in to check on the office. She might be able to give her a lead.

By the end of the day, Jennifer had an appointment to see Martin Galloway, an attorney highly recommended by Herb, and on telling Galloway the circumstances he said he would have private investigator David Hennessy sit in on the meeting. David was also well known for his many successes at doing the impossible. Jennifer was starting to feel better, but the hardest part was still to come—how to tell her parents what had happened. She knew her mother would blame herself for inviting Jennifer to visit. If she had been home, maybe none of this would have happened. She wished she could avoid having to tell them, but she had to have someone on her side. The children might try to get in touch with her, and not finding her home, they'd call her parents. She had to keep all the channels open. It would certainly come as a shock. Her parents had never been aware of any tension in her home life.

Jennifer tried to compose herself and give her parents as little as possible to worry about. It was the hardest of all calls to make.

TWO

Jennifer sat patiently waiting for Martin Galloway at ten o'clock the next morning. He was late. If Jennifer hated any one trait, it was lateness. Or was it just that she was overly anxious because she was very early? It was vital to get the ball rolling, to get David Hennessy on the trail of her children. The door to the office opened and Mr. Galloway's secretary addressed her. "I'm sorry for the delay. Can I get you a cup of coffee?"

"Yes, please. Cream, no sugar," Jennifer told the girl. "Do you have any idea how long I'll have to wait?"

"Mr. Galloway should be here in the next fifteen minutes. His breakfast meeting ran a little overtime. He sends his apologies," the young woman told her.

"Accepted," Jennifer said, and sank back into the deep green velvet couch in Martin Galloway's office. His secretary came back a few minutes later with Jennifer's coffee. "David Hennessy's outside. Would you like to talk to him?"

The private investigator! Jennifer jumped up. "Yes! Please! We'll save some time this way. There's so much I want to ask him."

"Jennifer Wells, David Hennessy." The secretary introduced them. Jennifer took David's extended hand. He was a large man, about thirty-five, she thought. Ruddy, good looking, in a rugged way.

"Sorry we have to meet under these circumstances," David began. "I understand the counselor is a bit late," he went on, taking a seat next to Jennifer. "Well, there are a few questions I'd like to ask, if you don't mind. Martin called me last night and filled me in a bit about your case. Your husband disappeared and took the children with him, is that right?" he questioned.

"Yes. I'm going out of my mind. I know this is going to sound awful, but I don't give a damn about my husband. I want the children," Jennifer told him.

"I can imagine what you're going through. This is becoming quite common," he comforted her. "I know how you feel. Did you bring photographs?" David asked.

"Yes. I wrote down their most recent statistics— age, height, weight, coloring, every detail I could think of," Jennifer babbled on. David looked at the pictures.

"Beautiful kids," he smiled. "They look a lot like you," he said, trying to get Jennifer to relax. "Do you have any idea when they left?"

"I'm not sure. I returned home from my trip two days ago. I was gone a week. I spoke to the children

28

two days before I returned, so the most they could be gone is four days. Is that a good lead?'' Jennifer questioned.

''Any lead is better than none. Do you have any idea where they could have gone?''

''No. I asked my mother-in-law, Frank's secretary, his lawyer. No one seems to know anything—or if they do, they're not telling me,'' Jennifer went on.

''Is your husband financially independent? I mean, can he afford to go away for an extended amount of time?'' David asked, writing down every word Jennifer said.

''Yes. He closed all our accounts, the house. It seems as though I'm evicted.''

''What does he do for a living?''

''He owns a stock brokerage house. WELLS, RICHMOND AND FIELDS,'' Jennifer said.

''Oh,'' David remarked, impressed by the firm. ''He's well off, and we have another complication. He can conduct his business from anywhere in the world. Does your husband have a favorite sport or hobby? A favorite place . . . hideaway?''

''Not in years. His only preoccupation has been making money,'' Jennifer said thoughtfully.

''Do you have any gut feelings about where he could have gone?''

''He could be anywhere in the world for all I know. As you said, he could conduct his business from anywhere.'' Jennifer was impatient.

''He could have headed for Europe. He'd be safer there under International Law. We can't really go after him and demand he come home. After all, the children are his, too. But the legal questions we'll

29

leave for Martin," he said.

"I wish I could be of more help," Jennifer said.

"You've given me a few leads. Now I'll have to do some leg work. It will take some time. He could have driven, taken a boat, plane. We haven't any idea at the moment, but we have ways of checking. One last question. Do you think his mother could be hiding him? He has to have a contact somewhere, and that seems to be the most likely one. Was she shocked when you told her he was missing?"

"At first . . . I don't know, but the more I think about it, the more I feel she knows exactly what he was up to. We can't force her to tell us," Jennifer said, frustrated.

"No, we can't. But we can watch her, see what we come up with," he said and cleared his throat. "I hate to bring this up . . . I realize your husband has left you high and dry, and hiring a private detective for an indefinite period of time could be very costly. Did Martin tell you what I charge?"

"Yes. I've sold a few belongings, and I've made some plans . . . well, living arrangements. I should be able to cover your expenses. I hope, really hope, this doesn't drag on too long."

"For your sake, so do I . . ." David began as Martin came into his office.

"My apologies to both of you. I'm very glad you got started without me," Martin said, placing his brief-case on his desk.

Jennifer appraised him as he picked up a sheaf of messages and gave them a brief once-over. He was exquisitely handsome, graying, with piercing blue eyes and a deep tan lingering from the summer. Martin was physically fit, well dressed in a three-piece gray wool suit and light blue shirt. His smile was warm and inviting. "Now, Mrs. Wells, let's introduce ourselves properly." He smiled, extending his hand. "Again, I don't like to keep my clients waiting. Please forgive me."

Jennifer said nothing, just nodded her head and smiled back. She knew she would forgive this man anything.

"I understand the predicament you find yourself in, but what is it exactly you want me to do? Start divorce proceedings, or find your husband and children?" Martin asked.

"I'm not sure I want a divorce. But I am sure I want to find my children. That's my first priority."

"I agree. And I want you to know you're in the best of hands with David. If anyone can find your children, he can," Martin stated. He addressed David. "Have you gotten all the information you need for the moment from Mrs. Wells?"

"Yes. Oh, one more thing. Where can I reach you if I do find something?" David asked.

"I'll be staying at my family's place in Marble Lake. I don't have a phone yet, so you can leave a message with my parents. I'll write down their number for you," she told him. "As soon as I get settled, I'll give you a call, and a number where I can be reached."

"Fine, then I'll wait to hear from you," David said, getting up and taking Jennifer's hand. "I'll do the best I can, I promise."

"I know you will. Thank you for your time," Jennifer said, and watched him leave the room. Then she settled back on the couch to talk to Martin.

"Where do I stand legally?" she asked.

"Well, you know the law. At the moment your husband has every right to take the children on a vacation—if he wants to call it that. I'm sure, knowing who your husband is, he's under very good legal counsel, and he'd never put himself in jeopardy. You will have to do the same," Martin stated.

"Do you have any idea why your husband would want to leave you and take the children? Have the two of you ever talked about separating?"

"No. When I left to go to my parents, things were a bit strained between us. He was under a great deal of pressure at the office, but our marriage, as far as I knew, was in good shape," Jennifer said. "I don't understand the entire thing. I don't know what to say."

"I hate to bring this up, but do you think you could be overreacting? Could Frank have just gone away for a few days on business, and decided to take the children with him?" he asked.

"No. I would believe that too, but he left me a note. I brought it along with me," Jennifer said, taking the note out of her purse and handing it to the lawyer. He sat back and read it. "No. He means business."

"As I told you on the telephone, he left instructions for me to leave the house. He's cut off all my charge accounts, bank accounts, and the utilities. As of Friday, I'm out on my ear," Jennifer told him.

"Well, I'm afraid we can't do anything about that right now. When we take this to court—that is, *if* we take this to court—things may change. But for the moment, the house and utilities are in his name. He has the right to ask you to leave. I know it isn't fair, but it's the law. You did say you had a place to go?" Martin looked concerned.

"Yes. It isn't the most ideal spot, but I'll have a roof over my head," Jennifer told him.

"Good. Well, I think it's too soon to think about divorce. In all honesty, Frank may come to his senses, come home and all will be forgiven. I've seen it happen many times. Let's sit tight, let David do his job and keep in touch," Martin said. "Remember, don't hesitate to call me at any time. If you come up with any leads about the whereabouts of your family, please call me day or night."

"Thank you. I will," Jennifer said, getting up to leave.

"We'll find them," Martin said, and Jennifer believed him. She knew it would take some time, but they would be found.

Jennifer left the office with renewed hope. Though she didn't believe in miracles, and knew it could be a very long, drawn-out process, she felt as though her life was taking shape. Her final chore was to go home, pack, and move into the cottage.

Her parents were worried about her, shocked that Frank could have pulled such a trick. They offered their daughter all their support, their home and money if she needed it, to help her to get her life in order, but Jennifer had promised herself that, unless she were in dire need, she'd try to make it on her own. She didn't want to take anything more from them. They had their own lives to worry about. Dad was retired, and what little they had, they had saved all their lives for. They had been more than generous in giving her the cottage.

She drove home and thought about the conversation with Martin. Divorce had never entered her mind. Murder had, but she had never given a thought to her marriage being over, though it had to be. Hadn't Frank said he was leaving her? Disposing of her as if she was a used object? Forgetting the years they had spent together? In all the confusion of the past two days and her worry over the children, she hadn't really thought about the collapse of their marriage. If Frank were to walk in the door when she got home, could she forgive him for what he had done to her? Could she forget her grief and anxiety and start again? The answer was definitely NO. She couldn't. He was dead to her. She felt no grief at that. In some strange sense, she felt relieved—relieved not to have to deal with his moods, his demands, being treated as a possession rather than a person.

She wanted no part of it. To her own shock and surprise, she almost looked forward to starting a new life. She knew instinctively that she was strong enough to make it on her own. Given the opportunity, she could support herself and her children. She wasn't sure at what, but she knew that if she had them with her, she could be whole again. Jennifer suddenly felt a sharp, stabbing pain of grief and loneliness. She wished she had them in her arms. She wished this was all a bad dream. She wondered if Frank was filling their heads with stories about her, telling them it was she who had deserted them. She did leave first. God, she was frightened! She wondered if they were frightened, too.

For the first time in two days, Jennifer cried, shedding tears of grief and of pain. She sobbed uncontrollably as she pulled into the circular driveway for the last time. She made her way into the house, and threw herself on Cassy's bed, hugging one of her large stuffed animals. She remained there till morning, paralyzed with pain.

"Cassy, Jonathan, where are you?" she whispered over and over again. "Please don't be frightened. Mommy will be with you soon. I didn't leave you. *I didn't leave you.*"

THREE

The trees were turning a bright crimson as Jennifer approached the lake. Her parents' cottage was nestled in the woods several hundred feet from the road. The gravel driveway which led to the cottage was narrow and unkept. Her parents hadn't used the place in several years, and it looked it. Putting her new home in order would keep her busy for a while, take her mind off the past.

Jennifer had walked out of the Wells home this morning, slamming the door behind her as if she were shutting out the past. From today on, she would be starting a new life, a life that wouldn't include Frank. She placed the last of her suitcases in the station wagon, and drove off, never looking back. Off to Marble Lake, her new home. Her new beginning.

Jennifer found the key her parents kept under the milk box at the side of the door. She looked around the small living room in dismay. The old furniture, covered with sheets, was in sad shape, and in need of a good cleaning. She walked past the tiny kitchen, and through the narrow hallway that led to the bedroom. Jennifer was glad her father had remembered to have the water and electricity turned on. She walked out the back door, picking up kindling wood and a few logs to start a fire to take the dampness out of the cottage. The wood-burning stove was going to be her only source of heat all winter. It would take some getting used to. As soon as she got the place fixed up a little, it wouldn't be so bad, she told herself. That is, if she didn't die of pneumonia first.

She rolled up her sleeves and went to work, cleaning up the cottage, re-arranging the furniture, unpacking her clothes, and marveled at the difference a bit of elbow grease could make. The following day, her phone was to be installed.

Her first call on her new phone was to David, giving him her new number. He didn't have any news for her, but wished her well. Jennifer also gave the number to her parents, just in case the children called there. Her next move was to start a bank account with the money she had left after paying David and Martin their retainers. She'd use her money sparingly, and hope she'd find employment to tide her over. Jennifer drove through the small, picturesque town of Marble Lake, and found its residents friendly and helpful.

She did her marketing daily, getting acquainted with the local shopkeepers. They were gracious, and as she drew herself into conversation with each of them, Jennifer asked if they knew of any jobs. Marble Lake, making most of its living during the summer months, employed few people during the winter other than the local police force, shopkeepers, fishermen and ranchers—nothing Jennifer found herself suited for.

She wondered after two weeks if she had made the right decision coming up here. What good was free rent if she couldn't make any kind of living to pay her other expenses? With this on her mind, Jennifer couldn't sleep. She walked to town early one morning, and walked into the Marble Lake Inn for a cup of coffee. Mrs. Rafferty, who ran the Inn, joined her.

"You look as though you have the weight of the world on your shoulders," the woman said. Jennifer looked into her friendly gray eyes, and nodded.

"I need a job," she blurted. "You wouldn't happen to need a chambermaid, desk clerk, waitress . . . ."

"Not this time of year," Mrs. Rafferty said. "But I do have an idea. If you're game, and if you're willing to work your tail off, and although the pay isn't the greatest. . . ."

"I'm willing to do anything. It's been years since I've had a job, but I'll do whatever I have to," Jennifer told her. "What do you have in mind?"

"Well, if you walk down Main Street about two blocks, on the east side of the street, there's a bar called Phil's Tavern. A local place, noisy, sometimes a bit crazy. But the people who frequent the place are harmless enough. And Phil, he's a real good-natured slob, willing to give someone like you a chance. He finances half the fishermen during the winter months —you know, keeps a tab for them. They're good for it, mind you. Pay him everything in the spring. Go to see him. You're pretty and he'll like you. You'll spruce up the place. Tell Phil you need a job. He may let you tend bar for him a few days a week. Maybe a few nights," Mrs. Rafferty told her, much to Jennifer's amazement.

"Bartend! I've never done it before in my life. I don't know the first thing about mixing drinks. Maybe a martini or two," she said, as Mrs. Rafferty laughed. "What's so funny?" Jennifer asked.

"This ain't no high class bar. You'll get no call for fancy drinks. A bottle of beer, rye on the rocks, Scotch. It isn't that hard. You're a smart girl, you'll catch on quick enough. Give the customers a friendly smile, an ear, a few kind words, and you'll be fine. Like I said before, the pay isn't much. You'll have to live on your tips, and to tell you the truth, they ain't big tippers in these parts, but it's something," she went on.

"I'll walk right over and talk to him. Oh, it's only eight-thirty in the morning. What time does Phil open?" she asked.

"Oh, he's open. If he wasn't, I'm sure half the fishermen in town would be clawing at the door by now. Smile pretty, and talk to Phil. If you don't get anywhere with him, I'll talk to him later," she told Jennifer.

"Oh, Mrs. Rafferty, thanks a million! You don't know how much this means to me."

"Oh, don't thank me. And don't come screaming after me either, when your feet ache. I'm not sure I'm doing you any favors, but it's worth a try. Let me know how you make out."

"I will. Wish me luck," Jennifer said, getting up and straightening her skirt. "How do I look?"

"Beautiful. Best in town," Mrs. Rafferty said. "Phil would be a damn fool not to hire you. You'll boost the morale of the male population."

Jennifer walked to Phil's Tavern, stared at the door for a few minutes, composing herself, and rehearsed her speech. She opened the door, and was surprised at what she saw. The Tavern was an old rustic *saloon*—the only word Jennifer could find to describe it. Fish nets and old ships' wheels hung from the walls. The wide shipboard floors were in need of a good polishing and a long, angular bar stretched to her left, with its twenty odd, mismatched stools. A large pool table sat on the right, with a reproduction of a Tiffany lamp hung above it. Odd tables and chairs filled in the gaps. Old photographs, in need of a good dusting, hung on the walls.

The smoke-filled room burned her eyes, until she became accustomed to the haze. Several men, dressed in old clothes, rubber boots and fishing caps, sat at the bar conversing noisily with the short, stout, round-faced man behind it. Whiskey bottles were in total disarray on wooden shelves behind the bar and a cash register sat in the middle of the two sets of shelves. All eyes seemed to turn in her direction as she stood staring back at the customers. The man who had to be Phil shouted at her, "Can I help you?"

"I'm looking for Phil," she said nervously, wondering if she had made the right decision. But then she remembered what Mrs. Rafferty had told her—the patrons were harmless enough.

"I'm looking for Phil," she repeated. "Mrs. Rafferty at the Marble Bay Inn told me I should speak to him."

"Well, you're talking to him right now. What can I do for you?" the man behind the bar asked. Jennifer was too nervous to ask him for a job in front of everyone.

"Could I speak to you in private—when you have the time that is," Jennifer stammered.

"Sure thing. It isn't often we get a beautiful girl in here, asking to talk to me," he joked, moving toward her. "Are you selling something?"

"No. Well, in a way I am," Jennifer stammered.

"Well, I ain't buying anything," Phil said, starting to walk away from her.

"I'm not selling a product. I'm here to ask you for a job," she said quickly before she lost her nerve. Phil turned around and stared at her in disbelief.

"You want to work *here*! Why?" he asked.

"To be perfectly honest with you, I didn't know where else to go. There aren't a great deal of job openings in town. It was a thought. I'm sorry if I bothered you." Jennifer started to walk away.

"Hey, wait a minute. I didn't say no. I didn't say yes, either. Why don't you sit down, and we'll talk a bit. I'll introduce you to some of the boys," Phil said, taking her by the arm and leading her to a vacant bar stool. She sat down hesitantly, feeling very uncomfortable. "What is your name?"

"Jennifer . . . Jennifer Wells," she answered.

"Jennifer Wells, I'd like you to meet Allie, Johnny, Charlie, and Mike," Phil made his introductions. Jennifer smiled quickly, appraising the men.

"Why don't you hire her, Phil? She's sure a damn sight prettier than you behind that bar. I'm getting tired of looking at your ugly face," Allie said. Jennifer guessed his weight to be three-hundred and fifty pounds. His missing three front teeth added to his charm. He got up to extend his hand to her, and Jennifer realized how tall he was—about six-foot-five. She took his large hand.

"I'm not crazy about looking at your face, either," Phil joked, as Jennifer sat in her seat uncomfortably. "What can I get you?" Phil asked her. "It's on the house."

Jennifer didn't know what to order. She didn't want to be rude, but she also didn't feel like a drink at nine o'clock in the morning. "Can I have a Coke, please?" she smiled.

"A Coke, coming right up," Phil said, as Charlie chimed in. "Another good quality. At least you won't have to worry about her nipping at your liquor supply." He smiled.

"Don't mind them," Phil said, handing her her Coke. "Now why does a pretty girl like you want to work in a place like this? Be a bartender? Look at all the harassment you'll have to take. I don't know if it's a good job for a dainty lady like you," he said sincerely.

"I'd like to give it a try," Jennifer said, deciding to be honest. "I need the money. It's personal. If you'll try me out, you'll see how sincere I am. I'll work hard," she went on, not knowing why she was pursuing this endeavor. She watched Phil a moment. He seemed to be appraising her. Jennifer knew he wanted to say no, but as Mrs. Rafferty said, he had a heart of gold and couldn't resist giving her a try. He felt sorry for her.

Phil watched the nervous girl sitting on his bar

stool. She was definitely from good stock, probably running away from something. But that was none of his business. He knew she probably did need the money. She looked as though she could use a good meal, too, but today that was hard to tell. All women wanted to be thin. Phil liked women with a little meat on their bones, and Jennifer didn't have any to spare. He thought a minute. She couldn't do the place any harm, and might do it some good. She was pretty, had a lot of class, and would certainly be different than anyone else he'd ever had behind the bar. He needed another bartender since Charlene got pregnant and up and quit on him last week. He watched Jennifer sitting there nervously, awaiting his answer. He prided himself on being a good judge of character, and she could be good for him. He had a feeling about her. Winters were gradually slow—if he had something pretty to look at, he might draw more than his usual customers. The wheels were turning, and he decided to give her a chance.

"Have you tended bar before?" he asked.

"Well, in college. . . ." She started and stopped. "No, but I catch on fast. I've mixed drinks before," she rambled on.

"Don't worry about it. No one in here gets too fancy. Most of these guys drink their beers right out of the bottle. Come on, walk around behind the bar. I'll show you around," he stated.

"Does that mean you're going to hire me?" Jennifer asked excitedly.

"Yeah, for a week's trial. If you don't work out, you'll get a week's pay, and be better off, and me, I'm not going to lose anything but a couple of bucks," Phil

43

told her. Jennifer was afraid to ask how much "a couple of bucks" was. She got up and walked around to the other side of the bar. Phil showed her the beer cooler, its contents—three varieties of beer—one beer on tap, the glass racks, the refrigerator where he kept the juice and fruits for his fancier customers, the ice machine, and the speed gun, a small nozzle which had six buttons—Coke, tonic, soda, Seven-Up, ginger ale and water. Each button was labeled. Jennifer made mental notes as he spoke, soaking it all in. He demonstrated how the glasses were washed in each of the three sinks: soapy water with brushes, two rinses. He showed her how to change the water. Despite the broken-down exterior, Phil kept a very clean bar, much to Jennifer's surprise. He brought her into the back room where he had once had a full restaurant. The room was closed off now, empty except for cases of empty bottles, boxes of pretzels and potato chips. They walked to the back where the large walk-in cooler contained the kegs of tap beer and the regular cases. Although she was a woman, she was expected to stack the beer in the front cooler like anyone else. At the end of her shift, she'd carry out the cases and re-stack the cooler for the next person—the next person being Phil, because he'd fired everyone else.

"Do you still want the job?" he asked.

"Yes." Jennifer was determined.

"I pay twenty-five dollars a shift, which means ten hours. And you make whatever you can on tips. I keep a close watch on the cash register. You get a bank when you start, and you're responsible for it all coming out even. What you lose gets taken out of your pay. I'll start you on days first so I can be around to help you. Then you'll be able to work a few nights. You start at eight in the morning and finish at six. Nights, start at six, close at four or a little earlier if it's slow. Be here at eight tomorrow morning," he said. Jennifer agreed, left and reported back to Mrs. Rafferty.

Jennifer woke at six the following morning. She wondered again if she had made the right decision, working for Phil. But she didn't really have a choice. She wished she had slept better; she knew she'd be dead tired by mid-morning. For fear of sleeping too late and missing her eight o'clock call, Jennifer dragged herself out of bed, made herself a cup of coffee, and stared out at the lake. It was such a beautiful view from her window. The leaves were steadily falling off the trees, and as one by one they fell to the ground, Jennifer felt that one more piece was put together in her life. Every time the phone rang, she expected it to be Martin or David, but neither called. Still no word on Frank and the children. She dressed and decided to walk to work, clear her head of all the cobwebs, and start fresh. She got to the Tavern fifteen minutes early. Phil was already behind the bar, fixing himself a cup of coffee. He greeted her with the same warm smile she remembered from the day before.

"How do you like your coffee?" he asked.

"Milk, no sugar." Jennifer returned his smile. "How are you this morning?"

"Same as usual. Sit a bit, you have time to enjoy your coffee before I put you to work," Phil told her. "Sure you want to work here now?"

"I'm here, aren't I?" Jennifer came back.

"You know, I was wondering whether you'd show up. I had my doubts. But now that I see you sitting here, I know you're serious. Do you mind if I get personal?" he asked quizzically.

"It depends," Jennifer said.

"What are you running from? I mean, I don't think it's the law or anything like that, but you're running from something." He was perceptive. Jennifer decided to tell him the truth.

"My husband left me a few weeks ago. He took our children with him. I'm working to help finance a detective to find them," she told him. Looking him straight in the eyes, she saw him soften.

"I'm sorry. I wondered if it was marital problems, but I never dreamed it could be anything like that. What a bastard . . . sorry."

"That's okay. I've called him worse myself," she smiled.

"Well, I don't know how much financing you're going to be able to do here, but if you stay as sweet as you are right now, the guys will cough up a decent tip every now and then. And after a while, you'll learn how to wheedle it out of them," he told her. "Now it's time to get to work. They'll be crawling in any minute. I've filled the beer cooler for you, so you'll do the same later this afternoon. I won't be far away today, so holler if you need anything."

"Thanks, I will. I think I remember everything you told me. I'm sure, though, I'm going to need your help," she said, then, feeling his compassion, added, "I promise, Phil, I'll do the very best I can. You won't be sorry you gave me a chance." She felt him melting, and realized he was a real softie.

"Now one other thing," he said, clearing his throat. "The guys might try to give you a hard time at first, but let me clue you in. One, they're all harmless, all talk, no action. Get my meaning? They have their own old ladies at home that would beat their asses if they made a pass at you for real. Two, you're allowed to give as much lip back as they dish out. They'll calm down soon enough," Phil went on, Jennifer standing beside him behind the bar.

She watched Allie walk in the door. She hoped she had dressed appropriately, in a sweater and a pair of slacks, her small bust concealed by the bulk of the sweater. The thin-soled shoes she wore gave no support—Jennifer realized she'd have to invest in ones more suitable.

"Good morning, lovely lady," Allie said, sitting himself down toward the middle of the bar.

"Jennifer," she corrected him.

"Jennifer," he repeated, and smiled. She smiled back. "Scotch and water, that's my drink. You'll never have to ask me again. Always drink the same thing," he told her and she made a mental note.

"I'll remember," she said, handing him his drink and watching him put it away in one gulp. He placed the glass back down on the bar and she filled it again. This time he drank more slowly. Johnny walked in with Charlie and Vinny. They sat next to Allie, and all greeted her. They were beer drinkers. She found herself being able to enter easily in conversation with these men. As amazed as she was at the hour they were drinking, she was even more amazed at the hour they got up, and were out on their boats. By eight in the morning, they had done a day's work. The alcohol warmed them up, since they were chilled to the bone.

Their hands were chapped and cut from their hard labor.

They were wise beyond her comprehension. None of them had book learning, but they had acquired their knowledge the hard way, through trial and error. She felt herself warming to them, her fears subsiding. And Allie, the biggest, was the tenderest of them all. He had five children of his own, and another three he had picked up along the way—strays no one wanted, but everyone was welcome in his home, and he treated them as if they were his own, giving them love and responsibilty. All his children worked his boat from time to time. There were no free rides.

Vinny had a different outlook on life. He had worked himself to the bone the first thirty years of his life, and he was bitter. Now he'd work long enough to go back on unemployment, contented to spend his check at Phil's. When it ran out, he'd work a day or two on one of the boats to pay the rent.

Charlie had his own hours. He'd drink at Phil's until two in the afternoon, then go home to his family. He went to bed early, and was never seen out at night. He always had a smile on his face, and no matter what blows life struck, he never seemed touched by it.

Then there was Johnny. He was a bit younger than the rest. A born loser, he couldn't make it as a fisherman, rancher, or a husband. He drank to get himself drunk enough to go home to face his unhappy marriage. Johnny was a dreamer, always talking about making it big one day. The big score. He was a gambler, but he didn't know when to quit, and his luck never changed. He always lost, even when he was the big winner. He'd stay a little too long, double the odds, and lose his whole pot.

Jennifer learned their quirks the first day. They all were eager to talk to her. They had a new ear, and a pretty one, too. The other customers were very much the same—friendly, helpful, and eager to make a good impression. Jennifer sensed Phil's presence even though he stayed in the back most of the day, letting her get the feel of the place. Allie would point out the bottle she was looking for every now and then when she seemed lost. The customers knew the bar as well as Phil, and knew where everything was hidden. They told her the prices of drinks when she wasn't sure, and included her in on jokes and stories, making her feel at home.

The pool table was in constant use, and now and then, Jennifer had to step in and arbitrate who was next in line. Not wanting to hassle her, they let her call the shots. She'd buy the loser a drink and everyone felt better.

Phil was pleased with the way she was catching on. Even Jennifer was amazed at her natural ability to communicate with these people. It was as if she'd had it stored up all these years. In a strange way, she felt she had something in common with these men. She too was misplaced, searching for something and setting up goals for herself. It was as if she were making a new family to fill the void of the one she had lost.

"Buy Vinny a drink on me," Charlie said, as Jennifer pulled another beer out of the cooler.

"Beat you again, huh, Charlie?" Jennifer smiled.

"He's on a lucky streak," Charlie said, but Jennifer

could see beneath the surface. Vinny was running out of money, and Charlie really didn't believe in charity from the boys. "I'll get him tomorrow," Charlie came back.

"As long as you're buying, how about one for me?" Allie laughed across the bar.

"Sure, fix him up with one too. It's only money," he said, and Jennifer wondered how much they all had left from the day's pay after they left the bar. But that was really none of her concern.

If Jennifer learned one thing, it was that these men had a sort of camaraderie among themselves. They felt comfortable together; no airs, no one better than the other, they all mixed well—farmers and fishermen, ranchers and businessmen. Their occupations didn't seem to matter inside this hideaway. Jennifer realized how limited her knowledge was about the workers. She listened with a new insight. She was learning about a new world, and she enjoyed soaking it all in.

The afternoon seemed to fly by. She went to the large walk-in cooler, carried the cases of beer to the front, and when Allie saw her, he jumped up from his seat to give her a hand, for which she was grateful. She signed the petty cash slip and took her twenty-five dollars from the cash register before emptying it into the pouch. Phil refilled the register with his own bank.

"How'd you like your first day?" he asked, knowing the answer.

"I liked it. But I'm dead. My feet are killing me," she confessed.

"I'd advise you to buy yourself a pair of comfortable shoes."

"I'm one step ahead of you. I'll do it the first chance I get. I'm really sorry I didn't bring my car to town. I'm too tired to walk home," she said.

"Hey, Allie, if you don't go home your wife's going to come down here and beat your ass," Phil shouted. "On your way, drop Jennifer off, she's had a long day with you guys."

"Sure thing. Don't you have a car?" Allie was concerned. "Because I got a friend who's selling one real cheap."

"I have a car, but I decided to walk to work today. Thanks anyway."

"Come on. I'll give you a lift home," he said. Jennifer wondered how he could be sober after polishing off a quart of Scotch. But in comparison to his size, it was a drop in the bucket.

"Are you sure I won't be taking you out of the way?"

"Nah, I got to get home anyway. The old lady hates it when I don't show up on time for dinner. You know, two chickens could go to waste," he poked fun at his large body. Jennifer laughed as they left the bar.

The cold air felt good. Jennifer took a deep breath. It smelled fresh and clean, unlike the stale tobacco and beer odors she'd been breathing all day. It was as if she'd come alive again. Jennifer was almost sorry she'd decided to take a ride with Allie. The walk would have done her good.

Allie opened the door to the pick-up truck for her, and she got in. She was drained, and felt like retreating inside herself for a bit, taking a hot bath, and climbing into her bed.

But she never made it into the tub. She decided to

lie down for a few minutes, and woke up to find the sun in her eyes. It was six-thirty the following morning. She couldn't believe it. She had barely enough time to shower, change and eat a small breakfast before reporting to work. But she felt good. It was the first peaceful night's sleep she'd had since the start of her nightmare. Her bones ached, but she felt alive again. Her life had some purpose. She figured it would take her at least a week to get used to this new routine.

Phil was waiting for her with a cup of coffee when she walked in. "You were a big hit yesterday. I'm thinking of retiring and leaving the place to you." He laughed.

"I liked them, too. I have to admit at first I was a bit skeptical. I didn't know if I could relate to them. I know nothing about fishing, and even less about farming. I thought we'd sit here all day and stare at one another, but they really opened up. Made me feel like one of the family," Jennifer said happily.

"I have something for you," Phil said, taking a spare key out of his pocket. "I thought you might need this from time to time. Sometimes I have the habit of oversleeping," he said, handing it to her. She took it.

"I thought I was on a week's trial. Are you sure you want to give me the key?" She was proud of her accomplishment.

"Sure. You're a hard worker, everyone likes you. So who am I to complain? But one thing. Use the shot glass when pouring drinks. I'll go broke, the way you dump the liquor in the glasses. I know that's one of the reasons the guys love you. But they'll have to get

52

used to the old treatment. One day of doubles is enough."

"I'm sorry. I didn't know." Jennifer was genuinely embarrassed. She fixed drinks here the way she would have at home—no need to measure. But Phil was right. They were paying for one ounce. "I don't know what to say."

"It's my fault. I should have told you. After using the shot glass for a while, you'll be able to feel the cut-off. Pouring will come naturally."

"Then Allie drank *two* quarts of Scotch, not one!" Jennifer laughed nervously.

"Well, it wasn't that bad. But you did make a big dent in my liquor supply," Phil teased, and Jennifer knew he wasn't mad, but he was going to tease her no end.

"How about if I give them all half a shot today?" Jennifer teased back.

"You do, and you'll not live to see the end of the day," Phil came back.

"I'm really glad you're not mad at me. It was one big error," Jennifer told him.

Phil got more serious. "How are things going? I mean, did you hear anything about the children?"

"No. I fell asleep as soon as I got home. And I worked all day and didn't have time to call."

"Well, you make sure you take a few minutes and call today. I mean, that's why you're working here to begin with. Not that I want to see you go. But you're a nice lady. I'd like to see you get your kids back," Phil went on.

"Thanks, Phil. You're the first person I've told and I appreciate your concern," Jennifer said, feeling the tears well up inside her. "Well, we'd better get things set up." She turned and walked to the other side of the bar, took the broom and started sweeping up the leftovers of last night's debris. Phil let her; he knew he had upset her, and didn't know what to say.

Johnny was the first one to walk in. He sat down in his usual seat, and Jennifer immediately served him a beer.

"Want to play a fun game?" he said. "Hand me a shot glass." Jennifer gave it to him. He took three dimes out of his pocket and placed them in the shot glass.

"What do you want, heads or tails?" he asked her.

"Heads," Jennifer said, leaning over the bar so she could watch what he was doing. He shook the glass, and threw the dimes on the bar. Two dimes came up tails, one came up heads. "You lose." He smiled.

"What does all that mean?" Jennifer was puzzled.

"Well, it's usually a betting game. See, if I call heads, and two dimes come up heads, I keep rolling until tails come up. I'll put up, say, ten dollars and my opponent covers my ten dollar bet. Then anyone watching can take a piece of the action. Like, if you don't want to bet ten, only five, then someone else will cover the other five. Do you follow me so far?" he asked. Jennifer nodded. "When tails comes up, then the other guy gets a chance to roll, until heads come up again. The other night I rolled heads fourteen times in a row," he told her. "I would have cleaned up."

"But you kept going," Jennifer said knowingly.

"Yep. I sometimes don't know when to quit. I broke out even, though. It was fun," he said. "I'll play you for a dollar," he challenged.

"No. I don't gamble. I see no future in it. If I lost, I couldn't justify it to myself. I wouldn't have anything to show for the loss," she told him, remembering Frank, and how much money he gambled with every day.

"Aw, come on. What could one dollar hurt? You might win . . . then you'd have two," he baited her.

"But if I lost, I'd be out the dollar," Jennifer said, weakening. He could see that. "Okay, one roll," she told him.

Jennifer took the dimes, placed them back in the glass and shook it. She was about to throw them on the bar when Johnny stopped her. "You forgot to call."

"Heads," she said and threw the dimes. Two heads came up and one tail.

"See? You won. You made a dollar and it's only eight-fifteen. Easy enough?"

It *was* easy, she thought. She was ahead; it beat yesterday's take of twelve dollars in tips. The guys were nice, but she could tell they weren't used to parting with anything more than the cost of a drink. She was sure they tipped waitresses and waiters, but why were bartenders different? It was a subject she'd tactfully bring up when the time was right. Jennifer put the two dollars in her pocket.

"How about double or nothing?" Johnny asked. "At this point you have nothing to lose." Jennifer thought about it for a minute and decided to take the chance.

She took the money out of her pocket again, and placed it on the bar. Johnny took two more dollars out of his pocket. She rolled again, still calling heads. This time she threw three heads. She was as surprised, as he was. She scooped up the four dollars.

"Won again. But then again, I'm a good target," Johnny told her. "I'm a natural-born loser."

"You just don't know when to quit." She tried to humor him.

"I guess you're right." But before they could finish their conversation, the others started coming in.

"Good morning, Jennifer," they said in unison. She moved over to them, and gave them their beers.

"I see the shot glass on the bar. Who'd Johnny hit this morning?" Charlie asked.

"Me. I went two rounds with him," Jennifer said.

"Did you win or lose?" Allie asked.

"I won. Beginner's luck." Jennifer shrugged it off.

"Still feel like playing?" Allie asked. "I'll put ten up." Johnny moved down to where Allie was sitting, and put ten dollars on the bar. Allie rolled first. Jennifer watched for two hours, pouring drinks. To her amazement, she watched three hundred dollars change hands. Several of the others took side bets. Secretly she hoped Johnny would quit when he was ahead. Most of the money was not sitting on his side of the bar.

"Why don't you pocket some of that?" Jennifer suggested. "At least a hundred. That way, if you lose you'll leave with something." Johnny looked up at her and took her suggestion. She looked at Allie as if to say, "A hundred dollars of it is his money anyway." She knew he understood. They played for another hour, and every now and then someone would ask her if she wanted to take a side bet. She could feel herself wanting to say yes, but practically she couldn't. They were playing out of her league.

Johnny was down again. She saw him take the

hundred dollars out of his pocket and start playing with it. She couldn't believe it. It had to be every penny he'd made this morning, and he was going to lose it all. Twenty minutes later it was all over. Allie and the others had the money and Johnny was broke. She felt sorry for him.

Give everyone a round on me," Allie shouted. "Better luck next time, John," Aliie said, laughing his hearty laugh, and slapping the frail man on the back. Johnny sat there quietly, taking a long chug of his beer. Jennifer knew from what she'd heard from the others that he'd be in big trouble with his wife. She didn't blame the woman. They had children to feed and rent to pay, and all the money was gone.

"Hey, Jennifer, will you cash this check for me?" Vinny asked, endorsing the back.

"Sure." She took the check. New York State Unemployment. She gave him the cash.

"It's your turn to buy today, Vinny. It's payday," Charlie laughed.

"Sure. Give everyone a drink on me," Vinny said reluctantly. He wasn't the last of the big spenders, but he had obligations, and he knew it. The others came through for him when he needed it.

Jennifer moved behind the bar with a little more ease than she had the day before. Now she was familiar with where everything was, and found a scrutinizing eye or two on her when she started pouring with the shot glass.

"Boy, this is some skimpy drink," Joe told her, hoping she'd pour a bit more in his glass.

"I just work here." Jennifer shrugged.

"I thought it was too good to be true, getting a

57

halfway decent drink yesterday," he said. Jennifer couldn't tell if he was joking or not. "Phil's finally broken her in, boys. The party's over," he continued.

"Sorry to disappoint you," she retorted, embarrassed. "I think it was kind of lousy of all of you to let me keep making the same mistake yesterday," she joked.

"Are you crazy? We love bartenders with heavy hands. We'd never turn you in, but we knew Phil had a watchful eye on you back there," Vinny said, loud enough for Phil to hear.

"You all could have gotten me fired." Jennifer played up to them.

"Never! Us?" Charlie said. "We wouldn't do something like that. Then we'd have to look at Phil's ugly puss again," he smiled at her, and she knew it was all right. Harvey came in then, with a small package for Jennifer.

"Thought you'd like to try these," he said, handing her the package.

"What is it?" Jennifer asked.

"Bay scallops. Bread them, broil them in butter and you have yourself one good meal. You could use some meat on those bones," Harvey said.

"Thanks so much. I'll make them for dinner tonight. I really do appreciate the thought." And for the first time Jennifer knew what her tips really would be. Not money, but little thoughtful gestures—fish, corn, other vegetables. That's how these men exchanged their favors. Well, it helped. It didn't pay the detective bills, but it would keep her going, and she wouldn't have to buy so much food.

"Deep fry them, you'll like them better," Joe said.

"What do you know, Joe? Do it like I said," Harvey butted in.

"Aw, let the girl alone. Cook 'em the way you like 'em. Don't listen to anyone," Allie said. "Hey, I'm feeling lucky. Anyone for a few rounds of poker?"

"Sure, I'll go a few hands," Joe said.

"You got two more," Harvey and Charlie shouted.

"You want to play a few rounds, Phil?" Allie yelled out.

"Maybe later. I'll play the winner," a voice called from the back.

The guys got up from the bar, and sat at one of the empty tables near the pool table. Allie bent over the bar and took the cards from the shelf. Phil came out from the back and joined Jennifer.

"Do they do this often?" she asked.

"Play cards or gamble?"

"Both," Jennifer asked.

"All the time. It gets them through the winter," Phil told her. "Why?"

"Just wondered. They don't seem to be rich men, but they sure know how to throw away their money," she said.

"Thinking about yourself?" Phil asked. His perception amazed her. "Thinking about how much you could use the money they lose?"

"Yes, I guess I am," she admitted.

"You'll get used to it. They work damn hard for the money they make. And when it gets really cold, they're half dead when they come in here—froze to death. They're looking for diversion or maybe a better way to make a living. I've won and lost more money in my lifetime, more money than you'll ever see," Phil told her. He didn't know how wrong he was. He really didn't know anything about her background. He could never imagine her living in the large home Frank and she shared, and she was content to leave it that way.

"Give us another round here, will you, Jennifer?" Allie asked, and Phil and she stopped conversing. She handed the guys their drinks, waiting around a bit, watching them play, then returned to her station. Her eyes never left the poker table.

"Could you do me a favor?" Phil asked.

"Sure."

"I'd like you to work two nights a week. I think you might make yourself a bit more money. It's kind of a different crowd in here at night. Do you mind?"

"Not at all. You still want me to work days?"

"Yeah. Two nights and three days. We'll start you on Friday. You'll have Saturday off. You'll need it. And then you'll work Sunday night. I think you'll be able to handle it."

"I'm sure I can," Jennifer reassured him, leaning against the beer cooler. Her feet were killing her again, and she made a mental note to buy shoes on Saturday, her day off. She hoped she could last until then.

"Phil, as long as you're behind the bar, do you mind if I make a call?"

"No, go ahead, I'll cover for you," he said. She took her purse, went to the phone booth and dialed David's number.

"I don't have very good news for you, Jennifer," he said. "Frank isn't in this country. He's traveling with the children in Europe. I tried to get you yesterday but no one answered."

"I'm sorry. I got a job. Let me give you the number here," she told him. "What does that mean, his being

60

in Europe? I thought that would be good news—at least we have a lead."

"Yes, but technically we can't force him to come home. He's protected under International Law. And he isn't staying in one place long enough for us to get a firm grip on him. I wish I could be more positive."

"I wish you could, too," Jennifer said wearily, feeling herself slipping into a depressed state. "What do we do next?"

"Wait. See if he settles in one spot, and take it from there. I don't know what else to tell you," he said.

"Well, it's something," Jennifer said trying to sound optimistic. "Do you think he'll come back to this country?"

"It's hard to say. You know the man better than I."

"What about the children? Are there some legal grounds we can get him on? If they're traveling, it means the children aren't in school. Shouldn't they be?"

"Yes. That's something you'll have to talk over with Martin. He could be traveling with a tutor, and in that case, he's giving them a proper education. Let me see what I can find out. I'll call you as soon as I know anything new," David told her and hung up. Jennifer tried to pull herself together before she left the phone booth. She didn't want to look worried or upset. She wanted to keep her personal life to herself, no questions asked.

Jennifer got through the remainder of the day and looked forward to being alone with her thoughts that night. She started a bath and threw the scallops in the oven. The quiet was getting on her nerves. She rattled around the tiny cottage until she couldn't stand it any longer. Her body ached from the long day, but more importantly she felt herself coming apart at the seams.

She needed someone to touch her, hold her and say everything was going to be all right. Jennifer felt a physical need, and a bit of guilt twinged inside her. How could she be so selfish when her children were out there somewhere needing her? But it didn't make her physical needs any less. She sat in the hot tub and tried to take her mind away from her body.

Jennifer remembered the last time she'd felt like this. She was sixteen years old, a late bloomer, almost unaware of her body and its functions. She never huddled in the corner with the rest of the girls and giggled about sex, nor had she ever experimented with her own feelings. She had been taught to wait for the right boy; she wanted sex to be perfect the first time, to make love to someone she was really in love with. She stood apart from the other girls in her school who were already sexually involved, and for the most part enjoying it. She hadn't realized then that what held her back was fear, fear of disappointment for the most important act in life. If she was let down, what had she to look forward to? Yet she remembered feeling an aching between her legs that wouldn't stop, not until one night when she lay in bed under the sheets, sleepless.

It was a dawn of a new era. Women were allowed to express themselves, feel the same pleasure men felt without shame. Jennifer wanted to touch herself, but she felt as though a million eyes in Heaven were on her. She tossed and turned most of the night until she gave in to her own desires. She brought herself to a beautiful climax, and suddenly she felt relaxed, and sleep overcame her.

During the nights that followed, she learned more about her own body, experimenting, touching, feeling, until she knew herself better than any man could, and when it was time to have sex for the first time with a man, she'd know what to expect and how to derive pleasure from it. Then why now, so many years later, were the old fears back, the old shame? Why couldn't she touch herself, and relax? Had she become so used to Frank that the thought of masturbation was unacceptable, second best?

"Well, there isn't anyone else," she said out loud. She could remain frustrated or give her body what it desperately needed.

Jennifer sat down deep in the hot water, closed her eyes and felt her body rise to her touch. She started and stopped several times, making her pleasure last as long as possible and, when she couldn't hold back any longer, she let go, feeling the strain of the past few weeks float right out of her body. The tension was gone, and she was truly relaxed. She felt she could sleep for a week.

Phil's night crowd was very different from the day crowd. Some of the regulars came in, but on the whole, the Tavern attracted a much younger group of people, too young for Jennifer to think about. They were interested in drinking their beers, playing pool, and listening to the jukebox. Most of the songs they played, Jennifer had never heard before—Country Western. They dressed in jeans, flannel shirts, work boots and down jackets, or some in army jackets. It seemed as though they were in a time warp, their hair too long for current taste and they weren't very different from the kids she'd gone to college with ten years earlier. The girls dressed very similar to the guys, drank beer out of the bottles, and generally were a fun-loving group. They had all grown up together, gone to school together and worked together. Still she felt the same camaraderie between these kids as she felt for the day crowd.

Jennifer recognized some of the boys who bore a strong resemblance to their fathers whom she served during the day.

"Hey, you're new around here," one of the boys said.

"Yes, I only started working here about a week ago," she answered.

"No, I don't mean working here. I mean new around Marble Lake. I've never seen you before."

"Just moved into my parents' cottage."

"You going to stay?"

"I think so. It's different, quiet. The people are very friendly," Jennifer said.

"Where you from? If you don't mind my asking."

"I'm from a suburb outside of Manhattan. I don't think you'll know it," she returned.

"I haven't been locked up here all my life. I've been to Manhattan many times. Too crowded, though. I don't think I'd like to live there. Nobody talks to anyone else."

"I lived in Bedford. And I think you're right. Manhattan *is* crowded. I lived there for a few years after college. It has some advantages though if you like concerts and theatre. I miss it sometimes."

"If you went to college, what are you doing bartending?" the boy asked.

"I sometimes wonder myself. In a way it's enabling me to meet people, interesting ones like you." She smiled. "Now you've asked me about myself, what about you. What's your name?"

"Hank. Hank Willard, and I grew up here. We own a farm a few miles down the road. I'm going to take it over soon."

"You like it?"

"Yes. If I wasn't farming I don't know what else I'd be doing," he told her, pushing the sandy hair out of his eyes.

"Have you ever thought about leaving here? Oh, I don't mean for good, but to see what the rest of the world is like."

"I did for a bit, hitched around the country after high school, but I didn't find much of a difference. Everyone I know is here, friends, family. I'm comfortable here. I suppose when I have kids, they're going to grow up here, too," he went on. Jennifer listened.

"Hey, Jimmy," Hank called to one of his friends. "I want you to meet Jennifer. She's just moved out here from the city," he went on. Jimmy extended his hand to Jennifer who took it readily.

"Good to meet you," Jimmy said.

"Same here," Jennifer returned.

"Will you be working every Friday night?" Jimmy asked.

"Yes, unless Phil thinks he needs me other times. I work Sunday nights too, and three days," she went on not knowing why. Jimmy returned to the pool table, and Hank joined him. Jennifer waited on the rest of her customers and conversed with them pleasantly.

It was after two and the crowd was starting to thin out. Jennifer was leaning against the beer cooler for a moment when the door opened. She couldn't see who entered, but she heard some of the locals shout, "Hello" across the room. Jennifer had never seen the man before. He nodded as he recognized some of the customers, walked to the end of the bar and sat down a few barstools away from anyone else. Jennifer watched his every movement. He was tall, lean, confident, and strikingly handsome. She walked over to him.

"What can I get you?" she asked, her eyes fixed on his. They were deep blue, and they seemed to look right through her.

"A beer, no glass, and change for cigarettes," he said, cutting her short. He placed two dollars on the bar. Jennifer took it, and returned a few minutes later. She watched him get up and walk over to the cigarette machine, and it was as if she had been struck by lightning. She couldn't remember ever meeting anyone who had this effect on her. He sat back down, said nothing to anyone, finished his beer and walked out of the Tavern. Jennifer didn't say another word to him. She felt his armoured shield, his aloofness. A quality that screamed out, "Don't talk to me until I talk to you first."

"Well, good night, Jennifer," Hank said, making Jennifer focus on the present.

"Hank, who was that?"

"Ross Davin. He owns a horse-breeding farm about ten miles up the road. We went to school together. He was a few years ahead of me. He doesn't say too much to anyone. Keeps to himself," Hank went on, not really telling Jennifer anything more about the man's personality than she had already figured out for herself.

"Thanks," Jennifer said, wishing she could have asked more questions like: Was he living with anyone? Was he married? What was he interested in? But she knew she couldn't be so obvious.

"Why did you ask?"

"He seemed a little different than anyone else I've met here. Not as friendly." Jennifer covered her tracks.

"Well, he's okay when you get to know him. The trouble is he's hard to get to know," Hank said. "I've got to go, my girlfriend has to get home. Hope I see you again."

"I'll be here next Friday, same place," Jennifer smiled.

"We'll be here, and if I'm not too tired, I may stop in on Sunday to say hello," he smiled back and left.

Jennifer waited on her few last customers, and started cleaning up the bar, emptying ashtrays, stacking up the empty beer bottles, and washing glasses. With each movement, she thought of Ross. She couldn't seem to get him out of her head. She'd never found his type attractive before, yet she remembered every feature . . . his reddish blond beard, his finely-honed, chiseled, sensitive face, his large hands, clean and smooth. He was unlike the Ivy Leaguers she usually found attractive.

When the last customer left, she decided to close the place and go home. It had been a long night, and she was tired. She wasn't used to staying up until four in the morning. She shut off the lights, locked the door and got into her car. Jennifer looked up and saw Ross's truck stopped at the light. Her heart stopped for a moment as she recognized him at the wheel. The light changed and he took off. Heading home? she wondered. Or did he have a late date with someone? She could picture him appearing at a young woman's door late at night, not saying much—she just knowing what he was there for.

Jennifer got into her own empty bed and pulled the covers up around her neck. She fell asleep thinking about Ross, wondering if she'd see him again, and if she did, what would she have to do to get him to talk to her, notice her—make love to her.

Ross Davin sat in his living room alone, opened up a beer and kicked off his boot. He had noticed Jennifer all right. She was new in town. She wore a wedding band and, for Ross, that meant safe. No involvement. He sensed she was as attracted to him as he was to her. He had watched her move behind the bar. It wasn't the type of work she was used to, he could sense that. She was different than anyone here in Marble Lake, and he wondered for a moment what she was doing here. But he quickly put it out of his mind. He wasn't up to getting involved with anyone new, starting again. He was happy with the way his life was. When he wanted to get laid, he knew where to go, no questions asked, no dating, dinners, conversation. Yet there was something about Jennifer he couldn't get out of his mind. He knew he wanted her.

Ross had been almost tempted to stop his truck when he'd seen her closing the bar. He knew she saw him at the light, but he trusted his first instinct. Get to know a little more about her first. He let the opportunity pass. There would be others, it was a small town. They were bound to run into one another again. He closed his eyes and drifted off to sleep.

FOUR

Jennifer dressed more carefully for work Sunday night. She felt a bit foolish, wondering if Ross would come in. She took extra care with her hair and makeup and when she felt ready, she was off.

Phil had a small group around him when she entered the Tavern. Everyone looked up and greeted her.

"What are we playing tonight?" she asked when she saw the money on the bar.

"Bill here has a new toy. A punch board. Pick a number, and whoever gets high or low, if that's what they call, wins. A dollar a shot," Phil said. "Want to play a round?"

"Just one," Jennifer said, feeling lucky. She made a mental bet in her head that if she won, Ross would come in. If she lost, he wouldn't.

"High number wins." Bill handed her the board to punch out a number. She drew 999, and felt a sense of joy fill her. The others picked their numbers and showed them. She won six dollars.

"God, you're lucky," Bill said.

"Only with numbers," Jennifer came back.

"Want to go again?" Phil asked.

"No. I know when I'm ahead," she told him. "Something some of you guys should learn," she added, feeling close enough to the group to be frank.

"If we always played it safe it wouldn't be fun," Charlie said.

"I guess not. But don't you feel badly when you lose your entire day's pay?"

"But for every penny we've lost, at some point we've won. You can't take it to heart. As the winter goes on, you'll learn, Jennifer. We'll make a gambler out of you yet," Phil said. "You'll get a chance tonight. Sunday night's usually slow, we play poker. You're welcome to join us."

"Not me. I haven't played poker since I was a kid. Don't know much about the game. Besides, I can't afford to play for your stakes," Jennifer said.

"Why don't you watch a few hands? We'll go easy on you," Vinny laughed.

"It's only money, Jen," Phil laughed, knowing how much it meant to her. "And if you win. . . ." She saw the twinkle in his eyes. "What can it hurt?"

"Well, we'll see. I want to watch a bit first," she insisted.

"Are you going to be out front the rest of the evening?" Jennifer asked Phil.

"Yep. Why do you ask? Do I make you nervous? You know I've stayed away all this time until you got used to the place." He was genuinely concerned.

"No. You don't make me nervous. I was just wondering if you were going to be here, why you needed me. I don't want you to think you have to put

71

me on extra days,'' she said, knowing Phil was trying to help her out.

''No. When I play poker I'm very serious. I don't want any interruptions. And these guys get thirsty constantly. I'd rather sit back and get waited on for a change.''

She thought about what Phil said. She did seem to have a lucky streak when it came to gambling, and she could use the extra money. She'd watch, and see. She couldn't hold a candle to these guys, but she'd try. She'd set a limit for herself and when she lost, she'd quit. Same with winning. It could be interesting.

As Phil said, the bar was slow. The time seemed to crawl by. Each time the door opened she half expected Ross to walk in. The boys were hours into their poker game, Phil being the lucky winner. She watched intently, trying to keep her mind off the door. When Vinny quit to go home, Phil asked her to sit in.

''I don't know. I really didn't bring any extra cash with me,'' she stalled, thinking about it.

''Take your pay out of the cash register,'' he told her. ''I don't mind. It's coming to you anyway.''

On impulse and out of frustration, Jennifer did it. She decided to gamble her day's pay. Wasn't that the same lecture she had given the guys earlier? But she hadn't lost it yet.

Jennifer sat down at the table and Joe dealt the cards. She was nervous. She'd never done anything like this before. Then she thought, what the hell! She'd been so good during this past month, not spending one cent more than she had to, cooking the fish some of the men brought her. She told herself to relax and enjoy the evening.

"Dealer's choice," Joe announced. "Ante up, jacks or better to open."

"Don't be so uptight," Phil said. "It's just a friendly game. We're not professionals," he went on, feeling her hesitation.

"I know." She sat back and looked at her hand. She couldn't open but she had the possibility of making a straight. Phil opened and Joe dispensed the cards. Jennifer asked for one, and everyone looked at her. She needed a three to complete her straight. She was almost afraid to look at the card she was dealt. Joe raised and Phil saw him. Jennifer put in her money when she got her three. She wasn't sure she'd win, not knowing what everyone else had, but she had more confidence.

"What have you got?" Phil was addressing her.

"A straight," Jennifer said, putting down her cards. Charlie threw his in, so did Joe and Phil. Bill did the same.

"Shit . . . Oh, I'm sorry," Bill said. "I thought you said you never played this game before."

"Not since I was a kid. I'm sure it's beginner's luck." Jennifer smiled, scooping up the pot. She continued to play, losing a few hands, getting uptight, then winning again. She mentally calculated her winnings and found she was definitely ahead. The next two hours seemed to fly by. Phil and she took turns waiting on the customers. It was after one when she looked up at the clock. If the card game did one thing, it kept her from thinking about Ross. She remembered how late it was when he'd come in Friday night.

There was still some time.

It was her turn to deal. "Dealer playing seven card," she spouted out like a real pro.

"You learn fast," Joe said, glad she was having a good time. She won that hand, and all the guys teased her about always winning her own deals. Could she be fixing the cards?

It was after two when they decided to break up the game. They all sat back at the bar for one last round, on the house, before calling it a night. Jennifer put her money in her purse. She was fifty dollars ahead, and very relieved.

"Didn't do badly tonight, did ya?" Phil whispered.

"No, but I can't be this lucky all the time," she said.

"You can if you're careful," he suggested, and she had to think about that. There was a message somewhere.

The last of the guys left, and she and Phil were alone in the bar.

"You go upstairs to bed. I'll clean up. You have to open in the morning," she told him.

"I don't mind."

"Go on. I didn't really earn my pay tonight. You tended bar as much as I did. And this was supposed to be your night off," she reminded him, pointing to the door. He shrugged his shoulders and followed her order, waved good night and disappeared.

Jennifer decided to clean up the ashtrays before closing the bar window lights. She heard the door open and without turning around, could feel Ross' presence.

He walked to the end of the bar and sat down. Jennifer walked over to him.

"A beer, no glass and change for cigarettes," she mimicked his order from the other night.

"Very good memory," he said, putting his money on the bar. Jennifer panicked, wondering what she could say next. She handed him the beer. "If you had waited a few more minutes we would have been closed."

"Do you want me to leave?" he asked, throwing her off guard.

"House rules. I have to stay as long as I have customers," she came back as cool as he, she hoped.

"I wouldn't want to keep you longer than necessary," he told her, his blue eyes penetrating hers. She stared back.

"No problem, I have nowhere to go," she said, hating herself for what seemed to be a come-on. She was definitely out of practice.

"No husband and kids to worry about you?" he asked staring at her wedding band. She'd almost forgotten she had it on.

"No." She didn't explain further. "Work nights?" she asked.

"What makes you think that?"

"The hour you usually come in," she told him.

"I didn't know I was punching a time clock. Are you keeping track?"

"Not really. It just seems like when I'm about to close up, you come in." She tried to hide her anxiety. She didn't want to seem too eager.

"I like a bar when it's quiet. I don't like crowds," he said, and finished his beer. Walking over to the cigarette machine, he threw another dollar on the bar. "I won't keep you. Finish locking up." He turned and walked to the door and was gone before Jennifer had a chance to say anything else. She stood in place, staring at the door, at first wondering if she had said anything to turn him off. Then, changing radically, she was infuriated by his power over her. Two could play this game. Next time he came in, she wouldn't say a word to him. She grabbed her coat and shut off the lights. She wouldn't have the chance to play his game for another week though. Her next night was Friday. She'd have to wait him out.

Jennifer lay in bed staring at the ceiling. She was exhausted but sleep wouldn't come. Men! she thought. Her mind was flooded with thoughts of Ross —but why? She had just ended a disastrous marriage with an impossibly self-centered husband. Why Ross? Why not Bobby Bahr? He was sweet, attentive, helpful. They had a common interest, both being between marriages. He also owned a bar. Bobby would stop by each chance he got to have a drink at Phil's, say hello, leave a sizable tip, and ask her out for dinner or a drive, but she always said no. He wasn't bad looking, pleasant, as a matter of fact, with a sensitive smile that always seemed to brighten her day. It was time she got out of this cottage for a night and met some people her own age.

Jennifer didn't feel the same physical attraction to Bobby that she felt for Ross, but she knew one thing, Bobby made her feel important, and she knew she'd be comfortable with him. He had the kind of sensitivity she needed. She could talk to him. She felt as though they were life-long friends. But why then did she have to talk herself into going out with him? Why wasn't it as spontaneous as it would be with Ross? If he asked her out, she wouldn't hesitate for a minute. But Bobby—Bobby would always be just a friend. She could never think of him as more than that, and she valued their newly-formed rapport. Jennifer knew in her heart, as she pounded the pillow for the tenth time that night, that if Bobby were to want to be more than friends it would ruin everything, and this she feared more than anything else. She could never give herself to him.

"Why are all these absurd thoughts going through my head?" Jennifer wondered out loud, sitting up. "What the hell is the difference? My children are out there somewhere, my husband has gone crazy, and I'm thinking about men. I must be going out of my mind. Suffering from cabin fever or something." She continued to talk to herself. "Damn you, Frank! Where are you? I want to get my life in order. I feel like I'm in limbo—not married, not divorced, a mother one minute and childless the next. Having a home, friends, going to school, and in a flash, living in a three-room cottage a hundred miles from civilization, and tending bar in a saloon, yet! No wonder I'm talking to myself. Any sane woman in my position would be doing the same. Jesus, I wish I could sleep, turn off the world, shut out all these thoughts, and wake with the morning sun. I always feel better in the daylight. I hate the nights, the darkness. It's like my life—dark and empty."

Jennifer got out of bed and poured herself a brandy. She put more logs in the wood-burning stove, and sat hunched up in the large club chair by the fire, wrapped in a blanket. The warmth of the fire and the liquor started to make her feel better—less frantic, less apprehensive. She began thinking, and the memories flooded her mind. . . .

It was ten years ago. She was sitting in a place similar to her present setting, arms around her legs, her head resting on her knees, staring into the fire in the large fireplace at the lodge. It was a cold January night in Vermont. Her roommate, Joan, had talked her into a ski weekend, and Jennifer had never been on a pair of skis in her life. But skiing wasn't foremost in Joan's mind. Harvard boys frequented the lodge, and Joan was going to secure herself a prestigious boyfriend. Jennifer wasn't that liberal. She knew the girls were into sleeping freely with the mate of their choice, but Jennifer still hadn't found it in herself to give away what her mother had always told her was her most priceless possession. Back in their room at school, Joan would spend hours trying to convince her she was wrong. "This is the dawning of a new age. Women have as many rights as men," Joan would tell her. "Why should men have all the fun anyway? No one expects *them* to be virgins when they get married."

"But what if you fell in love with someone special? What if he was put off by your having slept with other guys?" Jennifer would ask innocently.

"Then the hell with him. It isn't important what I did before we met. It's only important how I treat him, and what I do after we're together. I mean, what if I married someone and didn't sleep with him first, and he turned out to be a real dud?"

"Yeah, but if you didn't have all that experience you wouldn't know," Jennifer said unconvincingly.

"Great, so I live the rest of my life a frustrated hausfrau," Joan said. "Besides, I think of it this way. If I get all the adventure out of my system now—have fun, sleep around—when I'm ready to get married, I'll be ready to settle, won't have any doubts about what I missed in life."

"I guess you have a point," Jennifer said thoughtfully.

"I do. Just imagine yourself at forty, looking at the same face for fifteen years or so, and wondering if there was something better out there. I don't know a marriage today that isn't in trouble, and it all boils down to sex. If men go out and have a one-nighter, that's acceptable. If women do it, they're whores," Joan went on, exasperated. "It isn't fair!"

"I guess when you put it that way . . . but women have been doing it that way forever," Jennifer said, in defense.

"And it's time things changed. Sure, I want the usual things—a husband who makes a good living, who can give me a house, some snotty kids, and a place at the country club. But, shit, if I'm going to give the rest of my life to one man, then I want what's mine right now. And to tell you the truth, Jennifer, sometimes I lie awake at night and think about marriage, the total commitment, forty years with one person, and it scares the hell out of me."

"It doesn't scare me," Jennifer said.

"Well, you remember Alex, the first semester. I thought the sun rose and set on him. I was so in love, and even then when I'd see another good-looking guy pass me, I couldn't help looking," Joan went on.

"Sure, but that's natural. Women are human," Jennifer said.

"Yeah, but I would sometimes go home and fantasize about making love to that stranger or . . . now, I've never told this to another human being, so keep it a secret . . . I'd close my eyes and pretend Alex was that stranger. And it was so much more exciting. I wonder if there's something wrong with me," Joan reflected.

"There isn't," Jennifer tried to sooth her friend.

"Yeah, but, Jennifer, Alex and I were only together six months. That isn't long. The romance isn't supposed to wear off so fast."

"But you two broke up. Apparently, he wasn't the right one for you. You'll know when the right man enters your life. You won't want anyone else."

"You're such a romantic. A dreamer. That's one of the things I love about you. For you, Jennifer, romance is not dead. Get yourself out of those books you've been reading. Life isn't what it seems," Joan went on, plopping herself on her bed.

"You know, for a minute you almost had me convinced that my thinking was all wrong. But you've become so jaded—the more you live, the harder it gets. I think I'd rather keep my own ideals, have them stand or fall on their own. I know I'm better off," Jennifer told her roommate.

"Maybe you're right, but to sit in your room night after night, studying, waiting for Mr. Right, would drive me up the wall. God, Jennifer, there are so many men who want to take you out. . . ."

"Take me to *bed*," Jennifer corrected her. "Not one of them sticks around past our first date. None of them are interested in a meaningful relationship. They're looking out for their own interests, and that isn't good enough for me."

"Tell me the truth. Don't you ever get tempted? Don't you ever get horny?" Joan asked.

"Yes. I'm human too, but I don't want a one-night stand, or a series of them," she said.

"But maybe if you gave some guy a chance, he'd stick around longer."

"Maybe if some guy gave *me* a chance, got to know me, had some patience and compassion for my feelings, he'd stand a better chance." Jennifer turned her roommate's statement around.

"All right, we have to find you someone with a bit more staying power. Someone who doesn't go to this school. I say we go away next weekend. Go skiing."

"I'll find my own dates, thank you, and I don't know how to ski."

"We're not going just for sport. Although hunting for a mate is a sport in itself," Joan laughed, and Jennifer joined her.

"You're impossible! If I refuse, you'll haunt me all week until I give in, so make the plans. I'll go. But don't embarrass me. I'll pick someone out all by myself, Mommy," Jennifer told her.

"You're on. I have this feeling in my bones, you won't be sorry," Joan said, her eyes twinkling, and her long black hair swaying with every movement.

"One more thing," Jennifer added. "Ten years from now, even if we lose contact with one another, let's promise to meet. I'd like to know where both of us are in our thirties . . . if either of us is content with her life."

"We both may be, in our own way. I can see it all now. I'll be bitching and moaning, taking care of the kids, fantasizing about making love to Paul Newman, and you'll be happily cooking in the kitchen, probably still in love with the man you married—faithful, lily-white. If I'm lucky, I'll be able to sneak away for a romantic interlude once in a while with some gorgeous young delivery boy," Joan laughed, and Jennifer wondered if she were right. . . .

How different things have become, Jennifer thought. It was ten years later and she had long since lost contact with Joan. She was sitting by the fire fantasizing what Ross would be like in bed, her husband was gone, and it was probably Joan who had lived her life to the fullest, and was securely married and happy. But in a way all her problems had been thrust upon her. She never would have left Frank. She would have stayed, worked harder at making their marriage work.

"Why am I thinking about Joan's speeches? Why now, at my age, am I trying to free myself sexually? Am I trying to free myself from guilt so that if Ross ever came to me, I can justify an affair?" she wondered aloud. Why couldn't she just do it because it felt good? Why did she always have to have an excuse? She was thirty years old, and she'd only slept with Frank. She was the last of the old breed. Jennifer didn't want to think about that now. She'd push the negative thoughts from her mind and retreat to happier memories of ten years ago. She found herself slipping back to the ski lodge. . . .

She remembered Joan rushing toward her in the lounge, out of breath and excited. "I found the perfect guy for you! Very straight, Harvard Business student, money, nice looking, and after spending a few hours with this guy and some of his friends, I know he wouldn't lay a hand on you on your first date. So we're all having dinner tonight," Joan shot off, out of breath.

"Did you embarrass me by saying, 'I have this straight friend who's a virgin?' " Jennifer was aghast.

"Are you kidding? I told Frank . . . that's his name by the way, Frank Wells . . . that I had a friend with me who is a real knockout, bright, sensitive, and a charming dinner companion," Joan said.

"Just as bad. And you left out, 'has a wonderful personality.' It's like having to give him the hard sell, like I'm some kind of loser. I don't want to go. I'd be too embarrassed."

"Don't be silly! Believe me, the two of you will get on very well. I'm your best friend. Would I steer you wrong?" Joan said, putting her arm around her friend and leading her to their room.

"I'm not so sure." Jennifer was leery. "Don't I get to see him first before I say yes?"

"No. There isn't enough time. We have to shower, change and make ourselves beautiful."

"What's in it for you?" Jennifer asked.

"Oh, Frank has a beautiful friend. Totally corruptible. I have my own work cut out for me tonight," she told her friend devilishly.

"Joan, you're unbelievable!" she said, laughing at her insane friend.

"Listen, if I've made the right match, which I think I have, and you want this room all to yourself, be my guest. It clears the way for Larry and me. We'll take their room," Joan went on, throwing her clothes off to the floor.

"Oh, no. Listen, I'm not going to be stuck with Frank all night while you seduce his friend in their room. Forget it."

"Listen, you'll love him. You'll be doing both of us a favor."

"No. Now it's all coming to me. You want Larry, so I'm stuck with Frank. I'm to keep him out of your hair so you have a clear shot at his friend. No way! I'm not going." Jennifer balked.

"Okay, okay. We'll play it by ear. Whenever you want to go to sleep and leave our wonderful party, I won't stop you," Joan said, but she sounded optimistic. "And I don't think you're going to want to. Now get dressed. We have to meet them in half an hour," she ordered, and Jennifer reluctantly changed her clothes.

Both girls, looking radiant, entered the bar a half hour later. Jennifer was not prepared for what she saw. Had Joan not chosen Frank for her, she would have picked him out of a crowd herself. She felt her heart quicken as Joan introduced them. His wide, boyish grin, as he extended his hand to her, captured her heart immediately. She was glad she'd come. She smiled back at him, at a loss for words. She was grateful they were ready to go to their table before the moment became more awkward for her.

"Larry and I have a drink coming from the bar. What can I get for you?" Frank asked, his easy manner relaxing her.

"I'll have a glass of wine." Jennifer tried to think.

"Red or white?"

"White, thank you," she told him, wondering if he was as relieved by her appearance as she was by his. Frank ordered her drink and turned his attention to her. She felt his warmth and sincere interest and felt like having a grand time. They both started talking at the same time, and laughed. "I was just going to say that, as a rule, I hate blind dates," Jennifer said. "But

I think this one is going to work out all right," she added, feeling it was a dumb statement.

"Well, I have to confess," he said as he moved his chair closer to hers, "Joan would like to take credit for fixing us up, but I saw you first, realized Joan was traveling with you, and since she seemed the more gregarious of you two, I let her arrange our dinner party. I knew she was more interested in Larry anyway," he confessed. "And I'm glad."

Jennifer felt much better. He wasn't put on the spot. He liked her.

"Let's never tell her. There's no harm in letting her take the credit," Jennifer stated.

"None. I was getting worried, though. I might have had to come up to you cold turkey and get to know you. I'm not so good at that," Frank went on, his brown eyes looking straight at her. She couldn't believe it. She was sure he could have anyone he wanted. She also couldn't believe he could be shy. He was so good at making people feel comfortable. It was a gift people were born with.

"We'll finish dinner with Joan and Larry, then slip off by ourselves," he said, squeezing her hand under the table, then turning his attention for a moment to the other couple who were locked in their own world.

"I'm dying for a rack of lamb. Who'd like to share it with me?" Frank asked.

"Not me," Joan stated. "I'm going to have the veal and Larry 's going to have the fish special. We've decided to share."

"I'll share the lamb with you. It's one of my favorite dishes," Jennifer said.

"Good. How do you like it?"

"Medium, if it's okay with you?"

"Perfect. A girl after my own heart. Now that we've gotten the ordering out of the way, I want to thank Joan for setting up this very nice dinner party. Here's to an enjoyable evening," Frank said.

"Hear! Hear!" Joan cried. Larry touched his glass to hers, and they retreated back into their own little world, leaving Frank and Jennifer to make conversation.

"Joan says you're at Harvard Business," Jennifer stated.

"Yes, the family is grooming me to take over the company someday. When dad retires, that is. I'm looking forward to it. I finish in June. And you have two more years?"

"Yes. I have to admit, I'm still not sure what I want to do when I get out of school. I guess teach, but for some reason, it doesn't really appeal to me. I wish I had more definite plans," she confessed.

"Unlike me. I had definite plans when I was born. I'm the only son of a large family stock brokerage firm. My destiny was planned for me at birth. I never had a chance to see it any other way."

"Do you think you'll ever resent it? I mean, being forced into a life you didn't decide for yourself?"

"I don't know. Maybe. If there was another son, and he could take my father's place . . . maybe. But there isn't, so I have to do it."

"I may be talking out of turn, but I detect a spark of skepticism, as if deep down inside you would like to do something else, but won't even let yourself think about it," Jennifer said perceptively.

"Oh, the usual—a racing car driver, a daredevil

pilot," he joked, putting aside his feelings. Jennifer dropped the subject: she could tell he wanted to avoid it.

Dinner arrived, and all four sat eating and making idle chatter, eager for the chance to leave the table and couple up, going their separate ways, which they did as soon as they had finished coffee.

Jennifer went back to their room, grabbed her coat, and went for a walk outside with Frank. She didn't bother to ask Joan where she was going. She was much too caught up in her own thoughts of Frank and the evening in store for them. Frank put his arm around Jennifer when they were outside, and it seemed so natural. She moved closer to him. They talked more about the past, their childhoods—hers was so different from his, since she was one of four children, born and bred in a middle-class family. No country clubs, no fancy cars, but plenty of family traditon, love and understanding. She tried to imagine being rich and he, in a way, envied her contentment. They went back to the lodge, sat quietly in the lounge by the fire, and felt comfortable with their own thoughts. There was no need to talk, no need to force anything. It would all come in time. Jennifer was the first to break the silence.

"I wonder where Joan and Larry went."

"They're probably up in our room, snuggled up under the covers," he said.

"Where does that leave you?" Jennifer asked, wanting to throw her inhibitions to the wind.

"Out in the cold, dark night," he smiled.

"If you want, you can come up to our room. We have two beds," she blurted.

"Miss McKinley, are you suggesting we sleep together?" Frank teased her.

"Yes—but not in the way you mean. I mean *sleep*," she told him.

"Lead the way," Frank said, extending his hand to help her get up. They walked silently through the hallway and Jennifer unlocked the door to her room. It was empty. She was feeling nervous again, afraid she might not be able to resist if Frank were to make a pass at her. Deep inside she wanted him, but she also felt he would be disappointed in her if she gave in too easily. This was only a ski weekend. They might say goodbye to one another tomorrow and never see each other again. She had to be sure. She wanted to see him again, many times.

Frank felt her uneasiness, and tried to comfort her. "I don't have to stay if you'd rather I didn't."

"No, it's okay. I can't imagine your sleeping on the couch in the lounge. It will be fine," she said, sitting on the edge of her bed. Frank sat down next to her. He turned toward Jennifer, moved closer and kissed her softly on the lips for the first time. Jennifer kissed him back. She felt the magic between them she had always dreamed of. They parted, still gazing at one another, and Jennifer reached up and brushed the hair from his forehead gently.

"I want to hold you. Spend the night holding you, Jennifer. I won't go any further than you want me to. We have a lot of time to get to know one another. I plan on seeing you often after we leave here tomorrow," he whispered. She melted next to him and, a man of his word, Frank held Jennifer close to him, kissed her, stroked her long blonde hair until she thought she would explode, and they fell asleep in each other's arms. She knew the next time they were together, she'd give herself to him. She trusted him, and knew he'd never hurt her. He left before Joan came back, promising to meet her for breakfast. Joan came bouncing into their room before Jennifer left to meet Frank.

"So what have you been up to all night? Frank never came back to the room," Joan said, her eyes dancing with possibilities.

"Nothing. We talked, went for a walk, and spent a very nice night together, but *nothing* happened."

"Oh, Jennifer, you disappoint me sometimes! I saw the two of you locked together at dinner and thought for sure the old vibes were brewing. I rushed here this morning to hear all about it."

"Sorry to disappoint you but, if you must know, I've been thinking about it. Maybe the next weekend we spend together will be different."

"You're going to see him again?" Joan gasped with excitement.

"Yes, next weekend I'm going up to visit him," Jennifer couldn't hide her excitement.

"I'm so glad! Gee, I've never seen you so excited about a guy. I knew I was right. I don't know if I'll see Larry again. He didn't thrill me as much as I thought he would. We'll see. I wouldn't mind going up to the Harvard campus, though, if he invites me. Maybe we'll double next weekend, if I won't be cramping your style," Joan joked.

"No. It's okay with me if it's okay with Larry. But I thought he didn't thrill you," Jennifer said, pulling her green ski sweater over her head.

"Who knows who I'll meet up there? Maybe the man of my dreams." Joan smiled.

"You're impossible! I have to go or I'll be late. Frank's meeting me for breakfast. You know, I've had about twenty minutes of sleep and ordinarily I'd be exhausted, but I'm fresh as a daisy."

"It must be love. Watch out—he'll be having you darn his socks next," Joan smiled.

"Are you having breakfast with Larry?" Jennifer asked.

"Yeah, but not until ten. I have to get some sleep. I don't have the stamina you do. *I'm* not in love," she winked at her friend, throwing herself on the bed. "Do me a favor and call the room in about an hour. It will give me time to shower and get ready."

"Sure thing. See you later," Jennifer said, leaving Joan in peace. She dashed out the door and down the stairs to the dining room. Frank was waiting for her. She watched him for a moment before entering. He looked so handsome, sitting at the table in his light blue sweater and brown pants, contemplating the breakfast menu. She imagined the way he'd look contemplating the *Wall Street Journal*. She visualized Frank sitting at the breakfast table in their apartment, reading the paper as she finished cooking the eggs, then put the thought aside. She didn't even know if Frank liked eggs! She really didn't know much about him at all. But she knew she was in love with him. She walked to the table.

"Good morning," she said smiling and began to sit down. He jumped up to hold the chair for her. She didn't care what women were fighting for, she loved all the social amenities, like men opening car doors, holding chairs, lighting cigarettes. Frank had obviously been brought up to treat a lady like a lady.

"Good morning," he smiled back. "Did Joan get back okay?"

"I left her asleep."

"Did she give you a hard time?" Frank asked knowingly.

"Not really. She does have an active imagination though," Jennifer stated and then became more serious. "Frank, I had a wonderful night. One of the best of my life. I do want to come up to see you next weekend. I only wish we had more time together. We have to leave by two in order to get back to school in time."

"I know. So do we. But you'll come up Friday night, and we'll have a very long weekend to catch up on the time we missed," Frank said, taking her hand in his. She held on to it. "We still have the rest of the day. What do you say we go up to the slopes?"

"I don't know how to ski," Jennifer confessed, and Frank started to laugh.

"I'll teach you. You've never been on a pair of skis before?" he said in disbelief.

"Never," she said, her face turning a deep crimson.

"I'll have you skiing like a champ in no time. Finish your breakfast and we'll get started," he ordered and she obeyed.

"Promise me one thing," Jennifer said. "You must spend some of the day on the slopes by yourself. I want to watch you ski. Joan told me you were very good. I'd like to watch. Who knows, maybe I'll pick up a few pointers," she said excitedly.

"I do love to ski. Some of my fondest memories as a

child were skiing in Switzerland during school holidays. Even as a small boy, I remember getting out and skiing maybe eight to ten hours at a clip. My father would literally have to carry me inside,'' he went on.

For the rest of the day, Frank gave Jennifer her first ski instruction, and then Jennifer watched Frank fly down the mountain as gracefully as the expert dancers she watched on television. He was incredible. . . .

Jennifer looked up. The sun was rising, and she got up to stretch her legs. She had grown stiff frolicking down memory lane. Then it dawned on her. Frank's fondest memories were of when he was in Switzerland. The children were about the age he was when he started to ski. He also traveled there from time to time for the firm. He had to be in Switzerland! She reached for the phone but it was too early to call David.

She sat down again, feeling stupid. Why hadn't she thought of it before? Many nights Frank would talk about taking the kids abroad, teaching them to ski. How he missed it! He never seemed to have time for fun anymore. Jennifer remembered how he resented it. She knew in her heart where they were. Now all David had to do was find them and talk Frank into letting her bring the children home.

Jennifer paced until she could call David. The secretary was cordial, telling Jennifer that David was out of town for a few days, but she would be happy to give him the message as soon as he called in. Jennifer was impatient. It was the first important lead since Frank had left. Why did David have to pick this time to be away? She told the secretary her suspicions about the whereabouts of her family and hung up. Exhaustion finally overcame her, and she crawled into her bed, thinking of no one and nothing, and fell into a dead sleep.

The next few weeks grew more frustrating. David returned her call, thanked her for the information and told her he'd do everything to check it out including, if need be, flying to Switzerland, but again Jennifer had to pay all expenses. She was almost out of money and desperate to come up with the financing for the trip.

FIVE

The winter had set in full force in Marble Lake and each afternoon the gambling at the Tavern was in full swing. Occasionally, Jennifer would try her hand, and come up a winner. She had discovered a sure-fire way to beat the odds. She watched the players gamble and drink, and only when the liquor had gotten to them would she enter the game. It was at this point that the group usually got careless, or the big winner got overconfident, bet too much or didn't care if he won or lost, usually because he had covered his own stake. Jennifer never played too long, won maybe fifty dollars or so, and feigning having to go back to work, quit. But she knew fifty extra dollars every now and then wasn't going to help her plight.

Also at this time of year, Phil neglected the bar, spending more time playing cards. He appreciated Jennifer even more. She was eager to keep busy, to learn the business, and take some of the burden from his shoulders. She was learning who the suppliers were, and how to order liquor, and sometimes she would wander into the large empty room in back and imagine what it must have been like, full and lively as it once was. The place was actually mammoth. Its twelve-foot high ceilings and storage bins accounted for nearly 20,000-square feet. Having scrutinized the area closely, she discovered the century-old molding beneath the many coats of paint, its recessed shelves, the large oak doors, and the charm the Tavern must once have possessed intrigued her. She was beginning to love the business, and it comforted her many times, helped her from slipping into deep depressions, kept her busy talking to people, learning more about life in Marble Lake and slowly falling in love with the area and its residents.

Ross, on the other hand, hadn't come into the bar in the last two weeks, and Jennifer had almost given up hope that she'd see him again. She pushed any thoughts of him to the back of her mind.

"Jennifer," Phil called out. "Are you going to stand behind the bar all day or are you going to play some cards? Bill here is quitting."

"Oh, I don't know if I feel like playing today," Jennifer lied, hating herself for being elated by taking money from these men. But she learned the harder she tried to get out of playing the more anxious they were to have her play.

"You know how I feel about gambling. I work hard for my money, which is more than I can say for the rest of you guys," she laughed, walking over to the table. "You all must have a private stash somewhere, losing hundreds of dollars the way you do every day."

"For Christ's sake, Jennifer, it's the only game in town! Cut the crap and come sit down. You know you're dying to get in on the action," Allie told her.

"Well, I'm not playing long. I don't want Phil to get the idea I'm goofing off," she continued.

"No big deal," he smiled, eyes twinkling, knowing she needed the extra cash she won. He couldn't afford to pay her more, and it eased his conscience. "Sit down, and stop making such a fuss. Women! You're going to give everyone here the impression that I'm a slave driver," he smiled, dealing her in. "Dealer's choice, seven card. Ante up, everyone," Phil ordered. Jennifer played the first few hands cautiously, as always. Watching the faces of the other players, she sipped her usual club soda, although everyone kept buying her drinks. They all figured she could hold her liquor because it was only she or Phil who mixed the drinks, and neither she or Phil ever put any hard liquor in the glass. She lost steadily the first few hands . . . watching, waiting, then, when she knew the others were playing in full swing again, trying to go easy on her, she bet more heavily and took the next pot. She had nearly sixty dollars in it. She was way ahead, and feeling better. She could relax now and start winning since she was no longer playing with her own money.

The afternoon flew by, and Jennifer excused herself a little before six to finish up at the bar, and go home.

"You can't leave yet. I want to win back some of my money," Jack said.

"No deal. I said I was only going to play for a little while, and my time is up. I want to go home now," Jennifer insisted, getting up and smiling at the group. She picked up her winnings.

"Phil, tell her she ain't welcome in any more of our games," he went on.

"Shut up, Jack. Jennifer is under no obligation to stay. You should have quit when you were ahead. That's why they call it gambling," Phil said and turned to Jennifer. "Go on home, I'll take care of the bar."

"Thanks, Phil. And thank you guys for letting me sit in on the game. I'm sure it's only beginner's luck. You'll get me the next time," she said, knowing they wouldn't.

"Don't worry, we will," Allie confirmed her statement.

Jennifer turned to leave, when she saw Ross' truck pull up in front of the Tavern. She proceeded with what she was doing, getting her coat and purse. She started out the door as he was coming in. "A little early for you, isn't it?" she told him, her heart pounding faster.

"I could say the same for you," he turned back.

"Wrong night. I'm off tonight," she said, turning and leaving him behind her. She walked to her car without looking back. She could feel his eyes on her and it almost unraveled her. She couldn't wait to get home and calm down. She drove quickly through the snow filled, dark streets which led to her cottage, smiling to herself at how coolly she had handled Ross. She thought about giving him too much leeway the last time they talked, coming on too strong. Now if he wanted her, he'd have to do the pursuing.

Jennifer heard the phone ringing as she stepped out of the car. She rushed through the front door to the phone. It was David. "I have a good lead on them, Jennifer. I thought I'd call you right away," he said.

"Where are they?" she gasped, feeling excited.

"Switzerland. As you suspected. Now I know Frank is doing some trading in Zurich, but I don't have a line on the kids. I'm not sure they're with him, and that's what bothers me."

"What do you mean, they're not with him. Where else could they be?"

"Calm down. He may have put them in a private school in or around Zurich. I'm not sure yet. But I do know one thing, I'm going to have to go over there and see for myself. I'd like to leave as soon as possible," he told her.

"Of course. Leave whenever you must. I'll get you the money," she told him.

"You don't have to pay me until I get back . . . a big plus about credit cards. But if you could mail a check to my office for, say, five-hundred dollars, it would be helpful."

"I'll put it in the mail first thing in the morning," she told him, opening her purse and recounting her winnings. "When do you think you'll be back?" she asked.

"I hope within the week. If I have any news whatsoever, I'll call you," he told her.

"When do you think you'll leave?"

"Probably tomorrow night. Don't worry about a thing. If we know where Frank is, the children can't be too far away. Keep smiling. It may all come to an end sooner than you think."

"I hope so," Jennifer told him. "I really hope so." She hung up. She had three-hundred dollars poker money for the day. She had a few hundred in the bank that would cover the check he had to have tomorrow. But what about the expense of the trip to Switzerland? She needed at least another thousand dollars.

As much as she hated to admit it, the only way she could make that kind of money was to continue to gamble. But she'd continue to be cool about it, never become desperate, show the least sign of weakness. The day she did that was the day she'd lose her edge over the other losers at the Tavern.

Jennifer realized for the first time since she walked into the cottage how cold it was. She started a fire and sat in front of it to warm her freezing body. It was only the beginning, the middle of December, and she was finding it hard to live in the cottage. She wondered how she'd make it when winter really set in. And what would she do if her children *were* returned to her? Maybe if she was lucky, really lucky, she'd have them home for Christmas, but that was too much to hope for. She didn't want to have her spirits lifted too much because she knew if she had to spend Christmas without them, she'd fall to pieces.

It was hard enough to get through Thanksgiving. She had tried to be cheerful then for her parents' sake, but when she was surrounded by her nieces and nephews, brothers and sisters, she felt so alone—so isolated from the happiness everyone else felt. She decided not to stay the entire weekend, as planned. She'd much rather be here alone than pretend she was having a good time. Her parents felt hurt when she left. They wished they could help her, convince her to stay with those that cared for her, but in the end, they reluctantly let her go. Jennifer knew she was hurting them, but she had to think of herself first now. She had to stay strong for the long battle ahead of her. She came home, asked Phil to let her work her usual nights, and pushed the holiday behind her.

Tonight she let herself think about Christmas for the first time. Wasn't it about this time of year when she was usually rushing around the stores, trying to find the right Christmas presents for Jonathan and Cassy, picking out just the perfect gift for Frank, the in-laws, her family, sitting up in their bedroom, wrapping the presents and hiding them so no one would find them. But they sometimes did. As Christmas grew nearer, Frank would pack the kids in the car, and they all would ride around trying to find just the right tree. They'd bring it home and, on Christmas Eve, the whole family would have a hand at decorating it, then placing their gifts underneath to be opened in the morning after a large family breakfast. It wasn't going to happen this year. Jennifer would drive up to her parents' house, hoping to keep her spirits up, and reluctantly watch her family opening gifts she cared nothing about. No. She'd have to find a way out of going. She'd much rather be here and block out the entire holiday, pretend it was like any other day of the year.

Jennifer heard someone at the door, which snapped her back into the present. She walked to the door and couldn't believe her eyes. Ross was standing on the other side. Jennifer opened the door, speechless.

"Just get home?" he asked matter-of-factly as he let himself in, looking at Jennifer wearing her coat.

"No. It's a bit brisk in here. My only source of heat," she said, pointing to the stove.

"And if you keep it lit like that, you'll freeze to

death before January," he told her, walking to the stove, repiling the wood already burning. "Where do you keep the wood pile?"

"Out back."

"I'll be right back," he said, leaving her standing in the small living room. Jennifer couldn't believe his self-confidence. His easy manner. She heard him coming back in, loaded down with wood.

"Firstly, you don't burn a wood-burning stove the way you do a fireplace. Watch what I'm doing," he ordered. Jennifer obeyed, watching his every movement. "In a few minutes it'll be so hot in here, you'll be able to walk around in a T-shirt," he continued.

"I can feel the difference. I think I can even take my coat off, so can you if you want to stay," Jennifer told him.

"Thanks, I will."

"How did you know where I lived?" she asked, knowing it was a stupid question.

"It's a small town, everyone knows where everyone lives," they said together and laughed.

"I'm learning," she laughed again. It felt good. "I don't have much in the house to offer you."

"That's okay. I brought a bottle of wine. It's in my truck."

"Why didn't you bring it in?"

"I didn't want to be too forward, give you the wrong first impression. Shall I go get it?"

"I'd like that," Jennifer told him. She took off her coat, and went into the kitchen to find some glasses. He was sitting on the sofa when she got back.

"White. I hope you like it." She smiled, wishing she could say more to him. Why are you here? Why did you stay away all those weeks? What do you want? But for some reason, she felt strained. She couldn't be free to say what was on her mind. She had the feeling she had to treat him more carefully than anyone else she knew. It wasn't like the instant understanding she and Frank had from the moment they first met. ''Corkscrew!''

''Oh, I'm sorry,'' Jennifer said, getting up again and fetching one. She hated the awkward first dates, the long pauses, the silly questions. She had hated them as a young woman, and in ten years she hadn't changed one bit in that respect.

''So what made you come over tonight?'' she blurted out.

''Honest, I don't really know. I stayed and had a beer at the Tavern, and decided it wasn't the place I wanted to be. I drove around a bit and my truck somehow made it here. It was an impulse. I should have called first, but that's the way I live my life, from moment to moment. I do what I feel like doing. If you had been busy, I would have left and maybe come over another time. I'm not sure,'' he rambled on in a monotone. Jennifer could feel his nervousness, and she started to adjust to the situation. They were both apprehensive about the evening. She wanted to say something to make him feel better.

''I'm glad you did. Do you know you're the first person who's ventured up here since I moved in,'' she told him, as he filled her glass.

''I thought I might be. I've noticed you're a loner. Oh, you talk to everyone at the bar, but you seem to set yourself away from the rest. . . .''

''Like you,'' she said.

''Very good. Yes, like me,'' he smiled.

102

"I know why I do it, but why do you?" she asked. "You were born here."

"Even more reason. Most people bore me. I can't muster up the enthusiasm to spend hours making small talk. I really don't much care to listen to gossip, or the everyday mundane events in people's lives. I guess in short, I don't like very many people."

"But everyone seems to respect you. At least that's the impression I've gotten."

"They respect what they don't understand. They know nothing about what I do, where I go, who I see. They just wonder and, after a while, even wondering gets boring, so they don't talk about me. They don't think about me. It's the way I want it," he went on, gulping down his first glass of wine and pouring himself another.

"Then why don't you live somewhere else? Like a big city where you can get lost in the crowd?"

"I do from time to time. My ranch is here, my livelihood. When I think I've had enough, I leave for a while, but I always come back. It's my home. Why are *you* here?" he switched the subject.

"I'm at the crossroads of my life. Marble Lake is a nice place to do some soul searching," she told him, and left it at that.

"Why don't you get off the floor and sit up here on the couch?" He was direct, and Jennifer started to feel apprehension again. With all the small talk, they both knew what he was there for.

"Before I do, I haven't had dinner yet, have you?" she asked.

"No and I never turn down a meal. You feel like whipping up something?"

"Why not," she said, getting up, stalling for time.

Jennifer didn't have any idea what she could whip up. She hadn't really bought food since she came to live here, and the refrigerator looked like it. She scurried around, putting whatever leftovers she could find together into a casserole. Panic set in. She wished she had washed her hair this morning, put on some makeup. She hated his spontaneity. And yet, it was what she needed tonight. Ross remained on the couch, contented to let her do her job in the kitchen, not offering to help.

"I hope you're going to like this," she yelled from the kitchen. "Living alone, one doesn't buy much food. And, after a day at the bar, I don't feel like doing much but sitting down and relaxing," she continued.

Jennifer came back out to the living room fearing Ross had gone. It was all too quiet. He hadn't physically left her, but mentally. He was far away and off in a dead sleep. Jennifer used this time to her advantage. She put the casserole in the oven, took a shower, and washed her hair. When she returned to the warm living room, Ross was still asleep, the glass of wine still in his hand. She reached down and gently removed the glass and put it on the small table at the side of the couch. He stirred and curled into the sofa as if he had been sleeping there all his life. She watched him for a moment, so peaceful, contented, as she remembered Jonathan sleeping. She brushed the hair away from his eyes, and took a blanket from the closet and covered him. She decided to leave him where he was, let him sleep.

She turned the oven off, picked up her own glass of wine and crawled into bed. Jennifer knew she should feel let down, insulted for the lack of attention, but she didn't feel any of those things. She felt relieved. She was glad he could feel so comfortable with her that he could be natural. She sipped her wine, picked up the book she was reading and eventually drifted off to sleep herself. It was dawn when she first heard stirring coming from the living room. She lay quiet in her bed wondering if he would find her. She would not coax him. She heard his footsteps coming toward the bedroom, and her heart leaped. He peeked in to see if she was asleep. When he saw that she wasn't, he came into her bedroom and sat down on the edge of the bed.

"Sorry I fell asleep. You should have awakened me."

"You looked as though you needed it. You were sleeping so soundly."

"I have a habit of doing that," he said awkwardly, deciding whether to go or stay.

"I'd offer to make you coffee and some breakfast, but it seems whenever I offer you food you fall asleep," Jennifer told him, trying to ease the situation, not moving a muscle under the covers. He looked at her for a moment and leaned over and kissed her softly on the lips. She remained still.

"I wanted to do that last night, but you chose to make dinner instead."

"Well, that settles it. I definitely won't make breakfast," she said, kissing him again.

Jennifer watched him remove his clothes, scattering them on the floor. He joined her under the covers. His body was warm and fit perfectly next to hers. They melted together, touching, exploring one another shamelessly, and urgently. She wanted him to take her fast the first time, she needed him. But he wouldn't. He wanted more. He gently and wordlessly maneuvered her into the position he wanted. She drew him into her mouth slowly, feeling no shame, as if it were the most natural thing she could have done. His large hands gently caressed her hair, pushing it away from her face. Jennifer moved her hands over his chest, stroking him, massaging his thighs, until he had had enough. As gently as he placed her there, he moved her away and onto her back so that he could enter her. She felt his body shudder. He kissed her deeply, his tongue finding hers, until she couldn't hold back any longer. She felt herself climaxing, reaching new heights she never thought she could reach. The excitement of a new body, the second man in her life, brought her to a peak she had never shared with Frank. He held her close, following her lead, as she came. He kissed her gently on the forehead, on her cheeks and her eyes. He moved his hands under her bottom pushing her up toward him, and with a deep thrust, released himself inside her with the same passion and fervency Jennifer felt a moment earlier. He held her for a moment longer, then moved her to her side, still remaining inside her. They both lay facing one another, holding on, feeling the warmth and goodness only lovemaking can leave. They said nothing for what seemed like an eternity.

Ross looked over at the clock. "It's almost seven. I have to go soon," he said, kissing her again on the forehead. Jennifer feared these words. She didn't want him to leave, not yet. She didn't want to stay in an empty bed.

"I know," was all she could muster. He moved

away, reaching for the clothes on the floor and started to dress. She wanted to ask when she'd see him again, but said nothing. She remained quiet, watching him dress. He sat back down on the bed, held her one last time, pulled the covers up around her neck, and let himself out of the bedroom and out the front door.

He had said nothing. Nothing about seeing her again or calling her. Was he going to show up at her door-step again unannounced when he wanted her? Was he going to keep her in suspense again for another few weeks? Instead of feeling elated, as she should have, she felt empty, let down, disappointed, and she didn't even have to go to work today, she didn't have anyone to take her mind off her despair.

"Of course you'll see him again," she tried to tell herself, but she wasn't convincing. She fell back to sleep, smelling his scent on her sheets and for the moment it would have to be comfort enough.

SIX

The next few months dragged by for Jennifer. She had slipped into a routine of work, sleep and once in a while seeing some friends. She managed to avoid spending Christmas holidays with her family, feigning exhaustion and her need to work. The call to her parents was a phone call of pretenses, her family pretending to believe her, and Jennifer pretending to believe them. Ross had not come by the bar nor the cottage, and she found herself driving by his ranch on her days off, hoping to catch a glimpse of him, but always, to her relief, she didn't. David had gone to Switzerland, discovered where Frank was staying, but the children were nowhere in sight. He'd checked all the private schools in the area, but neither child was registered. Now that the investigation was mostly in Switzerland, the expenses were heavier, and Jennifer had to continue to gamble to make the extra money she needed. She was still a few thousand dollars behind in her payments. David was patient, never slowing down, relentlessly following Frank, giving Jennifer glimpses of hope every now and then. But still nothing concrete.

To counteract her continued state of boredom and anxiety, she reluctantly agreed to have dinner several times with Bobby Bahr. She found him warm, generous, and helpful. He sensed her "no hands on me" moods, and never once overstepped his bounds. He respected her wishes, and for this Jennifer was very grateful, making their dinners together enjoyable. She listened to him talk about big business, learning all she could, and being pulled into the challenges. It was also a safe subject and one they both felt comfortable with. She realized, within Phil's own reach, he had a gold mine in the Tavern. With better management and a little more elbow grease, he could turn the business around, but Jennifer found Phil to be content with the way things were. He was making a living, enjoying what he was doing, and that was all he cared about.

Jennifer found herself being absorbed into the bar business. She liked it enough to think about opening a place of her own someday. Bobby was the only recipient of her thoughts. He agreed that with time and her ability, she could run a very fine first-class establishment. The hours were long and hard, of course, but the payoff could be rewarding for someone who liked the challenge. The bar had been her saving grace, keeping her in touch with people and keeping her mind off her problems.

From time to time, she even found herself going into Bobby's place when she felt blue. He was opening new doors for her, introducing her to new people —females as well as other males, and she enjoyed the diversion. Jill was one; one of Bobby's favorite people, and Jennifer found out why. She was a few years older than Jennifer, divorced, warm and open. She greeted Jennifer with none of the hostilities two women might have for the same man. Jill was pretty —tall, slender, with chestnut hair, always in high spirits as if life's problems never touched her. She seemed content and happy all the time and Jennifer admired her. She had also spent many years tending bar in the area, confiding in Jennifer some of the tricks she had learned over the years. She'd invite Jennifer to her home for a drink or a potluck dinner, and the two became close friends quickly. Something Bobby knew Jennifer needed—another female to relate to, to confide in, and count on.

Jill was well liked by everyone, and quickly introduced Jennifer to her friends in Marble Lake and the surrounding towns, making Jennifer feel more at home than she had ever felt in Bedford with Frank. They all seemed to have one common bond: they had all tended bar at one point in their lives, and eagerly exchanged funny stories, which lasted some nights until dawn. Jill, on occasion, would help Bobby when he needed an extra barmaid, and as Jennifer would learn, she was allowed to enter a tightly-knit group. They all helped one another out when the going got rough, and when one bartender lost his job, another who was working five shifts would relinquish one or two to his friend to keep him eating.

"You know, tending bar isn't a secure occupation," Jill told Jennifer one evening when they were having dinner together. "You may have your job today and for no apparent reason, be fired tomorrow. Owners are strange people. They think if they keep turning in one bartender for another, their business will pick up. It doesn't, but we've all learned to live with it. You're very lucky to have started with Phil, he's more relaxed than the others. As long as you show up for work, he'll keep you. The other places around here, a different story," Jill continued.

"But don't the owners have to show cause for firing?" Jennifer asked aghast.

"Not really. They use the old standby 'business is off so I'm going to get behind the bar myself.' So you'll go into the bar a few days later and find a new face waiting on you. That's how Rachel got started. I was working five shifts over at The Apple, and she had gotten fired from Harry's place, and needed to work. I gave her two of my shifts, and when it was time for me to leave, she got all my days. She's really one of the best in the business. Honest. Good with the customers, and loyal. I have to introduce her to you sometime. You'll like her," Jill went on.

"I'm sure I will. Everyone I've met through you has been very nice to me. I can't believe that after a few short months of living here I feel as though I've lived here all my life. I find myself driving down the street, smiling and waving at half the town. And they wave back. It's a nice feeling. It's helped me get through this time, I appreciate it. If there's anything I can ever do for you, please let me know—except, of course, giving up some of my shifts. I really do need every penny I'm earning at the moment, but someday . . .," Jennifer paused.

"Of course, don't worry about it," Jill told her, sipping her wine in the large country kitchen which she had just finished painting with Jennifer's help. Jill owned the type of house Jennifer had always dreamed about. An old farm house, large, spacious, and in need of a great many repairs which Jill was doing slowly. It had a multitude of possibilities which always intrigued Jennifer.

"I love this old place, I really do," Jennifer told Jill again. "You're so lucky to have found it."

"I know. I looked for years. I didn't have much money, and I had to resign myself to the fact that I'd have to purchase something that needed years of work. But it gives me such a feeling of satisfaction whenever I finish a room. You should have seen this place a few years ago when I bought it, it didn't even have indoor plumbing. No one had lived here for nearly thirty years. The doors were left open, piles of dirt, leaves and other debris were inside. It took weeks just to clean the place out. Then I saw what was ahead of me! Most of the floors had rotted, the walls were too thin, and the electrical system antiquated. It left a lot to be desired. So I tackled it, one step at a time. First the necessities, then the small luxuries. I still have more work than I want to think about," Jill said proudly.

"I know, but it's what I've always wanted to do. When I first married Frank I moved into the family home—large, beautiful and completely decorated—it was like moving into the White House, everything was too precious to move. After years of working on my husband, I finally got him to let me redecorate the kitchen. I felt such a sense of achievement, it was the only room in the house I felt was truly mine. But for some strange reason, I'd never want to build a new house. I've always wanted to find a place with character, a history of sorts, and restore it to its original heritage. Maybe someday I'll get the chance."

"I'm sure you will. I was where you are five years ago. Well, not exactly," Jill stopped. "I wasn't looking for my kids. But I mean, starting over. It was frightening, I thought I'd never make it. I have, and it was worth the struggle. This place is mine and I love every inch of it. I've even learned to do gardening, which for a city girl who never mowed a lawn in her life, was an achievement. I enjoy watching things grow, seeing the colors of spring. It consoles me. I'll have to teach you this spring," she went on. "For future reference, that is."

"I couldn't possibly plant anything around the cottage, it's so thick with trees and bushes," Jennifer began, enjoying having a female friend.

"Don't worry, I'll find somewhere to plant flowers. I always do. Do you want more wine?" Jill asked. "I have to go upstairs and make sure the kids are in bed, they have school in the morning."

"Go ahead, I'll start cleaning up," Jennifer offered.

"Don't. I'll do it later."

"I want to. It makes me feel useful. Say good night to the boys for me."

"I will, they really like you. I can't wait for the day when Pete and Roy can meet your children, I know they'll get along," Jill said.

"I can't wait either, and for other reasons. My mind is on them all the time, wondering what they're doing, if they're okay, if they miss me. Sometimes I don't think I'm going to make it."

"Sure you will. You have to. The children have to

113

find their mother in one piece when they finally come home. It's easy for me to say, I know if I were in your shoes, I'd be going to pieces," Jill told her, leaving her alone in the kitchen to tend to her own two boys.

God, Jennifer ached to be doing the same thing, tucking her own children into bed.

Jill came down a few minutes later. "I know this isn't any of my business, but what are you going to do about Frank? Do you think the two of you will ever reconcile? When you find him, that is."

"For a time I wondered about that myself, but now I know I can never forgive him. I want him out of my life entirely, and not just for what he's done but because of what he tried to do to me all these years—control me, never allow me to have friends of my own or do what I felt was best with my life. I've become too independent to ever want to go back into a controlled home life again. In some ways, I feel free for the first time in my life. And it isn't entirely Frank's fault. I was so in love with him when I married him that whatever the master said, I was willing to do. I was the one who set the ground rules, and once he got used to it, there was no turning back. My whole world centered around him and the children," Jennifer went on. "I guess it was no one's fault, but now I just want out."

"Then why don't you file for divorce? Get the ball rolling at least," Jill told her.

"I can't. Not just yet. At least that's what my lawyer tells me. I don't want my kids to disappear for good. We know they're in Switzerland someplace, it's just a matter of time," Jennifer told her friend. "Besides, I'm not about to walk down the aisle again, so what's the hurry?"

"No hurry. I thought maybe deep down, you might be hoping Frank and the children would come back to you. It isn't an unrealistic thought, you did spend ten years with the man," Jill said.

"I know I did, but I'm sure, surer than I've ever been about anything else in my life, that it's over."

"You know, Bobby really cares for you," Jill said throwing Jennifer off guard.

"I know, but I only like him as a friend." Jennifer blushed.

"You could do worse you know. He's one of the sweetest people around. He'd do anything in the world for you. Finding a new man may take your mind off the old one."

"I tried that once. It didn't work," Jennifer blurted out before she realized it.

"Out here? You mean you're holding out on me?" Jill teased. "Anyone I know?"

"I don't think so. Well, maybe you do. Ross Davin."

Jill almost gagged on her wine. "What! Why would you want to get involved with him! It's a no-win situation, no one gets close to him. I admit the man is sexy as hell—but strange. He isn't sitting around welcoming the world with open arms. He may have done you a favor by leaving. Or was it you that left, but somehow I doubt that," Jill told her knowingly.

"How do you know so much about him?"

"To be honest, when I first moved here I was looking to get involved right away. Wanted another man in my life, and I met many tending bar. Ross was one of the men I saw occasionally. He'd fly into your life and out of it just as fast. I was seeing other men, so it wasn't so painful. But one day, when he was having dinner here, and I started to try and figure out what made him tick, I realized he wasn't the sort of man I wanted to waste my time with—too introverted, too self-centered, and a taker. He does a good job at taking all he can and giving nothing back. Do yourself a favor, stay away from him. If you don't, you'll have your hands full. I know he can wrap himself securely into your heart, and you'll be in for a fall—a big one," Jill rambled on. "I think you've had your share of disappointments for this year, for the next five years. Leave well enough alone, but I must admit I'm curious. What happened?"

"Nothing really. He came into the bar a few times, and one night he appeared at my door. We spent the night together, and he was gone. That was before Christmas, I haven't seen him since."

"Oh," Jill said, not surprised. "You must have been a big threat. You frightened him off the first time."

"How?"

"He was feeling too close to you, afraid he might get involved. So he ran. He's done it before and he'll continue to do it."

"Do you know why?" Jennifer asked, hanging on every word, hoping to find the answers she was looking for.

"Nope. No one does. I told you, he doesn't talk much. Listen, hon, you're better off with Bobby. So what if the bells don't go off every time you see him. Understanding, warmth, compassion—they're much better in the end. They last—the bells don't."

Jennifer knew Jill was right, but she was much too young to settle. She wanted it all, and if she couldn't have it, then being alone didn't really frighten her.

"Well I could sit here talking all night, but I have to work in the morning," Jennifer stated, and got up to leave.

"You're welcome to stay here tonight, if you don't feel like being alone," Jill offered.

"Thanks, but if I stay out, I may miss a call or something," Jennifer said.

"I know. Hey, thanks for giving me a hand with the kitchen. And call if you need to talk. Or come back—you know you're always welcome."

"I appreciate it. I really do. We'll get together again soon. Give my love to the boys," Jennifer said, making an abrupt exit before she was tempted to stay. She was beginning to hate going home.

"Hey," Jill yelled out to her when Jennifer was getting into the car. "Don't let Ross in again if he should appear at your door," she laughed.

"I won't. Well, I can't promise," Jennifer answered, closing the car door against the cold March night.

David called early the next morning, making Jennifer glad of her decision to come home. He had received word on the children, they were definitely in Geneva. He was going to fly out and investigate the situation the next afternoon. Jennifer was grateful and relieved, but that meant she needed more money for the plane fare and expenses. She felt her head was in a vise. She was already behind in her payments, and now that they were getting closer she couldn't quit. She gave David the go ahead. She had to get the money.

Jennifer knew Phil was aware of what she was using the gambling money for, and that made it all the easier for her to get into the games. She even knew that when she was losing, he threw an occasional hand to her, but she couldn't count on his generosity forever. After all, these guys didn't play for small stakes, and she couldn't always be the big winner. She could make a great many enemies that way. But she had to try again. She had to get the money to finance the Switzerland trip.

Jennifer arrived at work to find Phil and the others still sitting around the poker table. "Have you guys been playing all night?"

"Sure have, and Phil here's the big winner. We're not leaving until we win some of our money back," Jack said. The pile of money on the table was staggering. She'd never seen them play for so much before.

"Allie, who's the biggest loser?" she asked, walking behind the bar.

"Most of the money came from this guy none of us have seen before. Came in last night for a few beers and joined the game. Phil wasn't happy about it at first, you know, you can't trust everyone, especially someone you don't know. Well, anyway, he dropped nearly five-thousand dollars."

"You're kidding. Where is he now?"

"Gone. He left about an hour ago. Johnny has a few thou at stake, so does Billy and Jack."

"Those guys can't afford to lose that kind of money. What will they do for the remainder of the winter? And then they won't have any financing to get started again in the spring. We have to put a stop to it." Jennifer was indignant.

"We can't. They'll play all day if they have to. Jack's waiting for the bank to open so he can get more cash. I've never seen anything like it in all my life. There has to be ten-thou at stake. Everyone has big hopes of winning it, and to tell you the truth, Phil isn't giving it up. He's on a hot streak," Allie continued, his large frame sweating profusely from the heat of the pressure everyone was under, and the stale cigarette smoke stank up the place.

"Anyone over there want some coffee?" Jennifer yelled out. "Sorry, Phil, but it might help."

"Never mind the coffee. Keep the beers coming," Phil answered back, feeling jolly over his new-found wealth.

"You got it. I just want to say, whoever the winner is, I expect a large tip," Jennifer joked, trying to get into the spirit of things and wondering what she could do to get into the game. God, some of that money could solve all her problems.

"Everyone relax for a half hour," Jack demanded. "I'm going to the bank."

"Are you sure you want to do that, Jack. Haven't you lost enough," Jennifer tried to be helpful.

"I don't need any advice from you, lady," he snapped. "I've been playing poker longer than you've been around. Butt out."

Jennifer stepped back and said no more. She had never seen everyone so irritated. The onlookers were as tired as the players and the losers had blood in their eyes. This was no longer a friendly game. She wasn't sure she should even consider playing in it.

Phil was the first to break the silence. "Going to join in later, Jennifer?"

"This game is a bit rich for my blood," she answered, still thinking about it.

"Nah. As soon as I clean Jack out, you'll sit in," he ordered. She said nothing.

"Listen, I'm going over to the Inn to get some breakfast. Anyone want anything?" Allie announced.

The orders came flying at him. The group was preparing for a long day, and food was on their agenda. Jennifer made a fresh pot of coffee and served those who wanted it. Phil came behind the bar.

"Listen, Jennifer, play a few hands later. There's plenty to go around. Jack and the others should really quit, but I can't make them. They're getting careless, and for that I don't feel sorry for them. But you—fresh blood, you have a good chance of winning," he whispered, slipping her five hundred dollars. Jennifer was shocked.

"Phil, I can't take it. You won it fair and square, you don't have to stake me," she told him.

"I know I don't. I want to. You can't win everything anyway. But you might make a few dollars to pay that detective. I told you, there's plenty to go around."

"Then why don't you let the others win back some of their money?"

"I've tried. I don't like cleaning them out any more than you do. But they're trying too hard, and nothing they do seems to go right."

"But Jack is out there cleaning out the family's savings. You must stop him," Jennifer demanded.

"You don't know the nature of the beasts here. They're proud. He'll lose, but he'll be okay. It isn't the first time this has happened," Phil said. The phone rang behind the bar, interrupting their conversation. It was Allie's wife, Norma.

120

"He's over at the Inn getting breakfast," Jennifer said. "I'll ask him to give you a call when he gets back," she said, hanging up.

"Oh boy, Norma is pissed. She's been calling here all night. She wants Allie home. If she comes down here to claim him, the shit will hit the fan," Phil said.

"I'm sure half the wives in this town are pissed that their husbands didn't come home," Jennifer stated.

"She's a little different. Glasses and dishes fly when she comes here. She's got a real temper, that one."

"I'm sure Allie can take care of himself," Jennifer laughed, thinking of his size. There wasn't a glass or a dish that could penetrate his thick exterior.

"Don't be so sure. If there's anyone Allie's afraid of, it's Norma. She throws a mean punch," Phil started to laugh. "I remember the night she was so mad, she stabbed him."

"What!" Jennifer was aghast.

"It was an accident. I don't think she really meant it, but she stabbed him all the same. What a sight. Allie sitting at the bar drinking five scotches, to get up the nerve to pull the knife out."

"Was he hurt seriously?" Jennifer asked.

"For anyone else, it would be serious. For Allie, with all his layers of fat, it was only a flesh wound. I don't think he even went to a doctor," Phil continued.

"I'm glad I wasn't around for that scene. And I have a feeling I'm not going to enjoy the one coming up," Jennifer said, seeing Allie come through the door with the food. Jack was behind him.

"Allie, call your wife," Jennifer said quickly.

"She haunting me again?" he started. "That

121

woman's going to be the death of me yet." He shrugged his large shoulders. Jennifer agreed in more ways than one.

"Everyone's got five minutes to eat, and back to the card table," Jack ordered. Jennifer said nothing, knowing how he had resented her interference earlier. Her heart went out to his family.

"Two-thousand fresh, new dollars," Jack said, plunking them on the table. Phil cashed them in for chips. He put the money in the safe with the rest of the cash. Jennifer put the five-hundred dollars Phil gave her in her pocket and wished she could send it right off to David, but she couldn't. Phil wanted her to play and that was that!

The gaiety ceased and the tension mounted during the next hour. The first few rounds Jack lost consistently. He was down to nearly half his new stake, and Jennifer felt sorry for him. She felt his panic. The phone rang again, breaking her thoughts. It was Norma again. This time she handed the phone to Allie. She heard one side of the conversation— Allie's. "Yes, Norma. I will, Norma. Right away," and he handed the phone back to Jennifer.

"I think you'd better go," she told him.

"I will later. She can be a real pain in the ass," Allie teased. "But I can't complain. She's a good woman most of the time. But she's got a real thing about my coming home. You'd think she'd see enough of me, she's got eight kids to keep her company."

Jennifer didn't answer, she waited for the hurricane to come through the door. She didn't have long to wait. Norma must have broken the speed record flying down to the bar. She stormed into the place a few minutes later. Allie jumped up and ran into the men's room. Jennifer wasn't prepared for what she saw. The woman couldn't have weighed more than a hundred pounds soaking wet. She was a little bit of a thing, five-feet-two at the most. She stormed into the men's room after him and no one tried to stop her. Jennifer realized they must be used to the scenes these two played.

"Allie's in big trouble now. He's going to get it," were some of their off-handed comments, mingled with an abundance of laughter.

Allie rushed out of the bathroom, Norma flying out after him, her purse banging into his chest constantly. Allie didn't try to stop her. He knew he could knock her over with one strong breath.

"Sit down, Norma," he ordered. "Have a beer and join in. This is the best poker game ever," he tried to appease her. Jennifer stood there mute.

"Jesus, you get me so mad," Norma said, calming down and plopping herself on an empty bar stool. She eyed Jennifer's expression.

"A bottle of beer," she ordered, and Jennifer handed it to her. "Surprised you, didn't I," she smiled. The mousy, dark-haired woman was calming down, and ready to join the others.

"Well, I can't say I've seen anything like this before," Jennifer blurted out.

"Don't let it worry you. Allie and me's been fighting for years. I know how far I can push him. He's never laid a hand on me though," she said proudly. Jennifer was relieved. He could kill her with one punch. "I got to tell ya, Jack's wife ain't too pleased, either. I see he's the big loser," she stated.

123

"He isn't the only one. But you all must be used to it by now," Jennifer said.

"We should be. Especially around this time of year. I wish for once, we wouldn't be so broke before spring. I don't know what gets into these guys," Norma stated frankly, which surprised Jennifer. "Hey, how much did you lose?" she shouted at her husband.

"Not much," he said. "I was smart. I got out fast," he told her, and it seemed to quiet her down.

Norma turned her attention to Jennifer again.

"Do you play?"

"Sometimes. But not seriously," Jennifer lied.

"Allie told me. It's poison, you know. Gambling . . ." she drifted back, "I don't know what Jack and his family are going to do if he doesn't win some of his money back. Poor Kate," she whispered, seeming to contemplate their plight.

Jennifer walked over to the table and refilled everyone's drinks. She saw Jack sweating profusely.

"Jennifer's going to sit in a bit," Phil announced. "I think we can all use some new blood and some new money," he winked at her. She didn't answer him.

"At this rate, we could be going at this all day," Billy said.

"Got anything better to do?" Phil came back.

"Me? No. I'm in to the end."

"Good. See what everyone wants and then cash in your money," Phil ordered. "Hey, Norma, watch the bar, will ya?" he said, with a motive. Phil wanted to keep Allie around in case of trouble. No one would dare get out of line.

"Sure, I guess I'll keep busy doing nothing. After

all, I don't have any money to play with," she said, glaring at Allie, who smiled back at her sheepishly.

"Just make the drinks, Norma," he told his wife. She walked behind the bar and took Jennifer's place. Jennifer took Jack's chair. He had lost the entire load. He didn't have anyone to borrow from, and he retreated, taking the last twenty dollars out of his pocket. "Guess I'll go for broke. Buy everyone a beer," he said joyfully, and Norma served them. Jennifer sat back down, nervously, the resentment filling the room. She knew she really didn't belong in this game and everyone felt the same way. It was quitting time, but Phil insisted, and got a few more takers. It was going to be a long afternoon.

Jennifer played out the first few hands cautiously. She felt the mood of everyone at the bar tense, it wasn't the usual friendly game. There was too much money at stake, and everyone wanted to win it. Even Jennifer. In the depths of her being, she wanted to win the entire pot. It would solve all her problems, but that was absurd, she couldn't even imagine her luck holding out that long. She sensed one other thing. She couldn't just get up and walk out of *this* game whenever she wanted to. Everyone was playing for blood, no one dared to move; unless, of course, they ran out of money.

The cards were changing, Phil was losing steadily, dividing the money evenly with the other players. Jennifer had a few thousand dollars on her side of the table and thoughts of running out had entered her mind, but quickly vanished. She felt herself getting greedy, taking more chances than usual. Winning was foremost in her mind as the afternoon dragged on.

It was growing dark outside, Norma was still tending bar, and tempers were soaring from too much booze and not enough sleep. Jennifer could feel Phil's natural vitality wilting, along with the others, yet no one would quit. Bill's eyes were bloodshot, and Jim had to look at his cards more than once to make out what he was holding. Jennifer certainly had the advantage if she wanted to go for it. She had had a good night's sleep, she wasn't tired, and her energy level was up. She could make a killing. It was a tough decision—take advantage of the people who had been nice to her and win; or play cautiously, giving in to the disadvantages of the other players. She made one ill-fated attempt at it.

"Hey guys, you've been playing for nearly twenty-four hours, don't you think we should all quit, take our winnings and maybe continue this game tomorrow after a good night's sleep?"

"Are you kidding, and maybe lose all this loot?" Jim said. "No deal, I'm just getting my second wind, that is if Allie'll go out and get us some food."

"Sounds good to me," Bill stated, rubbing his eyes. "After a little food, I'll be as good as new."

"You heard them, Jennifer," Phil said. "They want to stick it out." He grabbed fifty dollars from his side of the table and handed it to Allie. "Go get us something." Allie took the money, shrugged his large shoulders and left. He too, Jennifer felt, was growing weary from the long night and day.

"Hey, are we all going to sit around staring or are we going to play poker," Jim shouted. "It's your deal, Jennifer."

Jennifer picked up the cards, shuffled, and called,

"Jacks or better to open." She dealt out the hand.

Jennifer looked at her cards. Possibilities, she thought, but not good enough to open. Jim passed, so did Bill. She was about to throw in her hand when Phil announced gleefully, he could open. She studied her hand closely and decided to go for a straight. She dealt out the other cards and took only one herself. She needed a ten. She felt her heart quicken, and her face flush, as she reluctantly looked at the card she had dealt herself. It was a three, she had lost the hand. Jennifer threw her cards on the table and waited to see what the others did. She watched the expressions of their faces, Phil was chuckling silently to himself, while Bill and Jim were thinking hard on what they should do. She knew there and then that Phil was going to win, and win he did, leaving the others far behind him. If things kept up the way they were going, it was soon going to be a match between Jennifer and Phil, and relief flooded through her. She knew she could get out of the game and home to her bed with her winnings.

The foursome played for another three hours, everyone getting weary and irritable. Jennifer was on a hot streak, winning almost every hand. Jim and Bill were playing cautiously, losing slowly and steadily, while Phil was the biggest loser in the group at the moment. She figured they had two, maybe three hands left before they would finish, and the other two would be without funds. She had no idea what was in store for her; Phil was drinking heavily, becoming careless, and yet never relenting for a moment. He wanted the game to continue when he knew Jennifer had reached her limit.

"I think I'd like to take a break. Deal me out of this hand," Jennifer said.

"No. Absolutely not," Phil said adamantly. "No one is going to leave this table until the last card is dealt and there's only one winner," he said. This was certainly out of character for Phil. Jennifer was surprised, and so were the others. It was almost as if he was counting the money he was going to win, and wanted it all.

"Phil, it's only one hand. I can't sit this long, I'm tired," Jennifer protested.

"*You're* tired," he mimicked her. "Sit down. You wanted to play a man's game, now play like a man," he ordered, and she obeyed. "You're the big winner tonight, and I'm going to take it away from you."

"Phil come on, stop kidding," Jennifer chuckled, trying to make light of his foul mood. "It's only a game."

"It might be a game to you, but I'm dead serious about what I'm doing here. And I don't intend to lose tonight."

"Hey, Phil, knock it off," Allie chimed in. "Just because you lost a few hands doesn't mean you got to take it out on the lady. You were sure singing a different song when you were winning."

"Okay, okay, knock it off," Phil said. "Fix me another drink, it will calm my nerves." He continued dealing out the cards. Jennifer looked up at the clock, it was nearly ten, and she didn't know how long she could continue to sit there. Phil was out for blood and she couldn't count on his support nor could she think of leaving. The stakes were too high, and the tempers too fierce. She took the cards Phil dealt her and stared

128

at them. She yearned to get some fresh air, she had been cooped up all day and half the evening. She needed a few minutes to clear her head. Regardless of what Phil said to her, the next hand she was going to excuse herself and go to the ladies' room. He'd have to excuse her for that. Without giving it much thought, Jennifer won the hand and knocked Bill out of the running. The stubby man got up, stretched his legs, and Jennifer took the opportunity to excuse herself.

"Don't panic, I'll be right back," she said sarcastically to Phil, whose eyes darted at her. It felt good to walk across the smoke-filled room. Her back ached, and her shoulders could use a good massage. She hadn't realized until she got up how tense her body was during those hours of playing. On her way back to the table, she poured herself a cup of coffee. It tasted vile, strong and bitter, yet she needed it. All eyes were on her as she walked to the table.

"How long do you think it's going to take you to beat the pants off Phil," she heard a voice say.

"I say we all quit and go home with our winnings," Jennifer chimed in, taking her seat.

"Oh, no. We're going to play until the bitter end," Phil said.

"It serves you right if you lose everything," Allie shouted at him. "The lady gave you a chance to bow out. Now you go for the kill, Jennifer." Everyone laughed.

"This isn't funny," Jennifer shouted out. "I'm too tired to continue playing. Why don't we all go home and meet here tomorrow." She looked straight at Phil.

"No way. If you're going to beat me, then do it, but

129

do it now," he defied her. She couldn't read him anymore. She couldn't figure out what he was up to. It was so out of character for him, yet on the other hand, had she read him wrong all this time? She put all other thoughts out of her head, and took the cards Jim dealt her. It was almost as if she felt a surge of anger building up within her. She didn't feel sorry for Phil anymore. If he wanted to play until the bitter end, she'd give him a run for his money. And she didn't feel one ounce of guilt for beating him. Her entire attitude changed, and she almost felt enjoyment as she won the next few hands. She could feel the money beneath her fingers as she pushed it to her side of the table. Jim was now out of the running and it was a private war between the two of them. She continued to sip her cold bitter coffee, and stared deeply into Phil's eyes. What had he to gain by continuing the game? Was his ego more important than losing his shirt? But there was an attitude out here she had never been exposed to—All or nothing, no happy medium. Or was it too shameful to lose to a woman?

Jennifer was dealing the next hand when she felt Ross' presence. She hadn't seen him come in, but she knew he was there. She knew he was watching her and for a few quick seconds, she resented his intrusion. She felt embarrassed at being at this table with a room full of men, stooping to their level. She composed herself quickly, and continued to play, but he had thrown her off guard, and she lost the hand.

"Aha," Phil said. "I knew my luck would change if I pressed you long enough." He pulled in his money.

"Lucky hand," Jennifer said glibly. She turned to look in the other direction, her eyes meeting Ross'.

130

He lifted his drink to her as if to salute her, and she felt irritated at his nonchalance. How dare he think he could come in here after all this time and pick up where they left off. Then she changed her thinking. After all, it wasn't her night to work. How would he know she was going to be in the bar?

She couldn't think about Ross now, she had to concentrate on the game. It was going to buy her children back for her. She needed money and that was all that was important. She made a mental note of how much money she had won, and was astonished. She wanted to get up and run, even if it meant losing her job. She wanted to take the eight-thousand dollars, it could buy a great deal of sleuthing. But she knew she couldn't quit, she had to stay and finish it all out.

The tormented anxiety was unbearable. She had to change her philosophy. She wanted to get this over with, and she had the capital to do it. Jennifer started doubling her bets, playing harder, giving Phil a tougher time. She didn't care. She wanted to leave. It was after midnight, and she wanted to go home. Phil was playing harder, too, but he also wanted to win. He was getting careless, making the wrong moves, trying to psych her out, but he was no match for her determination. He was getting mad, and Jennifer sensed it. So did everyone in the bar. They were egging her on, cheering each time she won a hand. It was as though they were taking sides, and the mood was against Phil. She couldn't believe it. Had they become hostile because of all the money he had won during the two days from the other men, or could it be they felt as she did? Get the long overdue game over with!

Phil didn't appreciate the new mood and he

withdrew into himself. They stopped communicating with one another. The silence during each hand was deafening and unnerving. Jennifer sensed Phil was getting nervous, he was sweating under pressure, and drinking heavily. She knew that now he wanted to quit, but couldn't. Something was driving him to go on, and go on he did, until he had very little money left. If Jennifer pushed him, he could be finished in one more hand. Everyone sensed the mood and quieted down. The silence was deafening. Everyone knew it would be over soon. It was the last hand and Jennifer had all the money.

She was about to get up, her back still aching, when Phil spoke. "One more round. Just one more hand—all or nothing," he said.

"No, Phil. I've had enough. I don't want to play anymore," she told him.

"You have to. And you haven't heard the stakes," he said, his eyes searching.

"Why do you want to take the chance of losing more money? I don't think it's sensible. We're all tired, and this isn't the time."

"I say it is," he shouted. "I'll play you everything you've won for this place."

"You're joking. Why do you want to play with stakes like that? This isn't the old West. People don't put up their real estate." Jennifer tried to humor him, while everyone else stared in disbelief.

"You've got to be kidding, Phil," Jim said.

"I'm not. I could win everything," he continued. "It's only one hand. How long could it take, another five minutes? Look how much you'll have if you win. All the money and this place too."

"What would I do with it? And what if I lost? No

dice," Jennifer told him, and looked around the room at all the solemn faces.

"Play him, Jennifer," Allie said. "If the old ass wants to put up this place, let him. I bet you win."

People started taking side bets.

"This is ridiculous. Stop it," Jennifer shouted. "Stop putting bets on us—we're people, not race horses."

"Hey listen, lady, you've got all the money. What's the difference to you if we make a little on the side? Don't be greedy," Bill yelled, remembering how much of his own money Jennifer was taking home.

Phil sat at the table shuffling the cards, defying her to say no. He had her, and she knew it. She couldn't say no now. She looked up and saw that Ross was no longer sitting at the bar. Somewhere in the confusion he had gone. She turned back to Phil, "Are you sure? I don't want to go on," she pleaded.

"Don't worry. If I win, I'll take care of you. I wouldn't want you to go home empty-handed. And when I do win," Phil shouted to the others, "all the drinks for the rest of the night are on the house." He turned to Jennifer again. It was settled. She sat down reluctantly, wondering what she had gotten herself into. Her gut instinct was to stop all this nonsense, but she had to be fair, everyone was watching her. She had to play out the role she had created. She made up her mind that if she won, she was only going to take the money. She wouldn't take the bar. It was Phil's and she was not going to take it from him.

"Okay, but let's take a few minutes break. I want to stretch my legs," she said, as Bobby Bahr walked into the bar.

"Jesus, what's going on in here? All I heard at my

133

place this evening was that the bartender at the Tavern is beating the pants off all the guys," he said, trying to mimic one of the locals.

Jennifer laughed. "Well, it's about over. Phil wants to go one more round, he's putting up the bar," she said, crossing her eyes in disgust.

"You're kidding. You can't let him do that."

"I said no, but the boys in the peanut gallery are egging him on. I wonder if they'll all be around in the morning if he loses."

"What if he wins?" Bobby asked. "You could lose all your money."

"At this point, I don't care. I'm too tired to care. I don't know how to get out of it," she said. "I better get back to the table, the natives are getting restless."

"Listen, stay a bit longer after the game. I'll buy you a drink," he told her.

"Not tonight. I can't stay in here one minute longer than I have to," she said, touching his arm affectionately. "I have to get out of here."

"So who said we have to stay here and drink? I know a better place down the road," he smiled. "Mine. I can't stay too long either. I have to close the place up tonight."

"We'll see. It depends on if I win or lose," she told him and headed back to her seat which hadn't even cooled since she left it.

"My deal or yours?" she asked sarcastically.

"We'll cut the cards," Phil told her. "High card deals."

"You're really making a ceremony out of this. Does anyone want to make a side bet on who deals?" Jennifer called out.

"Not a bad idea," Allie laughed. "But I think we've got all the side bets we can handle for one night. Deal the cards," he shouted. "My money is on you."

Jennifer drew first, an ace. There was no reason for Phil to take his card. He conceded the deal to her.

"That a girl, Jennifer. Now play this hand as good as you picked that card. Don't give the sucker a chance," Jim shouted.

"Dealer's choice. What's your game?" Phil asked gleefully.

"Five card, Jacks or better to open," Jennifer replied. She dealt out the cards. The place was so quiet you could hear a pin drop, each team holding their breath, waiting for the two to say something. Jennifer looked at her cards, she couldn't open, and again she had a possible straight. The last time she tried to finish the straight she had lost. She felt nervous, and was ready to call defeat for the first time all night. She hoped Phil couldn't open either.

"I open," he said, chuckling. "Two cards, dealer, please."

"Dealer takes one," she said, holding her breath. She needed the same ten, and God, she prayed she got it. She imagined herself walking out of the place with nothing, all this card playing being in vain, losing the pot, on one stupid game. She made a silent promise, if she won this hand, she'd never play another game of poker again. She'd never gamble again. She was making so many silent promises, she couldn't stand it. She looked up and all eyes were on her. She hadn't dealt her own card yet. When she did finally, she was afraid to look at it. She couldn't stall any longer and picked up the corner of the card to peek at it. Her heart jumped. It was the ten! She had gotten her straight! She couldn't believe it. She looked at Phil, who had a shit-eating grin on his face, like, "try and beat me, lady, you can't, my hand's too good." The game wasn't over yet—not by a long shot—she still had a fighting chance.

"We might as well get it over with. There's no bettin' this game. All or nothing. What you got?" he said.

"I'm the winner," Jennifer calmly announced. "Why don't you put your cards down first," she was stalling.

"Three aces, and you dealt them to me," he laughed. She put her cards down slowly, feeling a sudden letdown, the big moment wasn't as exhilarating as she had hoped. She felt sorry for Phil. She had him beat. He took her reluctance as a sign of loss. He jumped up and yelled, "Drinks on the house."

"Phil, I have a straight," she said quietly, and everyone who had bet on her jumped with enthusiasm. She looked at Phil. He felt sad and she knew it, but he wouldn't let on to anyone.

"It's Jennifer's place now. Only she can say whether the drinks are on the house."

"Of course they are. But, Phil, I wouldn't take this place from you. I don't want it. It was all too stupid. You played a good game . . ." she rambled.

"Hey, a deal's a deal. It's all yours. You'll meet me at my lawyer's office in the morning and I'll sign over the place to you. And I'm going to say this in front of all these witnesses. I want you to treat Jennifer with the same respect and patronage as you've given me all these years. I'm even going to let her use my liquor license until she gets one of her own. I wouldn't want any of you to suffer," he laughed.

"Hey, Phil, you really weren't serious," Jim said. "I thought you were only trying to humor all of us—give us a side bet. She don't want this place."

"I don't," Jennifer chimed in.

"I don't care what she wants. She beat me and the place is hers," Phil went on. He pulled Jennifer aside. "Listen, keep all the money in the safe for the night. I don't want you walking the streets until the banks open," he said, his old self again.

"Phil, please. Don't do this. I don't want this place. It's been your whole life," she pleaded.

"Jennifer, I want a change. I want to leave this place, travel a bit. I have some money saved. It's time I got out from behind the bar. I want to do this. You just go and get those kids of yours. You'll have something to bring them home to now," he told her and Jennifer felt a total sadness she hadn't experienced since the kids left. She didn't want to do this. Phil wrote down the name and address of his lawyer and told her to meet him there at eleven. It was all going to work out fine for both of them.

Jennifer took the paper, and decided to say nothing more until tomorrow in the lawyer's office. Maybe the two of them could talk him out of this foolishness. She realized he had to keep up a front. Maybe when he sobered up in the morning things would be different.

Jennifer walked over to Bobby. "I think I'll have that drink now," she said. "But let's have it here. My legs are falling out from under me. I can't believe I won all that money. I'll be able to send a check to

David in the morning. It feels so good."

"Are you going to try to talk him out of giving you this place?"

"I tried, but it's no go tonight. I was hoping tomorrow he'd feel differently. I don't know what I'll do if he insists. I know nothing about running a bar," she said, "I wouldn't know where to begin."

"At the beginning. And you know you'll have all the help you'll ever need from me. I'm not worrying about the competition," he winked.

"Ha! If I really did take this place over, it would be a whole different ballgame. I'd make a lot of changes."

"So you have been thinking about it."

"Not winning it, per se. But sometimes when the place was slow, I'd think about what I'd do to liven things up a bit. I was going to give my suggestions to Phil, as a matter of fact," she said defensively.

"Well, if you do keep it, I'll have to give you a run for your money," he told her. "But I'll still help you. Actually, I think you'd make a great tavern owner. You seem to have a natural flair for the bar business," he went on. "How about dinner later on this week? I've got to get back," he told her.

"I'd like that. Thursday night is fine. I have Friday off, I don't have to be in until six," she smiled. "I don't know why I'm telling you that. You seem to know my hours better than I do. Thanks for the drink, and the support," Jennifer said warmly. Bobby smiled back at her, touched her shoulder gently, and left. The others were drifting out now, and she and Phil were alone.

"You know if you hadn't given me the money to get

into the game, I wouldn't have beaten you," she said.

"I've thought about that," he looked up at her. "But if I had to do it over again, I would have done the same thing. Now go home. You've put in a very tiring day," he smiled slyly.

"Not any longer than you. You look exhausted. Try to get some sleep. We'll talk tomorrow. I won't let you give me this place," she said adamantly, picked up her coat as she left the bar.

SEVEN

She stood outside for a moment and breathed in the
cool fresh air. It felt so good. Her lungs had been
crying for this all evening.

She closed her eyes for a moment, and remained
rooted to the spot. She didn't know how long she was
standing there, but when she opened her eyes again,
Ross' truck was parked in front of the bar. She looked
at him, and didn't move. He took his long arm and
pushed open the passenger's side of the truck,
beckoning her to get in. She hesitated a minute, and
decided to go with him. She got into the truck. He said
nothing. Jennifer was the first to speak.

"Where are we going?" she asked as casually as she
could.

"My place, if that's okay with you."

"You mean, you're going to let me into the inner
sanctum?" she said, not knowing why.

"You're right, I don't invite many people over. I

don't remember when I've had someone there last," he responded.

"Why am I so privileged?" she kept goading him.

"I didn't like your bed. It was uncomfortable," he came back, and Jennifer laughed to herself. Was she that easy that he could assume they'd go to bed together again?

"You assume a lot."

"I know I owe you an apology for not calling or stopping by, but that's the way I am. Besides, I was away for a while. I have to get away from here every now and then," he continued. "Please don't try to figure me out. You won't be able to, and to be honest, I won't let you. I never get too close, I never get involved."

"Are you giving me the ground rules?" Jennifer turned to look at him.

"Maybe. I don't know. I just thought, well, she's had a big night, she's all keyed up, and it would be nice to get together with her again."

"I'm glad you told me. What if I don't go along with your ground rules?"

"It's up to you. I'll turn the truck around and take you back to your car, and we'll part friends," he told her bluntly, making Jennifer feel uncomfortable. She wanted him tonight, she needed him, but she didn't want him to take her for granted.

"I can play by the rules you set up, until they don't suit me anymore. You're a bit of an egotist. What makes you think that I want to get involved with you in the first place?"

"You don't. That's what makes you so convenient. We could be good for one another. You have your life

141

and I have mine. We are good together in bed, and we meet one another's needs. What more can we ask for?''

"Nothing," Jennifer said. But she didn't believe him. He was looking for something, and she didn't know him well enough to figure it all out. But she had intended to get through the shell he had put himself into. She knew she had her work cut out for her. She'd have to tread slowly, walk lightly, and watch her every word. She'd get to know him better, she was sure of that, and maybe he would trust her enough to open up a bit. She smiled to herself as he stopped the truck, remembering Jill's words.

"What's so funny?" he asked, pulling her over to him.

"You. You're funny. And I don't believe a word you said. But I can assure you, you're perfectly safe with me. I don't want you, not in a serious way. I only want your body," she joked. He leaned over and kissed her, and helped her out of the truck.

Jennifer looked up at the old farm house. It looked so large and overpowering for one person to live in. He let her in the front door. The house was even larger than she had imagined. She let him lead the way, through the enormous living room, with its stone fireplace, and heaps of papers, magazines, clothes, and empty bottles strewn around. She looked at it in disbelief.

"I should get someone in to clean. It's not one of my strong points," he said apologetically.

"I can see that. May I look around the rest of the house? It's beautiful. It has so many possibilities. . . ." She stopped herself suddenly. She didn't want him to

142

get the wrong idea.

Most of the house was in the same condition as the living room. The kitchen was also large, an old wood-burning stove in the corner, piles of dirty dishes around the sink, stove and table. The dining room was in better condition. He probably never comes into this room, she thought. There was a small study on the main floor which Ross used for an office, the trail of dishes finding their way into this room, too.

There was a small bathroom, off a narrow hallway, and then another half-empty room.

"What are you going to do with this room?" Jennifer asked, still shaking her head in amazement.

"I'm not sure yet. There are four bedrooms upstairs, so I have enough guest rooms . . . if I had any guests. I don't know. I was thinking of breaking through and making my office bigger, but it's still in the planning stages."

"Why do you have such a big house?"

"Got a deal on it. I needed the land for the horses, the house came with the land," he told her in a matter-of-fact tone. "Can I get you a drink?"

"No thanks. I've smelled enough booze tonight to last me a lifetime."

"I heard you made quite a killing."

"I'd say news travels fast around Marble Lake," she told him.

"What are you going to do with the bar?"

"How did you know?"

"Good news travels faster," he smiled. "Do you want to go upstairs?"

"To bed, or do you want to show me the rest of the house?"

143

"Both. There's nothing much to see, just a lot of beds. The upstairs isn't as interesting as the rest of the house."

Jennifer followed him up the stairs. He turned on the lights to brighten the way. Ross walked into the front bedroom but Jennifer didn't follow him, she roamed the upstairs. The house was neater here and the other bedrooms were in order. She stayed a bit longer, giving Ross time to put his things in order in his own room, as she would do when bringing someone home unexpectedly. But to her surprise, he was naked and sitting up in bed when she found her way to him. The bedroom was in total disorder, a month's laundry on the floor. She pushed some of it out of her way so she could walk over to the bed.

"How in the world do you ever find anything in this room?"

"I do. Sometimes I have difficulty distinguishing the clean clothes from the dirty ones," he laughed.

"You mean all the clothes on the floor aren't dirty?"

"No. They get mixed up when I'm trying to find something to wear. I'm sure when it comes right down to it, I'll be able to tell the difference."

"I don't want to be the maid you hire. She'll go out of her mind! Before you get to the cleaning, you have to put this place together," she said, picking up a pair of overalls and putting them back on the floor.

"Don't start tonight," he said. "I'd much rather have you here in bed with me."

"I had no intention of starting ever, I don't have the time. This project will take at least a month," she laughed, getting into bed with him.

"Take off your clothes," he told her, warming up her cold body.

Jennifer did what she was told, dropping her clothes on the already cluttered floor, and sliding under the sheets next to Ross' warm body. Her body was trembling both from the cold and from the anticipation of what was to follow. She snuggled next to him remembering how well their bodies fit together. He turned over on his side facing her, his arms and legs wrapped around her and kissed her gently. His lips felt smooth and cool on her face. Even his beard was soft and comforting. She wanted to lose herself inside of him, stay near him and be protected from the world.

Jennifer looked up at the man beside her. Her mouth found his, and she kissed him more urgently than he had kissed her. She savored every moment, waiting, watching, wanting him. She didn't know when she'd ever see him again, he might disappear once more. She held him tighter, feeling her body move, responding to every one of his movements, wanting to give to him, as well as take all there was. She felt uninhibited, touching him, taking him, knowing very little about the stranger she was making love to. She opened up to him, letting him explore her body, savoring it, kissing it, and bringing her to each climax as if it were the first.

He held back as he had the first time, filling her up, exhausting her until she had had enough, and even then she wanted more. She was insatiable where he was concerned, and he enjoyed the power he had over her. When Ross could hold back no longer, his breathing grew heavier, his pace quickened and he came inside her. His body shivered. Jennifer held him tighter, wanting to be close, not wanting him to move away. He didn't. They fell asleep wrapped in each other's arms.

Jennifer woke with a start. Ross wasn't in bed with her. She sat up and looked around the bedroom, it looked worse in the daylight. She lay back on the pillows again. She couldn't believe the series of bizarre dreams she had had during the night. Everything was so confusing. Her children were home, Ross was with her, they were sitting around the poker table at the Tavern, and no one was talking. They were all smiling and watching. Then the bar turned into Ross' bedroom, the curtains billowing in the cool spring breeze, the room neat and clean, and Jennifer and Ross were in bed making love, touching, holding one another, feeling closer than they had ever dreamed possible. Jennifer felt good about the dream. Was it a premonition of things to come? Would everything come out all right? Would they all live together in this house?

Jennifer stayed quiet a moment longer, savoring her good mood, then decided to dress and find Ross. She found her way to the kitchen, and discovered a freshly-made pot of coffee on the stove. She had a hard time finding a clean cup so she rinsed out a dirty one and took her cup of coffee outside.

The day was clear and cold, but it had the promise of Spring. She noticed a few men working around the barn and decided to walk in their direction. Ross was talking to one of the men. He held up his hand to her, as if to tell her to stay where she was. She didn't move. She waited for a few minutes, then saw him coming toward her. Jennifer smiled at him. He didn't seem as relaxed this morning as he had been last night. It was as if he felt awkward about having her here in the daylight. She'd been seen by some of his men, and she felt it didn't sit right with him. It would be all over town by evening.

"Hi," she said, trying to lighten up the mood. "I found the coffee."

"Good. I'll take you back to the bar in a few minutes. I have a call to make first," he said curtly, leading her back into the house.

"Sure, don't rush. I'd really like to take a look at some of your horses if you don't mind," she said.

"No, go ahead. The guys saw you anyway."

"Does that bother you?"

"I don't know. I guess it does. I told you, I don't like to advertise my private life," he told her as she followed him into the office.

"Then why did you bring me here?"

"I don't know. It seemed like a good idea at the time." He paused. "I'm sorry. I didn't mean to start anything. It's me, not you. It isn't your fault. Go out and take a look at the horses, it's fine with me."

Jennifer turned on her heels. She felt as if she'd been hit with a ton of bricks. Would she never be able to figure him out? He never let his guard down for a moment. He was so sensitive in bed, so loving, so warm, and when the sun came up, he turned back into a cold defensive human being, with "don't touch me or come close" written all over his body. She wondered if she should pull out while she had the chance,

147

while she wasn't in too deep. She walked slowly and quietly to the barn.

"Good morning," Jennifer addressed one of the ranch hands. He looked up and tipped his hat. "I'm going into the barn to take a look at the horses. I hope you don't mind," she said defensively.

"Sure, go ahead. Take a look at the new filly, born two days ago. She's a fine specimen of a horse," the older man went on. He followed her inside the barn, gabbing. "Never saw you around here before."

"I've never been here before."

"Kind of surprised me to see a lady. Don't see much of them around here," he went on, and Jennifer listened. It gave her renewed hope. Ross was certainly a loner, and he wasn't much with the ladies. He was taking a chance, bringing her here. She wondered again why he did it.

She walked toward the stall where the filly was sleeping. "Oh, she is beautiful," she said. "May I touch her?"

"Be careful. The mother don't like that much. So go in gentle-like," he instructed. Jennifer did, and knelt down beside the new foal. It was soft to her touch, much like Ross' beard. "How many horses do you have here?"

"Depends, sometimes fifty, sometimes more, sometimes less. It depends on what Ross has in mind."

"For instance," Jennifer tried to coax.

"Rodeo. Most of the guys here travel the circuit. Ross did too for a time, but he doesn't anymore. Now he watches and teaches, only rides once in a while when the mood strikes him, but not like he used to," the man rambled.

Jennifer was intrigued. "When did he stop riding?"

"About two years ago, maybe a little longer. Time goes by fast, it's hard to keep track."

"Did something happen to Ross? Did he fall?" Jennifer pried.

"Don't know for sure. He doesn't talk much, and I never heard. He loves the horses, but in a funny way," the man told her.

"I don't understand," Jennifer said, hoping to get as much insight into the situation as possible.

"He keeps his distance. He's harder on the beasts than he used to be. . . ." the man started to say when Ross came in the barn.

"Pete, did you fix the fence on the south fork?" he asked.

"Not yet, I thought I'd do it this afternoon." Pete got up, gave Jennifer a quick look, and moved on to what he was doing before she had interrupted him.

Ross walked over to her. "Are you ready?"

"Sure, I have everything. I have to go home, change, and meet Phil at his lawyer's office."

"Oh, yes, about owning the bar. You going to let him give it to you?" he inquired.

"Not if I can help it. I think the entire game was ludicrous."

"But you played all day and half the night." He stared at her.

"Yes, but sometimes we all have to do things we wouldn't ordinarily do. We can't all be as guarded as you, or as self-controlled," she darted at him.

She got into the truck and rode part of the way in silence. She was the first to speak. "Ross, I'm sorry if

I embarrassed you this morning. I didn't know I wasn't supposed to go outside.''

"No. I told you it isn't your fault. I'm sure it did my reputation a bit of good,'' he smiled, trying to make her feel better. "And if you're not too busy with your bar next weekend, I'd like you to come with me to the rodeo. That is, if you still want to have anything to do with me,'' he said, behaving like a little boy.

"I'd like to go. And you can bet I'll remember the ground rules,'' she assured him. "Are you going to ride in the rodeo?''

"No. I don't ride anymore.''

She knew not to ask any more questions. They pulled up next to the Tavern. The place looked deserted, no cars, and no lights. She wondered what was going on with Phil. Jennifer moved over to Ross, gave him a kiss on the lips and moved quickly out of the truck. He didn't stop her. He pulled away and was moving out into the traffic immediately after she closed the truck door.

She looked at the Tavern again. It seemed to be locked up tight. Phil probably had had a long night and decided to sleep. She'd go home, and meet him later in the lawyer's office. She hoped he was okay, and almost decided to unlock the front door with her key and find out for herself, but decided against it. The man had a right to his privacy and it wasn't her day to work.

On the drive home, Jennifer tried to put the pieces together from what the barn hand had told her about Ross. The way he acted, the way he lived indicated that he was avoiding life. He seemed to be closing his eyes and his heart to everything around him. She was intrigued and wanted to know more, but she knew it wouldn't be Ross who told her. The people in town didn't seem to know much about him either. She'd have to sit tight and listen carefully, picking up all the leads she could find and following them. Maybe in time, if she was very careful and very gentle, he'd confide in her.

Phil was already waiting in Matt Hemsely's outer office when she arrived promptly at eleven. Phil jumped to his feet as soon as she walked in. He greeted her warmly. "Thought I'd change my mind?"

"I was hoping I could talk some sense into you," she replied. "Phil, we don't have to go through with this. I don't want your bar. Please believe me," she told him.

"Well, you won it."

"Look, this is only foolish pride. You don't have to make a grandstand play where I'm concerned. You can make up any story you want to the guys. I'll go along with it, if you feel you must. But don't do this foolish thing. It won't do anyone any good. What will you have left?" she tried to reason with him.

"I have a few pennies saved, I told you that. And I want to travel before I die. The bar only tied me down. Now, I talked to Matt this morning. He has all the papers drawn up, and I even asked him to include a clause about letting you use my liquor license until yours comes through. I'm dead serious and you're not going to talk me out of it," he said adamantly. Jennifer shook her head sadly. "I think we should go inside. Matt is waiting for us, and I have a million things to do today," he continued.

Phil opened the large oak door which led to Matt Hemsely's office. He stepped aside and let Jennifer enter first. She saw the small, balding man sitting behind his desk. Hemsely rose as soon as he saw her and extended his hand. "Good morning, Mrs. Wells. I hear you won my client's bar last night," he kidded.

"I know. I'm trying to talk your client into keeping it, too. It seems he won't hear of it. Can you do something?"

"I've known Phil for almost twenty years. When he makes up his mind to do something, he does it, and no one talks him out of it. So my advice to you, my dear, is to sign the papers we've drawn up, and become the new owner of the Tavern."

Jennifer sat down in the large green leather chair opposite Hemsely. She read over the papers he handed her. They were simple enough, no loose ends that she could see. Everything was cut and dried. As soon as she put her name on the papers along with Phil's, she'd own the bar. Clean and simple. She couldn't believe it. It was more than she bargained for.

"What if I want to sell the place?" she asked the lawyer.

"It's yours to sell. Do with it as you see fit. But, of course, the liquor license can't be transferred," he told her. Jennifer looked over at Phil one more time. "Are you sure you want to do this?"

"I'm sure. Now stop stalling and sign the papers," Phil demanded, but he did seem a bit on edge. "I've written down all the information I thought you'd need. The combination to the safe, where you'll find the ledgers, who we owe and how much. On the whole, the bar is in good standing. I never bit off more than I could chew. You'll also find the list of suppliers," he went on.

"How do I know that?" Jennifer asked hesitantly. She didn't know if she was opening a Pandora's box. What if Phil was in debt up to his ears?

"Take a look for yourself. You've worked there long enough, answered enough calls. Does it seem to you the creditors are beating down the doors?" Phil was embarrassed.

"I'm sorry. I should have known better, but, Phil, you seem awfully anxious to get rid of the place, and I'm not knowledgeable about these things. I'm taking your word. Working on blind faith."

"Hey, listen, Jennifer, you're getting a bar for absolutely no money. You can't complain," Phil answered defensively.

"Hey, this isn't my idea," Jennifer raised her voice.

"Stop it this instant," Hemsely intervened. "Now what are we going to do here? I can understand Jennifer's apprehension about taking over a bar she knows nothing about. And I know you, Phil. He's never been in debt in his life," he spoke to Jennifer. "Now are we going to sign these papers or not?" Hemsely demanded.

"I'll sign the papers," Jennifer said, taking them and putting her signature at the bottom. She initialed where necessary and than handed the papers to Phil. He did the same.

Phil got up and took her hand in his. "Take care of the place, make it into something big. I know you can do it. I didn't have it in me anymore," he said sadly. "I'll send you all a postcard from wherever I am."

"When are you leaving?" Jennifer panicked.

"As soon as possible. I have no reason to stay."

"But can't you stay around for a while, show me the ropes, answer my questions?" Jennifer implored.

"Listen, I knew from the first day you started working for me that you were a survivor. You can handle anything. It doesn't take much talent, just a lot of work. You'll be fine. Anyone I could introduce you to, you've already met. Just don't take any lip from anyone. And do yourself a favor, take the day off. Everyone is tired from the long game. Open up tomorrow. The place will be swarming with people wondering what happened," he told her and started to leave the office.

"Phil, what about the money in the safe? Shouldn't I put it in the bank?"

"Sure, do what you want with it, but talk to Matt about it. Start a business account," he stated, looking over at Matt. "Give her a hand with the details, will you, Matt? She can use your help. I have to go," Phil said, disappearing through the doorway. Jennifer sat back down again.

"I really can't believe this past twenty-four hours. Yesterday, I came into work as usual, wanting to do my job, and by nightfall I had won all sorts of money, and after that I own a bar. Help, Matt. I need some help," she cried out.

"Sure you do. I'll call the bank and have the officer set you up with an account. I'll vouch for you. And I want you to feel free to call on me whenever you need help. I'll try to straighten out all problems you may have," he said, comforting her for a moment.

"Well, I don't agree with Phil. I'm going to go over

to the bar, take the money out of the safe and deposit it safely in the bank," she told the lawyer, getting up.

"I'd do the same if I were you. Let me make the phone call first to the bank officer, Alvin Strong," Matt said, writing the man's name down on a piece of paper for her. "See him, and he'll get you settled," he said, walking her to the door.

"One more question. What if in two weeks Phil decides he didn't want to give away the bar. What happens?" she asked.

"Nothing. The papers are all signed. He can't go back on his word now. He's out in the cold, no turning back. So don't worry your pretty little head about it," the lawyer told her, opening the door to his office. "Do me one favor," he said. "Phil did put his name on the line for you by signing over his liquor license. I don't know if you realize how serious that is. He's taking full responsibility if anything happens. Do him proud! Keep his name as flawless as he's kept it. Do that favor for me. Phil's one of my favorite people."

"I will. I certainly will. I'd never want to do anything to hurt him. He's been very good to me, more than you'll ever know," she told the lawyer, and meant it. Phil had been good to her, giving her a job, and treating her like family. She'd never do anything that would hurt him.

Jennifer didn't feel like going straight to the bar. She walked over to the Marble Lake Inn to have some lunch with Mrs. Rafferty. After all, it was she who started the ball in motion. The woman gave Jennifer a big hug when she saw her standing in the doorway of the dining room. "I can't believe what I've been hearin' all mornin'. Did you really win the bar?"

"Sure did. We signed the papers this morning. I don't know what the hell I'm doing. My head's still somewhere on Cloud Nine. I can't believe it. I think I'm going to have to pinch myself to see if I'm dreaming. Mrs. Rafferty, I don't know the first thing about running a bar," she said, confidentially.

"Here, sit down, have some coffee, and I'll join you in a minute. I want to hear every detail, from the beginning. Don't leave anything out. It's time I heard some news first hand," she laughed, that large hearty laugh Jennifer adored.

She sat down and mulled over the morning. Phil was giving up too easily. There had to be more than met the eye, but what? She had to remember to write a check out to David today. She could give him everything she owed him, and be even for the first time in months. It felt good. Jennifer saw Mrs. Rafferty coming toward her with a large hot bowl of soup.

"Eat this, it will make you feel better. Now, tell me all about it," she said, her eyes gleaming, ready for a story as a little child would be at bedtime. She sat down and made herself comfortable.

Jennifer explained the facts as best she could remember them. Mrs. Rafferty nodded every once in a while in disbelief.

"It's the biggest story this town has heard in years," she said. "And I can genuinely say I had a hand in it. I introduced the two of you. I don't know if you should thank me or shoot me," she smiled.

"I don't know either," Jennifer said. "But I do know one thing, I'm going to give it a good try. I want to make that bar the best place this town has ever seen. It's mine, and I'm going to make it work. It's going to be a good place for my kids to come to," she went on. "Now you can fill me in on something too, if you will, Mrs. Rafferty," Jennifer asked.

"Anything. What is it?"

"I want you to tell me everything you know about Ross Davin," Jennifer said, shocking the woman.

"Why do you want to know about him?"

"I just do, and I don't want you to repeat this to anyone . . . or I won't give you anymore first-hand information," Jennifer played up to her.

"I don't really know much. He's quiet, keeps to himself, passes in and out of this town, doesn't stay put. He isn't like any of the other boys around here," she stated.

"You're not telling me anything I don't already know. I mean, was he ever involved with anyone seriously? Did he have an accident or something?" Jennifer asked, not knowing where she was headed with the conversation, and hoping she wasn't saying too much.

"If he ever was involved with anyone seriously, it wasn't with any of the girls around here. I've never seen him with a woman, come to think about it. Whenever he's in here, he's always alone. And as far as an accident, I don't think so. He may have fallen off one of his horses when he was a kid, that's what made him so peculiar," she laughed at her own humor. "But as far as anything else, I never heard about it. Now tell me what you're going to do with this information."

"I don't know. I've met him a few times. You know, waited on him at the bar, and I noticed he was

157

different from the others. I'm just curious. He doesn't seem to fit in. I thought there was more to the story than meets the eye. I may be wrong," Jennifer lied.

"You may be right. But what it is, I don't know. I'll keep my ears open for you. If I hear of anything, I'll let you know," Mrs. Rafferty said and Jennifer nodded.

"No. It isn't important. I just wondered." Jennifer tried to cover her tracks.

"Are you sure? You ain't thinking about making a play for him. He's good lookin' and all, but too strange for my blood. I like my men open, warm and talkative," Mrs. Rafferty laughed.

"No, it isn't anything like that. Just wondered. When you're an outsider looking in, like me, things don't always seem what they are. I thought it was my imagination, I know now it isn't. I thank you for the conversation, the information, and the warm soup. Please come visit my establishment," Jennifer joked, as she got up. "Keep your fingers crossed for me. I'm going to need all the prayers I can get."

"You got 'em," Mrs. Rafferty told her, walking out of the dining room with her. "Listen, if things get too busy over there for you, and you just want to sit and talk, come on over," the woman invited, and Jennifer was grateful.

Jennifer pulled her coat tighter around her chest and walked the few blocks to the tavern. The place looked deserted and eerie. She never remembered it looking that way. Even when she opened in the morning, Phil was around, coffee was brewing and there was movement. But now the place was perfectly still.

She heard the sounds of her own footsteps as she paced the front of the bar, taking a whole new long look at it. She walked to the back, and climbed the stairs to the apartment that Phil had occupied. It was empty now. He must have stayed up half the night packing and moving. She wondered what the hurry was. The apartment wasn't too bad. Four large rooms, in dire need of repair and a fresh coat of paint, but it could make a better home for her than the cottage, especially now that she had to spend more time in here.

She had to think about hiring someone to cover for her when she had errands to run, and the thought of being open twenty hours a day, seven days a week didn't appeal to her. She must certainly call Bobby and ask him to help her find another bartender. She walked downstairs again, and took out the combination to the safe.

She opened the heavy door and looked in. She picked up the ledgers, put them aside, and looked for the box of money she was to take to the bank. Her fingers touched the steel gray box, opened it and looked in. It was empty! The money was gone! Phil had taken everything. No wonder he was in such a hurry to leave. She rushed to the phone to call Matt. She didn't know what to do.

"Phil's gone and he's taken all my money . . . " she blurted out half hysterical.

"What! Slow down. What money?"

"The money I won last night. The cash. It's gone," she told him a bit more calmly.

"Are you sure? Did you look around, maybe he put it someplace else," Matt told her.

"I didn't look elsewhere. Last night I left it in the safe, and I expected it to be here this morning. It isn't. Phil's gone, all his clothes are gone, and so is my money," she screamed.

"Do you want me to call the police?" he asked.

She stopped for a moment, and nodded to herself. He had her over a barrel. Phil knew what he was doing all along. He knew he was going to take the *few* pennies he'd saved. He knew she'd never turn him in.

"No," she told the lawyer, and hung up.

Jennifer walked over to the cash register. It was filled with the money from yesterday. At least Phil didn't take that, she thought. Thank God he'd left her with some working capital, but now she was in the same shape as yesterday. No money for David, and a bar to run. She was going to have to stall as usual, pick herself up, and start again. She was getting used to it by now. But at least she'd have a cash flow from day to day, if half the town didn't hate her for taking this bar away from Phil. She hoped she could depend on their patronage. She was hoping they would continue to come in, bail her out. But she couldn't be sure.

She locked the door to the tavern, and kept the window lights off to avoid any intrusion. She had to pull herself together and read over the ledgers to find out exactly where she stood. She counted the money in the cash register. Nearly six hundred dollars. It was a start. Not a great start, but something.

She wondered how much of it she owed to others. She sat down to read the ledgers.

EIGHT

Frank Wells sat quietly in his suite at the Richemond Hotel in Geneva. The children were in the park with Maryanne, their tutor. He read over the stock reports for the third time but he was not concentrating. He couldn't concentrate. His mind kept wandering off to his home, his wife and his life. He wondered sometimes why he had left her. She was a good wife, devoted, understanding, but when the pressure started to mount, he took it out on her. Took his children and ran!

Now he wondered how she was. His latest report on her was that she was doing fine, bartending in a little local place up near her parents' summer home. For the life of him, he couldn't picture Jennifer tending bar. She was so delicate, fragile. The thought of her hoisting cases of beer and waiting on customers made his stomach turn.

The children were unhappy, too. They missed their

mother and wondered when they were going home. At first it was an adventure. The morning he decided to leave everything behind him, he walked into the children's room, helped them pack, and told them they were going on a fun vacation. He was finally going to teach them how to ski. Jon and Cassy were excited, but their first question had been, ''Is Mommy coming too? Shouldn't we wait for Mommy to come home before we leave?'' Frank said very little. He told them that mommy was away and would join them as soon as she could. They seemed to be satisfied with his answer and continued packing happily.

But life with them wasn't all it was cracked up to be. Cassy had a series of nightmares, and he couldn't comfort her. Jon stopped eating, and refused to dress himself. They missed their home, their friends, and most of all—their mother.

But Frank couldn't turn back now. He had to stand firm. He was waiting for Jennifer to make her move. He knew he was being followed, that Jennifer was hot on his trail. It didn't seem to bother him much. He was still two steps ahead of her. He'd know when she was getting too close, and then he'd make his move.

Geneva was getting to him, the cleanliness of the city, the beauty and the charm wasn't as appealing as he had hoped or remembered when he was a boy. The old adage ''you can never go back'' disturbed him because he knew it to be true. He wasn't happy here. He missed the office and all the little nuances that had unnerved him. Frank called home regularly. His mother told him about her conversation with Jennifer, and how Jennifer had no idea she knew where he was. The last report he had from her, mother hadn't heard a word from Jennifer. She hadn't called in over two months. Even his lawyer, Herb Gardner, hadn't heard from her. If he hadn't gotten his weekly reports from his own detective, he wouldn't know she existed anymore.

Frank got up, stretched his legs, and looked out at the busy Geneva traffic. It wasn't Wall Street by any means, and even his weekly trips to Zurich didn't content him. He needed to be home. He needed his life to take on a new order, a new excitement. He couldn't stay here hidden away for very much longer. Jennifer had to make her move soon. She had to motivate him to build up his creative juices, run again, take on a new city, a new lifestyle. Let her get so close she could touch him, yet far enough away that she couldn't.

Frank thought about the children. They weren't wearing well under the strain. He had planned an elaborate Christmas for them. His mother even flew over to join them, but the children weren't in a Christmas mood. They couldn't care less about what Santa Claus had under the tree. They didn't even get excited over the nine-foot tree he decorated especially for them. They moped around all day, looked out the window, and wanted to know why their mother wasn't with them. They wanted to call her, see if she was all right. After all, she had to have had an accident or something worse not to be with them for Christmas!

The children weren't buying the stories Frank was feeding them about her being too busy with the house to come visit. They knew something was wrong and they wanted some answers. It was his mother who helped him out a bit. She told him to tell the children the truth—that he and Jennifer were getting a divorce and he was going to take care of them from now on with her help, of course. This didn't make them any happier, it only made the day sadder for them. They didn't want to hear that their mother wasn't going to be there for them anymore . . . that she was living all by herself. Cassy started to cry and dropped her new doll on the floor. In tears, she picked it up, broken beyond repair.

"Mommy is going to be so lonely without us. She loves us and can't be alone. Maybe I should go live with her and Jonathan should keep you company," she said in her very young voice. Jonathan cut in. "No. I want to live with her. You stay with Daddy." The two began to fight over who was staying with whom, leaving Frank out in the cold. He didn't know what to do to help himself or his children.

"Stop it, both of you. We are not separating. You're both going to stay with me. I love you and want you with me," he told them, trying to hug them, but they pulled away.

"I want my mother," Cassy started to scream, Jonathan joining her. "Why can't we go home?"

Frank lost his temper. "We can't, that's all. We're all staying here. And I don't want to hear any more about it," he shouted.

Both children looked up at him, tears still streaming down their faces, but they were too frightened of him to continue to cry openly. They cried silently into their pillows for the next week. Frank thought he was going to go out of his mind. His heart broke for them, but he also knew that in time they'd get over it.

Three months later things seemed to be calming down. The children fell into a daily routine, but he knew in his inner soul they still longed for their mother. Frank was like a madman, obsessed with hurting Jennifer, obsessed with teaching her what life could be like without him. There were times when he thought he was going out of his mind. The reasons for his leaving home weren't as sharp in his memory as they once were. He felt so strongly about teaching her a lesson months ago, but now it didn't seem so important.

Maybe he should give in, let her see the children once in a while. But how could he now? She was not the woman he had known, hanging around bars, relating to fishermen and farmers, and staying out half the night. She had even taken a lover. The hurt was building inside Frank again. She had betrayed him. How many times had she betrayed him in the past while he was busting his ass to make them a good living? How many lovers had she taken on the side? No, he would never let his children be a part of her new life. He would never let them be exposed to the shabby way Jennifer was living in that tiny little cottage, in the middle of nowhere. Jonathan was meant for better things, and Cassy, his precious little girl, exposed to the roughnecks Jennifer was associating with? No way. Never! He'd fight her to the finish. The children were getting used to him, and in time they would forget her for good. He tried lying to himself, deluding himself, and it was working.

He got up, poured himself a drink, and waited for the children to come home from the park. He'd plan a nice dinner for them at Le Gentlehumme. They liked to go there, and he wanted to treat them tonight. Treat all of them. He needed to get out, too. He needed to find himself some female companionship, someone to take his mind off the past and put it where it belonged, in the future.

Frank hadn't been near another woman since he'd left Jennifer. He didn't seem to want to try to be sociable. He couldn't bear the thought of touching another woman. He had gotten so used to Jennifer, feeling her, making love to her. But she didn't care, so why should he? It was about time he got dressed and went out and behaved like a man. He thought about putting the children to bed and going out by himself, maybe hitting some clubs and trying to meet one of the local beauties. He deserved it.

Frank went back to his desk, put away the latest report on Jennifer, and wondered what the next one would bring. What would she be up to next? What other man would she be sleeping with? The resentment built up in him, and he felt more justified in going out this evening and having himself a good time, that is, after he spent some time with the children. Jennifer had them nearly all to herself all these years. Now it was his turn. They'd learn to love him the way they loved her. He'd have to sit and wait, but all good things would come to him.

NINE

Jennifer sat excitedly at the rodeo. She stayed behind the lines, watching Ross intently. This was the first time she had seen him in action. The crowds were roaring, and everyone dressed in jeans, cowboy hats and boots, joined in the gaity of the moment. Even Jennifer was feeling excited today. Ross had been especially warm to her this morning when he picked her up and introduced her—first name and last—to everyone whom they met. She felt she was making some progress. The work this past week had totally drained her. After going over the books, she talked to Jill who suggested a friend to help her. Rachel Crosby, a young, pretty brunette with a lot of experience, could help Jennifer and also be an asset to the bar. She'd be good for the customers. Jill set up a meeting between the two immediately since Rachel had just lost her job and was looking for another one. The timing was perfect. Jennifer remembered the last talk the two had had about bars and bartenders being bounced around. She made up her mind that she wouldn't be that kind of employer. Rachel was grateful for the job and Jennifer was delighted to have her. Together they organized the bar, giving Jennifer the opportunity to get acquainted with the inventory.

Phil had told her the truth about his not being in debt, which eased her mind a great deal. She was still behind the eight-ball with David, but she could put something away for him each day out of the cash register. The guys came into the bar the following day when she opened, in disbelief that Phil was really gone. They accepted Jennifer as they always had. It was a bit strained at first, but Jennifer was confident that all would work out.

She asked Rachel to work irregular shifts for a while, filling in whenever Jennifer needed her, days and nights. Jennifer had decided to move into the apartment upstairs and had to spend some time cleaning and getting it in order. All in all, it had been a very long week, the first of many to come, but Jennifer felt she had the worst under control.

Bobby came into the bar every day, helping her with the organization of the storeroom, giving her tips on how to stock the liquor, what to reorder, and how to deal with the suppliers. He was a godsend, and she utilized his every suggestion. Bobby felt good about it, too. He was sure he had found a way to get into Jennifer's heart, but he was in for a big surprise. She wasn't biting. She wasn't even tempted. She would keep him as a friend, and that was all there was to it.

Ross had surprised her, too, by calling to see if she needed any help. She screamed, "Yes." She needed his truck to take some of her clothes to the apartment and also he loaned her the use of two of his men to paint the apartment and help her move. Jill brought over dinner the first night and all night long they talked about the future.

Jennifer heard everyone cheer, and the sounds brought her back to the present . . . the rodeo. The men were getting ready for the big event—riding the bull. She had seen it many times on television but she had never once seen it in person. She was as excited as everyone else. She wished Jonathan was with her now, he'd love it all. She wasn't so sure about Cassy.

One by one, men came out of the stall riding the bull, arms flying in the wind, trying to stay on. Everyone cheered, and even when the men fell off, it didn't bother anyone. Of all the events of the day, the bull was the highlight. Jennifer looked around at the people, they were very much like the residents of Marble Lake. If Jennifer could find a way to duplicate the excitement of the bull in her own bar, she'd make a fortune, draw in a new crowd of people, and bring a new excitement to Marble Lake. She knew she'd have to check out the particulars, but she was so excited, she wished she could talk to Ross about it right away, and if she could get it done fast enough, she'd have the place ready for the summer crowd. Like everyone said in Marble Lake, "If you don't make the money in the summer, you won't make it at all." It was perfect! The timing was perfect, and she knew in her heart she was on to something. . . something BIG! It could give her financial security. So much so that she'd never have to worry again.

Jennifer zipped up her jacket. The sun was going

down, and the stadium was getting cold. Her mind was still on her mechanical bull. Ross was packing the truck when Jennifer found him.

"How'd you like your first rodeo?" he asked.

"I loved it. You certainly do work hard. I wish you could have spent more time with me, I could have used an explanation or two," Jennifer told him, getting into the truck.

"I'm sorry. I told you you were on your own today. I can't be in two places at the same time," he went on, "but if you'd like to have dinner with me, I'll fill you in."

"I'd like that. Besides, I have something to ask you. A thought came to me when I was watching the bronco event. Did you ever hear of Gilleys in Texas?"

"Yeah, why?"

"I think if we brought a mechanical bull to Marble Lake—you know, open up the back room of the tavern and put it there, maybe bring in a band—I'd have myself one hell of a summer business. Do you know anyone who could make the bull for me?" she asked excitedly.

"I do, but I think you're crazy. Do you know the kind of repercussions you'll have? What if someone falls off and hurts himself? You can be sued for everything you own."

"I don't think so. I'll check it out with Matt, but I'm sure they ride at their own risk and also have to sign releases saying they don't hold the bar responsible."

"I don't care what a piece of paper says. People can hold you up in court anyway," Ross told her.

"I think you're being pessimistic. I think I have a really good idea here. Are you going to introduce me

170

to someone who can build the bull or not?'' Jennifer was firm.

"I'll introduce you. But I still think you're crazy. I don't want to hear about it when things start going wrong,'' he told her.

"You'll be the last to know. One other thing, how long do you think it will take to build it? I'd like to open the summer season with the bull. It will be great! I'm definitely going to hire a band,'' Jennifer said firmly. "Music, bull, new atmosphere, it's what the bar needs. I've been studying it ever since I started working there. Did you ever notice the details, the old woodwork, the high ceilings? It can all work to our advantage.''

"Hold on, take it one step at a time. You've just opened the place. You haven't even learned how to run it the way it is. What makes you think you can run a first-class establishment like that one? It will take up all your time,'' he told her, trying to concentrate on the road.

"I can. I know I can. But I can't change it too much, I have to keep the regulars happy. I don't want to alienate them. After all, when the summer folk leave, they're all I've got.''

"True, and remember that. They're your real bread-and-butter. I think the changes will be more harmful than good,'' he tried to discourage her.

"Why are you being so negative? I can just see Allie, Jim, Bill, and all the guys trying to ride the bull. They'd love it. They'd even find a way to make bets on who's going to stay on the bull the longest,'' she laughed.

"You've got a point, it isn't beyond their comprehension. They would love it, and they'd probably break their necks trying to prove themselves, too."

"So you'll help me?" she asked again.

"I'll help you," he told her. "I don't know why. You're roping me in here, lady, and I can't figure out why I'm letting you," he told her quietly.

"Because you can't stay in that shell you've made for yourself all your life. You have to come out and join the living every once in a while. Besides, remember me? I'm no threat to you. I don't want to rope you in to housebreak you. And speaking of housebreaking, can I do a favor for you?"

"It depends."

"Why don't I help you find someone to clean your place up? Once the initial cleaning is done, you shouldn't need anyone more than once a week. They'll even put away your clean laundry so it doesn't get mixed in with the dirty," she joked.

"The place really upsets you," he said thoughtfully.

"Well, it's beautiful. Or what I saw of it was. It needs work, fixing and repapering, painting, small cosmetic surgery, but on the whole, the lines are beautiful and it deserves better. You'll even feel differently about yourself when you can walk in a room and sit on the couch without having to clean off a spot first. I really can't see how you can live that way. I used to laugh with my kids when we watched *The Odd Couple*. I thought Oscar was a figment of Neil Simon's imagination, but he must have met you," she laughed, feeling good about herself and her ability to talk to Ross with a bit more ease than before.

"Okay, you win, but I want a tall redhead, nice legs, good body, who might want to sleep in once in a

172

while," he kidded. Jennifer listened and didn't answer him right away.

"You'll get what I can find in this town. If she happens to fit your qualifications, you're in luck," she told him.

"Okay, but she has to do windows," he joked along with her.

"Do you mind if we stop off at the bar a minute before dinner? I want to check on Rachel. I've been gone all day."

"I don't mind. I'll wait in the truck."

"You can come in. I'll buy you a drink," she told him.

"No, I'd better not. It's been a long day, I might fall asleep at the bar."

"Yes, I remember you're very good at falling asleep at the drop of a hat," Jennifer teased him.

"Well, those are the breaks. I told you I could never change, do things that make me feel uncomfortable," he murmured. Jennifer could feel his mood changing, and she was saddened by it.

Ross pulled up in front of the bar. The place seemed lively enough, plenty of cars parked in the lot.

"I'll only be a few minutes," she told him, jumping out of the truck.

Rachel greeted her as she walked into the bar. "Well, boss, how was your day at the rodeo?"

"Very eventful. I have a million things to talk to you about tomorrow. It's still my day off, that is if you think you can work the night shift?"

"No sweat. It wasn't so busy this afternoon, had time to put my feet up a bit. Ha, ha," she giggled.

"How's the register?" Jennifer asked, walking behind the bar and smiling at some of the customers she recognized. "Buy everyone a drink on the house," she told Rachel, who quickly made the announcement.

It was nearly ten o'clock, and the register had nearly five-hundred dollars in it. Not bad, but not so good either. She had to pay Rachel for two shifts, and there were other expenses. She might clear a couple of hundred dollars for the night if this kept up.

"It's got to get busier this evening," Rachel told her. "You know, college kids getting home, people coming out because the weather's nice, early summer people. It happens like that all the time."

"I know. I'm still at the overprotective stage. I feel guilty when I leave the bar too much but I just needed some time for myself."

"Go ahead. The ship is in good hands," Rachel told her. "Have a good time with Ross, if anyone could have a good time with Ross?" she joked.

"Why did you say that? How well do you know him?" Jennifer asked.

"Not very. I met him once or twice when Jill was seeing him. He always struck me as trouble. I don't think he's your type. Honest, that's all," she told her.

"I know what you mean, but I think he's worth the trouble. He's really very nice," Jennifer defended him.

"I'm sure he is. Everyone says that, but no one really knows him very well. Maybe we'll all be pleasantly surprised," Rachel tried to cover her blunder. "Now, go on, the man is waiting."

Jennifer started to leave, but she didn't like the impression Ross had made on everyone. There was more to him than that. She tried to push the remark out of her heart, but she couldn't. It bothered her.

Ross was half asleep in the truck when she got in. He jumped up quickly.

"We don't have to go to dinner if you'd rather go home to bed," she started.

"I'm starved," he told her, "but I don't want to hassle with a restaurant. Why don't we buy some sandwiches or something to take out and go home to eat?"

"Sounds good to me," she told him.

"I'll make it up to you. We'll go out for dinner another time."

"No problem. I'm tired myself. All that fresh air can get to a body. And with the work all week. I'm really exhausted myself. But like you, I'm starved. Where can we get sandwiches, and pick up some good sweets?"

"Sweets! They're not good for you."

"Neither is sex, but that doesn't stop me," she felt giddy.

"Oh, I've met myself a real winner here. I can sense it." He felt the same way Jennifer did.

Ross pulled into the large delicatessen on the main highway. Jennifer went in with him, she wanted to pick out her own food. When she looked at all the delicacies, she realized how hungry she really was. In addition to the enormous sandwich she ordered, Jennifer picked out a large piece of chocolate cake, two bottles of soda, and a bag of potato chips. Ross looked at her in disbelief. She looked back at him shyly.

"I think it would have been cheaper for me to take you out to dinner," he sighed, as he pulled the truck out of the parking lot.

"Oh, I didn't know you were counting pennies."

175

"I don't usually, but I'd like to see you eat all the food you bought."

"Don't let this thin frame fool you. I can really pack it away if I put my mind to it," she told him, pulling out the bag of potato chips and starting to munch. He stared over at her.

"I'm hungry. Believe me, it won't spoil my appetite," she said, as if reading his mind.

"I didn't say anything. It's your body, but salt and sugar aren't good for you."

"Are you one of those health fanatics?" she asked.

"Not really, but I watch what I eat. No use taking any chances."

"Not me, I could live on junk food. If it wasn't for the kids and wanting them to eat right, I'd snack all day long," she told him, downing her last potato chip.

Ross entered the long driveway that led to his house. Jennifer wasn't looking forward to sleeping in that messy room again, but she didn't put up a fight. They walked into the house and Jennifer looked around the kitchen in disgust.

"I've got to find you someone to clean this place in a hurry. Ross, we're not even going to find a clean dish to eat on," Jennifer said.

"Never fear, I keep a supply in the cabinets. I have about four sets of dishes so I can eat off them for months," he told her, handing her a plate.

"Then what?" she asked.

"Then I have to break down and wash them. I sometimes talk my neighbor into doing them for me. The lady needs money from time to time and she's more than willing to clean up."

"Why don't you ask her to do it regularly?" Jennifer asked.

"Can't. She doesn't have the time. And there are days she says she's coming and she can't show up because the kids are sick or some such nonsense. I don't want to hassle her."

"Then we go back to Plan A. Because, my dear, I wouldn't know where to start," Jennifer told him.

"You could try," Ross joked as he took a bite out of his sandwich.

"Oh, no. I don't do dishes for strange men I'm not living with."

"Oh, is that a hint?" Ross was offended.

"No. I'm simply telling you that I won't do your dishes, or clean up your room, or do your laundry. I have enough trouble keeping track of my own life, which by the way, I'd like to get in order. Please call the guy you had in mind to build the bull."

"Oh, yes. I was hoping you'd forgotten about it," Ross replied.

"Why does it offend you? I'd like to know."

"As I said before, people don't know how to ride those things. They'll get hurt, I don't want to be a part of that. Do you know how long people train to ride the real bull? It's dangerous," Ross went on.

"But it isn't the same thing. This bull isn't going to run you over if you fall off. I remember reading about it, some of the mechanical bulls are made with different speeds. It's all safe enough," she tried to convince him.

"I don't buy it. People in bars are drinking, they think they can handle something they can't. Or they're bullied by their friends to go on, and they're scared stiff. There's bound to be accidents. Don't you understand what you're introducing here?" Ross continued. He got up and walked to the living room.

Jennifer realized she'd hit a nerve and wanted to drop the subject, but she couldn't. It was too important to her.

"If you don't want to get involved, I'll find someone else who will. I don't mean that as a threat, but I'd like to save you the aggravation," she told him as she followed him into the living room, pushing some of the debris from the couch to make a seat for herself.

"No, I'll help you. I said I would. I'll introduce you to Sal. He'll make a machine that will be safe, I can count on that. I don't want to talk about it anymore," Ross said, but Jennifer didn't know when to quit.

"Did someone fall from the bull once? Is that what upsets you?" she asked.

"No. You're barking up the wrong tree, and I want you to forget about it. I'm tired. Let's go to bed," he told her, getting up and starting up the stairs. Jennifer followed him. She, too, had lost her appetite.

Ross remained silent, crawling into his side of the bed. Jennifer did the same. She wanted to undo the damage she had caused. She had pushed too hard, making Ross move away from her. She moved closer to him in bed, but he remained still. She moved her hand over his chest, and laid her head on his shoulder.

"I'm sorry," she whispered, "I didn't mean to pry. I was caught up in the excitement of the day. I know I stepped out of bounds." Jennifer waited for Ross to reply. He didn't.

Jennifer rolled over to the other side of the bed and tried to fall asleep. She couldn't, and she could tell from the way Ross was breathing that he wasn't asleep either. But she didn't know what more to say.

What could she do to change his mood? She decided to say nothing. Do nothing. Let him make the first move. She remained lying on her side, facing the wall.

Ross moved over toward her and pulled her closer to him, but Jennifer didn't turn around. She felt the warmth of his chest against her back, and fought the temptation to turn around toward him and pretend that nothing had happened. If she gave in this easily this early in their relationship, she'd give in all the time. He'd expect it.

"I didn't mean to snap at you," Ross started to say. "There are things about me that you don't know and you will never know about them. I don't like to talk about my feelings, nor do I want to have any feelings toward anyone. But I don't want to hurt anyone, either. I don't like it when I hurt you," he said, pausing for a moment to reconstruct his thoughts. Jennifer remained still, waiting for him to finish. "I don't go along with what you want to do. It isn't right for me. Most of what I do and think isn't right for anyone else, and I have to stop imposing my feelings on other people. I'll help you, but promise me you won't try to pry into my life any more. I like things the way they are, I don't want to change. I don't want to pull away from you, but I will if you keep thinking you're going to get close to me, figure me out, and everything is going to turn out all right between us."

Jennifer turned around and faced him. He was more sensitive to what she was doing than she realized. She'd have to tread lightly from now on.

"I won't, Ross. I apologize. It's just that when I see you're hurting, I want to help you, stop the pain. But I realize now it was wrong of me. You *want* to feel that pain, you *want* to suffer. There isn't anything I can do, or anyone else for that matter. You're the only one who can put an end to the suffering. When you're ready, you will. You won't have any interference from me," she told him.

He pulled her closer to him, holding her, and gently and tenderly, they made love.

TEN

Sal Marino invited Jennifer to see his shop. He'd received a call from Ross the day before, explaining as best he could what Jennifer had in mind. Sal was very enthusiastic. He'd never done anything like it before, but was confident he could.

Jennifer liked him immediately. He was a short man, not more than five-feet three-inches, slightly built, with dark curly hair and a thick mustache. He was warm and friendly, making Jennifer feel at home the moment she walked into his immaculate work-shop. Everything had its place, neatly organized, Sal's pride and joy.

He pulled a chair out from the corner and invited Jennifer to sit down. Sal took out a large sketch pad, and waited for Jennifer to make the first move. She started slowly, not really sure how to go about making a mechanical bull.

"As Ross told you, I've taken over the Tavern, and

I'd like to make it an even bigger and better place to go. I think the mechanical bull is just the right touch for the people out here. I believe they'll get a kick out of it, if you don't mind the pun," Jennifer smiled, choosing her words carefully.

"I think you're right. I saw it all as Ross was explaining it to me. I know I can build it," Sal told her with pure confidence.

"I'm sure you can, too, but where do we start? And, most important, how much do you think it will cost?"

"It all depends. How fancy are you planning to get? How many speeds? Leather trim? What kind of mounts?" he shot out at her.

"I don't know. I was hoping to leave it up to you, you're the expert. I do know I want the bull to be absolutely safe. I want to be able to let my grandmother get on it to ride without worrying about her. You know what I mean?"

"I do. I was thinking along the lines of five speeds, from very slow to very fast. Look, you'll have to have someone working the bull at all times. And you'll have to be able to say to someone, "No, it's too risky the way you want to ride it. You can only go to speed . . . let's say, three. Then the real cowboys who are used to riding can work up to five, as the others can do in time," Sal explained. "Get my drift?"

"I do. Sounds good. I do think, however, it's the idea of the bull, not what it looks like that counts. If you want to decorate it with a good western saddle, trim, we can talk about that later, and cost it out. Right now, I'm only interested in building a sturdy, safe machine," Jennifer told him, remembering Ross' hesitation.

"You got it. Anything I build will hold up to any wear and tear. I'll do up some rough sketches and plans for your approval and give you a call when they're ready to show you."

"Fine. I'll be waiting to hear from you then," Jennifer said, getting up. "One more thing. Just a rough guess, mind you. I don't want you to feel under any pressure, but how long do you think it will take to finish? I'd like to re-open the place for the summer crowd, bull and all."

"We're talking about the end of May. It gives me a little over two months. If I put a second man on, and you approve the plans right away, I think I'll be able to meet your deadline, give or take a week. I'll know better after I show you the first set of plans," Sal told her.

"Good, then I'll be anxiously awaiting your call. Thank you for seeing me," Jennifer smiled, extending her hand out to him. He took it firmly.

"Thank you for giving me this opportunity. I'll do the best I can to keep the cost down. I know you have a great deal to contend with, being a new bar owner and all. I really want to do this, we'll work it out somehow," he told her.

"I'm sure. Thanks again."

Jennifer left the shop, got back into her car, and headed to the Tavern. The meeting with Sal was the first of the day. Rachel was working the day shift for her so she could conduct her business, and she felt very lucky to have her. The old customers still drifted in and out as usual, hardly mentioning Phil's name. It didn't take the town long to find out about the theft of the poker money, and this was helpful for Jennifer.

She didn't come out the big winner everyone had thought.

"How'd it go today?" Rachel asked, handing Jennifer a cup of coffee over the bar.

"Good. I think Sal's our man. He can deliver on time, and he'll try to keep the cost down, which is a major accomplishment. How's business this morning?"

"Fair, as usual. Bobby was in looking for you. He said he'd be back later," Rachel went on.

"He's another man I don't know what I'd do without. He's made this entire transition period much easier for me."

"I know. But he's got the hots for your fair frame," Rachel chuckled.

"Don't be ridiculous, we're just friends. I can't believe you people. If a woman sees a man more than once, and they seem to have a halfway decent relationship, they jump from friends to lovers. Why can't a man and a woman just be friends?" Jennifer snapped.

"Don't yell at me, I was just making an observation. The man is nuts about you. I think you've been too busy to notice, but sooner or later, his patience is going to wear thin," Rachel whispered out of earshot of the other customers.

"I hope not. What I don't need right now is an affair. I'm having enough trouble dealing with the one affair I'm having."

"Ross giving you a tough time?"

"No tougher than usual. I find myself trying to figure him out every spare moment, and taking moments when I shouldn't. The man is driving me crazy," Jennifer said, throwing her hands up, loving the challenge.

"How're things on the other end? With the kids?" Rachel seemed more discreet.

"I have a meeting next week with my lawyer. He has a new plan of action. I'm anxious to get this over with. If I didn't have this place to occupy my mind, I'd go crazy."

"I know sort of what you're going through," Rachel confided. "I was married once myself."

"You were! I didn't know that. I'm always shooting off at the mouth about my problems. I've never stopped to think that everyone else had a life before coming here, too. Were you married long?"

"No, just about two years. My husband had a macho idea he had to reproduce himself, have a son, an heir. An heir to what? But he wanted kids. And five years ago, it seemed like a good idea for me, too. After a year of trying, I finally got pregnant, but the sperm cells were too weak, or some such nonsense. The doctor tried to explain it to me. Anyway, I lost the baby. Don, that's my husband, he was beside himself, and in a funny way so was I. I didn't know your body changed or something when you get pregnant. You feel so maternal, and I was in love with the idea of having a baby. I went into my own depression, that mixed with Don's and the marriage was a total washout. We kept blaming one another until we destroyed any happiness we might have shared. I decided to come out here to get closer to nature, and to start a new life. I became a bartender, and lo and behold, here I am today still tending bar."

"Are you sorry? I mean about moving out here?"

"Sometimes, when I have to fight petty battles with tavern owners, but no, not really. There's a sense of peace and tranquility I've found here, I thought I'd never feel again. And I've made some very nice friends," Rachel told her.

"I sort of feel the same way. I feel more at home in this place than I've ever felt before. I think I can live the rest of my life out here. I know the kids will love it," Jennifer said, then changed the subject. "Do you think you'll ever get married again?"

"Maybe. If I find a man who can support me in the grand style I've become used to," Rachel slipped back into her jovial tone.

"Me, too. That gives us a large range. Poverty level," Jennifer laughed, having something in common with Rachel, and feeling closer to her.

"I think one night you, me and Jill should go out and terrorize the town, find ourselves some good looking men. And here are our choices," Rachel laughed, looking down at the men sitting at the bar.

"Depressing, isn't it?" Jennifer laughed along with her. Heads turned toward them.

"What's so funny down there?" Jim shouted.

"Private joke between us girls," Jennifer answered. "I think I'll stick with Ross. He's the best there is," she whispered.

Rachel nodded approvingly. "I wouldn't turn him out of my bed."

"Hands off. I don't share."

"Are you kidding. Never! I have a job to protect," Rachel smiled.

"Well, I have to get back to work. I'm going to call the managers of a few bands. I'm trying to set up our entertainment for the summer festivities. Now that's a thought. I might hire a musician who'll waltz his way into your heart," Jennifer told her friend.

"I'm counting on it. Why the hell do you think I work in this hell hole, anyway? The money ain't fantastic," she said, taking on the local lingo.

"Now, now, one never knows what can happen. You might win the bar from me one day."

"No, ma'am. I don't need the headache," she shouted at Jennifer, and went back to wait on her customers.

Jennifer sat down at her desk in the small office, and picked up the pictures of the kids she kept there. Her mood changed. "Please come back to me soon," she sighed and went back to making her calls, trying to snap back into the good mood once again.

Jennifer heard a knock at the door. Bobby poked his head in. Jennifer waved for him to come in. "I'm on hold, I'll be off the phone in a minute . . . Yes, as I said to the gentleman on the line a few minutes ago, I want to book talent for my bar this summer. Yes, Country Western, and I need a firm commitment. Next month I intend to start advertising and I don't want to make promises I can't keep. Now Mr. . . . Brewer, I can't understand why this is taking so long. I've agreed to your price, and I want a contract sent out to me immediately. If you can't deliver, then I'll find someone else who can," Jennifer heard herself shouting into the receiver. She was losing her patience. "Well, that sounds more like it. But I warn you, Mr. Brewer, if the contract isn't here by the end of the week, I'll go elsewhere," she told the man, hanging up.

"My, my, that's telling him," Bobby smiled. "I told

you, you'll get the hang of it very soon. You're on your way."

"I doubt it. I may be shouting but am I getting any results? I don't think anyone takes me seriously. A commitment is a commitment," she continued.

"Calm down. It will all work out. Now, aren't you going to ask me what I'm doing here?"

"Sorry. I've been rude, sitting here running off at the mouth. What can I do for you?" Jennifer composed herself.

"Thought I'd take you away from all this. How about going out to dinner tonight? Monday night is really slow, I can afford to be away a few hours myself," Bobby continued.

"I don't know. Rachel worked the day shift for me. I don't think I can ask her to work the night shift as well," Jennifer hesitated.

"What you need, lady, is another bartender. You're going to have to start thinking about it anyway as we approach our busy season."

"I know. I feel so lucky to have found Rachel. I don't think I can find anyone equally qualified."

"Solved that problem for you," Bobby told her.

"I knew there was another reason for this visit," Jennifer smiled at him.

"I received a call last night from an old friend of mine. His daughter wants to visit relatives out here this summer, and he insists she doesn't sit on her tail all summer long soaking up the sun. Wants her to earn her college spending money. He asked me to try and find a spot for her. I thought of you immediately. She's beautiful. Tall, redhead, lots of class, and I think Rachel could train her in no time. Her name is Janey Wilkes. Of course, at summer's end she goes back to school and you can go back to your original schedule. The young local kids will eat her up."

"Hm, it's a thought. I'm looking to get in a younger crowd, with the bull and all. And music, too. She just might work out. When can she start?"

"I think she'll be here the second week in May," Bobby told her.

"What do you think about having only female bartenders, though. I mean, the men could ask for equal time," Jennifer half laughed.

"I don't think it matters, but I would hire a male back-up bartender. If you think this place will be as busy as you hope with the bull, you may have to put two people on during the weekends. There's going to be just so much that you can do alone."

"I know, Bobby, but I have to keep the cost down. I'm nowhere near being rich yet."

"I realize it, but think about it. The bartenders don't get a geat deal of money per shift, they count on their tips. I don't have to tell you that. It might be worth another thirty dollars or so a night."

"You're right. Keep your eyes peeled for someone for me. Someone who doesn't do fancy footwork with the cash register," she smiled knowingly.

"I did say you'd learn fast, and honest people are hard to find. But with Rachel, you'll have a pair of hawkeyes the likes of which you've never known, not even your own. You're very new to the business. And Janey, she's too new to know how to steal. She's not the type anyway."

"Well, if the men have pretty girls to look at, let's find a very handsome guy. Equal time," Jennifer told him.

"And speaking of equal time, we've gotten off the

189

subject. Dinner, remember?"

"I don't think so. I don't want to impose on Rachel. Why don't we do it tomorrow night? I'll have her come in later, and she won't mind working a couple of extra hours," Jennifer tried to be fair.

"I'll have to settle for that. I'll pick you up here about seven. We won't make it a late night," he told her.

"Good. See you then. I'll be eternally grateful to you. Someday I'll have to return the favors," Jennifer started to say, and wished she hadn't. If Rachel was right, she was playing right into his hands.

"I'll find a way. Besides not taking all my bar business away this summer, leave me a few stragglers," he laughed, starting to leave.

"All's fair in love, war and business. You'll have to come up with your own gimmick. I've decided to make a killing."

"I believe you will, I'm beginning to get scared. I may have to ask you for a job myself."

"It's yours. Now let me get back to work, I'll see you tomorrow night," Jennifer cut him short and waited until the door had closed behind him before she picked up the phone again.

Bobby arrived at the bar promptly at seven the next evening, dressed in a sports jacket, wool slacks and a shine on his shoes. Rachel looked over at Jennifer.

"Hm, looks like he's all spiffed up for someone special."

"Don't get cute. We're just going out for dinner. That's all," Jennifer defended herself.

"I didn't say you had anything else in mind. But

190

Bobby seems to. I haven't seen him this dressed up in a very long time. He's trying to impress you, I feel it in my bones."

"I think you're getting the early stages of arthritis. Leave your bones out of this. Want to bet? Anything but the bar," Jennifer made Rachel giggle.

"No."

"Aha, you're not sure either."

"How can anyone be sure what's going on in a man's head? I don't claim to be an expert. What do I say if Ross calls?" Rachel asked her.

"Nothing. It isn't any of his business." Jennifer picked herself up and greeted Bobby. "Have a drink. I won't be a minute," she told him.

"Take your time," he smiled. "I've made reservations at a very nice French restaurant about twenty miles from here. I thought we could both use a change of scenery."

"Sounds nice." Jennifer started feeling uptight about the date. "I'll go get my things." She looked over at Rachel as she left. The woman smiled back knowingly.

Jennifer decided to make things perfectly clear to Bobby that evening. She didn't want him to get any wrong ideas about their relationship. They were friends, and could never be anything else. He had to understand. She waited until they were seated in the restaurant before broaching the subject.

"I heard the food was excellent here," Bobby started to say, feeling uncomfortable out of his own surroundings.

"I'm sure it is. And I thank you again for thinking of me. But, Bobby, you know I haven't been in town

191

very long, and I have many problems to work out within myself. I just want to tell you how helpful you've been, and how much I value our friendship. I hope we can go on this way for a very long time. No entanglements, two equals, being able to talk business, and feeling perfectly free to express ourselves however we need to," she said, watching his expression very carefully.

"I know that you think of me as a friend, and no one knows how much you've been through like I do. But to tell you the truth, Jennifer, I was hoping that when things started to calm down in your life, we could move this friendship to another plateau. You know I'm crazy about you. I think we'd make a wonderful team."

"I don't know, Bobby. Lovers are so easy to find, but good friends . . . that's another matter. I wouldn't ever want to do anything to ruin our friendship. And once we cross the threshold to another plateau, we can never return to where we were," Jennifer tried to explain as tactfully as she could.

"Is that why you've taken up sleeping with Ross Davin?" he shot back, to her surprise.

"I didn't set out to sleep with him. It just happened. He's good for me at the moment. You seem to have your doubts," she questioned.

"Of course I do. He isn't right for you. He's selfish, self-centered, and most times I think he's a bore. He'll hurt you, he wants things his own way. I don't want to see you suckered in again."

"How well do you know him?"

"Very well. We went to school together, and we were friends, loosely speaking. I didn't really like him then, and I don't care for him much now. He's trouble," Bobby went on, grinding out his cigarette.

"You're given me your opinion, but no hard proof of how he can hurt me. Finish what you started to tell me," Jennifer told him. They stopped talking while the waiter took their order.

"Go on."

"I can't, it's a story that Ross himself has to tell you. I promised never to divulge it. I found out about it one summer when I was camping in Colorado with my kids. It's nothing I can talk about, I just have to warn you. He isn't for you. He'll bring you more problems and heartache than Frank. Trust me. Have I ever steered you wrong before?"

"No, Bobby, but this is a lousy thing to do. You start a story and leave me hanging. I mean, my imagination could do more damage than what really happened."

"No, it couldn't. Believe me, he's a louse. A real son of a bitch. Look, Jennifer, if you were spending your time with a man who was good and kind, and would give you a future, I'd be very happy for you. I'd be the first one to move over. I'd bow out gracefully, as they say. But not Ross. I'll fight for you until the end. Don't let me have to watch you suffer. It would hurt me as much as it would hurt you," Bobby ended his speech.

"Could you give me a hint—is it animal, vegetable, or mineral," Jennifer asked him.

"I'll tell you this much. It had something to do with a woman. A woman he destroyed. . . ."

"In Colorado?" Jennifer prompted.

"Yes. But please don't mention it to Ross. If he's going to tell you the story at all, it's going to have to come from him when he decides the time is right. But

I doubt you'll ever get that close."

"Does he know you know?"

"I'm not sure, we weren't in Colorado at the same time. I never saw him or spoke to him very much when I returned."

"How long was he away?"

"A little over a year. Two years ago."

"Before he left, was he as distant as he is today?" Jennifer asked.

"In a way. He was never one of the boys, kept his distance. But I have to admit, not as much as he does right now."

"Maybe, just maybe, Bobby, Ross was affected by what happened more than you think. He's too guarded, too distant. The woman may have been hurt by him, but who's to say he wasn't equally as hurt."

"I knew I'd start something by confiding in you, you're going to make a romantic tragedy out of this. That's something I didn't want to happen. Jennifer, as I heard it, he walked out on her."

"That means nothing. I don't want to minimize your concern, but I am a big girl. I can make decisions on my own. And to be perfectly honest with you, Ross and I see one another, but we're not that close. It's okay."

"You don't sound satisfied," Bobby said.

"It isn't the perfect relationship, but then everyone has to make concessions."

"All the concessions are on your end, I'll bet," Bobby said knowingly. "And why pursue something that isn't giving you total fulfillment? Are you a glutton for punishment?"

Jennifer couldn't answer him. She wondered about

that herself. Ross was a mystery to her, a challenge, but beyond that, was he really meeting her needs?

"I don't know. I'm comfortable. No strings, no commitments. For now, it's fine for me. I don't know what's going to happen to my divorce, or what's going to become of my children. I'm not ready to get married again. I need my own space, and Ross gives it to me."

"You're wrong. You give it to him. You don't make any demands, or expect him to have to go out of his way for you. He's got a beautiful bed partner who lets him do exactly as he pleases. Why shouldn't he keep you around? When was the last time he took you out for dinner?" Bobby asked.

"Well, he never really has. We've both been too busy," Jennifer made excuses.

"Bullshit. How long does it take to eat? Jesus, Jennifer you make me so mad. Why do you need him?"

"I don't need anyone. I enjoy being with him," she told him.

"I'll tell you what you enjoy. The challenge. You can't have him, so you'll dig in, try to change him, and when you do have what you want, you won't want it. Women!"

"That isn't true," she lied. She knew in her heart that part of her attraction to Ross was her inability to have him.

"I say it is. But you're in for a fall. He isn't going to change, and he isn't going to wake up one morning and decide you're what he wants, and marry you. I'm telling you the truth," Bobby said.

"This is ridiculous. I spend a few nights with a man and the whole town has me married to him. I think this conversation is ridiculous. Men!" Jennifer retorted.

"Well, if it eases your mind any, Mrs. Wells, I'm not running away. I know I want you, and I'm willing to wait. When you get bored with your present lover, I'll be waiting for you. I know that isn't much of a challenge, but I've never been one for game playing. I'm getting too old," Bobby told her, placing his hand on hers.

"I appreciate it. I also appreciate what you were trying to do, really I do. But whatever happened in Ross' life before we met is none of my business, as what I did before I met him is none of his. We've both slept with other people, and we've had our problems. I want to start my life fresh, and I think in all fairness to Ross, he has the right to start again."

"Case closed. I'll sit and watch, thank you," Bobby said.

The waiter came and served their dinner. They both ate in silence, Jennifer mulling over what Bobby had said, and Bobby wishing he hadn't brought up the subject at all. He felt he had come on too strong. Jennifer had to think it was a jealous ploy.

They dropped the subject, and talked business the remainder of the evening. Jennifer didn't want to leave on a sour note.

When they returned to the Tavern, she looked up at Bobby. "Friends?" she asked.

"Always. I'm sorry about tonight, I feel like a fool. I'm no one's protector, and you are a big girl. Just be careful."

"I will, and thanks for a nice evening. Do you want to come in for a drink?"

"No, I'd better not. I have to check out my own place. I'll stop by tomorrow. I called my friend, and he's pleased about his daughter having a job. She's going to come down in a few weeks so the both of you can meet. I'm sure you'll get along fine."

"I'm sure we will. Thanks again," Jennifer said, getting out of the car. She watched him drive away.

Rachel looked tired when Jennifer got behind the bar.

"You wouldn't believe it, but for two hours we were packed. Johnny was having a going away party and they all decided to stop here for a few drinks. It was crazy. Felt good to move around again," she said.

"I'll take over for you. You can go home if you want."

"Nah, I'll stick around for a while. Maybe have a drink and unwind myself. By the way, Ross called. Twice."

"Does he want me to call back?" Jennifer asked.

"I think so, I think I may have gotten you in trouble. I didn't know you were going to be gone so long."

"What did you say?" Jennifer panicked.

"Instead of telling him you were out to dinner, I said you just stepped out for a minute and would call him when you returned. He called back a few hours later, and I said you were busy. I think he knows I was lying," Rachel said.

"Why would you do something like that?"

"You have one philosophy of life, and the people out here have another. Especially the men. I don't think Ross will understand your friendship with Bobby, so I didn't want to add salt to the wound."

197

"We don't have a commitment. We're not married, engaged, even going—God help me—steady. I can do what I want with my evenings," Jennifer said. "I wish you hadn't lied. I put up with enough jealousy tonight from Bobby."

"What happened?"

"He gave me a lecture on how bad Ross was for me. Some strange secret about his past. I don't know, I couldn't make any sense out of it. Now I have to explain where I was for Ross. I hate lying. I don't ever want to be put in this position again," Jennifer snapped. "I'm sorry, I know you meant well, but you should know better than I that when one person goes out to dinner with another in this town, the town knows."

"You're right. Blame it all on me, I have it coming. I just know the guy means a lot to you and I didn't want to screw things up. But lying isn't the answer. I'll stay on a few more minutes. Why don't you call him and straighten things out? It's my fault, anyway."

"I'll do that."

But Jennifer didn't have to call. The phone rang again before she had the opportunity to reach it. She looked at Rachel. It was Ross. "I'll take it in the office," she said.

"Hi, is anything wrong?" she asked. She heard Rachel hang up the extension phone.

"Nope," was all Ross said. There was silence on the other end.

"Ross, you called me. What is it?"

"Where were you tonight?" he asked, and Jennifer decided to tell him the truth.

"Out to dinner with Bobby. I know that isn't what

Rachel told you, and I don't know what got into her, but I'm not about to hide my whereabouts to anyone," Jennifer was firm. There was silence on the other end of the phone again.

"Ross, come out with it. What's bothering you?" she asked, exasperated.

"It doesn't look right. I wasn't snooping, but I knew Rachel was lying to me," he went on coldly.

"All right. I went out to dinner. It's all of eleven o'clock and I'm back to work. What does all that mean?"

"Nothing. I just don't see why you persist in that particular friendship, if you want to call it that," Ross was snippy.

"There's nothing else to call it. We are friends. He helps me, he's teaching me the bar business. He's been very generous with his time," Jennifer tried to be calm.

"And what's in it for him? He's giving a lot and getting nothing in return?"

"Yes, he's getting my friendship. And he knows if I can ever return the favors, I will. But so far, he's been a perfect gentleman, if that's what you're insinuating."

"I know men. And they don't do favors for nothing," Ross stated.

"How the hell would you know? You've been out of touch with the world for so long you don't have the right to make observations like that. My word should be enough. And besides, I don't have to make excuses to you. Remember, *you* set up the ground rules. We're not to get too close. It seems you're breaking the rules," Jennifer shot back.

199

"You're right. I've crossed the boundary. I'm sorry," Ross told her. "I'll talk to you soon," he said, hanging up.

Jennifer found herself sitting with the receiver in her hand. She couldn't believe it. It was the first time Ross had given any sign of his affection for her, and she blew it. Came on like gang busters! Miss Liberated Woman! But she hadn't done anything wrong. It was an innocent dinner. She dialed Ross' number.

"I'm sorry for blowing up at you. It's been a long day and I'm sure you called because you were concerned. I don't want to fight with you," Jennifer purred.

"I don't want to fight with you, either. I guess I want to have my cake and eat it, too. I want you on my terms, and I don't want you to sleep with anyone else. I never said I was anything else but selfish. I believe you that nothing happened, but will everyone else?"

"What difference does it make. Since when do you really care what other people think? You live your life the way you see fit. Most people don't agree with it, and the way I live my life shouldn't affect you, either. We know what we're doing. Let them talk, they're going to anyway. I can't live guarding my every movement. I resent living in a goldfish bowl. I'm disappointed in you for lowering yourself to the standards of the local gossips. If I were to believe every story I've heard about you, we wouldn't be talking at this very moment," Jennifer snapped.

"I know what you're saying is true, but logically I can't go along with it. I guess it's my upbringing, my brainwashing. See you tomorrow as usual," he said, changing the subject.

"Yes. See you tomorrow," Jennifer hung up. But

instead of feeling disappointed in him, she felt elated for the first time since they met. He cares, and he's jealous, she thought. If he wasn't, why would he care whom she had dinner with? She sat a moment to savor her mood, and then returned to the bar.

"Everything all right?" Rachel asked.

"Fine. But please don't lie again. I can't take the accusing eye. Nothing happened, and it looked as though it did."

"You're right. I'm sorry," Rachel apologized.

"Now go to the other side of the bar. You've had a long day," Jennifer ordered.

"So have you, and if it keeps up like this for the next few hours, you'll be able to close early. You can use a good night's sleep yourself."

"I know. I'll work the day shift tomorrow, and you, the night," Jennifer told her.

"Yes, boss. I'll be here at six. Going to Ross'?"

"Where else? By the way, Bobby is sending over a girl in a few weeks. Thinks she'd be good for a summer job. I want you to meet her too and besides, I thought I'd tell you before you panicked and thought you were being replaced."

"Thanks, and he's probably right. We may need two people on the weekends."

"Bobby mentioned that. I thought of hiring a man."

"When you're ready, let me know. I have a friend who'd be perfect. A nice guy. Honest, hard worker, and not bad looking," Rachel told her. "Toby Ellwood. You'll like him."

"As soon as business picks up, we'll talk. No one should have to work seven shifts a week, it's inhuman."

"You're telling me," Rachel reminded her. "But for

now, I can use the money. And breaking it up days and nights, makes it a whole lot easier. Well, I'm going to say goodnight." Rachel gulped down her drink., "I'm dead, and I want nothing more than my pillow and blanket. See you tomorrow night. Chin up," Rachel waved goodbye.

Jennifer waved back, and slid three beers toward the end of the bar. It had been a long day and an eventful one.

ELEVEN

Martin Galloway greeted Jennifer warmly as she walked through the door. David Hennessy was sitting in the chair opposite him. David rose and took her hand. They all sat down, and Martin was the first to speak.

"I think it's time to talk divorce, Jennifer."

"I was wondering when you thought it would be possible. I've had plenty of time to think and I don't believe there can ever be a reconciliation between Frank and me."

"I know. So this is what you'll have to do. It can't happen overnight. For your sake, I wish it could. I'll start drawing up the papers, but you can't really file for the divorce for another six months. I want to file on the grounds of abandonment, and of course, ask the court to grant you custody of the children. David has the whereabouts of the children in control, and we will continue to keep close contact with them, in case Frank decides to up and disappear again. I'll do everything as fast as possible, but we do have to stay within the boundaries of the law," Martin said.

"Damn it, you mean I have to wait another six months before I can see the children?" Jennifer asked, almost in tears.

"I'm sorry, but I want to build a strong case, make sure the courts award you your children. Then, when they do, we can fly to Switzerland with a court order and bring the children back. We can demand that Frank turn them over to us. Until then our hands are tied. They are in another country and Frank is protected. It isn't fair, but sometimes the law isn't always fair. I do believe, though, that justice prevails in the end."

"Those words don't warm my heart at this very moment," Jennifer snapped. "What is all this going to cost?"

"It's going to be expensive. Especially if we keep someone watching the children. We'll try to cut down where we can, but I don't want you to have to go through the expense of locating them again," David said.

"I know," Jennifer replied.

"I'm going to need a retainer to start the proceedings, five-hundred for now. The time will fly by. I'll file the instant the waiting period is over, and I'll get you in front of a judge sooner than that," Martin tried to comfort her.

"I realize you're doing the best you can but six months is so long. So much can happen."

"Not if we're careful, and we keep on top of the situation. I doubt if he'll show up in court. He'll lose by default. Trust me. Frank is wrong all the way down the line. We have proof that he walked out on *you*, left you alone without funds and, without your permission, took the children away. As sure as I'm sitting here, he can't prove your character so unfit that you'd never see your children again," Martin continued.

"I don't know what to believe anymore. I don't know what's going on in that sick head of his. However, one question has been going through my mind for months, ever since I won the bar. Do you think that now that I own a bar and sometimes work nights, it could hurt my chances of getting my children?" Jennifer asked.

"You did what you had to do to earn a living after Frank left you. Today, many women who have families work. Your children are of school age . . . gone most of the day. I'm sure you can show the court that you can hire someone to run the bar in the evening so you can spend time with your children when they're home. How you make an honest living is of no concern of the court. I personally think what you did, in the short period of time after your life was pulled apart, is admirable. It shows strong character and determination. The court will see it that way, too, I'm sure," Martin told her. "But do keep it clean. I don't want you to be mixed up with any drugs at the bar, nothing that could mar your character."

"I have to be careful. I'm up for my liquor license, and you know how careful they are."

"If you can pass that test, you can pass any. You have a home to bring the children to?" Martin asked.

"Well, for now I live above the bar, but I don't have

to. It's more convenient at the moment. But as you said, I wouldn't want my children to live there. Besides, the apartment isn't large enough."

"You have time to make other arrangements. But remember, I want all the arrangements made before you appear before the judge," Martin explained. "Well, that's about it. I'll send you a rough draft of the divorce papers as soon as they are ready. And you have to tell me whether you want to sue for alimony, child support."

"I don't want anything for myself, but I do want him to aid in supporting the children. Between us, I won't fight for it, but if you think it's fair . . . he certainly can afford to do so."

"I think what I'd like to do first is get a cash settlement. You know, for your mental abuse, and then a monthly settlement for the children. One-hundred dollars a week is fair in today's market. We can go for more, but I want it to look as fair as possible in front of the judge since you're working."

"I'm working now, but I won't be putting in as much time when the children come to live with me. I don't want to take too much time away from them. And then we have the readjustment period to worry about. By the time the children come back, they'll have been through a lot."

"If I were running this divorce the way I'd like, I'd hit him for as much money as I could. Before I put a figure into the agreement, let me think about it. I'm going to prepare one hell of a case for our side," Martin told her.

"I'm sure you will. Call me if you need any further information," Jennifer said, getting ready to leave.

"One more thing," David interrupted. "I don't know if this will upset you, but I had some pictures taken of the children playing in the park. I want you to have a copy. It will ease your mind that they are fine," David said, handing Jennifer the envelope. She took it, not wanting to open it up in front of them.

She thanked them both and left the office. It wasn't until she was inside her car that she decided to look at the children she hadn't seen in months. They both looked well, but Jennifer noticed a sadness in their eyes that had never been there before. She wept quietly as she backed the car out of the parking lot. She'd make it all up to them when they came home. She knew now that they missed her as much as she missed them. How dare Frank put them through this anguish! She should go for the jugular in the divorce. Clean him out. She deserved every penny considering what he'd put them all through. But she wouldn't. She didn't want anything from him—ever! She knew she could take care of her children herself. All they needed was each other. She drove back to Marble Lake with renewed hope and her head full of plans to make a wonderful life for her children.

Instead of going to the bar, Jennifer drove directly to Ross' ranch. Ross was busy rearranging the furniture in the living room when she walked in.

"I can't believe my eyes. There's a rug on this floor," Jennifer teased.

"Don't get funny. I've having a burst of energy. Want to give me a hand?" he asked, giving her a quick kiss on the lips.

"Is this Spring cleaning?"

"Sort of. It didn't start out to be. I lost a file, and came in here to look for it this afternoon. One thing led to another," he told her, as he pushed the large couch in front of the window.

"How does that look?" he asked, standing back to see the effect.

"Not bad. I'd move it to the other side of the room though, so people can sit and look out at the view," Jennifer added.

"I don't have much company," Ross defended.

"So then leave it where it is." She looked at Ross as he pushed the couch across the room, taking her suggestion. She pushed two chairs out of the way for him.

"Did you find what you were looking for?" Jennifer asked, picking up a lamp and placing it on a table.

"Not yet. But I have hope."

"What would a file be doing in here in the first place? I thought you kept them all in the office."

"I was working in here a couple of weeks ago, and I know I was working on that particular file. I don't remember seeing it after that," Ross told her.

"In this mess you may never see it again."

"Now this isn't any way to talk. Think positive. We're being positive here tonight. How come you're here anyway?" Ross changed the subject.

"I returned from the city a bit down, and didn't feel like seeing people, so I came here."

"Thanks a lot."

"You know what I mean. Look, take advantage of it. I'm in the mood to do some physical work. I'll work off my hostilities," she said.

"Bad news?"

"Not really, but it will be at least another six months before I see my kids again. I can't file for a divorce before then. But I don't want to talk about it. What do you want me to do?"

"Look through those piles of papers. Look for a file marked 'Thoroughbreds.'"

"Can I throw out anything that looks dated. Like, everything?"

"If it turns you on. But be careful not to throw out anything valuable," he told her.

"Let's face it, if you haven't had use for these things in at least a year, you won't miss whatever I'm putting in the trash."

"Don't be too hasty. You never know," Ross teased. Jennifer liked the light mood he was in and joined him wholeheartedly.

The two worked in the room for two hours. Jennifer had piled four garbage bags full of junk to throw out, and she couldn't believe the difference. The room looked beautiful.

"Now if we could do this in the kitchen and, God knows, your room, we'd have a good head start."

"I knew you were going to say that. Walk into the kitchen," he coaxed. Jennifer was intrigued. The kitchen was immaculate.

"What happened? Did you get a troop of cleaning women in here?"

"Nope. One conscientious lady who needed some extra cash," Ross said.

"Whoever she is, bless her soul. This kitchen is wonderful. I never realized how large and spacious it was before. It certainly has character. A person can even think of cooking in it now," Jennifer bubbled on as she walked around the table, inspecting the cupboards and the counters.

"I was hoping you'd say that. I'm starved."

"Are you asking me to cook?" she kidded.

"Only if it doesn't go against the grain," he smiled.

"Is there anything in the refrigerator I can whip up?" she asked, walking over to take a look. She observed a few unappetizing leftovers. The look of disgust on her face made Ross laugh.

"Everything can't be perfect all at once. I have a can of chili, some Spam," Ross started looking through the cupboards, "a can of baked beans, some crackers . . ."

"Okay, I get the point, I'll put something together. You, my dear man, can take the trash out. What good is it to have mounds of garbage bags in the center of the living room floor?"

"Boy, there's no pleasing some women. They want it all," he mumbled as he started dragging out the trash in a woebegone manner. Jennifer shook her head in disbelief. She didn't know what had put him in this mood, but she was happy she had decided to stop by.

Ross returned and helped her prepare dinner. He looked at Jennifer and caught her watching him. "Anything wrong?"

"Not a thing. I was just wondering why you're in such a good mood. Don't get me wrong, I'm thoroughly enjoying it," she corrected herself.

"I don't know. The weather's getting nice, days are getting longer, I bought two new horses, and I'm just feeling good. Can't explain it any better than that."

She had hoped she was the reason for some of his good humor. "Glad to hear it. You should buy horses more often."

"Don't get spoiled. The next time you'll see me in a

mood like this will be next Spring," he was still guarded.

"That's if I'm still around next Spring," Jennifer responded.

"Going somewhere?" he asked.

"One never knows, to steal an expression of yours. I'm taking it one day at a time. I talked to Sal the other day, he's started working on the bull. It's looking good. He's putting in every safety device money can buy. I think you'll be pleased."

"It's not pleasing *me* that's important. I know Sal's a good man. He'll do right by you."

Jennifer dropped the subject when she felt his mood slipping into sobriety.

"Are you going to stay the night, or do you have to go to the Tavern?" he asked matter-of-factly.

"I have an idea. Why don't we stop by after dinner, and I'll come back as soon as I check the register and see how Rachel's doing?"

"All right," was all he said. Jennifer didn't pursue the subject.

"Okay, for what it's worth, dinner is ready," Jennifer announced.

"Good, I'm starved. Smells good."

"You do have a cast-iron stomach. You could eat anything."

"Hey, I've had to rough it many times. Life isn't easy. Only the strong survive," he quipped.

"You have me beat," Jennifer laughed, picking at the baked beans. "Next time the lady with the washcloth comes, why don't you ask her to do a little grocery shopping? You can use everything."

"Who said she was coming back?"

"She isn't?" Jennifer was disappointed. "This place will go back to looking the way it did in a week."

"I'll think about it," he teased. "She'll be back next week. Make a list and I'll have her go to the store. It will save me money. Everytime I need something, I go to the local delicatessen and pay twice as much. This place needs a little organization."

"Well, we have a great start, let's keep it that way. By the way, do you know the name of a contractor to do some minor repairs on the Tavern? I want to re-decorate before the grand opening."

"Where are you getting all this money? Don't you think you should slow down?"

"I can't. I've hired a band, and the bull will be in. I want the place to look fresh, new, more attractive without changing the rustic flavor. If I'm going to do it, I have to do it right. I'll be in hock up to my eyeballs, but if my calculations are correct, I'll make it all back double in spades by the end of the season."

"I hope you're right. It could also be bankruptcy court if it doesn't."

"Why do you have to always look on the dark side? Damn it! I know I'm risking a lot, but I can't make an adequate living for myself and the children on the bar the way it is. I have to take the chance, and so far my hunches have been right. Look where I was six months ago—no job, no place to live. I've come a long way," she shouted, sounding like a commercial.

"Calm down. I'll call a friend of mine and see if he can fit you in. He isn't cheap, but he's the best there is."

"Thank you. That's all I wanted to hear. I'm nervous enough about this venture, and you sound like my conscience. You're not saying anything to me that I haven't said to myself. But it sounds worse out loud," she softened.

"I know. I'm sorry, but I wouldn't want to see you bite off more than you can chew. The Tavern made a living for Phil for years the way it was."

"A living, but not a good living. Phil lived upstairs, kept his overhead down. I can't expect my children to come home to an apartment above a bar. I don't think the courts would be too happy with that prospect either, not with the life Frank could give them. I have to do this."

Ross didn't say anymore. He got up, kissed her on the head, and put his dish in the sink. Jennifer did the same. She started to wash them.

"Aha, you *can* do dishes," he laughed, trying to lift her spirits.

"Well, I don't want to ruin this place so soon. Don't get used to it, it may never happen again. Like your mood, I'll wash them again next Spring," she retorted.

"Very good. You do keep me on my toes. You never forget a word I say . . . and use it again as soon as you can."

"Remember, imitation is the highest form of flattery. Let's go. I don't want to be out too late."

"We'll take your car, I don't feel like driving," he told her.

The drive to the Tavern from the ranch was a silent one. Ross was lost in his thoughts.

"Do you want to come in, or wait out here?" Jennifer asked when she pulled up in front of the Tavern.

"No, I'll come in. I feel like a beer. I know the owner, and she's buying," he said, his blue eyes twinkling.

"I'll never make money at this rate," Jennifer said, letting Ross hold the door open for her. They walked in smiling.

Rachel was in deep conversation with Bobby at the bar. Two kids were playing pool, and several of the locals were sitting quietly sipping their drinks. On the whole, the place was very quiet.

"Put a couple of quarters in the jukebox," Jennifer told Rachel. She nodded to Bobby.

"I can't. It's broken. I called the guy this afternoon, but he hasn't made it down here yet."

"Shit! It's so quiet, it's like a morgue. I'm going to have to invest in a cheap stereo as a back up, or something," she said, handing Ross his beer.

Bobby looked over and acknowledged him. Ross nodded back, and turned away, leaving no room for unwanted conversation. Jennifer could feel the tension mounting between the men. She counted out the cash drawer as quickly as possible; She wanted this to be a short stay. Bobby, sensing her mood, got up and said goodnight.

Jennifer was finished by the time Ross finished his beer.

"Ready?" she asked.

"Anytime you are."

"Close about one, if it stays like this. I'll call the repairman again in the morning, if he doesn't make it out tonight."

"He may. Harry works some strange hours. I'm going crazy with the quiet, I could fall asleep," Rachel complained.

"You've had a very long day."

"It's almost over. Tomorrow it's your turn. I'm sending Toby in to see you this week. I think it's time you hired him. It will give him a few weeks to get the feel of the place before it gets busy. Besides, I think we could use the help."

"Good. Talk to you tomorrow," Jennifer said, leaving with Ross.

"Why didn't you want to talk to Bobby?" she asked as they drove home.

"I don't like him. I never did. Don't push it," he said quietly, deep in thought. "He wants more than friendship from you."

"Let's not go into that again," Jennifer said.

"I'm just making an observation. I saw the way he was looking at you. He likes you."

"And I was there with you. I like him as a friend, and that's all."

"I know, I'm just telling you what I see. What you want and what he wants are two different things."

"I'm perfectly capable of keeping a man at arm's length. I don't want to go into it. He knows exactly how I feel, and respects my feelings. Please trust me."

"I do. I just think encouraging him will only lead to an unpleasant scene. It isn't fair to either of you. It's as if you're using him."

"I didn't think you liked him," Jennifer snapped angrily.

"I don't, but I don't think it's fair for people to use other people. You're taking advantage of his feelings."

"Not any more than you do. You have rules and I

live with them. I have rules and he lives with them. What makes us different?" Ross said nothing. "Oh, you get me so mad. Whatever you do is right. Whatever anyone else does isn't fair. Think about it."

He started to laugh. "I do it all the time, but I'm me, and I want it all. I don't think anyone else should have it."

"You pompous ass. Sometimes I want to strangle you," she laughed, fully exasperated by his honesty about himself.

"I can be infuriating, but that's part of my charm," he teased.

"I really should have my head examined," she said, pulling into the driveway.

"You should. I'm never going to be any different," he told her, and she hated that phrase. Of course he was going to be different, even if she had to shake it out of him. He had been different today. He could be, he just didn't want to be, and she'd have to make him want to be. She put her arms around his waist as they walked from the car to the house.

Ross didn't bother to turn on the lights in the living room. He went immediately upstairs to the bedroom, and Jennifer was right behind him. In bed, Ross made love to her with more warmth and passion than she thought he was capable of giving. He stayed close to her all night.

He can't go back to the way he was, Jennifer thought. She couldn't stand it, now that she knew he was capable of giving. She, too, wanted it all.

TWELVE

Jennifer stood in the middle of the main room of the Tavern giving directions to her faithful employees. She had closed the Tavern for three days so that the construction crew could get the bar ready for its grand re-opening. Janey, Toby and Rachel came in each day to help clean, paint, and reorganize the back room where the bull would be installed. Jill also donated her time to the effort. Ross, as usual, was too busy.

His words had rung true, his good humor had subsided after their night together, and again he put distance between them. Jennifer was disappointed by the change but wouldn't let herself be pulled into his ill moods. She had too much work to do with the renovating and the re-opening.

"I have a surprise for you," Jill said, rushing into the Tavern. "Everyone come out to the truck and give me a hand." They all followed her. In the truck Jill had a large assortment of plants. Jennifer gasped with surprise. "They're beautiful."

"My gift to you. I didn't do it all myself, mind you. I rounded up donations from the customers, Bobby, and even managed to get a few pennies out of Ross. I felt what was lacking in this place were some live plants, some greenery. So here they are. Everyone take one and I'll arrange them inside later," Jill shouted.

"Thanks so much. It really is the touch we needed. It looked so barren in there, I was wondering what I was going to do. But will the plants survive? There isn't much light," Jennifer asked.

"That's why I picked them out. These plants don't need much light, they'll live through anything."

"Even alcohol and cigarette butts?" Jennifer smirked.

"Well . . . we'll see what we can do about that. And I'm going to take care of them," Jill announced.

"What a way to drum up business," Jennifer joked with her friend. "For a small fee?"

"Very small. I don't charge my friends full price, and I got a really good deal on all the plants. We'll work out something we can both live with."

"I know we will. Thanks for the thought and the work. I still can't believe you got some of my regulars to part with their money," Jennifer joked, trying to conceal her inner emotions.

"They like you, Jen, they really do. We all hope you make a go of it this summer. You have a great rooting section," Jill continued.

"I know. I'm very touched," she said, as Jill handed her a large cactus and pointed her to the door to the Tavern. Jill followed behind with another plant.

Jill placed the plants in strategic places that would enhance the atmosphere, yet far enough away from doused cigarettes and drinks. Toby ran the floor polisher while Janey and Rachel stacked the glasses, some of which hadn't been washed in years. Jennifer was fortunate to have found Phil's extra stock in an unmarked box in the back room. The jukebox was on full blast, keeping everyone going.

"Who's ready to take a lunch break?" Jennifer shouted, bringing in a supply of sandwiches, compliments of the Marble Lake Inn.

"It's about time," Toby shouted. "I was getting weak from starvation. It's nearly two o'clock."

"Boy, does time fly when you're having fun," Rachel cracked, picking up a roast beef sandwich and taking a hearty bite.

"Beer, soft drinks, coffee?" Jennifer asked.

"Beer for me," Toby said.

"Make that two," Jill shouted.

"I want a Coke," Janey said.

Rachel took a club soda.

Jennifer brought over the drinks, pouring a coffee for herself. They sat around the table in silence while everyone gobbled down their food.

"Oh, that was good," Janey said. "I needed a break. But now I don't feel like getting up and working again," she said as she lighted a cigarette.

"Me neither," Toby chimed in. "And this is just the tip of the iceberg. Tomorrow night will be the real test. We open for business!"

"I know. I'm so nervous. I want everything to go

just right," Jennifer told them.

"What time will Sal be here with the mechanical bull?" Rachel asked.

"Late this afternoon. He's putting the final touches on it. I can't wait to see it," Jennifer told them.

"I want to ride it," Janey said. "It's going to be so much fun. Does the help have to pay to get on?" she asked Jennifer.

"No. But the help have to sign the same releases for two reasons. One, I don't want anyone to break an arm, God forbid, and, two, I can't afford to lose you. I've put together a great team. We really work well together," Jennifer said.

"Hear, hear," Rachel cheered, holding up her club soda. Toby tapped his bottle against her glass.

"I have a toast to make," Toby announced. "Here's to making a lot of money this season for Jennifer, and to lots of tips for us poor bartenders."

"I'll drink to that," Janey said. "I didn't think I'd like working here, but it's really a lot different than I expected. I'm glad I have the opportunity to see history in the making, the first mechanical bull on the North Shore."

"The ads and the commercials I've heard on the radio are wonderful," Jill said.

"I know. I'm very proud of them," Jennifer answered. "I hate to break up this happy group, and I'm as tired as all of you, but we have to get back to work. I want the room all ready for Sal."

Jill stayed at the table a little longer than the others. "You do look very tired," she said to Jennifer.

"I feel as bad as I look. I guess it's the mental pressure as well as the physical work these past few weeks. I want this to work out so much. I'd feel so foolish if we were a real bust."

"You won't be. And running yourself into the ground isn't going to help any. If you feel this bad now, what are you going to be like in July when this place is running full steam? I think you need some time off, a few days to relax and rest up."

"I wish I could, but the grand opening is tomorrow night. There isn't any time," she said, pulling herself up from the chair.

"Look sit a bit longer. What is it that has to be done? I can do it. Why don't you go upstairs and lie down for a few hours. I'll call you as soon as Sal gets here," Jill told her friend, concerned.

"I can't. How can I expect everyone else to work if I don't?"

"Don't be ridiculous. They work for *you*, they have to be here. And, more importantly, they want to be here. I'm sure they'll understand. You look as though you're ready to drop," Jill continued.

"I could use a nap. I don't understand why I'm this tired. I haven't been working any harder than Rachel."

"That's not true. Rachel puts in a long day, but she goes home and forgets about it. Goes to sleep. You can't. You have books to do, bills to worry about. Look at what you've been up against these past few months. You've taken on a big challenge."

"I know. I sometimes can't remember if it's Tuesday or Sunday, day or night. Everything is so turned around," Jennifer said wearily.

"Go upstairs this very instant and take a nap," Jill ordered. "I'll take care of everything down here."

"Thanks. You are a real doll. You're worth every penny I'm going to have to pay you each month to take care of my plants," she joked.

"I aim to please. And I intend to get other accounts from this place, too," Jill said to her friend. "After all, I have to make a living also."

"Let's hope us independent women make it," Jennifer said, walking toward the back of the bar. She climbed the steps wearily, not knowing what had hit her, and threw herself on top of her bed. She was asleep in seconds.

Ross woke her up at five-thirty.

Jennifer felt groggy for the first few minutes. "What are you doing here? I thought you were too busy to come down today," she asked, still yawning.

"Sal's downstairs installing your mechanical device and I was curious," he told her.

Jennifer snapped awake quickly when she heard what he said. "How long has Sal been here?" she jumped up.

"About half-an-hour. When Jill said you were up here asleep, I asked Sal how long it would take him to install the bull. He told me a few hours, so I didn't see any reason to wake you."

"Thanks for your concern, but I left strict orders to wake me the minute he got here," she said, feeling light-headed.

"Are you okay?" he asked.

"Fine. Just tired, and wishing this whole grand opening was over with. I have to get downstairs," she told him, heading for the door.

"Wait a minute. Drink this first," he said, handing her a cup of coffee.

"Thanks. I have to wake up. I feel as though I'm in a fog."

"You are. You've been working twenty hours a day. How long do you think you can keep it up?"

"For as long as it takes to pay off my creditors and get this place moving on a steady basis. I'm young and strong, I'll be fine," she told him, taking another sip of the coffee.

When they got downstairs they found everyone just sitting around, watching Sal as he bolted the bull to the floor. They had pulled the mattresses that would cover the floor around the bull out of the storeroom and stacked them in the corner neatly.

"How are we doing?" Jennifer asked Sal.

"It won't be long now. Sit down, relax, and let us finish."

All eyes remained on Sal.

"Okay, everyone into the other room. Let's leave Sal alone," Jennifer ordered.

They filed out into the main bar area. Toby got behind the bar and fixed everyone a drink. "None for me, thank you," Jennifer said.

"Are you feeling any better?" Jill asked.

"Not really. I hope I'm not coming down with anything. I don't need to be sick right now," Jennifer replied.

"That's the risk you run working the way you do. You have to take better care of yourself. I hope you get a good night's sleep tonight. Anything else that has to be done, can be done tomorrow morning."

"I know. I plan to do exactly that. I'm not even going over to Ross'. If he wants to stay here, fine. But I'm not going anywhere."

"Well, he's already here. I'm sure he'll stay. I have

to admit, things have lasted much longer than I antici-pated," Jill chattered. "He seemes relaxed around you. Maybe he and I met at the wrong time in his life."

"I doubt it. Don't let looks fool you, we're still as far apart as we were when we met. We're just following a regular routine that's comfortable for both of us."

"Are you happy with the way things are?" Jill asked her friend, not meaning to pry.

"No. I've always been a person who either makes full commitments, or no commitments at all. This re-lationship gnaws at my insides, it goes against every rule of my life I've ever believed in. How can two people spend so much time together, make love, and still be so far apart? I know I can't. I've fallen in love with him. I want him to be with me all the time, it's harder and harder for me to tear myself away from him when I have to leave," Jennifer sighed, sipping her coffee. "Oh, why do I get myself into these messes? And mostly, I don't know why I'm pouring my heart out to you right now. I don't know what's come over me," Jennifer said softly.

"That's all right, I don't mind. You know you can talk to me whenever you want. I'm glad to listen."

"Thanks. I feel so foolish, and I'm so darn weepy today," Jennifer said, fighting back her tears.

"I always feel the same way when I'm coming down with something. When you feel better, life will look better," Jill told her. "Jesus, I sound like a fortune cookie."

"Well, I'd better go over to Ross before he gets par-anoid that we girls are discussing his private life."

"Does he really worry about that?"

"All the time. Don't you realize that's the reason he

stays so distant. He wants no one to know anything about him. You'd think he was hiding a murder or something," Jennifer teased. "Or a skeleton in the closet."

"We all have skeletons in our closets. We've all done things we're not too happy about and wish we could undo. Someday he'll grow up and realize he's no different than the rest of the world," Jill told her.

"I hope you're right. It's what I'm hoping for," Jennifer said, walking over to Ross.

She sat down beside him at the bar. "Do you mind very much if I don't come over tonight? Can you stay here instead?" Jennifer asked him.

"To the first question, no. To the second, it doesn't matter. I'll stay. You're not going to work anymore tonight?"

"No. When Sal leaves, and the others go home, I'm packing it in," Jennifer said.

"I can go and pick up a pizza or something, and we'll sit and relax. You have a big day ahead of you tomorrow."

"Don't I know it. And I'm not feeling very well."

"I can see it in your eyes. You're more than tired. I hope it's not contagious," he tried to lighten the mood.

"Don't worry. If I thought it was anything contagious, I'd send you packing. I know what a baby you are when you're sick," Jennifer joked along with him.

"That's hard to believe," he smiled.

"Remember last month when you called me? You were supposed to be dying, remember! All you had was the twenty-four hour virus, which lasted seven days," she continued.

"That was your opinion. I think I was far more ill

than the doctor said." Ross was serious.

"Ross, you had a virus. But you love the attention being sick brings, so why get better fast?"

"I do not. I hate it when people make a fuss over me. I like to be alone when I'm sick."

"Really? Then why did you call *me*? It's a direct contradiction, as usual. I don't think you're really sure what you want," Jennifer stated.

"I didn't want you to feel left out," he blurted trying to hide his confusion.

"Let's drop it. I have my opinion, and you have yours. And God knows who's right." He seemed to settle for that.

"It's ready!" Sal announced. Everyone jumped to their feet and followed him to the back.

"Which one of us gets to ride it first?" Toby asked.

"Me," Sal replied. "I want to make sure it's perfectly safe before I allow anyone to get on. Place the mattresses around the bull," he ordered.

Ross, Toby, Rachel and Jill, each grabbed a mattress and threw it close to the machine. Jennifer watched the commotion. Sal got on the bull. Mark, his assistant, ran the controls. Sal started slowly. The bull didn't ride any faster than the mechanical pony rides in the supermarket. Then Mark hit the second speed. The bull moved faster until, when they hit speed number five, Sal had to hold on tight, his arm flying in the air.

"You're too tense," Ross shouted. "Relax, move with the bull." Jennifer looked at him in surprise. "Damn it, people who don't know how to ride that thing shouldn't get on," he snapped. Jennifer could feel him tense up. His anger was building.

226

Mark shut the machine off. "That's it, folks. Your bull is installed," Sal announced.

Jennifer noticed for the first time the small gold initials on the saddle. J.W. It was her bull with her name on it. It must have been an added touch Sal thought up at the last minute. She had to remember to thank him.

"Listen, folks, we have to think of a name for this thing," Rachel said. "We can't keep calling it 'bull' or 'machine.' "

"Anyone have any suggestions?" Jennifer asked.

"I had an old man once who reminds me of that bull," Jill stated, "started slow and rose to high gear. Ornery like him, too."

"So what was his name?" Rachel asked impatiently.

"Bill, what else?" Jill laughed.

"A good name, short and sweet," Jennifer added. "We'll call him Bill," she laughed.

"Okay, Bill," Toby said, "ready to take me for a ride. It's okay, isn't it?" he looked at Jennifer who nodded her approval.

Toby got on, but Sal ran the controls. He started on one, as Mark had for him, but he wouldn't move the bull past three for Toby.

"Aw, come on. I want to feel how he goes full power," he griped.

"Not yet. You'll have to get on many more times before I put it full steam ahead," Sal told him.

"I'm next," Rachel shouted out, almost pushing Toby off the machine. "Let 'er go, Sal, I'm ready," she said, as Sal worked the controls. She slipped off onto the mattress on the third speed.

"Are you all right?" Jennifer ran toward her.

"I'm fine. Nothing to it. I'm getting on again. Bill isn't going to throw me and get away with it," she laughed, Jennifer could see the look of horror on Ross' face.

"It's going to be all right. No one will get hurt. That's why we have the mattresses."

"I know. I keep telling myself the same thing," he said quietly, his eyes never leaving the bull or Rachel riding on it.

"Come on Ross, you get on," Sal shouted out in fun. "You're the only one who can take her to the fifth speed and show us the proper way to ride her."

Ross put down his beer and got on. "You don't have to start with the first speed for me," he told Sal. "Start with three. I want to feel what it's like—how others will be riding at that speed—then take it up," he said. Sal did what he was told. Jennifer watched Ross, his grace and movements. That was the way the bull was supposed to be ridden. He looked wonderful on it. And despite himself, he was feeling good on it.

"It's going to be quite some time before any of us can ride that well," Jennifer said. "Come on, Jill, you haven't gotten on yet."

"I know, but I'm a coward. I might not want you to go past one," she laughed.

"Whatever you say," Sal told her, and helped her on. He started the motor.

"Hey, this is fun," Jill shouted.

"Ready for two?" Sal asked.

"Shit, give it a try. The worst that can happen is that I fall off. Rachel showed us all how easy that was."

"Go to hell," Rachel shouted back.

"You've got yourself a real winner here, Jen. The guys are going to eat it up alive," Jill said, as Janey took her turn.

"Wait until Allie gets on. That's going to be the true test of the bull's durability," Janey laughed.

"You're right," Toby agreed. "Hey, Jennifer didn't get on. It's her machine. She should have had first crack at it," Toby said.

"Do you think you should?" Jill asked. "Not feeling well and all?"

"I'm fine. Maybe Bill will shake it out of me," Jennifer laughed, and looked up at Ross.

"Remember," he started. "Hold on, relax and go with the movements. You'll be fine."

"I have no doubts," she told him, mounting the bull. "Okay, let it roll, Sal," she shouted and Sal started the machine up. "It's slippery. You need a good sense of balance," she shouted out. "Take 'er up." Sal pushed it to speed three and Jennifer felt herself slipping off. Her problem was not letting herself go with it. She held on, trying to recover her balance. She couldn't. Sal, seeing her dilemma, pushed the machine to five instead of one, and then off. She fell to the floor. Everyone rushed to her side.

"I'm fine. I'm fine," Jennifer assured everyone.

"I'm so sorry, Jennifer. I'm still getting used to the machine myself," Sal said.

"You should be more careful," Ross shouted.

"Hey, he made a mistake. Thank God I was the one on the bull," Jennifer told him. "It won't happen again."

"It won't, Jen, I'm sorry," Sal continued.

"I know. And I'm fine," she said, trying to get up.

Ross gave her a hand. "It was my fault more than his. I knew I wasn't feeling up to par. I shouldn't have tried to ride it tonight," she said, feeling worse. She had an ache in her lower back, which she tried to ignore for everyone's sake, especially Ross'. Jill caught her expression, though.

"I think we should call it a night. Go home. Let Jennifer get ready for tomorrow night," Jill said and everyone agreed.

"See you first thing tomorrow morning," Toby said.

"Not too early. About noon. We have a long day," Jennifer told him. "And we don't open until four."

"What time do we unveil Bill?" Rachel asked.

"Eight or nine. I'll see how it goes. The band comes in around the same time," Jennifer told her. "Now all of you go home, get a good night's sleep and I'll see you tomorrow."

Everyone left except Jill. "Are you really all right?" she asked.

"I don't know. I have a very bad pain in my back. I'll send Ross out for a pizza, please stay," she asked.

"You got it," Jill told her.

Ross was standing by the bar, talking to Sal who was packing up his equipment, getting ready to leave. Jennifer sat down at one of the tables, the pain in her back getting worse.

When Sal left, she could no longer hold back her tears.

"Jill, I don't . . . I don't feel very well. I don't think it was the fall. It's just the way I've been feeling all day," she looked up at Ross. He bent down next to her.

"What is it?"

"I'm not sure. Do you think you could get me over to a doctor?" she said, slipping from the chair to the floor, doubled up in pain.

Jill knelt down next to her. "I'll call Doctor Gilbert. I'm sure he'll see her right away." Ross held Jennifer in his arms. The pain was getting worse.

"We were in luck, he was just leaving his office when I called. Told us to meet him in the emergency room," Jill said as she grabbed a jacket.

Ross carried Jennifer to his truck. She sat propped between Jill and Ross while Ross sped to the hospital like a maniac.

Dr. Gilbert was waiting for them in the emergency room. Jill and Ross waited in the hallway while Dr. Gilbert examined Jennifer.

"What do you think it is? I'm sure it had nothing to do with her fall?" Jill rambled on nervously. Ross didn't answer her. "Do you want anything? I'm going to try to find myself a cup of coffee," Jill said. Ross nodded. She met Dr. Gilbert coming out of one of the examining rooms. "How is she?"

"She's going to be all right. I'm going to keep her here overnight, she'll be able to go home in the morning," he said.

"What happened?" Jill asked.

"I think it's up to her to tell you. All I can say is that she's going to be fine. She isn't in any more pain, and I've given her a sedative. As soon as we have her settled in her room, you can go up and see her." Jill forgot the coffee and went to tell Ross, relieved at the news.

Jennifer lay quietly in her bed. It all happened so

fast, she hadn't even had time to realize she was pregnant before she lost the baby. She felt numb. How could she have been so careless? How did she get herself into this position anyway? She was too tired to think.

Ross came into her room and sat down beside her. She looked drained.

Jennifer spoke first. "I wasn't trying to keep anything from you, Ross. I just didn't know. I guess with all the confusion for the past few weeks, I didn't even think," she said softly, and then realized from the expression on his face that he didn't know what she was talking about. She had assumed the doctor had told him.

"You were pregnant, weren't you?" he said slowly.

"I thought you knew," she whispered. "I didn't realize the doctor hadn't said anything. I'm sorry."

"Just as well," he said coldly. "I thought you'd be more careful."

"Then I guess it *was* just as well," Jennifer tensed, turning her face to the wall. She didn't want to cry in front of him. She wanted to scream; instead she said nothing.

"I hope you feel better," he said, getting up to leave. "Jill wants to come in to see you," he told her. Jennifer said nothing.

Jill walked in after Ross left. She sensed something had gone on between them, but didn't know what. "Ross looks as bad as you do. What happened?" Jill asked.

"I had a miscarriage. I told Ross because I thought he knew. I don't want to go into it now."

"More importantly, how do you feel?"

"Numb. So much has happened tonight. I lost a

baby I didn't even know I was having; I blew my entire relationship with Ross; and I have to be strong enough to open tomorrow night," Jennifer said.

"Look, I told you he looked very hurt when he left the room. Give him time to let it all sink in. I don't think you blew anything. And, if you did, the hell with it! It takes two to make a baby. The woman isn't all to blame. In my opinion, even without the fall, you would have lost the baby anyway. So what's his problem?" Jill asked.

"If I knew, we'd all be better off," Jennifer replied.

"Listen to me," Jill responded. "With all the help you have, me included, we'll have everything running smoothly tomorrow night. It will all be done. I don't want you to worry about anything. I'll tell the gang you have a virus. You'll be home from the hospital before they come into work anyway," she continued.

"I always seem to be thanking you," Jennifer said.

"Don't worry about him. Worry about yourself for a change. The man always recovers." Jill shot back. "You two really belong with one another, both masochists," she bent down and kissed Jennifer on the cheek. "I'll talk to you in the morning. Get some sleep."

"I will," Jennifer said, drifting off.

Ross was waiting in the lobby for Jill. They drove in silence back to the Tavern where Jill's truck was parked.

"I think you're a real bastard. The lady needs you right now, and the least you can do is be there for her."

"You don't understand—I can't."

"*Can't* is the wrong word. You don't *want* to. It's too much trouble. You'd have to stop pitying yourself for a minute. I don't know what she sees in you," Jill told him.

"I agree with you. I don't know what she sees in me either. I think it would be better for both of us if I didn't see her anymore," he told Jill.

"I'd love to agree with you, but I think this is a lousy time to pull that stunt. At least wait until she feels better," Jill was furious.

"Look, I think I'm doing her the biggest favor of her life. She doesn't need me. I can't give her what she needs. Tonight really put it all in perspective for me."

"You mean if she hadn't lost the baby, you'd be stuck with a commitment to make," Jill shot back at him.

"It wouldn't have made a difference. You know me a long time, Jill. The baby wouldn't have made a difference. It would have only pushed us further apart."

"I don't know what's eating away at you, but if you don't get it settled within yourself, you'll destroy anyone you come in contact with," Jill told him.

"That's exactly why I keep my distance," he told her.

She climbed out of the truck and slammed the door. Ross drove away.

THIRTEEN

Ross sat on the couch in his living room, in darkness. Why had he allowed himself to get close to Jennifer? He could never let it happen again. He wasn't good for anyone, not himself, not his family.

When he was put together it seemed something was left out. He couldn't get close to anyone. Even as a child, he always seemed to be watching, sitting at a distance, never joining in, staying within himself. He was happiest hunting, fishing, and walking through the woods alone, with no one making demands on his time. No favors received, none having to be reciprocated. His mind was always on other things—far away places, getting away from the regimen. He hated the daily routine, going to school, studying, doing chores around the ranch. Growing up to take over the ranch was his lot in life, and he hated the prospect. Even as young as ten years of age, Ross knew there had to be more to life than that. More than just getting married, raising a family, and sitting around doing nothing while the years passed quickly by.

When he was eleven, Ross ran away for the first time. He packed his belongings and decided to find adventure but he didn't get more than two miles outside the ranch when a hand saw him and took him home.

Neither his father nor his mother understood his need for adventure. They were born and raised in Marble Lake, their family was there, they wouldn't think of leaving their roots. But in all fairness to him, they tried to understand his point of view. They tried to give him the freedom to explore other avenues.

For all his resistance to people, Ross always seemed to be thrown into groups, and he was very good at teaching what he knew. He had a great deal of patience and sensitivity. He had a natural ability to ride horses, and to care for them. He had the ability to make people sit up and listen, ask him his opinion, and rely on his judgment. At times, Ross felt himself drawn in, enjoying their attention. But as soon as this sense of well being came over him, he felt himself pull back. Nothing was going to stand in the way of his getting out as soon as he finished high school.

He also found himself being invited to parties, and being asked out by girls as his high school years flew by. Despite his resistance, he was very popular. But he sensed himself watching people, sitting on the sidelines getting drunk, watching everyone getting comfortable. On occasion, he'd joke, tell a story or two, feel a sense of pride in doing so, make love to a classmate, but he was never one of the guys who went steady, taking any relationship seriously, and as soon as any of the girls he dated started getting possessive, he moved on.

Ross realized he had a magical power over women. No matter how he treated them, no matter how distant he was, they seemed to stay around, calling him at home, asking him to come over to their homes for dinner, take a ride, go to a movie. He never treated them cruelly—just kept his distance. He never encouraged their interest. They seemed to be aware of his sensitivity and assumed he was once hurt by a girl which was why he was so distant. He reminded the girls at school of James Dean, whose moodiness had swept the country in the fifties. Without trying, Ross had become a cult figure. Everyone wanted to be friendly with him, and the more he pushed them away, the more persistent they became, until he learned how to become friendly and stay at arm's length.

During his senior year of high school, his parents took him aside and told him they had made a decision. They hoped he'd come back and run the ranch, but if he felt he wanted to go away from Marble Lake for a while, they understood. They gave him the opportunity to go to college anywhere in the United States. At first Ross welcomed the suggestion, but then realized he would be pinned down to another area for the next four years of his life. After much thought, he decided it would be best to go out West. He would be away and still be able to feel the wide open spaces—to ride his horse and commune with nature.

Ross found himself becoming more open in his new environment. The kids he met at college didn't know him all his life. He had secrets from them. He could be himself, drink with them, party, be one of the boys, raise hell, and no one was going to talk about it the next day. No one really cared. He was a man to them, not a little boy they patted on the head as he was growing up. He became a story teller, regaling people for hours about life on the ranch, as well as becoming more confident about himself.

The women he met at school were different, too. They didn't seem to want to tie themselves down. They wanted to experience life, not get married next year and raise a batch of kids. His four years at school passed quickly and they enabled Ross to unravel the net he had woven around himself.

He didn't come home during his vacations. Instead, he chose to go to another part of the country, staying with a roommate or a friend. Slowly he found himself traveling through the States on one adventure after another, meeting people, and yet, being able to become friendly because he knew he would be leaving in a week or two. No matter how intense a relationship got, he had an out, he was leaving.

But, as graduation grew closer, the old fears returned to Ross. His parents expected him home. They had given him his four years, paid for his good times, and now he had to live up to his commitment. He wasn't ready and instead took a job during his senior year to save his money for his next expedition. He planned to fly to Europe after school was out, spend the summer. Just a few more months was all he needed before he went back to the ranch.

He did just that and returned in September, ready to work, but it didn't last. He was home only six months when he again developed cabin fever. He had to leave! He remembered the talk with his father. It was the most painful conversation they had ever had. They sat quietly across from one another at the kitchen table.

"I can't stay. I'm not happy here. It's a nice place to visit, and maybe in time I'll want to settle down, but not now. Why don't you let Philip take over the ranch? He loves it. He wants to stay on and he doesn't want to go to school. He needs it more than I do," Ross told his father.

"I built this place for you. I wanted you to take it over. It won't be the same if Philip takes over. He doesn't have your know-how, your natural ability to handle people, to handle animals. I'm very disappointed," he said sadly. He started to get up. "You have to do what makes you happy, son. I just wonder what will become of you," Mr. Davin said.

"I'm my own man. When I'm ready to come back, I'll buy some property of my own, build a place for myself. Run it my way. I have to have my own place because if I feel I have to go away again, travel, it's my ranch I'm putting on the line, not yours. Philip will be fine. He's your son, and my brother. Something had to have rubbed off on him all these years," Ross told his father sadly.

"When do you want to leave again?"

"I don't know. I don't have any definite plans. Maybe next month," he told him.

"How will you make a living?" his father asked.

"I'll find a way. I'll always get by. I don't need much," Ross said, and his father walked away. Ross hated himself for disappointing him. The man had always been more than fair.

The family kept track of Ross' travels through post-cards—Australia, New Zealand, Africa. And then they got a call from him. He was back in the States, living in Colorado. He was working on a ranch and hoped to get home for a week or two soon.

Ross worked for two months on the McKinsey ranch. He saved every penny he could get his hands on. Soon it would be time for him to leave again.

Ross remembered that June day as if it were yesterday instead of five years ago. He had ridden out into the desert to get away from the ranch. He had sat quietly on his horse as he watched the sunset, but sensed he wasn't alone. When he turned around he saw another horse approaching. The rider was a woman, her dark hair blowing in the cool breeze. She smiled at him as she approached.

"I've been found out," she said.

"What do you mean?" Ross asked, watching her. She was graceful, slight, at least a foot smaller than himself. Her features were finely chiseled, and her dark green eyes flashed in the sunlight.

"I thought I was the only person who knew about this spot. I feel invaded. I come here when I want to be alone," she told him.

"Sorry. I didn't mean to intrude. I've come up here a lot in the last two months and I've never seen you before," he said.

"I imagine we want to be alone on different days," she smiled slyly, moving her horse closer to his.

"Do you live out here?" he asked, not wanting her to ride off without getting her name and location.

"Yes, the Barnes ranch. My father owns it. And you?"

"I'm working over at McKinsey's for a while," he told her.

"Then what?"

"Then I leave, travel around more, until I run out of money. Then I have to go back to work again."

"Is that your ambition in life?"

"For now. My family owns a ranch back East. When I'm ready to settle down, I'll go back home," he told her without knowing why. He didn't want to give her the impression that he was irresponsible. A new feeling for him.

"Then you ride well?" she asked.

"Yep. Why? Are you hinting that I ride away from your spot?"

She laughed. "No. I'm not very good at conversing with strangers."

"You're doing fine," he said, trying to keep her with him. "It's going to be dark soon. I'll ride you back to your ranch."

"All right. You can join us for supper," she said, riding off ahead of him. He caught up quickly. He liked her, felt himself drawn to her, and he didn't know why. She seemed to be as distant as he, and he was intrigued. It was completely dark when they arrived at the Barnes' ranch. She dismounted, and walked her horse into the barn. Ross did the same, taking off the saddle and placing it on an empty saddle mount.

"By the way, Miss Barnes, I don't know your first name. I hate to eat with strangers," he smiled.

"Erica, and yours?"

"Ross Davin," he extended his hand to hers. She took it, her hand was soft, not calloused like his. They walked into the large house, Erica introducing him to her parents, and announcing he was staying for supper.

That was the first of many meals Ross would have at the Barnes'. He postponed his plans to leave Colorado, and stayed on. The McKinseys were glad to have him, and his relationship with Erica grew quickly.

She was more than beautiful. She was elusive. Every time Ross thought he was getting close to her, she'd move away, become distant, need time for her self. He had finally met a woman like himself. And as long as she remained unattainable, he remained safe. And in her own way she controlled Ross, and she loved him, more than she had ever loved anyone else in her twenty-three years. And Ross, with all his fears of commitment, longevity in a relationship, fell deeply in love with her.

Ross got up from the couch, walked into the kitchen and fixed himself a drink. Why was he thinking of Erica now? Why? Didn't he think of her every day in one way or another? Didn't he still long to touch her, to be with her? And yet, he had pushed away the need, threw himself into his work to forget the pain, the memories of the life they may have made together.

He went back into the office and tried to work, fighting the urge to take out the photograph of her he kept hidden in his desk drawer. He couldn't look at it anymore. It reminded him of his own inadequacies, his inability to be unselfish. Ross didn't want to feel those old feelings he had kept bottled up.

Ross couldn't concentrate on his work. Thoughts of Erica kept flashing through his mind. He gave in to them and thought back to the first night Erica had brought him home for supper.

Erica ran upstairs to change and left Ross in the study with her father to fend for himself. Ross felt uncomfortable trying to make conversation with a man who wondered what he was doing in his home. Ross knew nothing about Erica, except she rode horses and liked to spend time alone. He was relieved to hear Mrs. Barnes announce supper was on the table, and Erica would surely be there to relieve some of the tension. But she didn't. She remained quiet, listening to the men ask half-hearted questions.

"Where do you come from?" Mr. Barnes queried.

"East. A small town in New York."

"What are you doing in Colorado?"

"Making money to continue traveling," Ross answered, feeling for the first time his answer was empty, made him look like a drifter, with no roots and no ambition. It was the first time he looked at himself in those terms.

"When do you plan to leave again?" Mr. Barnes continued.

"Soon. I'm not really sure, I don't have any definite plans," Ross answered, looking over at Erica who was taking in the conversation.

"When I feel I'm ready to settle down, I'm going to take over my father's ranch back East," he lied, trying to put some substance into his existence.

"Then you've spent most of your life on a ranch?" Mr. Barnes asked.

"Yes, except during my years in college."

"Young people! I don't understand them today. Here you are, a man who has the opportunity to go home and take over a ranch your father must have sweated his whole life to build, and instead you go gallivanting around the world, trying to find yourself," he commented.

"It isn't that simple," Ross defended.

"Oh, but it is. What are you looking for out there? The only thing I can see is that you're running away from responsibility. Running from your duties," he went on angrily.

"Don't mind daddy," Erica cut in for the first time. "He believes in convention, sons taking over where their fathers left off. His only regret is that he never had a son. He had a daughter."

"Don't be ridiculous, Erica. I have a right to my opinion. All I see are long-haired boys running around barefoot, trying to find love, life, happiness. The truth is, if you can't find happiness within yourself, at home, you are not going to find it anywhere else. Happiness is in the soul, Ross. There isn't anything out there that you couldn't find in your own backyard."

"I don't agree. I've seen many interesting places, met good people. For example, if I hadn't gone traveling, would I be sitting here right now with any of you? Look what I would have missed," he said.

"Yes, an argument with daddy," Erica said laughing.

"Argument or not, I'm learning about someone new, hearing their point of view," Ross said. "Look, Mr. Barnes, I appreciate how you feel, and I don't expect you to understand. I came from a very small town, everyone knew everyone else. No one had any secrets, no one had any private thoughts. I wanted to become a man who cherished his privacy, and maybe someday, when I find what I'm looking for, I'll go home. But when I do go home, it will be because I want to be there, and I'll do a good job. It won't be because I don't have any other options. Forcing a person to do what they're not ready to do, doesn't work anymore. Can you understand that?'' Ross spoke softly.

Mr. Barnes remained quiet for a moment. ''I guess. If you don't like what you're doing, you won't do a good job.''

''Exactly. And I have a great deal of pride. Whatever I do, I want to do well. I want to be proud of my accomplishments and to do that, I have to like what I'm doing,'' Ross continued.

''Youth. You may be right, but we're losing tradition. And that saddens me.''

''Maybe, in the long run, we'll all be better off and tradition will continue in a somewhat different vein. It may be time for new tradition. New isn't always bad, it's just different, and takes getting used to.'' Ross was serious, and knew he had won over Mr. Barnes and in doing so, had won over Erica.

''Well, I thank you for a delicious supper, but it's a long ride to the ranch. I'd better be going,'' Ross said, getting up from the table.

''It is a long ride,'' Erica stated. ''Why don't you leave your horse here for the night. I'll drive you. You can pick him up tomorrow.''

''That sounds good,'' Ross said. Erica excused herself from the table. "It was very nice meeting you both," Ross said. "I hope I haven't offended you, Mr. Barnes."

"No. I've stopped getting offended years ago when my daughter brought her friends home from college. I guess in a way I'm jealous of this new generation. They have options we never had. Maybe if I was born now instead of fifty years ago, I would have led my life differently," he said, walking Ross to the door.

"Thank you again. I hope we get to talk some more."

Erica was sitting in the car in front of the house. Ross got in and they drove off.

"Do you really want to go straight home?" Erica asked.

"What did you have in mind?"

"I don't know . . . a drive? I sort of left you hanging back there at the supper table, but daddy has a way of digging out information I wouldn't have the nerve to ask."

"Thanks a lot. I think I won him over in the end."

"You did. But daddy's a pushover anyway. He's always been cordial to my friends, even when he doesn't agree with them. He's come a long way in the last five years. You should have seen the expression on his face the first time I brought home a guy with long hair. He went crazy. The old cowboys out here don't take to hippies. They want to take them out to the barn and shoot them," she laughed.

"I know, I've spent a great deal of time in this part of the country. But if you don't antagonize them, remain polite, and try to understand where they're coming from, then you have half the battle won," Ross told her.

"And you know how to do it, right? I watched you back there. I was impressed," Erica said.

"Impressed enough to see me again?" Ross blurted out.

"Yes. I'd like to," she said, stopping the car in the vicinity of where they had met. "Let's walk," she said, and got out of the car. Ross joined her. "I love it out here. It's so quiet and peaceful."

"I know. And I'm glad you've allowed me to share it with you," Ross said, bending down to kiss her. She kissed him back. Ross moved her gently to the ground, kissing her, touching her.

"I want to make love to you," he said softly.

"Yes, I want you too. I wanted to make love to you while I was watching you at the table. Take your clothes off," she whispered.

He did, and watched her undress, after she took a blanket from the trunk of the car. They wrapped it around themselves. The air was cool, and at first Erica felt cold. Ross warmed her, exploring her perfect body, taking his time, wanting to prolong the moment.

"I want to feel you inside me," she told him, straight to the point, as Ross would learn she always was. Erica knew what she wanted, and how she wanted to be pleased, and Ross would learn how to make her happy. As she learned to fulfill his needs.

He entered her, moving slowly at first, trying to hold back until she had climaxed, but for the first time, he seemed to lose control.

"Erica . . . I can't . . . I can't hold back . . . darling. . . ."

She rose up to meet him, his pace quickening, Erica moving with him. They came together, Ross pressing

247

his lips to hers, reaching inside her mouth for her tongue, holding her so tight he thought she'd break.

He wanted to roll off her. She stopped him.

"Don't. Stay inside me. Keep the warmth between us a little longer," she whispered, holding him. They remained entwined for what seemed like forever— and at the same time an instant. It was over.

"I don't want to move from this spot," Ross whispered, "but I think a rock is embedded in my knee."

"Move over," Erica said. "I don't want to leave but I have to drive you home soon and get back."

"I know. So do I," Ross said. "What time should I pick you up tomorrow?"

"Whenever you get finished work. What do you want to do?" she asked.

"I want you to come back to my room so I can make love to you again. And maybe we'll go out for a bite to eat, too," he teased.

"Only out for my body," she joked. "Well, I don't know if I want to see a man again with such shallow interests," she teased.

"Well then, I'll have to take you again, right here, and now if you won't see me tomorrow," he said, pushing her on her back, his large body on top of hers.

"Oh, no. The ground's too hard. I'll see you tomorrow. I promise," she stretched, wiggling away from him.

"Good. I'll pick you up at six," he said, winning his point, although he would have enjoyed making love to her one more time. He bent down and kissed her again, wanting her more than he had the first time. It could wait, wait until tomorrow.

Ross saw Erica every night. She'd come back to his room with him, and they'd make love. She showed him what pleased her, leading him, touching him, and exploring new avenues neither of them had tried before. They gave to one another fully, both sexually and emotionally. Ross loved her more than he thought it was ever humanly possible to love another human being. He hated being away from her, and found himself counting the hours during work to get to her. She was always there, waiting, laughing, and wanting him just as much.

Erica was every bit his match. She could ride as well as he could, shoot, hike, and loved competing. She wanted to be best in whatever she did. Unlike some of the women Ross had met in his travels, women who let a man win because they thought it made them more feminine, Erica would not. If she could possibly beat Ross in any sport, she did. And if she lost, she put up one hell of a good fight.

The weeks turned into months, and Ross made no mention of leaving Colorado. When he did have a free week, they drove together to California, visiting friends of his—they were a couple sharing, loving, and needing one another. He wanted to marry her.

Ross was working hard, practicing for the rodeo the following weekend. Erica came down to the McKinsey ranch to watch him. Ross was uptight about it. He wasn't having much luck on the bull, and he hated the thought of Erica watching him fall off.

She didn't run to his side like another woman would. She laughed, shouting "Get the hell up there again. How dare you let a bull throw you like that. He's nothing but a stupid animal. You can outsmart him, or can you?"

"I'd like to see you get up on him and stay on, smart ass," Ross shouted back.

"I could if I wanted to. But I think the whole thing is silly," she shouted back.

"Oh yeah? That's only because you're chicken."

"I'll get on someday. I've broken horses more dangerous than that bull."

Ross walked over to her, picked her up and carried her to the barn.

"You really think you can outdo me at everything." he jumped down on her, trying to kiss her, but she pulled away.

"I won't kiss a defeatist. And tomorrow, I'll show you I can ride the damn thing."

"No. I don't want you to try. All kidding aside, it's much too dangerous for you."

"Bull. Nothing is too dangerous for me. Just you watch," she told him, getting up and shaking the hay off her jeans.

"Erica, I don't want you to. What if you fall? What if you get hurt?" Ross pleaded.

"I won't. If I fall, I fall. It wouldn't be the first time. I've fallen off a thousand horses. I know how to fall right."

"It isn't the same thing, but it's senseless to try to talk you out of it. You're so pigheaded."

"I'm glad you gave in. Well, give in or not, I was going to do it anyway. Now go back there and get on that bull again. I want to watch you make a fool out of yourself," she laughed and ran out of the barn before he could grab her again.

Ross worked on the bull a few more hours. Erica

watched him. He'd hurt himself many times on the damn thing, and the thought of her delicate body being thrown off was too much for him. He knew she'd get hurt. And she'd be too proud to admit it. They went out that night and discussed her riding the bull the next day. She was relentless, once her mind was made up, no one could talk her out of it. Ross thought he had made matters worse by trying to protect her. She was perfectly capable of protecting herself. The case was closed. She'd meet him at the McKinsey ranch at two-thirty.

Ross made one more stab at it when he drove her home. "I've decided anyone as stubborn as you isn't going to be my wife," he told her, waiting for her response.

"I don't remember talking about getting married, ever," she said.

"Well, I've thought about it, and I've decided to take back my marriage proposal," he teased.

"Take it back. I don't want to be married to a man who thinks he can boss me around," she retorted.

"You don't want to marry me?" He was surprised and hurt.

"You know I would, but I can't be owned. I don't want to be protected. I'm your equal, and you have to respect my wishes, as I must respect yours. That's one of the things I love about you. You always let me be independent, be myself, give me my own space, and I know you need yours. I think we could be happy together, have a really fine marriage. As long as we don't try to push our opinions off on one another."

"You're right. You do what you have to. I know I love you and want to spend my life with you. That's all that matters," he said, taking her in his arms and holding her. "Believe me, Erica, I never thought I'd say that to anyone. Marriage was always the furthest thing from my mind. I never wanted to spend my life with anyone. I love you," he said, kissing her and holding her close.

"I love you, too. I'll see you tomorrow. And if it really means that much to you, I won't ride the bull. I know I shouldn't give in, but it isn't that important," she told him.

"No, I was wrong, and maybe a little jealous. It was my male pride. If you got on that bull and did better than I did, I'd have felt less masculine, and that's foolish. Come tomorrow at two-thirty, and ride the damn thing. But I'll tell you one thing, if you fall off, I'm not going to rush to your side anymore than you rushed to mine. I'm going to shout, 'get the hell back on . . .' " he laughed.

"I love you," Erica murmured. "I'll see you tomorrow," she said, starting to close the car door. "Oh by the way, when do you want to get married?"

"Tomorrow at three-thirty," he smiled.

"Sounds good. Gives me just enough time to beat your ass off on the bull, change my clothes, and find a Justice of the Peace. Good. I'll bring a dress with me," she laughed.

Ross got out of the car and took her in his arms. "You really want to get married tomorrow?"

"Yes, we can drive to Las Vegas. Isn't that tacky?" she laughed. "And spend the night, and come home Sunday."

"Doesn't seem very romantic," Ross stated.

"Remember what daddy said the first night you had

supper with us? Happiness is where you are. And wherever you are, it's romantic," she told him.

"Okay, I'll see you tomorrow. Wish you were spending the night with me."

"After tomorrow I'll be spending every night with you. It's a bit scary, when you think of it," she said.

"Like I said, once it was. If a girl said I want to live with you, or wanted to spend all her time with me, I ran the other way. You're different. I want to be with you," Ross said, holding her.

"I'm glad. I have to go in. I'm not going to say anything to the folks. We'll surprise them. Sleep tight," she said, and Ross watched her run into the house.

He drove back to his room feeling good, happier than he'd ever been. Wouldn't his own folks be surprised! He could go back to Marble Lake, buy his property, and start a ranch of his own.

He was tempted to call them, but remembered the time difference, and didn't. Tomorrow would be soon enough.

Erica arrived at the McKinsey ranch a little after two. Ross was in the corral, getting things ready for her. He rushed over to the car before she had time to get out.

"My suitcase is in the trunk. I had a tough time getting it out of the house without my mother seeing it. It's so exciting. Much better than planning a boring large wedding," she rambled on. "How about you? Getting cold feet?"

"No. I searched my soul. I think I still love you as much today as I did yesterday," he said. "Enough to drive halfway through the night to Las Vegas."

"Good," Erica got out of the car, grabbed her gloves

and walked with Ross to the corral. They looked at the bull.

"How's he doing today?" she asked.

"Ornery as usual. Threw me off three times, I'm embarrassed to say," Ross told her. "Remember, Erica, be careful. I want you in perfect condition for our wedding. No bruises, no broken bones."

"I'll be doubly careful," she kissed him on the cheek.

Ross moved aside as Wally and Jed got the bull ready for Erica to mount. She did it like an expert and took off. Ross watched intently as she held her own, bouncing in the breeze. Wally was timing her.

"Two minutes," he shouted out. "That girl is amazing, rides like a man. Three minutes," he continued, as Erica fell off. Ross wanted to go to her, but didn't. She got up, and moved quickly to the fence.

"See, I told you I could do it," she told Ross, his ego deflated.

"Set him up for me, Wally, willya?" Ross asked. It was Erica's turn to watch.

Ross was more determined then ever to stay on. He wanted to beat Erica's time of three minutes. His shoulders ached, his back hurt, but he wasn't going to let the bull throw him. "Three minutes, ten seconds," Wally shouted out, and Ross jumped off. He was beaming by the time he got to Erica.

"I broke him in for you," she teased.

"Can't stand to lose," Ross told her.

"I'll show you," her competitive spirit getting the best of her. "Set him up again, Wally," Erica shouted.

"Enough's enough. We have a very important appointment," Ross said.

"Another five minutes. I want to ride again. It was fun," she told him. Ross didn't say anything else.

"Tell me when it's three minutes, twenty seconds," Erica whispered to Wally. She was off again, and everything became a blur. It all happened to fast! Wally was timing her, Jed was reaching over to get the flag out of the way, and fell in the line of Erica. She jerked, not wanting to run over him and was thrown onto her back. Jed got up and tried to steer the bull away from her, but not in time. The bull threw her again. Ross and Wally ran into the corral to rope the bull, and move Erica out of the way. She was, conscious, but seriously injured.

Ross paced up and down the hospital corridors while Mr. and Mrs. Barnes sat quietly in the waiting room, deep in thought. Ross couldn't face them. He kept blaming himself. If he hadn't wanted to show off and beat her time, this never would have happened. They would have been on their way to Las Vegas. Why had he been so stupid?

Ross saw the doctor approaching the Barnes, and he rushed into the waiting room to listen.

"Mr. Barnes, I'm not sure how extensive the damage is to your daughter's spinal cord, I wish I could be more definite. I'm sure we won't know for days. But the few tests we have made show complete numbness in both her legs," he said. "It may be reversible with time, therapy and an operation. She may get back the use of her legs. This, we're not sure of. We must do more extensive testing. But she's alive and, overall, in good health. I wish I could say more, or the news could be better," he continued.

Ross felt his own legs weaken under him. His lovely Erica, paralyzed! She was so active, never wanting

255

any restrictions. She couldn't bear to live the life of an invalid. She couldn't! The doctor had to be wrong. There had to be something that could be done to cure her.

Mr. Barnes looked at Ross. He walked over to him. "I'm sure you heard," he said hoarsely. "I don't want you to blame yourself, and I can see that you are. My daughter was always headstrong. There wasn't anything you could have done to keep her off that bull, aside from tying her up. Right now, I'm standing here blaming myself for not being able to control her more myself. I know you love her, and want to help her, but do it because you want to. Don't do it out of guilt. Please try and remember that. Search your soul and your reasons. Pity never helped anyone."

"I love your daughter, Mr. Barnes. She and I were going to get married today. I still want to marry her. I'll never find another woman like her again. I'm going to stand by her side all the way," Ross said and meant it.

"We'll see," Mr. Barnes said, patting Ross on the shoulder and walking away. Erica was his only daughter, his only child. It was indeed a tragedy for him. Mr. Barnes took his wife by the arm and walked her out the door.

Ross remained at the hospital all night. He was rooted there, couldn't bring himself to leave, and after a few hours, the doctors agreed to let him see Erica, just for a minute. She was sleeping peacefully, as if nothing was wrong. She looked so beautiful. She never knew he was there.

As the weeks went on, the test results weren't any more positive. There was irreversible damage done to the spinal cord. She would never walk again. The doctors told her she was lucky. She had the use of her hands, arms, head. There was much she could do with her life, with her mind—but without the use of her legs.

Ross visited her every day. Some days, she'd talk to him, be warm, her old self, and other times she'd say nothing, turn her face to the wall and ask him to leave. She didn't want him around anymore. And as her moods changed, so did Ross'. He's sit for hours in his own room, wondering about their future. He knew he loved her, but a part of himself was repulsed by her paralysis. The sex life they thoroughly enjoyed was over. She could bring him pleasure in her own way, but he could never bring her pleasure. They could never ride, ski, or hike again. Her life would be virtually bound to her wheel chair. As soon as he found himself thinking like this, he stopped. He'd think of all the positive sides—her humor, the hours they spent talking and arguing about life, politics, religion and environment. There was still so much they had in common. Her legs could never stand in the way of that. He had to make her see he loved all of her, and if part of her wasn't right, there was still the rest, which was more than most people had.

Each day he'd go to the hospital with this renewed hope, and each day he'd see her lying there and the old fears returned. He never stopped blaming himself.

"I want you to go away and not come back to see me," Erica told Ross one evening when he was visiting her.

"You always say that, and you don't mean it. If I

257

had the accident, would you stop loving me?" he asked.

"I don't know. I really don't. I'm being as honest as I can be. I have to deal with living with myself like this. I don't want to have to deal with you, too. Can't you understand I know you're blaming yourself and I can't stand it anymore. I'd run like a thief if I were in your shoes," she said.

"No you wouldn't. I know you would be there for me."

"Stop it,"she shouted. "I wouldn't. I couldn't live with you this way. I might say yes in the beginning, but I know in time I'd be bored. I couldn't do all the things that made us happy together. Please, Ross, I need this time to be alone. Maybe in time, when I get things sorted out in my head, if you still love me we may have a chance. But for now, I want to be alone. Please don't come here anymore," Erica said. She was testing him. Ross kissed her on the forehead and left.

He didn't return to see her for over a month. He worked hard every day doing physical labor, beating out his anxieties, his anger and disappointment. He needed her. His body needed her. And he turned to other women to give him the physical satisfaction he craved. Each time he left the woman he had spent the night with, he felt guilty. These women meant nothing to him, he felt cold and detached, lonely, guilty, and the pain within himself grew more intense from day to day until he couldn't stand it any longer. He went to the hospital to see Erica.

She was sitting up in bed when he walked in. She looked hurt when she saw him.

"It's been a long time."

"I thought you might call me, tell me you were ready to see me again. I got tired of waiting. I took the chance and came here myself. Uninvited," he mumbled.

"Well, I didn't call you. I didn't want to see you then, and I don't want to see you now," she said, eyes facing straight ahead.

"Erica, please, I can't go on like this. I love you. . . ."

"If you loved me you would have been here day after day. You took the easy way out, and left when I asked you to," she said angrily.

"Erica, you asked me to. I thought you had the right to your privacy. Isn't that the agreement we made when we decided to marry? We promised one another we would never crowd the other one. I did what I thought you wanted."

"I didn't want you to go around sleeping with half the town," she shot back, and hurt Ross.

"I was miserable alone. I'm not making excuses for what I did. I've never been in this situation before. I'm playing it by ear, and if I made the wrong move, I'm sorry. I don't know what you want from me."

"I don't know what I want from me either. I'm so confused. I'm sorry I took my hostilities out on you. I destroyed my own life, I have no right to destroy yours."

"You're not. I want to be with you. Please believe me. I need you. Let me stay," Ross pleaded. Erica took his hand and kissed it. She started to cry and Ross hugged her gently. It felt good to hold her again, to smell her, to touch her.

"I missed you so," Erica said. "What kind of a life are we going to have now?" she whispered.

"Don't think about it. Just get well, and get out of here. I want to hold you in my arms again, spend the night with you, make love to you," he said.

"Oh, Ross, I don't know if I'm unselfish enough to let you go. I want to lean on you," Erica said, to Ross' relief.

For the next few weeks things seemed to go back to the way they were. Ross returned to see Erica every day, helped her with her therapy, until it was time for her to return home. Ross rented a larger apartment. He wanted Erica with him right away. If he was going to marry her, it was his duty to take over the responsibility of caring for her. The sooner the better.

But life with Erica at home was not what Ross thought it would be. She became moody, staying alone in the apartment during the day while he went to work. They had to hire someone to come in and look after her when she had a cold, or a virus, which seemed to happen more and more often these days. She took tranquilizers from time to time to combat her depression. She gave up doing her exercises. Ross was beginning to stay at work longer, hating to come home, not knowing what mood he was going to find her in, until they were at one another's throats. Ross worked late on their last night together. He returned home from work two hours later than usual and found Erica in her chair staring out the window.

"Where were you?" she shot at him.

"I put in a few extra hours. We need the money," he tried to explain.

"It's my fault. If I wasn't sick, we wouldn't be

scraping for money. You could take some from my parents. They want to help. That way you could spend more time with me."

"I don't want to. It's our life, and I can manage it," he told her.

"Sure. It's easier to work longer hours. Then you don't have to make excuses about coming home to me. I know it's getting harder and harder for you to face me. I see it in your eyes, in the way you touch me. You don't even want to make love to me anymore," she sobbed.

"That's not true. I'm tired," he was making excuses for himself. She was right.

"Are you sleeping with someone else?"

"No. I don't know what to do anymore. I don't know if I can handle it. I don't understand my own feelings," he said, trying to be honest.

"I want to go home. I want you to take me to my parents' house. I can't stay here anymore. It isn't any good," she told him.

"Are you sure? Do you want to give up?" he told her, not wanting to fight her on the subject. He needed some time alone to think, too.

"I'm sure. I've already packed a few things. Please take me home now," she told him in tears. He didn't say anymore. They drove to the Barnes' ranch in silence. A part of Ross was hurt; another part, relieved. He didn't know how to deal with what he was feeling. He hated himself at the moment.

Mrs. Barnes made Erica comfortable upstairs, and Mr. Barnes asked Ross to sit and talk to him.

"I know you tried your best. It isn't easy taking care of her. Please understand that I admire what you tried to do. No one could have done more. No man could be expected to do more. Erica has to find her peace before she can embark on a life with another person. The doctors warned you that you were taking on one hell of a responsibility. If you ran away now, I wouldn't blame you. I'd probably do the same in your shoes," he said sympathetically.

Ross sat there, saying nothing. A million things rushed through his mind. "I'm sorry," were the only words that would come out, and he left.

Ross went back to his apartment, packed his things and left for home. He couldn't stay in Colorado, not now, and when Erica was better, he might think of returning to her. But who was he fooling? He loved her the way she was before the accident, not the way she was now. He felt like a coward, a quitter. But he had to go home, to familiar surroundings, to start his own life. He dropped a note to Mr. Barnes telling him of his plans and giving him his address if he had to contact him. Ross returned to Marble Lake.

He stayed with his parents until he found property of his own to buy to start his ranch. He used money he had saved over the years and borrowed the rest. He found the house was run-down, needed work, but in time he'd be able to put it in order. He'd start small and build, take one step at a time. He needed a diversion, and he had to put distance between himself and Erica.

It was nearly three months before Ross heard from Mr. Barnes. He received a call a few days after he moved into his new house. From the combination of the sound of Mr. Barnes' voice and the lateness of the call, Ross knew it was only bad news.

"I wanted to call you myself and let you know that Erica is dead. I know you loved her, and only wanted her to be happy. Maybe now she's at peace," he whispered.

"How did it happen?" Ross asked.

"My wife and I weren't watching the amount of tranquilizers she was taking—or not taking—and she accumulated enough to kill herself," he said, choking up.

"When did it happen?"

"This morning. We're holding services for her the day after tomorrow."

"I'll be there," Ross said.

"No. Don't make the trip. Remember her the way you loved her. Please, don't make it any harder on yourself than it is already. You're twenty-six years old, you have your whole life ahead of you. Start again, learn to live with the pain, and in time it will subside. Please leave it the way it is," Mr. Barnes said.

"What can I say?" Ross went on.

"Nothing. Be happy," Mr. Barnes told him and hung up.

Ross sat in his house for days, not seeing anyone, not wanting to go out into the air. He felt as dead as Erica. The pain was overwhelming, and he knew he'd never put anyone through this pain. He'd never hurt another human being again.

No matter how many times Ross went over the story, the pain was still there. He looked out, the sun was coming up. He thought about Jennifer. Yesterday she was carrying his child, and she lost it. The bull had succeeded in destroying another human being. At least Jennifer was fine, she was strong. She didn't need him in her life anymore. And when he knew she was feeling better, he'd leave her alone.

FOURTEEN

"What are you doing?" Jill shouted through the room full of people attending the opening of the Tavern.

"I've rested all day, and I'm really feeling fine. I won't overdo it," Jennifer said, looking around, hoping Ross would show up. He hadn't called or been to the Tavern all day.

The band was about to begin their first set, and in an hour, Jennifer was going to unveil Bill. Sal had donated his time to working the machine tonight and, much to Jennifer's amazement, the place was packed —not just with regulars, but kids, both locals and some from as far away as thirty miles. The advertising had paid off. The register was busy.

Toby, Rachel and Janey were working, dressed in Western attire, as was Jennifer. Everything seemed to be going right. Then why did she feel so sad, so disoriented, like a piece of herself was missing? It was more than not having Ross here, she knew from the beginning he probably wouldn't come. He hated crowds, and wasn't too happy about Bill.

"Jen, you really did it," Bobby said, congratulating her.

"Thanks, but it's the first night. Let's see if it keeps up after the novelty wears off."

"It will, I mean I'm listening to people talk, this is the hottest thing for a hundred miles. It's great. I wish I'd thought of it first."

"I wonder what Phil would think if he walked through the door this very minute," Jennifer said.

"He'd eat it up. He always loved crowds. And as I was told, this place used to be this crowded all the time years ago when the back room was open."

"I'm glad."

"Come on, the band's about to begin. May I have the first dance?" Bobby coaxed, leading her to the dance floor.

"I really shouldn't. I've got a touch of the flu, and I'm having trouble keeping awake. I don't want to over extend myself, have to last until the last customer walks out the door, or four AM, whichever comes first."

"Hey, Jennifer, when you goin' to start up the bull? I'm goin' to be the first to ride," Allie said, to Jennifer's dismay.

"In about an hour. Hold on, Allie, if you break it, you have to pay for it," she teased.

"I'm goin' to give it a good run for the money," Allie laughed.

"I bet you will," Jim shouted. "I want to see your ass on the floor. I'll split my sides laughing."

"I bet I can stay on longer than you," Allie answered.

"Bet you can't," Jim said.

"How much you want to put down on it?" Allie asked.

"Five bucks. Any takers?" Jim shouted.

Oh, no! Jennifer thought. Here we go again. I knew this was going to happen.

Bobby was beside her, almost knowing what was going through her head. "Let them alone. It's all in fun. They can't get hurt. I know."

"I guess that's what I had in mind when I ordered it. Keep everyone happy," Jennifer said.

The band played. Everyone, already plied with liquor from the four o'clock opening, was dancing. People kept coming in, and no one was leaving. Sal had a list of about fifty people who wanted to ride the bull. At five dollars a shot, she could pay for the band, no matter how the register read.

At nine o'clock, the lights went up, and the band took a break. Jennifer walked over to the microphone. She got everyone's attention.

"I want to thank all of you for coming here tonight and making the Grand Opening of the new Tavern a success. Thank you to my old friends, and thank you to my new ones. We are going to open up the bull for riding now, and I'd like your cooperation. Stay beyond the mattresses, and leave the speed up to Sal's judgment. I don't want any casualties the first night. Thank you again, and have a good time."

Jennifer moved off the stage, everyone was shaking her hand as she moved through the crowd toward the bull. As Allie promised, he was the first one on. Jennifer looked at Sal who winked back at her in assurance. He started it up. Allie's body shook like a bowl of jelly, his left arm flying through the air. Jim and the others were beside themselves with laughter. Allie slipped off and thumped to the floor. He lay there a moment helpless with laughter and Jennifer was relieved. Jim was on next, and won his bet. The rest waited their turn patiently.

Jennifer had seen enough. She went back to the front of the bar. A sizable amount of people were there, but it was not as crowded as it had been an hour earlier. It was cooler and it felt good.

"How you doing up here?" Jennifer addressed Rachel and Janey.

"Tired. I can't believe the turnout. It is unreal! I hope I can make it until closing," Janey said.

"I think we should work out a schedule for breaks. Whichever one of you wants to go out for a half-hour first, go on," Jennifer said.

"You go ahead, Janey," Rachel said. "I'm used to it."

"Thanks. I have to get off my feet. And I'm starved! Is there any food left?" she asked.

"In my office. I made you all a plate. Go take one," Jennifer told her.

"Thanks a million. Is it going to be like this all summer?"

"It better be," Jennifer said, "or else I've invested all this money for nothing."

"I don't know if this is going to be so much fun," she smirked. "I liked it better when we had time to talk to the customers."

"You will. It will level off," Rachel replied as Janey walked away.

"How you doing?" Rachel asked Jennifer.

"Okay. I have to sit and rest every once in a while,

268

but on the whole I feel a great deal better than yesterday," Jennifer lied.

"What a time to get a virus. Jesus, you have all the luck."

"Speaking of luck, the guitar player hasn't taken his eyes off you all evening," Jennifer teased.

"I know, but he's too young. Maybe by two in the morning he won't look so young to me."

"You're impossible," Jennifer started to say, when Jill walked over.

"What are you laughing at?"

"First of all, we're punchy; and secondly, the guitar player. Rachel thinks he's too young for her, at the moment. She's hoping he'll age in four hours," Jennifer said.

"He probably will with this crowd. That bull is marvelous. Everyone loves it. They've signed up for another turn. Congratulations, Jen," Jill said, "and for you Rach, go for it. What the hell do you have to lose? He's over twenty-one."

"Not much," Rachel said. "Will you two leave me alone. Let me move at my own pace," she said, looking over at her friendly guitar player again. "He is cute though." They all laughed at her. "I hate one night stands."

"Who said anything about one night? You can have a meaningful relationship. They're here for the entire week," Jennifer laughed again. Rachel gave her a dirty look, and moved down to the other end of the bar to take care of her customers.

"You look tired," Jill said.

"I am a bit, but I'll make it," she said, glancing at the people coming through the door.

"Upset that Ross isn't here?"

"I don't want to talk about it. He has to get over the shock of yesterday," Jennifer defended him.

"Stop making excuses for him. You have a right to be angry," Jill said. "It didn't happen to me and I'm angry."

Jennifer smiled at her. She was right, she should be angry, she just didn't have the time to think about it.

Jennifer milled around the remainder of the evening. The crowd started to thin out about two o'clock and a rush of newcomers came in around two-thirty. Rachel, for the first time since she started working at the Tavern, had to announce last call. Jennifer felt she had accomplished her goal. Now if she could only draw a crowd like this every week, her troubles would be over. The next few weeks would tell the tale, and she had her fingers crossed that things were finally going her way.

Jennifer sat at her desk, she looked down at the full ashtray of cigarette butts that were spilling over. Papers, order forms, contracts were there, unread. Hours of work ahead of her. She doused out her cigarette, wondering why she had picked up the old habit again after all these years. But weren't there a lot of old habits—and new ones—she had picked up in the many months she had been separated from her husband and children?

The summer months were rushing by quickly, days meshed into days, and the crowds kept coming in. She became current on her bills and was able to put money aside for her upcoming trip to Switzerland, as soon as Martin gave her a court date. She was tired and almost looking forward to the end of the summer, and her bar going back to a somewhat normal schedule.

She continued to see Ross during the week, but he avoided coming into the bar when they weren't together. Their lovemaking was still good, but she didn't feel any closer to him now than she had when she met him. He still remained distant. Neither one discussed the miscarriage. It was as if it never happened.

Jennifer remembered the first night they spent together after she got out of the hospital. It had been almost two weeks and Jennifer hadn't heard from Ross. He'd neither called nor come into the bar. Jennifer was damned if she'd call him. If he wanted her, he had to make the first move this time. She was feeling pain again, another stab in the back from someone she had trusted. She knew in her heart he was fighting a private war, but so was she, and now was the time to be selfish, she had to think of herself first. She was tempted at times to pick up the phone, call him, and see how this was all affecting him, but she'd put it down quickly and resisted the urge.

Then the call came. Ross seemed strained on the other end, as if he didn't know what to say, feeling concerned, yet embarrassed that it had taken him so long to call. Jennifer remained quiet, she listened to "I hear the bar is a great success. . . . You've gotten what you want, I heard things are going very well, don't over extend yourself. Don't get yourself run down again. . . ."

Run down again, Jennifer wanted to scream, but didn't. She answered in monosyllables—"Yes, No,

Fine, Thanks." She wasn't going to make it any easier for him. Then he hemmed and hawed for a minute, and asked her to come over, have a quiet dinner with him away from the crowds. Jennifer was tempted to refuse, but decided against it. She agreed, promising to be at the ranch later that evening. They hung up.

Jennifer worked the bar the remainder of the day. The bull was now the main attraction, but the music started later in the evening. The band was sensational, everyone loved them, and Jennifer asked them to stay for another week, which made Rachel happy. She was merrily romping in the sheets with her guitar player, and was feeling down in the dumps that their engagement at the Tavern was drawing to a close. Her spirits lifted, and so did Jennifer's.

As Jennifer walked through the bar on her way out, Rachel shouted out at her, "Stepping out tonight? Leaving me here alone with the crowds?"

"I'm entitled," Jennifer laughed back, and walked to the other side of the bar.

"I'm kidding," Rachel said. "I'm glad Ross is back in the picture, you were a real bitch to work with last week."

"I wasn't that bad. And it had nothing to do with Ross. I was under the gun, it was make or break week."

"True, and for all good little girls, all good things are happening," she chuckled.

"I don't know about that, but I'm taking it one step at a time. Toby's coming in later to work the late shift. I'll see you tomorrow," Jennifer said, rushing out the door:

She did feel good, better than she had in a long time.

Physically, she was in better shape than she had been ten days ago. She felt strong again, ready to face anything, and going to Ross' she had better be ready to face anything. She didn't know what mood she was going to find him in. To her surprise, he was in a very good mood, greeting her warmly, kissing her at the door.

Jennifer sat in the kitchen and watched him cook. "Can't I do something?" she asked.

"No. I have it all under control. Sit, relax, and drink your wine," he ordered.

She obeyed. Jennifer watched him move around the kitchen ever so gracefully, cutting mushrooms, dicing onions, stirring the sauce, he knew exactly what he was doing.

"You've done this before," she felt good-humored.

"Right. Many times. I'm not a half-bad cook. As a matter of fact, I'm a very good cook," he told her.

"As I said, men make the best chefs. I think women should retire from the kitchen altogether, and leave it to the experts."

"Now I wouldn't go that far. I don't mind cooking once in a while, but all the time would get on my nerves. Women always amaze me. Night after night, they're expected to cook up a hot meal with imagination and expertise. I'd run away from home," Ross joked.

"I've heard it said that many women are running away from home, leaving their husbands with the dirty dishes and screaming kids," she rambled.

"But not you. You stayed until the last." He was testing her.

"You're damn right! I made a commitment, and I

rode out the bad times. I guess Frank couldn't do the same," she said quietly.

"How do you really feel about that?"

"Angry. At first very hurt, disappointed, now all I feel is anger. I'll fight until I die, but I'll get my kids back. He can go to hell."

"You'd write off all the years you spent together, just like that?"

"He did. Now it's my turn. When I let go, it's for good. I don't change my mind," Jennifer said firmly.

"But what if . . . just for argument's sake, the man went crazy, had a temporary breakdown, and really didn't know what he was doing? Could you forgive him and start your life over again?" he asked.

Jennifer was curious about this line of questioning. "I've thought about it, but I couldn't forgive him now. I've become a different woman. It isn't just what he did with the kids, it's more than that. It's my life! I've been able to make it on my own, and I'll be damned if I'll give up my independence and go back to the way things used to be. I have to be honest, Ross, our marriage was never what I thought it was. I was living in a fairy tale, it wasn't real, and it wasn't what I really wanted. I can see that now. Frank could never deal with the way I am now."

"But what would you really be giving up by giving up your independence? Would you miss serving booze to drunks and working days and nights in an atmosphere unbecoming to you? That isn't what you're used to. I understand your husband was very wealthy, and you had it made; moneywise, that is," he said as he cut the tomatoes for the salad.

"Let me get this straight. It would be better for me

to sit stagnating, working in the garden club or some such nonsense, and forgive my husband all the misery he put me through this past year, rather than lower my standards?" she spouted off. "In short, what you're telling me is that it's beneath my dignity working in a saloon? I'm a lowly bar owner," she said angrily, "not a prim, forgiving, little housewife."

"No. You've twisted my words to suit yourself. I think you have too much class to work behind a bar."

"Oh, even better, only people without class should own a bar. Or is it just the fact that I'm a woman, and a barroom is no place for a woman," she said, her voice rising.

"Okay, if you want to look at it that way. I don't think it's ladylike for a woman to spend so much time in a bar. I really don't think women should be in bars unescorted."

"Oh, really? Are you living in the dark ages? We are liberated, free to come and go as we please, or did you forget that? So you mean to tell me in all these years you've been going to bars you've never picked up a woman in one?"

"I didn't say that."

"Then what is it you're saying? Does my owning the Tavern embarrass you? That's it, isn't it. Although you sympathize with the humdrum life of a wife, you still think women belong in the kitchen, attending to the needs of men," she flew off in a rage.

"No. I think it's a two-way street. I believe in commitment when one is made. Two people take the good with the bad. They have to live through the rough times, they must understand one another. I think you've gotten a tough break, so you've had a taste of independence and you're ready to throw a great many years down the tube for it. I think in the long run you'll be unhappy, maybe when the so-called glamour wears off," he tried to explain.

"How the hell would you know? You never made a commitment that didn't suit your needs in your life. People change, they grow, and sometimes in a marriage it's good, but when the two people grow at different rates, they start to grow farther apart. That isn't good. Then they need to step back, evaluate their relationship, and sometimes go their separate ways. Two people marrying in their early twenties are not always going to feel the same way about one another after ten or twenty years of marriage. I'm not talking about those who find different men or women because they want to try something new. I'm talking legitimate changes. Nothing is forever anymore. There never should have been. We shouldn't have to feel guilty when a marriage fails. If I've learned one thing this past year, I've learned that. Sometimes our lives take a change and you can't go back. It's like you've put on a new pair of glasses and you see the world differently. It can never go back to the way it used to be," Jennifer stated with great conviction.

"I don't think people change that much. I think that deep down inside what they were at twenty-one they still are at forty-one. I know I haven't changed," he said.

"Then I feel sorry for you. With all the traveling you've done, and all you've seen, you've learned nothing. One has to change. The more you see, read, feel, the more you think, grow and change. Not always in a negative way, most of the time it's in a positive way. If you don't, then you stay constant, wither and die. No, Ross, you're not being honest with yourself. You've changed more than you want to admit, and the day you can admit you're wrong, you've grown. That's the day you can start living again," she ended her speech.

"I am living. I'm living the way I want to live. I'm happy with my life the way it is," he defended himself.

"Here we go again. I don't think so, but that's my lowly woman's opinion. I can see it doesn't count for much. I should be home forgiving my husband and working on saving my marriage."

"I just wanted to know if you had given it any thought. Instead of fighting so hard against it, maybe if you channeled your energies into trying to save the marriage, you might be happier in the end," he said softly.

"No. It can't be saved. I don't want it to be. I can't go back to what I used to be, and that ends that discussion. I hope I have eased your mind," she told him, wondering why he was so interested in getting her back with her husband. Or was it that he wanted to make sure she wasn't going to leave him when it was time to go off and get her children? Maybe it was Ross who didn't want to be left wide open to be hurt. Or was it that she was just being overly optimistic about how he was feeling about her?

"Ross, I know what I'm doing, and I'm sorry what I do for a living makes you uncomfortable," she said.

"It doesn't really, but it isn't a job I think well suited for you. You're not physically strong enough. I think you know what I mean," he stopped abruptly and Jennifer didn't answer him. He was referring to her losing the baby, because of the overwork and strain the bar thrust upon her.

She lit a cigarette and sat silently sipping her wine. She decided this was the time to say something she'd hesitated about for a long time. "Ross, what do you want from me? After all this time, do you feel nothing?" she looked straight into his eyes and saw his discomfort at the question.

"I don't want anything from you. I enjoy our time together, and I'm very fond of you. I like having you around," he said softly, and Jennifer decided to leave it at that.

Ross took the roast out of the oven. "Dinner is ready," he changed the subject.

"I'll set the table," Jennifer volunteered.

"You do that," he smiled at her, uncomfortable

They had both said a lot of things they didn't mean, but as far as Jennifer was concerned, it was a beginning—their first heated discussion. It was good for both of them.

Over dinner, Jennifer talked about the bar, the crowds, and how successful the bull was. She couldn't believe how many people from all areas it was drawing, but she was thankful. Ross listened, and kept eating. He kept looking over at her full plate.

"I guess I'm not as hungry as I thought. It's delicious, though," she told him, and it was.

"Then eat. You'll get run-down again," he said.

"I wasn't run-down," she snapped back, wanting to get everything out in the open.

"I don't want to talk about it," he told her.

"Okay, we won't," she answered, picking at her

278

food. "The place still looks nice. Someone coming in to keep it up?" she changed the conversation.

"Yeah. It seems to be working. I'm getting used to the order," he said, and Jennifer couldn't resist the dig.

"And you said you never changed?"

He smiled back at her knowingly. She knew when to hit.

They went upstairs after Jennifer finished the dishes. Ross moved close to her, holding her close, but didn't make any move to touch her. Jennifer rolled over and kissed him. He kissed her back, then stopped. She could feel his hardness against her.

"Ross," she whispered. "What's wrong?"

"Nothing, we shouldn't."

"It's okay. I'm fine," she told him.

"Are you sure?"

"Yes," she told him and kissed him again. This time he didn't resist. He wanted her.

"I love you," she whispered when they finished making love. He didn't answer her, but pulled her closer to him, and fell asleep.

FIFTEEN

Jennifer pushed the thoughts of Ross out of her mind. She had work to do. She was planning the Labor Day party at the Tavern, the official end of Summer, but she was told that people still came out well into the Fall if the weather stayed nice.

She wanted to rehire The Country Five—the original band she had when the bar opened—but their manager was putting the squeeze on her. He wanted more money, and she didn't know if she was willing to meet his price.

Jill came into the office. "Sitting back and relaxing again," she said, as she bounced onto a chair.

"Here to take care of our lovely plants?"

"As usual. And I want to thank you for the recommendations. The business has really taken off this summer. I even have enough money to construct my greenhouse. It's something I've wanted to do for years," she rambled on, but Jennifer was only half listening.

"I'm sorry, I wasn't paying much attention. I hate paperwork," she said through clenched teeth.

"Take a break. I'll get you some coffee," Jill told her.

"What were you saying about a greenhouse?"

"I'm going to start building mine next month. I have the plans drawn up, and hired the people to do the job. My dreams are coming true," she said, handing Jennifer a hot cup of coffee.

"It's ninety degrees out and I'm still drinking twenty cups of coffee a day," Jennifer stated.

"They say when you drink something hot when you are hot, it keeps you cool. It doesn't make sense, though. In the dead of winter, the last thing I want is a cold glass of iced tea," Jill chuckled.

"How are the boys?"

"Fine, but I can't wait until school starts. I love them dearly, but after two months, I can't take their running around the house all day with their friends. I want some time for myself."

"I remember it well."

"Oh, I'm sorry," Jill apologized.

"That's okay. This whole nightmare should be coming to an end soon. My kids will be home before I know it. Which leads me to another problem. I have to find a place to live, I can't bring them here. And I don't want them to go to the cottage. It was all right for me, but too cold for them."

"Do you want to rent something or buy? I can introduce you to a very dear friend in real estate," Jill offered.

"Do that. I think I'd rather rent for the time being. How's the market?"

"Rentals are few and far between, but they're out

281

there. If anyone would know it would be Monica. I'll give her a call for you when I get back home. Three bedrooms?'' Jill asked.

"Or four. Do I have much of a choice?"

"You'll probably get an old rambling farm house, somewhat on the order of mine. Maybe with an option to buy," Jill told her.

"Sounds good to me. It's just one more thing I have to find time to do. Jesus, I'm getting lazy. I feel like hiring a bookkeeper."

"I know someone who's very good at it, works cheap, and could use the extra money," Jill told her.

"Sounds perfect. Who?"

"Me. I'd love to give you a hand."

"But what about your business, and the greenhouse?"

"Even more reason I could use the extra cash. And since this place is open twenty-hours a day, the schedule isn't too tight. I could to it between other things," Jill said.

"Are you sure you want to take it on? It's b-o-r-i-n-g," Jennifer said.

"I know. I used to do it back in the dark ages when I got out of school. It might take me some time to acquaint myself with your system."

"What system? The bills come in, I pay them, and mark them down. I haven't set up a sophisticated system. And as you can see, I'm weeks behind in the filing. I tremble whenever the phone rings and I have to check an invoice. It takes me twenty minutes to find it. I just don't seem to find the time."

"Well, your prayers have been answered. Move over," Jill ordered.

"You're ready to start now?"

"No time like the present. I've saved your plants for last, and I'm free for the rest of the day," she said.

"Fine. See that pile of folders and papers on the chair over there? Put them in order and file them. We may as well start with the basics," Jennifer said.

"As you wish, Captain," Jill joked, saluting her.

"Just remember to tell me what your system is. I want to be able to find anything at a touch of a finger, if that's at all possible."

"It is. You know how organized I am. Do you want me to go as far as making out the checks for your signature?"

"No. I can do that. We'll keep a file of unpaid bills, and once I pay them, they can be filed away after they're posted," Jennifer told her.

"Seems simple enough," Jill went on. "I imagine once we get this place organized, it shouldn't take very long to keep it up. Much like Ross' house," she chuckled, then stopped. "I can't believe it. I've only been working for you five minutes and I've already cut myself to an hour a week," she laughed.

"I'm sure you'll find more to do. You're resourceful," Jennifer laughed back, "or else it won't be worth the gas to come in."

"How's the Labor Day party coming?"

"Good. I'm going to hire The Country Five again. That should make Rachel happy," Jennifer said.

"You've captured the hearts of the locals, here and in the surrounding towns. I think you're going to be surprised at how busy you'll be all winter," Jill told her.

"I hope so. But to tell you the truth, I could use the

quiet for a while I'm losing Janey, and when my kids get here, I won't have much time to tend bar myself. I don't think Rachel and Toby can handle it on their own," Jennifer said, thinking about Rachel's register lately. She reluctantly brought it up to Jill.

"You've known Rachel a lot longer than I have. I have something in my mind, but I hate to bring it up," Jennifer started to say.

"Shoot. What is it?"

"I've heard this, but I've never seen it," Jennifer said hesitantly. "Rachel hasn't been putting all the money into the register. She's been coming up over."

"Isn't that good? It's better than under," Jill said.

"No, it isn't. Bobby told me that a long time ago. If a register comes up over, it means that the bartender is putting cash in the register and not ringing up the drinks. They take it out later at a convenient time, if you know what I mean. If you're real good at it, you know exactly how much you didn't ring up, and take out the difference. But if you're sloppy, you sometimes make a mistake. Now Rachel used to come out even all the time, up until about six weeks ago. What I'm trying to say is, do you think she's capable of stealing?"

"Rachel! I never knew her to do it before but, Jesus, Jennifer, anything is possible. I hate to say absolutely no, and be wrong. Isn't there a way you can check on her? If she's innocent, no one will be the wiser; if she isn't, you'll be sure. You say you've heard about it?"

"Yes, some of the regulars. They say that when she sells a six-pack, she's been known not to ring it up. You know those guys have nothing else to do but watch. I hate to think they're right, and I hate to think that if she needed more money, she wouldn't come to me instead of taking it. But Bobby says it's the way of bartenders. They see all that cash and think, why not? The owner won't miss some of it.''

"That's awful. How can Bobby say such a thing?'' Jill asked.

"Because it's true. They have full control of the cash register, and they're dealing with cash, no receipts. It's too tempting not to steal,'' Jennifer told her.

"But to single out bartenders. I don't like that,'' Jill defended.

"I don't like it either. That's why I don't know how to handle this. I can't ask her, and I feel like a villain by setting a trap or watching her more carefully. She's such a hard worker, I'm wondering whether or not to forget the whole thing. How much could she be taking?''

"That isn't the point. If you don't get this straightened out, you'll never trust her again. Do what you have to do to ease your mind. If you find out she is stealing, then it's time enough to decide what to do,'' Jill said, disappointed. "I personally hate to think it's true. I recommended her.''

"It isn't your fault. She's wonderful. Maybe she needs the extra cash right now.''

"That's no excuse. But find out first,'' Jill said. "Cross one bridge at a time.''

"I will. Every day it's something else,'' Jennifer said. "I've got to go to the bank, and the post office, I'll see you back here later. I expect to see this place totally organized,'' Jennifer ordered.

"Sure, and I'll paint a big S on my T-shirt,'' Jill

laughed. ''Go to the bank, I'll do the best I can, I may be here for days. First, I have to find the file cabinet.''

Jennifer waved at Rachel on her way out the door. She hoped they were wrong. Rachel would be tough to replace.

Jennifer watched Rachel for the next couple of weeks and saw nothing. Jill had worked hard in getting her office organized and running it smoothly. The place was packed every night, people dressed in full country western attire—hats, boots and jeans.

Jennifer had special shirts made to give to those who stayed on the bull at full-speed. The shirts had become her trademark. The material fit the body snugly. It allowed the rider to move his arms with ease. They had been a huge success and many of the customers wanted to buy them. But Jennifer wasn't ready to get into the merchandising end of the business just yet. Not until the night she met Oliver Humphrey.

It was the Friday night of the Labor Day weekend, the place was packed as usual with The Country Five playing, the people dancing, and the bull on full steam. Oliver had come into the Tavern with a group of friends. He had docked his boat at Marble Lake that morning, and all he had heard about was Jennifer's Tavern. He had to go there to see what everyone was talking about. It didn't take him long to figure out. It was more than the bull, it was the atmosphere of the place . . . the easy manner, the ambiance, a place to go to relax, have a few drinks and a good time.

Everyone spoke highly of Jennifer, and he had to meet her. He asked one of the bartenders to point her out to him. He was equally surprised when they did. She was so young and pretty, a lady with class and refinement. He wasn't expecting someone like her. Jennifer was busy talking to a few of her other customers when Oliver walked up to her.

His Texas drawl set him apart from the others. "Miss Wells, may I talk to you a moment?" he asked.

Jennifer looked up and saw a tall, gray-haired man, deeply tanned, with a bit of a paunch, and large features. Jennifer excused herself from the others and walked to a corner with Oliver.

"My name is Oliver Humphrey," he said. "Your place is all I've heard about since I pulled in this morning. I had to check it out. You are doing a remarkable business. I feel like I'm back home in Texas," he told her.

"Thank you, Mr. Humphrey."

"Oliver," he insisted.

"Oliver. I'm glad you're having a good time."

"I'm having more than a good time. My wheels are turning, Jennifer. I think a place like this would go over big back in Houston. What do you think about opening another Tavern?" he asked, taking Jennifer by surprise.

"I've never thought about it. I have more than I can handle with this place," she told him.

"I don't mean run another place. Sort of franchise it out. Start a chain of Taverns. You're onto something here, and the timing is right," he continued, ignoring her first remark, which Jennifer would learn was a pattern. Oliver got what he wanted.

"Oliver, what about Gilley's? They're already in Texas," she told him.

"I know, and they're too big. I want you. There's an

287

informality about this place that's just what we need. I've heard a great deal about you, how you took this place from nothing and built it up in record time. It's as if one of my publicity men wrote the copy himself."

"I know, but I don't think I could do it again. I'm not sure I want to," Jennifer told him.

"I won't push right now. I'll let you think about it. I could make you a household word, merchandise your shirts, start your own label with new recording groups, make you the toast of the country. You're a young, pretty woman. They'll be receptive. Trust me. I'll give you time to find out about me. I've got lots of money behind me, and I'm the best promoter that ever lived," he said immodestly. "Together, we can make a fortune," he drawled.

Jennifer was intrigued. She either had to be dreaming this whole thing, or Oliver was the biggest bullshit artist she'd ever met. She hadn't decided yet.

Oliver returned to his friends, leaving Jennifer to think about his proposition. The more she thought about it, the more she liked the idea. Who wouldn't? It wasn't going to cost her anything to sit and listen to him. She watched Oliver leave with his friends and wondered if she had heard the last from him. She hadn't. Oliver was knocking at her door at nine o'clock the next morning. Half-dazed, Jennifer let him in.

"Sorry to burst in on you, little lady, at this hour, but it couldn't wait. I was up half the night putting together a package I think will change your mind," he blurted out with contagious enthusiasm. Jennifer watched him take out papers with numbers scribbled across the pages. She was too tired to argue. She sat down, poured herself some coffee, and offered a cup to Oliver. He took it black.

"Oliver, I'm elated by your enthusiasm, but it's very early and I only went to bed three hours ago. I have to reopen this place at noon and go all night again. I don't think I can do it on three hours sleep," she said wearily.

"Jennifer, I'll make this quick and let you go back to bed. I thought we'd start in Houston, I made some calls last night and came up with three locations. I talked to some friends, and they're ready to invest as soon as we can make a deal. You're sitting on a gold mine, so strike while the iron is hot. Next year may be too late. I'm telling you, it's a fad and fads make money. Look at the discotheque craze. It made millions. It changed fashion and brought back couples," he talked at high speed. "I'm telling you, along with the bull, there is a new mode of dress. Western boots, shirts, hats, jeans are really big. It's all there for the taking. Country music is on the rise and moving fast. Now's the time for you to make your move," he said without taking a single breath.

Jennifer stared at him. "What do you want from me?"

"That's the spirit. I want to use your name, your bull. You own the mold?"

"Yes, I had Sal sign it over to me," she told him.

"Good. The shirts you give away here, the material is wonderful. We'll use it! Also, I want you to go on talk shows. You're an intelligent girl, people will love you, and the name The Tavern, we'll use it and sell franchises all across the country. You'll decorate the places, set them up and then leave it to the owners. You'll receive a percentage of the sales. It's all down here, take a look.''

Jennifer wearily looked at the paper. Her eyes zeroed in on the bottom line, it was in the millions within the first year!

"What do you get?" she asked.

"A piece. A nice piece, but nonetheless, a piece. And I think it will be worth it in the end. You can make a nice living from this place for as long as it lasts, and after that, then what? This is a Summer town. I'm talking about setting up all year round. That will make a big difference," he droned on.

"But, Oliver, you're talking about my spending a great deal of time on the road, away from this place. I don't know if I can do that," she hesitated, thinking about Rachel.

"You hire someone to manage this place for you. You'll be able to afford it. And realistically, you won't be gone for long periods of time. More time in the beginning, but it will taper off," he said. "What do you think?" he was rushing her.

"Oliver, it's a great deal to think about. I know your heart is in the right place, but I don't think I can give you an answer right here and now," she told him. "I have some personal problems that need my attention. I may have to make a trip to Europe soon," was all she told him.

"We could work that out. You'll do what you have to do. You know, Jennifer, you're only as good as the people you hire," he said. "No one does it all alone. I know this whole operation is new to you, and you haven't learned yet how to let go, but you will, and you'll move on. Let me help you," Oliver said more quietly.

Jennifer sat back in her chair, threw back her head, her long hair brushing against her bare skin. It felt good. The backless halter top, and the shorts she wore, felt comfortable in the warmth of the early morning. She felt Oliver's eyes on her body and sat up straight. She wanted to say Yes I'll do it, what have I got to lose? but she hesitated. "What about this place? It isn't part of the bargain," she said.

"No, it's yours. It will always be yours. Unless you want to sell it someday," he told her. "I take it you're intrigued with the idea." He knew he had her.

"Yes. I'm intrigued. What's the next step if I say yes?"

"I call my lawyer, he draws up the contract. You have your lawyer look it over. If we both agree, we sign it. Then you'll fly down to Houston, take a look at the locations I have in mind, and we're off," he told her.

"Well, then I have nothing to lose. Have your lawyer draw up the papers and send them to my lawyer. I'll write his name down on that pad of yours and we'll take it from there," she said coolly, her heart jumping. "Are you going to fashion all The Taverns after this place?"

"Yes, they should all look alike. It's comfortable," he told her.

"Plants and all," she said, her mind in motion.

"Plants and all. They give the place a feeling of the outdoors," he said.

"Good, then I want the lady who decorated this place to help in the decorating of the others," she told him.

"Fine with me. I'll have that put into the contract," he assured her, and Jennifer was satisfied. She couldn't wait to tell Jill. She could finance her greenhouse for sure. It would be fun taking her on the locations, a safeguard against Oliver.

Jennifer got up. "Well then, I'll wait to hear from you," she told him.

"You'll see me tonight. I'll send this off to Houston right now. My lawyer is waiting for my call. Get some sleep, and I'll be here for the festivities," he said, and Jennifer walked him to the door and locked it after him. She was feeling too good to work, and a bit self-indulgent. She was going to be rich. Not bad for a tavern owner, as Ross once called her.

The next few weeks passed quickly. Oliver had contacted Martin, and the papers were ready to sign. It was all happening so fast. Martin was excited for her. He had looked up Oliver Humphrey's company and they had a fine reputation. She was in good hands. She made her first trip to Houston and looked at the locations Oliver had in mind. They agreed on the right ones.

Upon her return, Martin had informed her that a court date had been set for her divorce, and she was to be in his office a week from Monday. They'd go over her testimony, and be in court the next morning. She should plan to spend the night. She wished the court case didn't overshadow her new-found fame . . . but it did. Her whole life hinged upon the judge's decision. If her children were taken away, nothing that Oliver said or did could make up for it.

She suddenly felt frightened, insecure, and moody as the court date grew closer. She needed to be close to someone and Ross was the only person who could help. Bobby had long since given up, to Jennifer's relief. They remained friends, but he didn't visit the Tavern as often as he once had. He told her it was because business was down, due to her new contraption. She hoped he was lying. She didn't want to win at his expense. She heard other rumors from bar owners that she was pulling their business too. This couldn't be helped. None of them had the space necessary to put in a bull, nor the moxy to do it. She was safe for the moment.

Jennifer phoned Ross the night before she was to leave for New York. She knew she wasn't going to get any sleep, and needed to talk to someone, be close, feel some warmth. She wanted to be away from the crowds. He could tell from the sound of her voice that she needed him, and he was receptive. He always knew when something was bothering her, knew from the tone of her voice, even when she thought she was being so poised and guarded. He sensed it, and tonight she was glad. He was there for her.

He was upstairs in bed when she got to the ranch. She fell into bed next to him without saying a word. She wanted to be held, more than she wanted sex. She felt like a little girl, curling up next to her father for protection. Ross held her and for the first time since they met, she cried, openly and shamelessly. She had the right to cry, she was hurting, the pain she had stored away this year was now open, and the court hearing would be putting salt in what should have been healed wounds. She let it all out, sobbing uncontrollably. He held her, stroking her hair, until she stopped. He kissed her swollen eyes, her red nose, and gave her a handkerchief, ordering her to blow. She did what she was told.

"I know," was all he said before they made love. Jennifer felt closer to him that night than she had ever felt before. He understood her pain, she knew it, as she understood his. He was still asleep when she left in the morning.

Jennifer was sitting across from Martin Galloway for nearly four hours. They had gone over the testimony countless times, and Jennifer was getting tired. She didn't want anything to go wrong tomorrow, so she continued. Martin was a perfectionist, he continued to drive her. He knew he was pushing her to the edge, but they didn't have too much time.

"Why are you doing this?" she screamed.

"Because everything you want in the world is at stake here. I want you to have all the facts down pat. It's been a year and I don't want you to leave a single detail out," he shouted back, his patience coming to a halt.

"But we're making Frank out to be a monster. I can't say that. He *was* a good husband and father when we lived together."

"Good, then let him have the children," he yelled back.

"But I want the children!"

"Then do as I say. Divorce papers don't read like fairy tales. Once upon a time there was this happily married couple who woke up one day and decided they wouldn't live together anymore, so the husband decided to leave and take the children with him."

"Well, that's the way it was," Jennifer defended.

"Well, that isn't how you're going to get your divorce. We have to have grounds, prove cruel and inhuman treatment, abandonment. We have to have a solid case." He tried to calm down. "Look, Jennifer, the papers are painted black, they always are. They're cold and impersonal, and it seems as though two people never once shared a happy moment, any compassion, warmth or love. But courts are funny. They want to see cold hard facts, or the judge may rule to try for a reconciliation. Do you want that?"

"No. You know I don't."

"Then let's do it my way. I know what the judge is going to ask and I know how," he told her more quietly. Jennifer calmed down, and they went back to work. She hated it and wished it was all over. Why couldn't it be tomorrow and she was on her way back to Marble Lake . . . with her children.

Jennifer went back to her hotel after nine o'clock that evening. She was exhausted. She ordered something to eat and called her parents as she promised. They wished her good luck and asked her again if she wanted them there for moral support. She had spent more time than usual with them this Summer when they came to the cottage. They had conveniently stayed out of her way, coming to the Tavern only once in a while for a drink, bringing their friends, so proud of what she had accomplished. Her father looked at her in a new light, and her mother admitted she had done wonders under the circumstances. They gave her the love and support she needed, but she didn't think they should be in court tomorrow. Jennifer didn't know what tricks Frank might pull, and she didn't want to take the chance of hurting them. What if he sent someone to testify about her behavior, her love affair with Ross? She didn't know what they'd think. Jennifer promised she'd call them after court recessed. She fell into bed and right to sleep.

Jennifer met Martin and David at the law offices and together they drove to the court house. She dressed in a simple tailored suit with her hair falling loosely to her shoulders. She clutched her purse tightly, her knuckles turning white. Martin noticed and patted her hand.

"Relax, I haven't heard a word from Frank, or his attorney. I don't think anyone will show up in court today. We're going to be fine."

"What if the judge rules against me?" Jennifer asked.

"As a rule, Jennifer, the woman always gets custody of the children, except in extreme cases of neglect. I don't think you have anything to worry about. The judge has all the depositions from the children's teachers, and your neighbors, in front of him. You're a nice, clean-cut girl. You're a model mother, you made a good home for your children, you were always there for them, a regular PTA member, neat housekeeper. Your children were neat, happy, contented, and loved you very much. It surprises me, I was hoping to uncover a bit of imperfection," he told her, to ease her nerves.

"Yeah? What were you hoping to find?" Jennifer smarted.

"Anything. Women aren't that perfect as a rule, not when you start digging as I have. If I had met you first, I would have married you myself," he smiled, and she knew what he was all about. He bolstered her ego, and she needed it. "And what's more, you're going to be a very wealthy woman in your own right. I may divorce my wife and run off with you," he laughed again.

"Martin," Jennifer blushed. She wasn't sure what he meant by that remark, it was the first time he had been personal with her since they met. She wondered if he was trying to put her at ease, or whether he was testing her.

"If everything goes well today, when can we leave for Switzerland?" she asked.

"In about thirty days. It takes that long for all the red tape. I may go with you, I feel as though I've lived this ordeal with you. I want to see the reunion of mother and children myself," he continued.

Jennifer felt weary. She joked with him. "Does that mean I have to pay your plane fare?"

"No. I'll pay my own way there. But in a year from now you'll be rolling in money."

"Do you really think so? I may have hindsight, but I don't see what the to-do is all about. It's not as if they haven't heard of the bull in Texas," she continued.

"This is different. I read over the proposal, it's a wonderful opportunity for you and guaranteed to make money. Oliver Humphrey only invests in sure things. Look at McDonald's, Burger King, Kentucky Fried Chicken," he rambled on.

"But they're all fast food chains," Jennifer stated. "This is different."

"Yes, but the principle's the same. You're making

money on a novelty. A fad. Remember hoola hoops? Who ever thought they would become the rage?" Martin was glad he had decided to take Jennifer's mind off the court room. She was coming around.

"But, Martin, it died?"

"So what? So will the Western craze, but capitalize on it while the going's good. I believe the timing is excellent. I may invest myself," Martin admitted.

"You're kidding," Jennifer was surprised.

"No. I'm impressed with you and with Humphrey's track record. I've thought it over, and I think it's a sound investment. I will get a good return on my money. Jennifer, you're onto something," he said, as they parked in front of the court house.

"I don't believe you. It's costing me money by the hour so you can make money," she laughed.

"My mother didn't raise any stupid children. All's fair in business, and one thing has nothing to do with the other. I told you I'd pay my own expenses to Switzerland." He laughed. She laughed along with him. Martin became serious. "I'm glad you're feeling better. Are you ready to go in?"

"As ready as I'll ever be," she said, as she took a deep breath and got out of the car. Martin held the door for her, took her arm, and they walked into the court room.

Jennifer sat on one of the benches in the long sterile hallway. Martin had gone off somewhere. When he returned, he escorted her into the judge's chambers. "Judge Stockton thinks it would be better to have the hearing in here. It's more informal," Martin told her.

"Is that good or bad?" Jennifer whispered.

"Good. I sent him over the file last night and he's

had time to look it over. It's going to be fine. Trust me," Martin told her.

They both sat down across Judge Stockton's large mahogany desk. The door opened again, and an older man walked in carrying a case. He sat down at the side of Judge Stockton's desk, and set up his machine. The court stenographer. He sat patiently, staring at the wall until something was said.

Martin was the first to speak. He explained slowly and methodically what their reasons were for appearing before the court. They were petitioning for divorce, the custody of the two children, Cassandra and Jonathan, a settlement for damages, and immediate recovery of the children from Switzerland.

Judge Stockton waved his hand, and Martin sat down. The judge was still buried deep in the papers. "I would like to ask you a few questions, Mrs. Wells, if I may," Judge Stockton said.

Jennifer's throat was dry, she cleared it, and shook her head. She looked up at the man who would decide her fate. He was a short, balding man, slight build, hawklike face, and deep sensitive eyes. Jennifer hoped those eyes would be sensitive to her, give her the go-ahead to get her children.

"Mrs. Wells, did your husband give you any indication that he was leaving and taking the children with him?"

"No, your honor. I had no idea," Jennifer said.

"Where were you at the time they left?"

"I was visiting my parents for a few days. They were gone when I returned," Jennifer continued. "I don't visit my parents very often," she added.

"That's fine, Mrs. Wells. It's okay to visit one's

parents on occasion. I don't visit mine very often either," he said.

"I didn't mean it that way. I meant, I don't go off and leave my children to visit . . . ," she rambled. Martin shook his head to tell her it was all right.

"When you returned, you found a note from your husband telling you he'd left, and then you received word to vacate the house," the judge continued.

"The letter from Mr. Wells is in the file, your honor, as is the rest of the information," Martin interrupted. The judge shuffled through the papers finding what he was looking for.

"Yes, I see," he picked up the letter from Frank and read it.

"Could your husband have thought you had gone off to see someone other than your parents, Mrs. Wells? A man, perhaps?"

"No, your honor. He called me and I was exactly where I was supposed to be. I never spent any time with other men while I was married to Frank," Jennifer said aghast.

"Just a thought, Mrs. Wells. I didn't mean to upset you. I'm trying to put the pieces together. It seems rather strange that a man in Frank's position would up and leave a business, his home, his devoted wife, and take off to Europe."

"Frank was under a great deal of pressure when he left. He thought he had lost his touch. He was too hard on himself. He was working day and night," Jennifer tried to explain.

"In your opinion, your husband had a breakdown of sorts," the judge looked up at her.

"I'm not a psychiatrist, your honor. I don't know. I'm only telling you what I observed during the last few months we lived together. He seemed to be dissatisfied with his life. I don't claim to know what was going on in his head. I've gone over it time and time again during this past year. I'm as puzzled as you are," Jennifer said.

"There are others who seem to agree with you," the judge said. Jennifer wondered who, but didn't ask.

"I see here you're gainfully employed. You own a Tavern," the judge said.

"Yes, your honor. I won it, to be perfectly honest with you. It all seemed to happen so fast." Martin disapproved of that remark. The judge picked it up.

"You won it?" he seemed surprised. Jennifer didn't know what to say. Martin picked up but the judge cut him off. He wanted to hear the story from Jennifer.

"The fishermen in Marble Lake, where I live now, like to play cards. They were playing all night when I got to work one morning. They asked me to join in. I didn't want to, but Phil, who owned the Tavern before I did, insisted," she rambled nervously. "So I played a few hands, and I won." She over-simplified the story, not knowing what else to do.

"How did you get the bar?"

"When everyone pulled out of the game, the only two people left were Phil and I. I wanted to quit, and Phil didn't. He said we'd play one last hand, double or nothing. He put up the bar. I played and won. I didn't want to take the bar, but he insisted. The following morning when we were in his lawyer's office, I tried to talk Phil out of it, but he wouldn't budge. I was a Tavern owner," she said.

"I see," Judge Stockton said. "Do you play cards for money often?"

"No. Before I came to Marble Lake I had never

played. And I haven't played since I won the bar. I don't want you to get the wrong idea, your honor. It's a small town, and it's the way things are done there. I needed the job to pay David to find my children. I didn't want to lose my job by antagonizing my boss. So I played," Jennifer apologized.

"The man should have quit while he was ahead," the judge commented. "Being a Tavern owner means long hours, Mrs. Wells. How are you going to find time to care for the children?"

"I have three able bartenders. They open and close for me. I plan to spend time at the Tavern when the children are asleep, and are staying with a sitter," Jennifer continued.

"I see," Judge Stockton said. "You seem to have your life neatly put together for such a short period of time. You're a determined young woman."

Jennifer didn't know if she liked that remark. She was nervous again. It didn't seem to be going well. She shouldn't have said anything about gambling.

"Well, according to the depositions Mr. Galloway has here, you're very well liked by your peers and your neighbors. You were a conscientious mother, a respected citizen, and have a clean record. I feel the settlement you've asked for is a fair one. Your diligence in locating your children at any cost is admirable. I, therefore, grant you your divorce, and the custody of your children, and all monies asked for in the petition," Judge Stockton said, much to Jennifer's relief.

She looked over at Martin who also looked relieved.

"I have only one piece of advice, Mrs. Wells. Don't gamble," he smiled. "I wouldn't want to see you lose everything you worked for. Besides, it's illegal," he chuckled. He rose and left the room.

Martin took Jennifer by the arm but said nothing until they were well out of earshot. "I wanted to kill you for that gambling thing," he said.

"I'm sorry. But what was I to say? I couldn't lie and say I bought the Tavern."

"We would have worried about that if it happened. I told you yesterday, don't volunteer any information," he said. "Oh, it doesn't matter. We won! Soon you can go get your children. It's all over. How do you feel?"

"Like I could collapse right here and now. My knees are buckling under me," she said.

"How about a victory lunch and drink?" Martin asked. "I'm buying."

"Fine. I have some time. Easy on the wine. I have a long ride ahead of me this afternoon."

They walked arm in arm out of the court house. It was as though a fifty-pound weight had been lifted from her shoulders. The judge's decision hadn't really sunk in yet. Jennifer was still in a daze. It was almost all over.

Frank placed the receiver back on the phone. Jennifer had won custody of the children. He knew she would. It was only a matter of time before she'd come to get them, take his children from him.

They were no longer married. She was free . . . free to keep sleeping with her cowboy, to run her new establishment, to start others. Yes, he was up on all the news that affected Jennifer's life. But it wasn't going to be as easy as she thought. She didn't think she was going to fly here and take the children without a fight! No. He wasn't ready to put her life neatly in order. After all, she had everything she wanted. He wasn't going to be left with nothing. She even wanted his money. She had enough of her own, or would have when Humphrey got through with her. What a bitch, he thought.

Frank tiptoed into the children's room. They were fast asleep. He pulled the covers over Cassy, she had a habit of kicking them off. She always did. Even as an infant in the crib. She looked so peaceful, so beautiful sleeping there. Jennifer wasn't going to come here and disrupt their lives.

He'd finally gotten the children into a routine and made a new life for himself. He'd found a new mother for them . . . Janette. She even looked like Jennifer, and the children were very fond of her. They had roots now, new friends, a new life.

They couldn't be torn away from him, taken to a honky tonk small town, away from everything they'd known, to make new friends and start in a new school. Not if he could help it. And if they did have to move, it would be with him and Janette. Not with Jennifer and her murdering cowboy. He had gotten all the necessary data on Ross Davin, too. Frank didn't leave a stone unturned. He didn't like losing, and he would use all this information as ammunition against Jennifer when the time was right.

Frank brushed Jonathan's hair away from his sleeping face, and tiptoed out of the room. He sat quietly in the living room, contemplating his next move. He had time, time to think, time to move, if he had to. But not too quickly, he wanted to catch them off guard. Let them think they had him, and right under their watchful eyes, he'd be gone. He smiled to himself.

"Jennifer, you're not as smart as I am yet. You've done a good job, I have to give you credit for that. You latched onto a hot idea and you're running with it. You'll make a lot of money, but the war isn't over yet. The judge said you won the children, but you have to find them first," he said softly to himself.

He walked to the phone and called Janette. A sleepy voice answered on the second ring. He wanted her now, he needed her to be with him. Janette loved him enough to come without asking questions. Something the new Jennifer would never do.

SIXTEEN

Jennifer sat in the Tavern alone. She decided to close early. Two o'clock. Weekdays had slowed and now she only had the bank on the weekends.

She was cold, it was going to be an early winter. It was freezing for November, and the bar was damp. She was looking forward to moving out of the apartment upstairs.

Jennifer, with the help of Monica Richards, had found a pretty little farm house. It needed work, but there was a lovely fireplace in the living room and another in the master bedroom. The kitchen was large and screamed for remodeling. The bathrooms were antiquated, too, but in time Jennifer knew she could get the place in order. The owners really wanted to sell the place, but with winter setting in, they knew it was going to be nearly impossible, so they agreed to rent it to Jennifer. Monica said that this would give her time to really get to know the place, find the kinks, or fall in love with it. She could make an offer to buy it at any time.

Jennifer had looked at the two-story house three times before she agreed to rent it. The house was on two acres of land with a small barn large enough for two horses. There was also a detached garage, and lots of trees. The children would love it. She would talk to Ross and if she decided to buy the place, ask him about getting two horses for the children.

Jennifer was counting the days till she could leave for Switzerland. She was a little disheartened, too. She had to pack and go to Houston first. She had no choice but to leave Rachel in charge, as she was her head bartender, and everyone was right. Rachel *was* stealing money. But Jennifer would have to let it go for now, she needed her. She'd deal with the problem after she returned from Texas. She couldn't leave Toby in charge to break in a new person.

Why was she doing it? Jennifer wondered. She was making more money now than she had when she started. Had she been taking money all along? It was getting harder for Jennifer to look Rachel in the eyes. She had been avoiding her for a week. Rachel had to sense that she knew. Maybe that would make her stop.

Jennifer dumped out the ashtrays and wiped down the bar. She'd let Harry do the rest in the morning, drag out the trash, and polish the floors. She started to turn out the lights when she noticed headlights outside the front door. It looked like Ross' truck, but what was he doing here at this hour? Jennifer wondered, coming toward the door.

Ross stumbled into the bar, knocking over two of

the plants he'd come in contact with. Jennifer stood rooted in front of him. He was drunk. She'd never seen him in this condition. He found his way to the end of the bar and sat down.

"I'd order you a beer, but I think coffee would be better," she told him.

"Don't you ever get tired of being nice? Don't you ever want to shout out, 'get the hell out of my life, you're not giving me what I want'?" he glared at her.

"Did you come in here to pick a fight?" Jennifer asked. "Because if you did, I'm not in the mood, and I don't think you're in any condition to keep up with me once I got started."

"You never lose your cool. You're always in perfect control, when it comes to me, that is. Don't you know I know you're watching me, making a mental note of my every movement, thought, saying? It's as if you're writing it all down, putting it into a journal, and analyzing it later. So you'll know how to deal with the emotional cripple. Stay on his good side. Worm your way into his heart," he rambled on.

Jennifer handed him a mug of coffee. "Drink this," she ordered. He took the cup and threw it across the room. Jennifer jumped at the sound of the crash.

"I don't want any coffee. I'm enjoying the mood I'm in. Don't patronize me," he yelled at her.

Jennifer could feel her anger building. "Ross, what is it you want from me? You set the ground rules, I'm living within them. What more do you want? Do you want me to scream? I want more, I want to see you whenever I feel like it, not just on designated days. I want to be able to take you to parties, have you here with me, living with me, making a life together. Well,

I knew from the beginning it wasn't going to be like that, or are you uptight because I could live with what you want, and you're disappointed that I'm not more demanding? That maybe there isn't a warm woman who has to cling to a man behind this exterior?'' she said in perfect control, deliberately getting his goat.

"Not demanding!" he shouted, as if he had missed the rest of the sentence. "You are the most demanding woman I've ever met. Oh, not openly, but subtly. You're always there. Relentlessly. Making me feel guilty when I hurt you, while you grieve silently. You're unpredictably predictable, understanding, not giving me a moment's peace, not being able to hate you or move you over, send you away. Because you count every word, say the right thing, you're always on guard. You're driving me up a fucking wall. You go after what you want and get it,'' he finished.

"So that's what you're afraid of, deep down. I'm going after you and you'll weaken, and I'll conquer you,'' she jeered. "It isn't me you're afraid of, it's yourself. You're feeling more than you want to, and that's why you're angry. Someone's broken through that wall you put up. So you've come in here half crazed, hoping to pick a fight, catch me off guard, so you'll have an excuse to run again, hide in your own loneliness. Well, forget it. I'm not biting. I'm not going to make this any easier for you. If you want out of this so-called relationship, then you'll have to be the one who does the walking, not me,'' Jennifer said calmly, defying him again. She stared into his dark blue eyes coldly.

"You bitch,'' he said, as she walked around to the other side of the bar and sat down next to him. Ross grabbed her by the arms and held her firmly. He was hurting her, but Jennifer didn't flinch. "I don't want you in my life, I was happy the way things were. I don't want your warmth, your kindness, I don't want you to love me. I want you to find someone else. A man who'll appreciate you and love you. No matter how long we stay together, I'll never give you what you want. I'm not interested," he yelled into her expressionless face.

"Then that's it. Go on your way. I won't call you, or see you anymore. My life will go on without you in it," she told him, but didn't mean it. Jennifer didn't want him to leave, didn't want to put him out of her life. She loved him, wanted to help him to wipe away the hurt. She pulled away from him, and walked into the back room.

She heard him follow her. "Why are you doing this? Why aren't you falling apart?" he shouted out at her.

"Because I'm not going to give you the satisfaction of hurting me. You're doing a fine job on yourself. You may have fucked up your life, but you're not going to fuck up mine. I've finally put together all the pieces. Go home and lick your wounds, fall back into the depths of self-pity. That's your choice," she told him, picking up a broom and sweeping the cigarette butts to the middle of the room. If she didn't keep busy, Ross would notice how she was shaking. How this conversation wasn't as easy for her as he thought it might be.

"And you? You'll pick up and go to Houston, open up another one of these Taverns with this goddamn contraption," he said, pounding his fist on the bull. "You'll get your kids back. Start your life again.

Without a trace of hurt or resentment," he shouted at her.

"Right," she screamed. "Does that bother you? Yes, I'd like you to be a part of my life, but if you choose not to be, then what is it you want me to do? Beg you? Shout out, 'Ross, come with me. Stay with me. I can't live without you.' So you'll feel guilty and you'll stay. No! I don't want you that way. I want you to stay because you choose to. Because you think that together we can make a good life, complement one another . . . and not always in bed. But in all things, share the hurt, our thoughts, our needs. I don't want a man who can't do that. I want to give myself to you, and you'll have to do the same. You're not the only person in this world who's been hurt. We all have. But we don't hide behind the hurt and say, 'I'm not going to do it again.' To feel the joy of life one must feel the pain, too. It's part of living, something that you haven't done for a long time. You're just existing, Ross. You don't think my marriage breaking up was devastating for me? I could have sat back feeling sorry for myself, and let life pass me by, but I didn't. I chose to fight back. I opted for happiness. I have my whole life ahead of me, just as you do. I'm too young to lie down and die. I want it all—my family, a new life, a career, to share my life again with a man. And there's nothing wrong with wanting it all, because God knows, I probably won't get it all, but if you don't try, then you won't get anything. I'm glad I did what I did, you've taught me a very good lesson. You showed me what life could be like, pitying myself for the rough deal I was handed. Jesus, Ross, if you walk out that door, I won't be sorry I met you, I will have learned an important leason—what not to do with my life. And if I learn from each new relationship, be it with a man or a woman, no matter if it hurts me or not, I'll feel the pain, experience it, and grow into the kind of person I want to be. A better human being," she finished her sermon.

He stood staring at her. He walked over to the bar and poured himself a drink. Jennifer felt exhausted, drained of all emotion. He was testing her, baiting her, but she didn't know for sure what it was he wanted to hear. She walked back to the bar. She sat back on a bar stool.

"Ross, talk to me, tell me what's bothering you. Trust me," she begged, hoping to get to him.

He looked at her. "There's nothing to talk about. You're a hopeless romantic, hoping for a deep dark secret to justify my moods. There isn't one. It's just me. I am what I am. I've been this way for as long as I can remember."

Jennifer retaliated blindly. "I know there's more to it. I know something happened to you in Colorado years back." She watched Ross' mood change from passive to fury.

He stood up straight. "How dare you pry into my life! How dare you think you have the right to ask questions about me," he shot at her, almost hitting her.

Jennifer jumped out of the way. "I didn't, Ross, it came up in conversation," she defended herself.

"Who told you about Colorado?" he screamed, grabbing her again.

"It isn't important. I don't know what happened, I just heard something that didn't make any sense to me at the time. It still doesn't," she tried to pull away from him but couldn't.

"What did you hear? I want to hear every word," he yelled, his face flushed with anger.

"Ross, it was nothing. Something about a girl you once spent some time with. I wanted to know more but the person I was talking to wouldn't tell me. He said I should wait until you were ready to tell me yourself. I didn't put much stock in it at the time. I promise you. I thought it was a ploy to make me stop seeing you. It all took place months ago," Jennifer panicked.

"It was Bobby, wasn't it. He was the one," he yelled.

"It doesn't matter," Jennifer said. But Ross was hurting her, his large hands squeezing her arms.

"It does matter. I want to know. Was it Bobby?" he stared coldly at her, almost breaking her shoulder blades.

"You're hurting me," Jennifer screamed.

"Tell me," he demanded.

"Yes, it was Bobby. Remember when you told me he liked me more than a friend? Well, he did, and when he told me about the girl in Colorado, I just assumed he was making up the story to make points for himself. Really, Ross, that's the way it happened. He didn't go into detail," Jennifer rambled on, until Ross let her go. She moved back out of his reach, tears of pain welling up in her eyes. Her back ached.

"Why do people have to pry? Why can't they leave well enough alone?" he shouted, throwing his glass of scotch into the mirror of the bar, smashing everything in its path. He'd gone crazy. "All this time I thought you were different, and you knew all along what had happened," Ross shouted, throwing everything he could get his hands on. Jennifer ran to the back of the bar, he followed her, turning on the lights. The bull caught his eye.

"Did he tell you all the morbid details," he shouted, picking up the microphone stand and smashing the bull, hitting it over and over again, as Jennifer kept screaming at him to stop.

"I don't know what you're talking about. He didn't go into details. I swear. Tell me, Ross. Tell me, what happened?" she screamed, wanting him to stop before he destroyed the entire bar. He looked at her, exhausted with rage. His look of hatred pierced through her. She felt herself shudder. Jennifer moved backward.

"I don't ever want to see you again. I want you out of my life for good. Go laugh it up with Bobby. Snicker over the gory details. I hate you," he spat at her, and ran out of the bar. She ran after him, after she came out of her shock, but he was gone. She heard the truck tires screech from the front of the bar in the direction of the ranch. Jennifer went back inside and looked at the place. Glass was strewn all over; the bull was lying on its side, mutilated; broken chairs.

"Gold help me," she whispered. "Give me the strength to help him."

In the next instant, Jennifer put on her jacket, locked the bar, ran out and got into her car and started toward the ranch. She decided to pull over at a gas station and call Bobby. If she was going to confront Ross, try to help him, then she had to play this hand with a full deck. She had to know the entire story. She didn't care how she had to squeeze it out of Bobby.

The sleepy voice answered the phone after the fourth ring.

"Bobby? Jennifer. I'm sorry to bother you at this hour, but I have to talk to you, I don't have much time. You've got to fill me in on all the details about Ross and that girl in Colorado," she said quickly.

"Is that why you woke me up? I said 'no' months ago, and the answer's still the same."

"Listen, Bobby, Ross just tore up the place tonight. The bull is gone, I don't know how much it will cost for the damages—all because he thinks I know the story and I don't," she went on pleading.

"How did he get that idea?"

"It's a long story. Believe me, Bobby, it's important. Please tell me. I have to help him. I want to help him. I love him," she blurted out, hoping he'd fill her in. "Tell me what you know," she begged.

She heard Bobby sigh on the other end. "Are you all right?"

"Yes, fine. He didn't hurt me. It isn't me he's after. He's out to destroy himself. Please, Bobby, I wouldn't ask you if it wasn't important. He seemed to be getting so much satisfaction out of destroying the bull."

"Okay, I'll tell you what I know," he said, and Jennifer thanked him.

Bobby told her about Erica, as best he could. He didn't know all the details, not the little ones, but the important facts he had—Erica's accident and her suicide. Jennifer listened and felt sick. It was worse than anything she had imagined.

"God, he's been keeping all that bottled up inside him all these years. It wasn't his fault," she commented.

"In a way it was. If she hadn't gotten on the bull the second time, she wouldn't have had the accident. Ross had to show her he was better than she was," Bobby continued.

"I got all that, but it was an accident. They were both playing a dangerous game."

"He did love her though, which I find hard to believe," Bobby said coyly.

"Thanks. I'm going up to the ranch now and see what I can do. I really appreciate what you've told me," Jennifer said, about to hang up.

"Let me know what happens. Call me," Bobby said.

"I will. I promise, and thank you," Jennifer hung up.

She stood in the phone booth, freezing. What could she tell Ross, how could she help him without his thinking she pitied him? Until tonight, she didn't know the story. She didn't know what had happened. She had to make him believe that.

Jennifer drove up the long driveway to the ranch. She saw Ross' truck parked in its usual spot. She thanked God he had gotten home all right. She walked up to the side door of the house which Ross always kept unlocked, and let herself in. The house was quiet and dark. She hesitated to turn on the lights. She sensed his presence in the living room, and jumped back. She turned on a lamp on the table. Ross squinted from the brightness. She walked over to him.

"I had to come to see if you were all right," she said. He wasn't looking at her. She touched his arm but he moved it away. She didn't know where to go from there. She played it by ear, changing the subject.

"You don't think I was going to let you destroy my bar and pick up the tab for it myself," she humored him. "I'm a very practical person; you break it, you buy it. You now own a mechanical bull," she tested him.

"I'm sure Sal could put it together for you," he said softly.

"Good. You can call him in the morning and ask him. I'm supposed to catch a plane for Houston," she rambled on nervously. At least he had answered her. She touched his arm again. "I'm sorry about tonight. I really didn't know the full story, but I do now. I made Bobby tell me." He shot her a cold stare.

"He wasn't prying. He was in Colorado camping with his kids, and he happened upon it. He didn't tell another human being about it. I know him well enough to believe that. And your secret is safe with me, too. I want to help you. You've lived with this too long. Ross, please, I love you," Jennifer said, leaving herself wide open for him to attack her.

"I don't love you," he shot back. "I want you to leave me alone. Go away, go on with your life without me in it. I'll take care of all the damages in the morning. You have my word, I'll pay for it all," he said deliberately and calmly, teeth clenched.

"That isn't important. What's important is how you'll put your life together. I can fix the mirror, buy some new glasses and stools, that's simple. Picking up the pieces of your life isn't so simple," she went on.

317

"Don't you listen to me? Don't you hear anything I'm saying. I don't want to. I want to be left alone. You opt for happiness, for a full life. That's fine for you. Not for me. I want to be left alone. Now leave," he demanded.

Jennifer stood up, looked down at him and turned to leave. She couldn't help him if he wouldn't help himself. She turned and glanced at the tall, lanky man sitting alone on the couch and walked away, closing the door quietly behind her.

She got into her car, hoping he'd rush after her, take her in his arms and promise that together everything would be all right. He needed her strength, her love . . . but he didn't come after her. She started the car and drove back to the Tavern, tears half blinding her on the dark roads. She wanted to stop crying. She tried to think about more pleasant things. Her trip to Houston, her children rushing into her arms again after fourteen months of being apart, but nothing lessened her misery.

She veered off the road and headed to Jill's house instead of walking into the mess at the bar. She had to talk to someone, and Jill was the only person she could trust. Jennifer saw the lights on at Jill's as she pulled into her driveway. It was after four AM. She hoped nothing was wrong.

Jennifer saw Jill potting plants through the large bay window as she walked to the front door. Jill rushed to open it. They both asked each other the same question. "What are you doing up at this hour?"

Jill went first. "If I'm going with you to Houston tomorrow, I have to catch up on all my work. I lost track of the time. I'm almost finished. Now you," she said, taking Jennifer's coat.

"It's a long story. I just couldn't go back to the bar tonight. I couldn't face the mess. Just let me sit here for a while and try to pull myself together," Jennifer told her.

"Sure. Can I get you something—a drink, tea, coffee?" she asked.

"Nothing. Go back and finish what you were doing. I'll be all right," Jennifer lied and sunk her weary body into the large wing-back chair in Jill's living room. She closed her eyes and drifted off to sleep. Her body too exhausted to fight back.

Jennifer looked down at the bags and looked over at the telephone. She was tempted to call Ross just to see if he was all right, but she didn't. Distance was what they needed, time away from each other to think.

Harry had the bar swept up and some order when Jennifer arrived. He looked over at her and didn't say anything. It was none of his business how the place got busted up.

Jennifer heard the sound of Jill's voice at the bottom of the stairs. "Ready?"

"Almost. Making one last check to see if I forgot anything," she shouted back.

"If you did, you can buy it in Houston. I'm sure they have stores," she joked.

"Very funny. I'll be right down," Jennifer told her.

"Hurry up. If we hit any traffic we'll miss our plane."

"I'm coming. I'm coming," Jennifer said, half out of breath from rushing down the stairs.

"You look awful. Better get some sleep on the plane," Jill told her.

"I plan to. Well, let's go," Jennifer said. "We'll miss

our plane," she mimicked Jill's voice.

Jennifer looked over at Rachel behind the bar. "Take care of the place while we're gone," she ordered.

"Better than you took care of it last night."

"Yeah, well, we won't go into it," Jennifer told her. "Call you later, and we'll see you in a few days."

"Oh, the life of a jetsetter," Rachel retorted. Jennifer didn't answer.

"I don't like leaving her alone with the keys while I'm gone," Jennifer said when she was in Jill's car safely out of earshot.

"You don't have any other choice," Jill told her.

"I know, but I plan to do something about it when I return," she said.

"Are you sure you're all right?" Jill asked. "You were very upset last night."

"That was last night. Things always look brighter in the daylight," Jennifer told her, "and we're off to start a new club. There will be press interviews, another grand opening, more papers to sign," Jennifer went on.

"Not unlike our last trip to Houston a few weeks ago when we were setting up the new bar. Isn't it exciting? I know I've said it before, but did you ever imagine you'd be head of a whole chain of Taverns?" Jill asked.

"I wouldn't call two bars a chain," Jennifer laughed.

"For now, but Oliver said within a year there might be ten, twenty other Taverns. It's so unbelievable."

"There's part of me that enjoys it and another part of me that doesn't. It's too much like big business.

The other Taverns will never be like the original. I'm too far removed from them. They have my name, my bull, my shirts, hats and everything else, but it doesn't have the personal part of me that the original has. And even then, I'm not spending as much time with the place as I should," Jennifer went on.

"I'm sure everyone feels as you do in the beginning. But think of all the money you'll make. Financial security. You'll be able to give your kids everything; good schools, a nice home, and you'll be able to spend more time with them, instead of concentrating all your efforts trying to make a living at the bar. Oliver is right, you know, the bull is a fad. Its time will end, and then where would you have been? Sitting around like Phil trying to make ends meet?" Jill rambled on, trying to lift Jennifer's spirits. "This way, when the fad ends, you'll laugh all the way to the bank. You'll never have to worry again. I think your problem stems from a short memory. You forgot how hard it was on you in the beginning when you were scraping together enough money to pay the detective. It isn't like that anymore," Jill continued.

"No, it isn't. But there was something rewarding in the struggle, brainstorming, taking chances, putting everything on the line to see if it would go. The challenge was very rewarding, kept me on my toes. Now I can sit back like a fat cat," Jennifer said.

"You don't have to sit back and die. I'm sure you'll find something else to dabble in. Think of a new challenge to keep yourself occupied. We'll open greenhouses around the country," Jill joked.

"Don't be cute, but it isn't a half-bad idea," Jennifer retorted. Jill looked over at her. "Keep your eyes on the road, I was only kidding. I was thinking about finding a new challenge, trying to outguess the new fad. It's a thought.'' Jennifer sat back and relaxed in her seat.

She remembered the rushing around she and Oliver did on their last trip to Houston, the fun they had scouting just the right location, a place with charm, warmth, and high enough ceilings to house the bull; auditioning country-western singers who might be worthy enough to sing at the club; the power her name held. She had talked to textile mills incessantly, trying to find just the right fabric for her shirts. The one she had used originally was good, but not good enough for manufacturing. Everyone was pulling at her, wanting to please her, hoping to get the account that would make money for all of them. The endless meetings with lawyers, picking up on every detail of the contracts. One point for her side, another point for theirs. Martin was wonderful. He almost killed the entire deal several times with what Jennifer thought were petty points, but he felt in the long run they would be very important. Jennifer trusted him enough to stand behind his decisions. They won.

Every day, Jennifer read about herself somewhere. *People* magazine, *US* magazine, *Life*, women's magazines wanted to hear the story of her rise to fame. It hit them all where they lived. Divorced with nothing, she was building an empire. No family money lurked in her shadows. Oliver's people booked her on all the local talk shows as well as the national shows. As a matter of fact, she'd be dashing off to Los Angeles on this trip to do the Carson show after the Grand Opening of the Houston Tavern.

She didn't have time to think much about anything else. And now her only diversion, her only piece of happiness and contentment amidst the hustle was Ross, and he chose this time to plan his exit. He was her only touch with reality. He kept her feet on the ground, unimpressed by her accomplishments. He kept her from being carried off into the whirlwind of glamour where Humphrey was taking her. Why couldn't she have told him that last night? Why couldn't she have reasoned with him, told him she needed him, that he was like no other man she had ever met. Beneath the hurt and the pain he suffered, he was a realist, untouched by the world around him. A truly pure spirit, she thought.

Jill interrupted her thoughts. "Do you want to talk about it?"

"About what?" Jennifer avoided her remark.

"About what's bothering you. I know you long enough to recognize the signs. I know something is weighing heavily on your mind. And it's more than this trip," Jill continued. "Do you want to tell me what happened last night, why the bar was in total disarray this morning? Sal was there trying to put the pieces of the bull together."

"Ross and I had an argument. We decided not to see one another again," Jennifer oversimplified the situation.

"I don't want to ask who did the throwing, but it was one hell of a fight," she sighed. "How do you feel about it?"

"Mixed. It was time to either move the relationship to the next plateau, or call it quits. He thought it would be best this way," she hesitated.

"And he had to wreck the place to make his point?" Jill gasped.

"There's more to it. I can't tell you, it's his secret. There was a reason, and if it took his breaking up the place to make him feel better, then it was worth it." Jennifer tried to make sense out of what she was saying. Jill wasn't catching on.

"If you say so. Better you than me. I couldn't deal with it," Jill said honestly. "Look, there's a whole new world out there, and who knows who you might meet? Put Ross behind you. Don't let it eat you up alive. The only way to get over a broken heart is to plunge back in and find a diversion . . . and another broken heart," she laughed at her own advice.

"So they tell me," Jennifer interrupted. "I'm not looking, but if some handsome Texan wants to sweep me off my feet, I won't fight so hard," she laughed, feeling better.

"That's the attitude. Save the leftovers for me." Jill wanted to keep up the front.

"Why the leftovers? You're a very attractive woman. You'll do fine on your own. As you once advised Rachel, go for it," Jennifer said.

"While mom's away without the boys, she can play," Jill said. "I deserve it. Houston watch out," she shouted, "you're being invaded by the North."

Jennifer laughed at Jill's good humor. She was glad she had decided to take her on the trip and get her involved in the project. It was time her hard life came to an end.

Oliver was waiting for the women when they got off the plane. His eyes twinkled as he gave them an official Texan bear hug.

"So good to see you all. Jill, you look wonderful. Jennifer, you look a little tired. I'm going to drive you girls right to your hotel so you can take a hot bath and rest up for tonight's festivities," he said merrily, leading the women to the limousine. The chauffeur took care of their baggage.

"This is the style of travel I like," Jill said to Oliver. "You certainly know how to treat the ladies," she told him, and his grin grew broader.

"I aim to please," he told her and turned to Jennifer. "More papers for you to look over. I don't want to bore you with paperwork so soon after your trip, but I think you're going to be pleased. My phone has been ringing off the wall since your last appearance on television. Everyone wants to open Taverns. We can't let everyone, of course, but take a look at these ten locations. They're going to make us some real money," he continued.

"Ten," Jennifer sighed. "My God, that's incredible. How many have you turned down?" she asked.

"At least fifty. Don't want to crowd the market, and some of the inquiries came from people who couldn't rub two nickels together to make a dime. We're only interested in big money. People who can afford to keep up our image," he continued. Jennifer only half listened to him, reading over the papers he gave her.

"And I get the decorating fee," Jill bounced. "Makes my whole day."

Oliver smiled over at her. "Do you know what that means, little lady?" he was addressing Jennifer. "As soon as we sign the deal, you are a millionaire," he said.

"I can't believe it. I know I'm going to wake up and

find myself sitting in the old creaky bed over the Tavern, very disappointed," Jennifer responded.

"It's no dream, Jennifer. It's real, and it's only the beginning. When we get finished with the bull franchises, the shirts, not to mention the record deals, you will top that figure ten times over. I'd advise you to get yourself a good broker and invest that money so it makes more money for you," he continued.

"Stop. Stop!" Jennifer shouted. "I can only deal with one million at a time," she laughed, feeling very good. The limousine pulled up in front of the enormous hotel. Oliver had booked the women into the penthouse suite overlooking Houston. A magnum of champagne and a tray of hors d'oeuvres waited for them. The bellboy opened the champagne. "Is there anything else I can get for you?" he asked.

"Nothing," Jennifer said. Oliver handed him a twenty-dollar bill.

"Thank you for your hospitality," he said, and the smiling young boy was off.

Jill looked at Jennifer in disbelief. This was what money was all about, she thought. It put her life into a new dimension, and even though it wasn't really happening to her, she was sharing in the fun, and in some of the profits.

Oliver left the girls to their baths and beds, but neither one could sleep a wink. Jill rushed over to Jennifer and hugged her. "Can you believe this?" They were looking out the window and inspecting the suite like two schoolgirls.

"Now listen here, my friend. We are supposed to be two sophisticated New York ladies. This behavior is ndignified." She tried to keep a straight face as she d Jill stuff her mouth with caviar.

"Oh, this is good," she said, pulling off her boots and sitting back in the white velvet armchair. "This is the life. I could get used to it. To think, until yesterday all I wanted was to finish renovating my farmhouse. How shabby it looks next to this place," Jill said.

"I thought you were so contented with your life until this took us by storm. That was what I was talking about in the car," Jennifer said seriously.

"I'm kidding. I love the old house, but who wouldn't enjoy taking a break and living like one of the chosen few," Jill told her. "I'm not going to go home and become dissatisfied with my life, my kids and my home. I might hate them a little," she joked, "but I'm grateful for the experience. This never would have happened to me if I hadn't met you. Thank you, Jennifer," Jill said, holding up her tulip-shaped champagne glass.

Jennifer bowed her head. "I'm going to take a long hot bath," she said, screeching when she got to the bathroom. "Would you look at this? This bathroom is bigger than my entire apartment above the bar—two sunken tubs, two johns, two sinks, all in white marble with gold fixtures."

"I think I'll join you," Jill said, "if you don't mind." She looked through the vanity. "I found bubbles," she exclaimed girlishly. "We could sit in the tub, immersed in bubbles, and dial room service for more champagne," she said, picking up the bathroom phone.

"Before I settle in, I want to take my dress out of the suitcase before it gets wrinkled," Jennifer remembered.

"Me too. I'm glad you reminded me. My head's in a

daze. I'm not sure if it's the champagne or the suite. It doesn't much matter," she purred with satisfaction. "What time did Oliver say he was sending the car for us?" she shouted from the next room.

"Eight-thirty. He's getting up a press conference first, before we go to the club. I have to study my questions and answers, so I can be ever so charming," Jennifer said, imitating a Southern accent.

"Please do. I wouldn't want you to humiliate me. I, on the other hand, plan to keep my mouth shut. I am only the plant girl, not the millionaire," she said.

Jennifer picked up on it. "Does it bother you?" she asked seriously.

"No. I was only keeping up with your mood," she replied. "No, I'll be honest. Sometimes I wish I were you, basking in all the attention, but I don't know if I could pull it off the way you can. You're calm, so poised. You have the background for all this. It's all foreign to me. I'd maybe want to change places with you for a day, just to see what it feels like," she told her friend. "But push comes to shove, I'm glad to be a small part of what's happening. To be able to enjoy the fun, yet not have all the responsibility. You're my first millionaire, you know. I've never been friends with one before."

"Yes, you have. There's always Oliver. I saw the way he was looking at you. He's not married, you know," Jennifer joked with her.

"And he isn't going to be, not to me. He's a very nice man, but I could never dredge up the sincerity in the bedroom. I guess I'll never grow up. I'm still hung up on the old goose bumps on the flesh when someone I like touches me. I know it's not supposed to be important, but it is to me," Jill said seriously. "Sometimes I wonder if it will ever happen again. That's why I understand what you're going through with Ross. He may be a bastard sometimes, but he excites you and I can feel that. It can be worth the trouble. Without it, life is empty," Jill said. Jennifer put her arm around her friend. She was right. "Fight for him, if you think you can win," Jill said.

"I plan to. But I think putting some space between us for a little while will be good for both of us. Now, how about that soak?"

Jennifer and Oliver stood before the Houston press. Jennifer looked radiant.

"Rumor has it, Mrs. Wells, that you won the original Tavern," one lady of the press asked.

"Certainly did, just like in the old West," she answered.

That question always got a rise out of everyone. She wondered sometimes if Phil was watching her from a television set in God knows where, getting a kick out of what he started.

"Where did you get the idea for the original concept?" another reporter shouted out.

"At a rodeo. I had no idea it would mushroom into such a craze. Not until I met Oliver Humphrey," Jennifer said, easing him into the interview.

"Now, now," he said, "all the credit goes to Mrs. Wells here. She did all the work, pulled in all the people. I just knew a good thing when I saw one. And you know how we Texans are—can't pass up a deal to make money." Everyone joining in his good humor.

"How many Taverns do you plan to open?" someone else asked.

"That's entirely up to Mr. Humphrey and his team.

I have the utmost confidence in his judgment," Jennifer replied.

It was Oliver's turn to answer. "Well, I don't rightly know. We're hoping for an even dozen by the end of the year," he told them.

The questions continued for nearly an hour. Flashbulbs popping Jennifer felt her face would crack from the constant smile. She was tired and wanted to get out of there. Oliver, sensing her mood, waved off the reporters and led her into the main part of the club. She stopped smiling.

"I don't know how celebrities do it, always on camera, on stage for the reporters. It's a lot of work," Jennifer complained.

"What price fame and fortune," Oliver said. "It's all part of the game, and you are a natural. I knew you would be. They love you."

The doors opened, and The Houston Tavern was officially open. The crowds poured in, Jennifer mingling with the cream of Houston society, and the reporters who had stayed around to photograph them. Her photograph would be in all the papers in the morning.

For the first time in months she thought of Frank. He read the American papers, she wondered what he thought about her new life. It was good for him to known she hadn't lain down and died without him. She had made something of her life. Jennifer turned and glanced over at the person riding Bill.

Her mind shifted to Ross, and the scene they had last night. So much had happened since then. She walked back to the small office, and decided to call him. It was late, but she didn't care. She dialed the number, no one answered. Jennifer wondered where he might be. She didn't have long to dwell on it. Oliver bounced into the office. "There you are. Everyone's been asking for you. What are you doing hiding in here?"

"It's cooler. I was trying to unglue my face, but I'm ready to face everyone again. Oliver, tell me something, will I have to be at all the openings?" she was concerned.

"No. Only the important cities where it will do us the most good. We don't have to think about it now. Let's get through this one," he told her and led her out onto the dance floor. The band was very good. Oliver pointed out a few scouts from several of the record companies. "It's starting already," he told her. "I think it's time to think about starting our own label, making money from our talent instead of letting someone else do it. I'll set it up and send all the information to Martin. What do you think?"

"I don't want to think tonight. I'm sure whatever you decide will be fine with me. I don't know anything about the recording business," she told him.

"Last year you knew nothing about the bar business, and now look at you," he built up her confidence. "You're a natural. You have a good ear for talent. The band that was playing at your place when I first met you was very good. I'd like to get them down here," he continued.

"You're right. They're good kids. I'd like to see them make it. Everyone loved them when they played for me."

"Good. We'll go over that point in the morning. You do plan to stay on a few more days?" he asked.

"Yes. Then I have to get back. I'm leaving for Switzerland at the end of next week," she told him. He still didn't know anything about her private life. Or the fight for her children. She liked it that way.

Jill waved at her across the crowded dance floor. She looked happy in the arms of a very handsome man. Jennifer was pleased for her.

Jennifer excused herself from Oliver and moved over to the bar. She leaned wearily against it. Her feet hurt and her head ached from the lack of sleep the night before. All she wanted to do was go home to her hotel and sleep for a week. But it was still early. No one realized she was one hour ahead of everyone else, still on New York time.

Jill found her there. "Having a good time?" she asked.

Jennifer just stared at her in disgust. "I'm not cut out for this. I think I might slip away and go home. You don't mind if I leave without you?" she asked.

"No. Go ahead. I'll find my way back," she twinkled back. "Don't wait up," she was gone.

When Jennifer awoke the next morning, Jill wasn't there. She ordered breakfast, and both room service and Jill walked through the door at the same time.

"There's enough food here for both of us," Jennifer said nonchalantly.

"Go ahead, all I want is some coffee. I'm not hungry," Jill told her.

"That's a first," Jennifer said. "You look as though you had a very nice time last night, in every way."

"I did. And I will until we get on the plane that will take us back to reality," Jill continued and fell into bed.

Jennifer closed the door, and went back to her breakfast and her paperwork.

Jennifer was grateful it was all over for the time being. She had to come down to earth and deal with the problems at hand, one of them Rachel. It was too small a town to start interviewing new bartenders without her finding out, so she chose to talk it out with Rachel first. She suspected that Rachel would deny everything, which she did, and she even walked out for a few days. When she returned, she was ready to talk, and Jennifer was willing to listen.

"I was jealous . . . ," she started to say. "You had it all, and I wanted a piece. I know that isn't much consolation for what I did. I wanted what you had, but instead of sharing it with me, you chose Jill. She went on the trips, she was your right arm. I thought I had contributed a great deal to this place, too," Rachel blurted out.

Jennifer knew it was hard for her to admit the truth. She tried to make it easier. "Why didn't you come to me, tell me what you were feeling, ask me to let you become more actively involved. I think you're minimizing your worth. You're the head bartender here. You keep this place running so I can go out and do other things like opening new places. You are a very important part of my life and this operation. Even more than Jill is. She could never do what you do," Jennifer tried to bolster her confidence. "But to steal! What was that going to prove? If you needed more money you could have asked for it," Jennifer said.

"It's not the same thing. If I was taking the money, I was getting even. Hurting you," Rachel said. "It's childish, I know. It didn't amount to very much, about five hundred dollars," she said, handing an envelope over to Jennifer.

Jennifer looked at the money inside, resealed the envelope, and returned it to Rachel. "From me to you. A bonus for a job well done," she told her.

Rachel stared at her in disbelief. "You're not going to fire me!" she said, stunned and moved by the gesture.

"Not this time, but if I ever catch you with your hand in the cash register again, I will. And if you're ever feeling used or left out, I want to *hear* about it, not *see* it in your actions," Jennifer said firmly.

Rachel got up and went behind the bar. The jealousy was gone and now she had an entirely new outlook of Jennifer. She is fair and honorable, Rachel thought, and she felt ashamed of her actions. If Jennifer had been anyone else, she'd have bounced me out the door and I never would be able to work in this town again. "From now on, I'll do the best I can," Rachel whispered to herself. She was grateful for the second chance.

On the other side of the bar, Jennifer was deep in her own thoughts. She decided to let Rachel manage the place full time, and give her a percentage of the profits each year. It would bolster her morale, and keep her honest.

"Now I guess I'd better attend to my personal problems."

Jennifer drove up to the new house to supervise the painting and papering. It already looked one hundred percent better. The furniture would be delivered on

Friday so everything would be ready for the children's homecoming. She was so excited.

Time was crawling by. It always did when you were counting the minutes. She fell into the regular routine of running the Tavern, working behind the bar for solace and to keep her mind off Ross.

Bobby came around to see how she was and also to tell her that Ross was gone. No one knew where, apparently just another one of his trips without a return date.

"I wish I wasn't always the bearer of bad news," Bobby commented one night when things had slowed down.

"It isn't your fault," she said half-heartedly.

"I've very proud of you, you know," Bobby changed the subject. "Every time I read about you in the paper, or see you on television, I take full credit," he tried to amuse her.

"As you should. You were my mentor, and you, too, can buy a franchise somewhere in these United States," she laughed.

"You looked gorgeous at the Houston opening. I meant to tell you. You're a natural for the publicity hounds. And you haven't changed, I'm glad to see. I would," he told her.

"Why?" she asked.

"I don't know. I guess all the attention would go to my head. For a while, at least. But you, you never lose touch. You take it all in stride, talk to everyone like you always did. Everyone's commenting on that," Bobby continued.

"I'm glad I haven't. I want to live here. My friends are here, the people I care about. No matter how much money this brainstorm makes, I don't want to be any different. Maybe I'll buy a house instead of renting one," she admitted.

"You could buy the town if you wanted to when Oliver Humphrey gets through with you. You could even run for mayor," Bobby ranted on.

"Forget it. I don't need anymore headaches. But I have to admit it's good to be home, see all the old faces."

"We're always glad to have you home," Bobby told her, taking her hand. Jennifer moved it away.

"Still no go?" Bobby asked.

"No. I can't. He'll be back when he's ready. He has a great deal of thinking to do," Jennifer defended Ross.

"And if he still wants to be left alone when he comes back? Then what?" Bobby smiled at her knowingly. Jennifer felt she had finally gotten through to him. They'd never be more than friends.

"I'm sorry, Bobby," she said.

"No need to be. Win some, lose some," he sighed. "We're still friends, right?"

"Of course," she told him.

- "When the kids come home, I'll pick mine up and we'll all go out to dinner," he told her.

"I'd like that. It should be fun," she told him and meant it. She didn't want to lose a valuable friendship. He got up and left the bar.

Jennifer walked over to Allie and Jim and joined in their conversation for a while. They always made her laugh. They even offered to take her a round or two of dimes. She declined, the others played. She remembered what the judge had said. "No more gambling. It was illegal," and she smiled to herself.

336

SEVENTEEN

David, Martin and Jennifer fastened their seat belts as the large 747 was ready for takeoff.

It is almost over, Jennifer thought. Soon she would be holding Cassy and Jonathan in her arms again. They must have grown so much, she thought, clutching the photographs David had given her in what now seemed a lifetime ago.

Some of the passengers on the plane turned around to stare at her in recognition. Jennifer nodded back nervously. She wasn't used to her new-found fame as yet.

Martin patted her hand, almost reading her mind. "You'll get used to it," he smiled.

"I don't know. I don't want it to get in the way of my private life with my children," she told him.

"It won't. It will wear off. Then you'll miss it."

"I don't think so. I want to settle in and be a mother again. God, I miss it," she told him. "None of the day-to-day little traumas and questions. We have so much catching up to do. I hope this change won't confuse them too much," she said.

"It's bound to be somewhat traumatic, but given some time and understanding, the children will be fine," he said. "It's going to be some Christmas for you this year."

"So much better than last year. I'm going to put up the biggest tree Marble Lake has ever seen. I'll import it if I have to," she laughed. "Presents under the tree too, to make up for last year. I bought out half the stores in Houston when I was there," she told him. "You would have loved all the pomp and circumstance of the opening, Martin. Sorry you had to miss it," Jennifer told him.

"So am I. But I had to be in court all that week. You looked wonderful in the pictures I saw of you. And while we're on the subject of Houston, Oliver sent more contracts for me to read over. He wants to start your own recording label, of all things," Martin told her.

"I know, we discussed it when I was down there. What do you think?"

"I think it's a good idea. Costly though. If anyone can pull it off, it's Oliver. I brought the papers along with me to read on the trip. Let me take a look and I'll be able to discuss it more clearly with you later," he said.

As the NO SMOKING sign went off, Jennifer lit a cigarette. Her hands were shaking.

"By tomorrow at this time, you'll be sitting in your hotel room with Jon and Cassy," he said, reading her mind again.

"I know, but what if something goes wrong? What

if Frank won't give them up?'' The old fears still haunted her.

"He has no choice. We went about this the legal and proper way. The children are yours, you have custody legally, and that's that. David has kept a close eye on Frank. He's still in the hotel. It's as simple as going over there and picking up the children. It's over, Jennifer. Keep telling yourself that.''

Jennifer looked over at David. "You're sure Frank's still in the same place?''

"Absolutely. Called the hotel right before we left. You know I have a man stationed there. You've been paying the bills,'' he told her, and she felt easier.

"How could I forget? Gee, after this is over, I'm going to miss writing out those checks,'' she half joked.

She had gotten used to having David and Martin around, helping her, they had become part of her life. It was going to be difficult to let go. "I'm going to miss you,'' she told him, "although I'm glad it's over. All of you come up to my house for the holidays, I'll fix dinner. I'll even give you a free ride on Bill,'' she laughed.

"We'd love to. Martin's been up to the bar, but I haven't,'' David reminded her.

"Well, it's time you did,'' she told him feeling depressed.

"We'll keep in touch. I feel the same way you do after the cases are over,'' he told her, but knew differently.

People grew so close so quickly during a crisis, and when it ended, everyone was happy, promising to keep in touch, but didn't. In the beginning, David would receive a letter or card, but soon after—nothing. His clients disappeared back into their normal lives. They rarely needed him again.

"It's been a long haul, Jen, I'd like to keep in touch," David told her.

Martin interjected, "I don't believe you two. I'm going to get my handkerchief out," he said.

"Well you and Jennifer are still doing business together. I'm through after tomorrow, unless she wants to hire me to investigate the wealth of her prospective clients," David said. "I feel as though I watched my own daughter grow, start a business and put her life together. I feel proud," he went on drinking his cocktail. "I remember how distressed you were the first day I met you in Martin's office," David continued.

They sipped their drinks, all deep in thought. They ordered another round, remembering, feeling sad, then getting giddy.

"If I don't stop walking down memory lane, I'm never going to get these papers read," Martin said.

"Go ahead, read those boring papers. David and I will continue without you," Jennifer said coyly, squeezing David's hand. It was more personal than they had gotten since they met over a year ago. They were all caught up in the good mood mixed with the alcohol. They stopped talking a moment, and Jennifer settled in her seat with her own memories, which she was now pouring out to David. She remembered giving birth to Jonathan, how frightened she was, how young and inexperienced. Frank was there, holding her hand, trying to share the pain. David listened to every word.

"He was so small. I remember holding him in my

arms for the first time. What a feeling, a thrill like I've never experienced before in my life, looking him over, making sure all the parts were there, counting ten fingers, toes. It sounds ridiculous," she told him, "but you do it. I did the same thing with Cassy. Then you sit back and think about the responsibility. This little life is depending on you for food, clothes, shelter, advice, love, understanding. And you get caught up in it. Creating a new life, molding it into what will be a substantial human being. Watching them struggle to stand up for the first time alone, stumbling to take their first step. Pacing the floors with them when they're sick and teething. They grow up so fast, they're running, jumping, dressing themselves, before you know it. When they start talking back, forming their own opinions, then you have to learn to reason with them and hope that your advice is right. You always hope you're making the right decision. Jesus, it's hard enough to keep up with them when you see them every day, but to be away from them as long as I have, I'm frightened. What will I say to them? How do I explain what happened?" she asked feeling weepy.

"You'll be surprised. As soon as you see them again, it will all come back. You'll find the right words, I know you will," David consoled her.

"I hope so. So much has happened to them. I don't know if I should ask them about it, or wait and let them tell me at their own pace. I'm so anxious to be filled in on every detail of their lives that I've missed. Then I have to contend with the problem their father might have caused. I don't know how he explained to them why I wasn't with them. Did he tell them I was the one who deserted them? They might resent me," she panicked.

"No, not when they see you, see how much you love them," David went on. "It will be all right, you'll see. I've been through this before. Many times. All mothers I reunite with their children feel the same way. And it all turns out fine in the end," he told her again. She thanked her lucky stars for him. He was a kind man. He knew what she was feeling. He really knew.

"I know I'm over-reacting. And I'm boring you. You don't need to hear about children's teething problems," she smiled, and he squeezed her hand again.

"I don't mind. If it makes you feel better to talk about it, then do. If anything, it helps the time to pass," he reassured her.

She looked over at Martin. He had blocked out the entire conversation. He was deep into his paperwork. "I don't think anything distracts Martin," she commented. "He puts on those ear phones, and is off in his own little world."

"Lawyers always remain impersonal, at least the ones I've worked with, do. If they don't, they lose their objectivity. I can't," David said. "I get so angry, so involved, I can't sleep nights sometimes for thinking I've forgotten something. Thinking up a new angle. I'm going to have to quit this game soon. I'm getting too old," he told her.

"Well, if you ever want to take up tending bar, let me know," Jennifer joked.

"I might. You may see a face peeking in your window some snowy night, looking for solace. It will be me," he laughed, Jennifer joining him.

The flight attendants were serving dinner, Jennifer was starved. She hadn't eaten all day. They remained silent during the meal. When they finished, Jennifer decided to watch the movie, David fell asleep, and Martin continued working.

Jennifer thought about the children again. She was pushing them on the swings in the back yard. Cassy was yelling, "Higher, Mommy, higher," and Jonathan was rushing around the back yard with some of his friends, dressed in his new cowboy suit and guns. Yes, Jonathan would definitely love the new place. He would have a horse of his own, space to run and jump and be free. It was the sounds they made that Jennifer missed the most, the giggling under the covers when they were supposed to be asleep. Jennifer pretending not to hear them, or pretending to be mad when she finally made her way up to their rooms. They'd rush under the covers and close their eyes, trying to fool her. She always let herself be fooled. She mourned for those days, as she mourned, for the first time, for the baby she had lost six months ago. A part of Ross and herself, a new life, a new beginning. The baby would be nestled inside her today, almost fully grown, she'd be feeling it move, feeling its warmth inside her belly. Tears rolled down her cheeks. She was grateful for the darkness around her. She wiped the tears away. She had to think ahead.

Tomorrow was the beginning of a new life. A life that included her children. And in time, Ross would be back, she'd be stronger then, ready to face him, love him again. Jon and Cassy would like him. Like his gentle spirit, his sensitivity, as he would like them. And in time they would learn to love each other, as she had. She had been patient up until this time, she could wait a while longer.

As the movie ended, everyone stirred in their seats. The flight attendants were serving a snack. Jennifer asked for another drink. The others had worn off. She needed fortification. In her heart of hearts she wasn't as optimistic about the day as David and Martin were. She wished she understood her feelings. It was the same sinking feeling she had when she was returning from her mother's, a premonition of what was to come. She pushed the negative thoughts from her mind. It was going to be fine. She was wrong.

Martin took his ear phones out, and handed her the papers he was reading. "Looks good," he said. "I think we should go for it," he told her.

The plane landed, they retrieved their overnight cases and filed through Customs. When they got to their hotel, Martin went over the procedure again. She was to wait in her room while David and he went to see Frank. She was to wait for their call. When it came, she was to take a taxi to Frank's hotel and pick up the children. Martin wanted to avoid a scene. If the children were to see her before they talked to Frank it would be harder on all of them.

"But why can't I go with you? I'll stay in the lobby. You can call me when you want me to come up," Jennifer pleaded.

"Listen to me. It's better this way. I want it to go as smoothly as possible. Trust me," Martin told her. "I'm going to my room, shower, change, and have a bite to eat. It's too early to pound on their door. We'll leave about nine," Martin said. "Why don't you try and do the same. Get yourself all fresh and smiling for your reunion. If you're looking all worried and uncertain, so will they," Martin ordered.

Jennifer did what she was told. She walked around the hotel room, not able to sit down. She kept looking at her watch, the time crept by: Eight-thirty, Eight thirty-five. She called room service and ordered some coffee. It took almost a half hour for it to arrive. Martin knocked on her door to tell her he was leaving.

"Call me the minute you talk to him. I'll be sitting here waiting," she told him.

"I will. Don't worry. It will all go smoothly. Keep the line open," he said.

"Of course. Who would I call?" she screeched at him. "I'm sorry, I didn't mean to jump at you."

"I know. I'll forgive you this time," he humored her. He put his arms around her and gave her a hug. "Just a few more hours. Keep telling yourself that. It will be over in a few more hours. You've waited a hell of a lot longer than that."

"I know," she said dousing her cigarette and lighting up another.

"When this is over, you'd better give those up," he ordered.

"On my word," she told him. "Martin," she yelled out as he was closing the door to her room. "Good luck. And call me."

He winked at her and closed the door. She took a deep breath, tried to sit and have her coffee. She hated to be on the sidelines waiting, she wanted to be in the middle of the battle, watching the action. Jennifer was always a doer.

This was going to be the longest two hours of her life. She continued to pace up and down the tiny room, staring at the phone, waiting for it to ring. What was taking them so long? It was after eleven. Something had gone wrong, she knew it. She kept telling Martin it wasn't going to be as easy to take the children away from Frank as he thought. No, she knew it. Something had gone wrong. Jennifer started to panic. She looked at the full ashtray and took out her last cigarette. She wanted to call room service and beg them to bring her up another pack. But she didn't want to tie up the line.

Jennifer heard a knock at the door to her room, and rushed to open it. She knew instantly upon seeing the expression on Martin's face that the children were gone. She stepped back, let her attorney in, and sat quietly in the soft armchair. He sat down on the edge of her bed and took her hand. Screams were rushing through her body, yet nothing came out. She sat staring at the ceiling, fighting back her tears.

David was standing at the door when she looked over. He came rushing toward her. "I'm sorry," he started to say. "I've been calling everyone as soon as we found out they had checked out of the hotel. I don't know what happened," he told her sadly.

"Don't know what happened!" Jennifer shouted. "How the hell could you have let something like this happen? I trusted you. I believed all the lies you told me about having everything under control. I flew over here expecting to get my children, and I've come up empty handed," she ranted. "How did they get away?" she screamed.

"I'm not sure," David replied. "I can't figure out how he managed to get out of the hotel without my man seeing them. I guess we underestimated Frank's determination."

"What are we going to do now," she asked quietly.

"Start again. Listen to me, Jennifer. Frank knew our every movement. He apparently was keeping close tabs on us, closer, I'm ashamed to say, than we were keeping on him. We slipped up. I have no excuses. I'm not going to lie to you. When we were on the plane, he made his exit, clean, fast, and with no traces of his whereabouts. I'm sorry, Jennifer, truly sorry."

"Sorry isn't going to get my children back," she snapped.

"I know how you feel . . ."

Jennifer interrupted Martin. "How the hell do you know? You're sitting there, your life in order, your children safely at home with your wife. How do you know how I feel? You can't even hope to imagine," she shouted, bursting into tears.

Both men sat there helpless. David spoke first. "Jennifer, I'm going to do all that's humanly possible to get a line on your children as fast as I can. Remember, Jennifer, we did trace Frank here. It was all the paperwork and your divorce that took so long and kept us from taking custody of the children. I know it seems hopeless and time is of the essence, but I can only ask you to sit tight and wait."

Martin poured Jennifer a drink and handed it to her. "Here, it will make you feel better," he tried to soothe her.

"Nothing but the sight of my children will make me feel better," she told him and gulped down the brandy, pouring herself another, and drinking it quickly. She began to feel lightheaded. "Why is life always a trade off? Why do we win some points at the expense of others?" she began to ramble. Martin stared at her. "I'm making a great deal of money, I've become the little darling of the press, and yet with my contacts, and my money, it doesn't help me now. It doesn't console me and it won't get my children back," she sobbed.

Martin put his arms around her and held her. He felt so helpless. How could he ease her pain? What could he say to make her feel better, to give her new hope? "We'll find them, I promise you, if we have to tear the world upside down. We'll find him. Frank can't stay buried forever. And when we do, Jennifer, I'll get the son of a bitch before he can unpack. I don't know if it will before Christmas, but you'll be with your children soon. I won't let anyone hurt you again," Martin consoled her.

"Me, too, Jennifer," David interjected. "He won't get away again. If I have to personally track him down, and sit outside his house until you and Martin arrive."

She turned to him and gave David a hug, feeling the effects of the brandy. She took another drink. Martin poured himself one, and another for David. The remainder of the afternoon became a blur to Jennifer. She continued to drink, but nothing seemed to soothe her pain. She didn't want to go home. Everyone was waiting for her; the house, her friends, all to welcome Jennifer and her children. Now the house would remain empty. She wouldn't move into it alone. It would be a constant reminder of her defeat.

Frank had won again, he had outsmarted her. How much did he know? A shiver ran up her spine. He was watching her, having her followed, knew everything she was doing. He knew about the bar, Ross, and he was punishing her. He was somewhere safe and sound with the children laughing at her. He had made a fool of her again. But this afternoon, she didn't care. She didn't care about herself, her life, her fame—nothing mattered. Her children were whisked off again, having to get used to a new life in a new place, being confused, not knowing what to do next.

The room was spinning whenever she closed her eyes. She caught a quick glimpse of Martin lying there next to her, the brandy snifter in his hands. David had disappeared. Martin felt Jennifer's eyes on him, and looked down at her, and kissed her tear-streaked face. His lips were soft, no fuzzy beard against her cheeks, no firm body which fit so nicely next to hers, yet he was there, available, tender, and he wanted her. Jennifer kissed him back, he was there and available to her. It didn't matter if she didn't love him or even care if she ever saw him again. They were both releasing a physical need, for the moment. He was older, more experienced, willing to please her, susceptible to her every movement. And more than anything else, he wanted to satisfy her. She was willing to take from him, but didn't care if she gave anything back. She let him do all the work, and lay back basking in her own pleasure. The afternoon seemed endless.

She looked up, and saw Martin, then she'd see David's face. It was all so confusing. Was it the alcohol, was it her own anger, her rage changing the blame from one man to the other? Or was she in bed with two men, both trying to comfort her, both wanting to please her? It didn't seem to matter, it all felt so good. Hands touching her breasts, her face, between her legs, so many hands. And she was sensitive to every touch, every movement.

When had David come into the room? Was he really there? Was she imagining the entire afternoon? She drifted off to sleep, satisfied, and when she awoke, she was alone. The room was dark and empty, as her life.

She picked up the telephone and placed an overseas call to Ross. She was hoping he'd returned, she needed to talk to him, needed him as an anchor, but there was no answer. He was gone as everyone else that was important to her life. She fell back to sleep, the next time awaking to the sunlight. She got up out of bed, her legs felt as though they'd give way under her.

She noticed the note under the door, and picked it up. David had gone back to the States, and Martin was leaving early this morning. If she wanted to catch the plane with him, she'd better hurry. She decided not to. She'd stay on here for a few more days, walking the streets, the same streets her children had been playing in all this time. She felt closer to them here. And she didn't want to let go as yet. She needed to stay. She telephoned Martin's room, and told him of her decision. He seemed distant, and neither one mentioned what had happened the day before. He wished her well and told her he'd talk to her as soon as she got back home. She ordered breakfast, but couldn't eat it. The sight of the fried eggs on her plate made her sick to her stomach. She placed the cover back on the tray and told the bellboy to take it away. She sat in the familiar armchair and sipped her coffee.

Jennifer walked the clean Geneva streets, passed Frank's hotel, and decided to go in. She talked to the desk clerk who remembered Frank and the children.

"They were very well-behaved children," he told her. "Well mannered, always running in and out with their nurse, and with Janette." That was a new development. Frank had gotten himself involved with another woman! And this woman was taking on her role as mother. From the clerk's description, Janette looked very much like herself, a bit younger perhaps, but the physical characteristics were the same.

Jennifer left the hotel feeling worse than when she had entered. There was no hope. She went directly to the travel agent in her hotel and made arrangements to go home. Then changed her mind. She wasn't going back to Marble Lake, not yet. She would fly to Houston.

EIGHTEEN

Jennifer walked directly into Oliver Humphrey's office. She sat down across from him. "I want to get involved in the new openings. All of them. I want you to keep me as busy as possible. If this is going to be my business, I want to know every last detail," she told him.

"I thought you didn't want to . . . ."

Jennifer interrupted him. "That was last week. Now I want to. Does that present a problem?"

"Not at all, I'm delighted. We can use as much as possible. I'm glad you came. I'm having a meeting with the people from the mill this afternoon on that material for the shirts, and you can be very helpful," he said.

"A problem?"

"No. We have to choose the colors we want to work with. Check the new designs. We're trying to keep the cost down as you advised, so the shirts can be mass marketed. It isn't as simple as you thought. Costs are skyrocketing," he told her.

"I know, but let's do what we can. I don't want to skimp, but we'll take a look this afternoon," she said.

"Good. Then you can leave day after tomorrow. Chicago. We're opening another Tavern. It's good to have you aboard full time," Oliver told her, extending his hand. Jennifer took it.

"How are the record negotiations going? Martin told me that you had a good handle on it," Jennifer said as they walked out of the office.

"I do. Tomorrow they're auditioning a few new groups to play here. If we like them, we send them to the Taverns. Do you want to listen?"

"Sure. Why not? If it's part of the business, then I want to be there," she told him firmly.

Oliver wondered why she had taken on this new attitude, but was too polite to ask her. Jennifer didn't volunteer any information.

She moved around each day attending meetings, listening, learning, adding to her own input. She became an emotionless machine, feeling her life collapsing more now than she had felt when she first started.

She found herself waking in one strange bed after another, sleeping with the young musicians who responded to her advances to improve their careers. They were eager to please her, to make her happy, so that they would receive a contract to play at the Tavern. And hopefully, that would skyrocket them to stardom.

But each morning, she felt emptier than the bed. She didn't like what was happening to her, what she was becoming. She hated herself more each day, but didn't seem to know how to pull herself out from under the depths of despair. She wanted to stay detached, to keep her feelings locked up inside her so tightly that even she didn't know how to get to them. They were buried, much like Ross'. She smiled at herself when she made the connection. All the lectures, all the time thinking about how he was hurting himself, not knowing how to let go, and now she was doing the very same thing. She realized how easy it was to fall into the pattern. It wasn't as easy to come out of it. So she continued to use her body as a butt against herself. She basked in the attention, and continued to play the game.

Jennifer left Houston a month later, still no word from Martin or David. No line on her children. She went home. Home to safety. To friends and familiar surroundings. To her small apartment on top of the bar. Home to the smiling faces, the roots of her life. Home was the only place she could find herself again.

Rachel greeted her warmly and Jill was in the office working on the books. She didn't give anyone notice that she was returning home.

Jill said nothing, she just walked over to Jennifer and put her arms around her, trying wordlessly to say it was going to be all right. "You look awful. But it's so good to have you home. This place doesn't run smoothly without you," Jill told her finally.

"Thanks, but that's not what my spies tell me," Jennifer retorted, looking around and seeing everything intact. "It's been a busy month. So much to do, and not enough hours in the day to do them all. I've actually come home to recharge my batteries. As busy as this place keeps me, it isn't as draining as at the other end," she began to make small talk.

Jill responded, "Why don't you let it all out? You can talk to me. I'm here. I want to help. Martin called us when he returned and told us what happened," Jill decided to tell her. Jennifer looked surprised. "He's concerned about you. We all are. But it will all work out in the end. Three people cannot just disappear into the woodwork. Oh, they can for a while, but they have to be smoked out. I know David and Martin will find them, it's only a matter of time."

"Time!" Jennifer shouted. "How I hate that word. Time . . . each day my children grow older and farther apart from me. It means more time to get used to having them with me again. It means more confusion, more disappointments. Time . . . how much time? Frank is playing with time, Ross needs time, everyone in my life needs time, and they're all running away from me," Jennifer sobbed. "Everyone I love and need in this world is running away from me. So it must be me. It must be something I'm doing wrong. Something I'm incapable of doing right."

"Don't do this to yourself. It isn't your fault. You're the most loving, giving person I know. It's more the men you pick to become part of your life. If I had Ross in my hands at this moment, I'd strangle him," Jill said.

"No. I finally understand what he's going through. It's Frank I don't understand. Why is he torturing me this way? What does he have to gain?" she asked.

"Think about it a minute, Jennifer. You want it all, and Frank wants it all. He's fighting to keep his family together, just as you are. In a way, keeping those kids is keeping you. Can you understand that?"

"No, because if he wanted me, he shouldn't have left," Jennifer tried to follow her friend's logic.

"All right, did you ever get so disgusted you made a split-second decision? One that will affect your entire life. Well, that's what Frank did. He ran out. He didn't stop and think about the repercussions. He was running from his failures, from himself. But he couldn't blame himself, that's too hard. He had to blame you. He conjured up this demon, this woman, who wouldn't comfort him anymore, who was starting to find herself, continue her education, breaking out of the house and finding a new life, one that didn't include him. Jennifer, he was losing his grip on his business—the one area where he felt secure. He was the head of the family, the provider. Instead of allowing you to share his problems, he hid them, moved away from you.

"He didn't want you to see his weakness. So he ran. I know I'm oversimplifying the explanation. If he was more open to you, you both might have been able to work out his problems, maybe with therapy, enabling him to take a more objective look at his life. See it in its proper perspective. A lot of men go through a stage when they find themselves insecure, not riding the crest of the wave. I've seen it happen before, and I found myself ignoring my own husband's needs. I didn't know until we talked months after our separation that I never understood his needs. I wasn't there for him after the boys were born," Jill continued. "They became the center of my life, and I wasn't giving him the tender loving care he needed. I wasn't making the time for him I once did before the children. It was wrong. I know it. But men sometimes are bigger babies than babies. So putting all the pieces together, Frank was going to take away your security, your children, your home, and let you see what you'd be without him. I really believe it was a lark, and once he started his charade, he didn't know how to untangle the web. He kept going. Then it got worse. To justify his guilt, he continued to make you the fall guy, the brunt of his misery," Jill explained.

"How do you know so much?" Jennifer was astonished. Jill was making sense.

"I talked to Martin when he called. He told me that Frank was keeping a close eye on you. Don't you see, Jennifer, you didn't fall apart. You went on with your life, and made something of it. You're not going to crawl back to him and say, 'Oh, dear Frank, I need you, I want you back as well as the children. I want us to be a family again.' He realizes you've beaten him, you're going to take those children, and continue your life as if he didn't exist, and he's scared."

"So what do I do?"

"You go on. You let David locate the children again, and you'll get them. You pull yourself together and not let this thing destroy you. Your dear ex-husband has had a serious breakdown, and you have to understand what you're dealing with. All of us think that no one loves their children the way a mother does. She carries them, gives birth to them, so she's closer to them. Well, men love their children, too. And in some instances, they could make very competent single parents. Sometimes better than mothers can. Not in this case, but in some cases. If you let Frank know that he'll be able to see the children as much as he wants, that he can still be a big part of their life, and can continue to love them, after he first learns to love himself again, then it might be easier. You won't appear so threatening," Jill finished.

"It's so complicated. There is one fact of which you are unaware. Frank does have another woman in his life. He is beginning to pick up the pieces," Jennifer told her.

"Good. A positive sign. Then when the children are living with you, he'll have someone to love him, to comfort him, and get him through the rough periods. Jennifer, I don't believe he really meant to hurt you in the beginning the way that it turned out. It's all confusing, and it's all speculation, but I do believe Frank loved you and just wanted you to sit up and notice him. We all do very strange things when we want to be noticed."

"I did notice him!" she shouted. "I did try to help him. But he always pushed me away. I knew what he was going through businesswise. I tried to help him," Jennifer said.

Jill responded, "It isn't the same thing. You were seeing the weaknesses he didn't want to acknowledge. He was human, there's nothing wrong with that. I know it and you know it. We're of a sound rational mind right now, but to Frank . . . he didn't have the right to crumble under the pressure. He didn't want you to see him in that light. He probably figured you'd lose your respect for him, or some such nonsense."

"That isn't true. I would have loved him more. I wanted to share the bad times as well as the good. I wanted to be there for him like he'd always been there to take care of the children and me."

"But men don't look at it that way. I've only met a very few men in my life who were capable of showing emotion, who could openly cry and not be ashamed. They're geared to think that crying and showing compassion is a sign of weakness. It isn't! It's a sign of humility, of strength. But we're not going to change the male population overnight. I hope I've been able to teach my boys that. And I hope you'll be able to convey that message to Jonathan. That is all we women can do for now," Jill continued.

"I will if I get through this waiting," she said.

"You will. You'll make it. I'm here, and so are all your other friends. And what I think we should do is plan a very large Christmas party, invite all the displaced persons. Christmas is next week, you know," Jill stated.

"I know it. I planned to spend it with the children, remember? I don't know if I could bear it now."

"Yes, you can. You'll close this damn place, and have Christmas dinner at my house. We'll invite Toby, Rachel, and I'll think about a few more people. We'll do it up. You can't hide your head in the sand and pretend the holiday doesn't exist, like you did last year," Jill went on.

"Okay. I'll come. And maybe the night before we'll have an early Christmas Eve party here. An open house, all the regulars and their wives, God forbid they should go out together," Jennifer laughed.

"I love the idea. I'll ask Rachel to make a sign, letting everyone know. We'll get looped, sing some carols. It will be fun, and maybe Ross will be back," Jill approached the subject carefully.

"No word from him?" Jennifer asked quietly.

"No. No one's heard from him. But you know, in

Ross' case that isn't strange, it's the norm.''

"I wonder where he is. I wonder where he's hiding," Jennifer said.

"Maybe he's trying to put his life together the way you are,' Jill offered.

"I hope so. We both deserve a break, a chance at happiness again. Even if it isn't with one another," Jennifer continued.

"What do you mean, even if it isn't with one another?'' Jill asked.

"I don't know what's going to happen between us. I'm not even sure we have a chance in hell of making it. We're so different. I don't think about it anymore,'' Jennifer lied.

"How long will you be home?'' Jill changed the subject.

"Until after Christmas. They're planning a large New Year's Eve party to open the Los Angeles Tavern. It should be fun. Why don't you come? As a matter of fact, I insist you come. You don't have a hot date here I don't know about?'' Jennifer asked.

"Me? No. And I'd be glad to go with you,'' she said, remembering the good time she had in Houston. "It could be *very* interesting.''

Jennifer thought over what Jill had told her, and she felt better. Better than she had in Geneva, anyway. And she was glad she let Jill talk her into spending time with friends for the holidays.

Jill worked overtime to make everything perfect for Christmas. The house was decorated beautifully, the tree was adorned with all hand-made ornaments. The mistletoe hung openly in the doorway between the

360

living room and the kitchen, everyone taking advantage of the gaiety and the free kisses.

"I'm still hung over from last night's party," Toby grinned, his large even white teeth shining in the candlelight. His date, a cute very young redhead, sat in the corner quietly. Toby rushed over and dragged her under the mistletoe and kissed her. She giggled, as he groped at her body. "Toby, stop it," she said half-heartedly.

"Can't I help you do anything?" Jennifer asked her hostess.

"Everything is under control. Sit, relax, drink your eggnog, and have a good time."

The boys were running around the living room, fighting over presents they had just received. Jennifer had given Pete, the older boy, the set of trains she had specially picked out for Jonathan. Roy wanted to play with them, too, which caused a fight, making Jill go into the living room to referee.

Rachel held up her glass. "Here's to another year. May it be better than the last."

Jennifer agreed. Three more people arrived, none of whom Jennifer knew, all laden down with gifts, food, liquor, and grateful for the invitation.

"Are we going caroling tonight, like we did last night?" Toby asked.

"I think this town has heard enough of us for one year," Rachel answered. "Jesus, what a sight we all were. All drunk, waking up anyone who wasn't part of our party, singing in their windows. We're lucky we didn't get shot," she continued.

"Yeah, but it was fun. And remember we had Allie on our side, if anyone put up a fuss. I think we had the

361

spirit of Christmas in our souls," Jill said.

"We sure did, and 100% proof vodka in our guts," Toby continued. "Jesus, that was good stuff," he told Jennifer. "Where have you been hiding it?"

"In my private stock, where you won't be able to find it. It's for special occasions," Jennifer continued. "We really did terrorize the town." Rachel chuckled. "If we didn't have Harold, the Police Chief, with us, we would have been arrested for sure," she laughed, thinking of the motly crew.

"Aw, come on, we weren't that bad. And Christmas comes but once a year," Toby continued.

"Thank God. I couldn't bear it anymore," Rachel said.

"Why are you so gloomy today?" Jennifer asked.

"I don't know. I always seem to get this way around the holidays. It makes one think about what should have been, or could have been," she sighed.

"Now, none of that talk in this house," Jill stated. "We only want happy faces. What could have been, isn't; and what should have been, didn't happen. So cut it out."

"What have we got here, Confucius? You sound like a fortune cookie," Rachel told her.

"Well, instead of thinking of what could have been, let's be grateful for what is. We're all gainfully employed, we have rosy futures, and all the rest will fall into place, if we let it," she continued.

"Our strength," Rachel waved her hand at Jill. "Let's drown ourselves in this good cheer," she said, picking up her drink and finishing it.

"I'm glad you're not going to be with us at the New Year's Eve party. You'd be a wet blanket," Jill told her.

"What New Year's Eve party?" Rachel asked. "I'm going to be working."

"We're going to be away," Jennifer said. "In the hot Los Angeles sunshine. How I hate the cold," she continued.

"Only the lucky ones can go away," Rachel dug at her.

"If you want to take a trip, then come with us," Jennifer said. "You have some vacation time due you."

"Maybe I'll do that. Get away, get myself a great tan, and come back the envy of Marble Lake. But I think I'll wait until mid-January or the beginning of February, when winter seems unbearable," she said, in better spirits at the prospect.

"Give me fair warning," Jennifer told her, and walked into the living room to play with the boys.

At five o'clock, everyone sat around Jill's large dining room table and stuffed themselves with one of the best home-cooked meals they had all had in months. The goose was perfect, adorned with mashed potatoes, yams, green beans, fresh salad, and plum pudding. It was right out of Dickens.

Everyone full and satisfied, sat around the table, talking, eating chestnuts, while Jennifer helped Jill clear off the table, and make the coffee.

"How about a little game of cards," Toby said, taking out a deck from the side table.

"Only if we play for fun, no money. And I'm not going to put up the deed to the bar," Jennifer shouted out.

"Spoilsport," Toby said. "I'm not talking about large stakes. Nickel and dime for fun," he continued.

"Sure, why not?" Rachel said. "I want to see those

magic fingers I've heard so much about," she looked at Jennifer.

"It was dumb luck," Jennifer defended herself. "I'm not an expert."

"Sure, we know," Toby said, dealing out the cards. They sat down and played until midnight, Toby the big winner. He sat back in his chair, finished his coffee, and took his girlfriend, who had fallen asleep on the living room sofa, home.

Everyone else left shortly after, Jennifer returning to her apartment, and her lonely bed. She was almost grateful to be leaving for California. It was only when she was away that she could let down her defenses.

The next few months dragged on. Jennifer and Jill went to the opening of the Los Angeles Tavern, Jennifer releasing her tension in the bedroom of one of the newly-signed drummers. The opening was a success, as was the one in Philadelphia and the one in Manhattan. All of the parties were the same press, smiles, attention, and romping through the sheets with a new face, a young body, neither satisfying Jennifer totally nor allowing her to forget for one instant about her satisfactory sex life with Ross. Some of the bodies were similar, but they were not his. She seemed to pick men who had his physical characteristics—sandy-haired, bearded men. But they didn't measure up. They didn't truly satisfy her, and each time she'd return home feeling more empty than when she had left.

Jennifer tried to get caught up in the excitement, the music, the enthusiasm, and openly she seemed to be having the time of her life. But the spark wasn't there, the once-in-a-lifetime spark that two people share. Sex was just a release without the love that went along with it. She realized she was doing all the taking, and not giving anything of herself, and she missed it. She missed the pleasure of pleasing her partner, wanting him to feel as satisfied as she did. She had never even felt that closeness with Frank. She never wanted to explore the sexual avenues with him which she was more than glad to share with Ross. She loved being held after the lovemaking was over, fitting into place next to him as they slept, waking up next to him in the morning.

Jennifer hated waking up next to strange bodies, trying to make small talk while they fixed her eggs or coffee, hoping for another night. But there were never second nights. She always rushed out of their apartments, not wanting to get to know the faces that went with the bodies. She hated herself for what she was becoming. And more than hatred, she felt frightened. She didn't want to do it anymore, and she didn't know how to stop the physical need she felt, the void she was trying to fill.

Jennifer decided not to go on any more trips. She had to stay home and try to salvage her sanity. It was over four months since she had left Geneva and still there was no new line on Frank. She was beginning to give up hope. He had disappeared for good. She was never going to find her children, so she had to learn to live without them in her life. She couldn't destroy herself totally. It was wrong.

She still hadn't moved into the house, and she thought it was time she did. Time she put together the pieces. She couldn't be afraid to go on, she had to.

Someday her children would be old enough to seek her out, and she had to be there for them.

Jill had helped her with her problems. She was the one who made her see the light. If Frank was keeping an eye on her when she was trying to salvage her newly-wrecked marriage, he was most certainly keeping a watchful eye on her now, too. How would it look if he decided to show the courts what she had become? What kind of a mother would she be to her children, jumping from one bed to another? Those were grounds to have her children taken away from her legally for good. Courts didn't want to hear about reasons, despair. They were only interested in cold hard facts.

Frank was diabolical, tormenting her and choking her in her own wrongdoings. If she was able to beat him so far, she had to learn to continue to beat him. And now, after almost three months of gallivanting around the country, she was willing to try to rectify an almost hopeless situation. She was going home for good.

Let Humphrey and the others take over the business from here on out. Maybe she should even sell her shares, keep Marble Lake, and let the others make their fortunes without her. She already had more money than she knew what to do with.

NINETEEN

Jennifer began taking a more active interest in her own bar. She went back to waiting on the customers like the old days, enjoying their conversation and feeling her feet touch the ground again.

Bobby would come around from time to time to take her to dinner and then straight home to her new house. He had given up on any romantic notions he once had, much to Jennifer's relief.

When life seemed to have calmed down for her, she received a call from David. It was three o'clock in the morning. "I found them," was all he said on the other end of the wire.

Jennifer jumped up from a dead sleep and turned on the light. "Where? When? When can I go to them?" she shot out at him, fully awake.

"They are in, believe it or not, Boston. I found them early this evening and I have a man stationed outside the house. I'm not taking any chances this time. I just

367

hung up with Martin, and he told me to have you meet him in front of your place in a few hours. He woke up a friend of his who's a judge, and he's rushing over to his house right now to have him sign the papers. He's also been in contact with the Boston authorities and they're ready for you. So get dressed and let's start moving," he told her merrily.

Jennifer couldn't believe it. It was almost all over, but this time she didn't have the feeling of gloom, She knew it would all work out. She dialed Jill's number, waking her up. "Sorry, but I'm leaving to get my kids in a few hours. Call Rachel about six and tell her to open up the bar," she ordered.

"I'm so happy," Jill cried. "I knew it! I knew that once you pulled yourself together it would all work out. I'm so excited. I can't think about going back to sleep. Do you want me to come with you?" Jill asked.

"No. Martin is picking me up in a few hours. They're in Boston. Can you believe it? Right under my nose all this time. I thought surely he had taken them to South America, or Tahiti, or something. But right here in the States! Less than five hours away," Jennifer shouted.

"Are you going to fly or drive?" Jill asked.

"I don't know. I didn't even bother to ask. I'll do whatever Martin wants," she told her friend. "Oh, Jill, I'm so relieved," she sobbed.

"I'm coming right over. I'll stay with you until Martin arrives," she told her friend and hung up.

Jill made it over in record time. Jennifer heard her footsteps rushing upstairs in the farm house. Jill was still dressed in her pajamas, a raincoat thrown over them, and a pair of sneakers.

"I can see you didn't stop to dress," Jennifer joked feeling good-humored.

"Who had time? What's the procedure?"

"Same as before, I imagine. Martin, bless him, is waking up a judge right now to sign the papers. They promised me they wouldn't waste any time, and they aren't. I'm so happy," Jennifer jumped around. "I'm even feeling sorry for Frank. Isn't that strange?"

"No, it's human. He's going to feel as you did yesterday. Remember that," her friend said. "I wish I could be there. What time do you think you'll be back?"

"I'm not sure. I'll call you as soon as I have the children in hand. I'll let you know. I have to much to do. I want everything connected with this homecoming to be perfect," she said, rushing to get ready. "How do I look?"

"Like a mother. You're not going to an opening, you're going to pick up your children," Jill laughed at her.

"I know, but I want them to feel secure. I want them to know me. I want to act just right."

"You will! Calm down, take a deep breath. I'm sure they'll remember you. You haven't changed much in a year-and-a-half. Just remember to slow down, let it all happen naturally. If they don't rush to your side when they see you, remember what they've been through. And then again, we don't know what Frank told them about your disappearance. What I'm trying to say is, don't expect too much. Don't be disappointed. It's only a matter of time before everything will be back to normal, and they feel they can trust you again. Frank's all they had."

"I know, and I'm scared to death," she confided to her friend. "I want them to love me again."

"They will. Give them time," Jill said, and she turned to look out the bedroom window. "I thought I heard something," she said. "I think Martin is here."

"You're kidding. He must have broken the speed record," Jennifer said excitedly as she rushed down the stairs.

Martin was standing in the doorway. "Calm down," he said. "We've got a few minutes. A friend of mine is flying us up there, where we're being met by the police chief. It's all under control."

Jennifer hugged him. It was the first time they had had any physical contact since that afternoon in Geneva. She pulled away as quickly so as not to embarrass him.

"Oh, let me introduce you to my very best friend, Jill Randall," Jennifer said, as both smiled in acknowledgment. "Well, I'm ready, shall we go?" she asked him.

"Yes, and this time I promise you no slip-ups," Martin said assuredly.

Jennifer kept her fingers crossed.

"Call me," Jill shouted as she watched the two get into the car. "And I'll call Rachel for you." Jennifer waved goodbye and they took off.

The small plane was waiting for them as promised, and took off immediately. They reached the Boston airport at seven AM. The Police Chief, Reilly, was there to greet them.

"We have three plainclothes men staked out around the house. He couldn't possibly leave," the fat, balding man said as he took the papers from

Martin. He gave them a quick onceover and held open the car door for Jennifer. This time she wasn't going to wait in any hotel room for a phone call. She was going straight to the house with them. She'd wait outside if she had to, but she was going to be there. Martin didn't put up a fuss. He agreed.

As they drove quickly through the Boston streets, Jennifer's throat was dry. She had to take deep breaths to ward off her own anxiety. She felt almost relieved when, as they were approaching the beautifully tree-lined streets where Frank had taken up residence almost three months ago, she recognized David's familiar frame.

He greeted her with a warm kiss on the cheek. He walked over to Martin. "He knows we're here. It isn't going to be a problem. The children are dressed and ready to leave with Jennifer. He's not putting up a fuss," David told them.

"You mean I can really walk in there and get the children?" Jennifer said in disbelief.

"Yes, you can," Martin stated. "Do you want me to come in there with you?"

"No. I don't want to confuse them. I'd like to go in alone," Jennifer said. Her heart leaping through her chest, she walked shakily to the front door and rang the bell. A very pretty young girl answered. She had blonde straight hair, and piercing blue eyes that looked tired from lack of sleep. It had been a long night for them, too, Jennifer thought.

"Mrs. Wells? The children are waiting for you in the kitchen," she said softly in a thick French accent.

"Where's Frank?" Jennifer asked.

"He's upstairs in the bedroom. He knew you

wouldn't want to see him. He's been through a great deal these past few months," the young girl said, finally introducing herself to Jennifer.

"He's wrong. I would like to see him. I'd like to talk to him," she told Janette. "Would you ask him if he'll see me?" Janette looked surprised and walked upstairs, disappearing from sight.

Jennifer walked through the living room to the kitchen and saw her children sitting at the table having breakfast. They looked up at her in amazement. They looked well, and had grown more than Jennifer realized. She wanted to rush over to them and hug them, but restrained herself. She was savoring the moment. Cassy put down the spoon in the cereal bowl and rushed to her mother, almost knocking her over.

"I knew you'd come back," she said. Jonathan hesitated, then also rushed to his mother. Jennifer knelt beside her children, not wanting to let go, smothering them with kisses, almost suffocating them. It was more than she had hoped for.

"I've missed you so much," she told them in tears. "I didn't know where to find you. I love you both very much," she tried not to say too much. She didn't know what Frank had told them.

"I told you, Jonathan, she was looking for us," Cassy snapped at her brother.

"Why didn't you come to Switzerland with us?" Jonathan asked.

"I couldn't. It doesn't matter, we have lots of time to talk about that later. It's just so good that we're all together again. You're going to go home with me," she told them.

"We're leaving again?" Jonathan complained.

"Oh, but it's going to be for the last time. Mommy bought a big new house in the country for you. It has lots of land and a barn for horses," she tried to explain.

"We got horses?" Cassy asked.

"Oh, not just yet. I was waiting for you to come back so we could buy them together," Jennifer tried to explain. She felt Janette's presence in the room and got up.

"He's in the study," she said. Jennifer nodded.

"Children, finish your breakfast. Mommy wants to talk to daddy a minute, and we'll pack your things and go home," she told them. She realized they were very confused.

Jennifer knocked on the study door before entering. She heard the sound of Frank's voice inviting her in. She was shocked at his appearance. He was thinner than she remembered him, and he had aged ten years. She knew she could no longer hate him.

"I just wanted to tell you that my taking the children with me doesn't mean I want them to forget about you. You're their father, and I know you love them regardless of your feelings for me. I want you to know I won't stop you from seeing them. I don't think you'll take them away again," she said.

He looked up at her. "I won't. And you're being more generous with me than I was with you. I don't know what got into me, Jen. I know what I did was wrong, what I did to you and the children. They missed you so much, and they needed you. And, in time, I hope you all will forgive me. But first, I have to forgive myself. I need help, Janette's been good to me, and she's helped me understand myself and allowed me to see what I was doing was wrong." He hesitated, then continued, "I'm sorry, Jennifer. I think the children understand, and you'll be glad to know I never said anything bad about you to them. They're old enough to understand that I was the villain, I took them away from you," he said.

Jennifer felt sorry for him. She stood there and wanted to assure him that everything was going to be all right in time.

He walked over to the other side of the desk and took out a large manila envelope. He handed it to Jennifer. "I think you might find its contents interesting," he said. "I've been following your success story. I am proud of you," he said, and Jennifer realized how hard it was for him to admit it.

"I couldn't have done it without you," she said. He smiled at the irony. "I have to go, but let me know where you'll be. And please come to see the children when you're feeling better," she told him. He nodded.

Janette had them packed and ready for the trip.

"I'll have the rest of their things sent to you," she told Jennifer. "I'll take care of Frank, he'll be fine when he seeks some help," she said, and Jennifer smiled at her. She had more patience than Jennifer did, but then again, you always seem to muster up hidden strength when you love someone.

Jennifer walked out of the house with her children. Martin had a car waiting to take them to the airport, and back home. Jennifer sat in the middle and tried to listen to both children talking at once. They wanted to know all about the new house, the horse barn she owned, and if they could ride on her bull. They had read all about her in the papers. Jennifer was relieved to know Frank had kept them up on the latest news. It made their reunion so much easier.

"I want a big white horse," Cassy said.

"You can't have a big white horse. You don't know how to ride," Jonathan fought back.

"I can too," Cassy shouted at him. And Jennifer reveled in the old sibling rivalry. How she had missed it!

Jennifer read the contents of the envelope on the plane. It was a complete file on Ross. There was more pain there than Jennifer had ever imagined. In a small way, Frank wanted to help her to understand, to go on with her life. Jennifer put the papers away.

Jill had everything waiting for their return once Jennifer called her. The house was lit up, the toys taken out of the closet and neatly displayed in their rooms. The children ran through the house exploring all the nooks and crannies. They loved the new place. Jonathan wanted to know where they'd go to school, and Jennifer assured him he'd like it. She even had two friends for him to meet, Roy and Pete Randall, sons of a very dear friend of hers. The children wanted to rush to the new bar and see the bull for themselves, but Jennifer assured them tomorrow was soon enough. They had had a long day, should have dinner and snuggle in bed together.

The house was alive again, just as she had hoped when she decided to buy it. She was happy again, happier than she ever thought she could be. Life was finally back to normal. And now she had to relearn how to devote her time to the children. She'd almost forgotten how much of her time they needed. She'd think about hiring a housekeeper tomorrow. She realized for the first time since they returned, and after they were both fast asleep, that she was no longer free to get up and leave at a whim. She had to stay put. Something she was glad to do for now. But in her business, she didn't know if she could always be able to do that.

It didn't take long for everything to fall into place. The children were enrolled in school, the house was running smoothly by Mrs. Benjamin, the newest member of the family. She was a sweet lady in her late fifties. Her children were grown, and her life seeming empty, she decided to apply for the housekeeping job Jennifer offered. Mrs. Benjamin was a good cook, and was very good with the children. She knew how to handle them, never letting them get away with anything. She was strict, something Jennifer couldn't bear to be at first. She wanted them to adjust to their new environment before she put any pressure on them.

Mrs. Benjamin straightened her out on that point. "Once you let them get away with something the first time, you'll be very sorry," she told Jennifer. "I believe in setting the record straight from the very beginning. Those young ones are very smart. They know exactly how to take advantage. It doesn't mean you love them any less, because you've taken a spoon to their bottoms once in a while," she went on, and Jennifer knew she'd made the right choice.

Jennifer tried to spend time at the bar when the children were in school, and then returned in the evenings after the children were in bed, exactly as she had promised the judge she would. Frank had sent down the remainder of the children's clothes and toys but had not made any mention of seeing them. Jennifer was surprised and relieved.

Jonathan had hit it off with Pete, the two becoming best friends quickly, and Cassy had become friendly with the little girl next door. It was as if all those empty months never took place. The nightmare had been just a bad dream, not a reality.

Cassy rushed into Jennifer's room early one Sunday morning three weeks after they returned.

"Come on, you have to get up. You have to see the two beautiful horses in the barn outside. Thank you, mommy. They're so pretty," Cassy rambled, to Jennifer's astonishment. She didn't know what Cassy was talking about.

Jonathan followed his sister into the bedroom. "I told you not to come in here. We promised we wouldn't tell her until the horses were set up."

"Who told you?" Jennifer tried to get out of her son. "What is everyone talking about?"

"The horses you bought us. Remember you promised in the car coming here that we would have horses of our very own to ride," Jonathan answered impatiently.

"I didn't buy you any horses," Jennifer tried to explain as she was dragged outside to see the two horses for herself. "What is going on here?" she asked.

"The big one is mine. The smaller one is for Cassy," Jonathan said.

"Jonathan, I want you to explain to mommy how these horses got here," she knelt down in her bathrobe and remained at eye level with her son.

"A man brought them over early this morning. He told us not to wake you. He said it was a surprise and you'd know who it was from," Jonathan explained patiently.

Jennifer jumped—it could only be Ross!

"Jonathan, where did the man go?" Jennifer asked excitedly.

"He left," Jonathan answered matter-of-factly. "He left two saddles, some hay, some grain," Jonathan sounded like an expert.

Jennifer couldn't believe what she was seeing. She rushed into the house and dialed Ross' number. He answered on the second ring. "Good morning," he sounded chipper.

"Good morning. I hope you weren't away all this time just to buy my children two horses," she tried to remain calm.

"Nope, and I didn't buy them, you did. You haven't gotten the bill yet," he told her.

"Oh, I hope I can afford them," she tried to sound casual.

"From what I read, I think so," he returned. "I told Jonathan I'd send some men over later to build a corral whenever you give me the go-ahead," he continued.

"Ross, I don't believe you. You pop up out of nowhere, enter my life again, and bring in two of the biggest surprises. . . ." She couldn't contain herself anymore, "Where were you?"

"Do I have to talk about it over the phone? I'd much rather tell you in person," he said calmly.

"When?"

"Now's a good time," he said, hanging up.

Jennifer rushed back upstairs and tried to put herself together. She looked awful, her hair needed washing, and she wasn't wearing any make-up. How dare he do this to her. "Calm down," she said to herself, and remembered the contents of the manila envelope Frank had given her, Ross' involvement with Erica. She understood now what kept him so isolated for so long.

Jennifer heard his truck pull into her driveway. The kids rushed up to greet him. Jennifer watched them from her bedroom window as she pulled on her boots, and then she rushed down the stairs to greet him. She looked up at him. He looked good—calmer, more peaceful, a look Jennifer had never seen on his face before.

"Are you going to put the saddle on the horse for me now?" Cassy asked.

Ross knelt down to talk to her. "In a minute. I want to talk to your mother first. Why don't you go upstairs and change into a heavy pair of pants and some boots, if you have them. I'll meet you in the barn when you're done," he told her, and she listened.

Ross looked up at Jennifer. So many questions came rushing to her mind. But she remained quiet. Ross would tell her what he wanted her to know.

"I'm glad everything turned out well for you. I wanted to come back when I heard your Switzerland trip was a fiasco, but I couldn't, Jennifer, I wasn't ready then."

"And you're ready now?" Jennifer interrupted.

"Yes. I'm ready to start living my life again. And I can't seem to think about doing it without you as a part of it."

"The way it used to be?" she wanted to clarify his statement.

"No. Not two days a week, or three days, but everyday. I can't promise you I'll change overnight. There's so much of me that's still selfish, not because I want to be but because I don't know how else to be. But if you give me a chance, I'd like to try," he stated.

"I don't know, Ross," Jennifer said. "A lot has happened to both of us since you went away. I still want it all. And I don't know if I'm capable of cutting myself into that many pieces. I know I have an obligation to my children, and to the business, and I don't know what's going to be left over for you," she told him honestly. "I can't spend my time worrying about your moods, your needs, counting my words. I can't do it again."

"I don't want you to. I want you to be there when you can. I understand the commitments you've made. I'd just want to be part of those commitments. I think we can make a go of it. I've had time to think, to get in touch with my feelings, and mostly to put Erica behind me. Please give me another chance," Ross told her.

Jennifer wanted to reach over and hold him, tell him she could. But she was more cautious now. She needed time to see, she didn't want to be hurt anymore. "We'll take it one day at a time. That's all I can promise you, Ross," Jennifer told him.

"That's all I ask," Ross answered. "I love you very much. I always have. I just wasn't ready to admit it to myself."

Cassy rushed out the door before Jennifer could answer him. "I'm ready, Ross," she said.

"I'm ready, too. How about you, Jonathan?"

"Me? I've been ready since the horses got here," he said. The children rushed over to the barn.

"We'll talk later," Ross said. "I missed you. I want to stay with you tonight."

"I want you to," Jennifer told him.

"And tomorrow. . . ." Ross interrupted.

"We'll see. Let's get through today first," she told him.

He bent down and kissed her on the lips. She kissed him back. He felt good. She wanted him, but she'd have to wait. Wait until later, and the children were in bed.

She watched him walk off to the barn. Ross picked Cassy up and put her on a small chestnut mare. Jonathan fought any assistance as he mounted the bay himself. Jennifer smiled to herself and remembered something Jill said to her a lifetime ago.

"Everything was going to be all right. It was only a matter of time."